P9-DOE-979

The Best
AMERICAN
SHORT
STORIES
2000

GUEST EDITORS OF
THE BEST AMERICAN SHORT STORIES

The Best
AMERICAN
SHORT
STORIES
2000

Selected from
U.S. and Canadian Magazines
by E. L. DOCTOROW
with KATRINA KENISON

*With an Introduction
by E. L. Doctorow*

HOUGHTON MIFFLIN COMPANY
BOSTON · NEW YORK   2000

Copyright © 2000 by Houghton Mifflin Company
Introduction copyright © 2000 by E. L. Doctorow

ALL RIGHTS RESERVED

No part of this work may be reproduced or transmitted in any form or by any means, electronic or mechanical, including photocopying and recording, or by any information storage or retrieval system without the prior written permission of the copyright owner unless such copying is expressly permitted by federal copyright law. With the exception of nonprofit transcription in Braille, Houghton Mifflin is not authorized to grant permission for further uses of copyrighted selections reprinted in this book without the permission of their owners. Permission must be obtained from the individual copyright owners as identified herein. Address requests for permission to make copies of Houghton Mifflin material to Permissions, Houghton Mifflin Company, 215 Park Avenue South, New York, New York 10003.

Visit our Web site: www.houghtonmifflinbooks.com.

ISSN 0067-6233
ISBN 0-395-92687-4
ISBN 0-395-92686-6 (pbk.)

Printed in the United States of America

QUM 10 9 8 7 6 5 4 3 2 1

"Black Elvis" by Geoffrey Becker. First published in *Ploughshares*. Copyright © 1999 by Geoffrey Becker. Reprinted by permission of the author.

"The Story" by Amy Bloom. First published in *Story*. Copyright © 1999 by Amy Bloom. Reprinted from the collection *A Blind Man Can See How Much I Love You* by permission of Random House, Inc.

"The Beautiful Days" by Michael Byers. First published in *Ploughshares*. Copyright © 1999 by Michael Byers. Reprinted by permission of the author.

"The Ordinary Son" by Ron Carlson. First published in *Oxford American*. Copyright © 1999 by Ron Carlson. Reprinted by permission of Brandt & Brandt Literary Agents, Inc.

"Call If You Need Me" by Raymond Carver. First published in *Granta*. Copyright © 2001 by the Estate of Raymond Carver. Reprinted from the collection *Call If You Need Me: Uncollected Fiction and Prose* by permission of Vintage Books, a Division of Random House, Inc.

"Bones of the Inner Ear" by Kiana Davenport. First published in *Story*. Copyright © 1999 by Kiana Davenport. Reprinted by permission of the author.

"Nilda" by Junot Díaz. First published in *The New Yorker*. Copyright © 1999 by Junot Díaz. Reprinted by permission of the author and the Watkins/Loomis Agency.

"The Gilgul of Park Avenue" by Nathan Englander. First published in *The Atlantic Monthly*. Copyright © 1999 by Nathan Englander. Reprinted from the collection *For the Relief of Unbearable Urges* by permission of Alfred A. Knopf, a Division of Random House, Inc.

"The Fix" by Percival Everett. First published in *New York Stories*. Copyright © 1999 by Percival Everett. Reprinted by permission of the author.

"Good for the Soul" by Tim Gautreaux. First published in *Story*. Copyright © 1999 by Tim Gautreaux. Reprinted from the collection *Welding with Children* by permission of St. Martin's Press.

"He's at the Office" by Allan Gurganus. First published in *The New Yorker*. Copyright © 1999 by Allan Gurganus. Reprinted by permission of the author.

"Blind Jozef Pronek" by Aleksandar Hemon. First published in *The New Yorker*. Copyright © 1999 by Aleksandar Hemon. Reprinted by permission of the author and the Watkins/Loomis Agency.

"The Anointed" by Kathleen Hill. First published in *DoubleTake*. Copyright © 1999 by Kathleen Hill. Reprinted by permission of the author and the Ellen Levine Literary Agency, Inc. Excerpts from *Lucy Gayheart* by Willa Cather copyright 1935 by Willa Cather and renewed 1963 by Edith Lewis and the City Farmers Trust Co. Reprinted by permission of Alfred A. Knopf, a Division of Random House, Inc.

"The Bridegroom" by Ha Jin. First published in *Harper's Magazine*. Copyright © 1999 by Ha Jin. Reprinted by permission of the author.

"The Thing Around Them" by Marilyn Krysl. First published in *Notre Dame Review*. Copyright © 1999 by Marilyn Krysl. Reprinted from the collection *How to Accommodate Men* by permission of Coffee House Press.

"The Third and Final Continent" by Jhumpa Lahiri. First published in *The New Yorker*. Copyright © 1999 by Jhumpa Lahiri. Reprinted from the collection *Interpreter of Maladies* by permission of Houghton Mifflin Company and Janklow & Nesbitt. All rights reserved.

"Pet Fly" by Walter Mosley. First published in *The New Yorker*. Copyright © 1999 by Walter Mosley. Reprinted by permission of the author and the Watkins/Loomis Agency.

"Brownies" by ZZ Packer. First published in *Harper's Magazine*. Copyright © 1999 by ZZ Packer. Reprinted by permission of the author. Excerpts from "Brownie Smile Song," words and music by Harriet Heywood, and "Make New Friends," from *The Ditty Bag* by Janet E. Tobitt, are used by permission of the Girl Scouts of the USA.

"Allog" by Edith Pearlman. First published in *Ascent*. Copyright © 1999 by Edith Pearlman. Reprinted by permission of the author.

"People in Hell Just Want a Drink of Water" by Annie Proulx. First published in *GQ*. Copyright © 1999 by Dead Line, Inc. Reprinted from the collection *Close Range: Wyoming Stories* by permission of Simon & Schuster.

"Basil the Dog" by Frances Sherwood. First published in *The Atlantic Monthly*. Copyright © 1999 by Frances Sherwood. Reprinted by permission of the author.

Contents

Foreword

TAKING A VACATION from short stories a couple of weeks ago, I picked up Graham Swift's 1996 Booker Prize winner, *Last Orders.* For several nights running, I grabbed the book at bedtime and read the opening chapters — and then read them again, and yet again. Unable to enter the world of the novel, I seemed to be stuck at the front door, trying to kick my way in.

Finally I realized that this book was going to require more of me than ten-minute late-night intervals. Determined, I started over once again, earlier in the evening this time, in a straightbacked chair, under a strong light, and with a little "who's who" chart penciled on the inside back cover. And lo, the door swung open, to reveal an astonishingly beautiful work. Once inside Swift's working-class London suburb, I was compelled to remain there, reading to the end. But real life does not allow for novels to be read at a sitting, not since the enforced leisure of childhood anyway, when entire summer days could be bequeathed to *Treasure Island* or Nancy Drew.

Stories, of course, give us a break. They're shorter, more compressed, occupying territory somewhere between a novel and a poem, offering us glimpses of lives in process rather than layer upon layer of lives viewed over time. But my stint of novel-reading reminded me of what I love about both forms — the total immersion a novel demands; the quick plunges into stories; the opportunity, in both cases, to slip out of my own everyday life and into someone else's reality.

Edgar Allan Poe maintained that a short story has to be read in a single sitting, and the best ones do seem to insist that we stay put from start to finish. In fact, if a short story *doesn't* reach out and grab me by the end of its first page, then all may be lost. My gaze wanders off to the ad for a Jamaican villa on the opposite page, or to the Roz Chast cartoon in the lower righthand corner. The magazines in which most of us encounter our short fiction are full of distractions that lure us away from the written word. There is way too much to read anyway, too much to look at, too much to take in. How easy it is, then, in this throwaway culture of ours, for a short story to elude its audience altogether. We leave this week's *New Yorker* behind on the subway seat; we never quite make it to the back pages of the current issue of the *Atlantic Monthly*; we somehow let the *Paris Review* subscription lapse. The coffee-table piles grow and gather dust, until finally, giving up, we sweep the month's accumulation of reading matter into the recycling bin. And the so-called little magazines — the journals published on college campuses, the fragile, fiercely independent publications that exist in part to discover and nurture new talent — well, most of us never lay hands on these at all. Yet the stories are there, waiting between all those covers, to be read and pondered over and shared. An annual anthology like this one ensures that the most distinguished of these works will be gathered up and served again — to a vast audience, an audience of committed readers who would just as soon skip the Gap ads and cake recipes and get to the real stuff, the important human secrets embedded in stories.

As the annual editor of this series, my greatest challenge is finding a way to give each of the 2,500 or so stories I read during the course of a year its due. My own piles encroach on me even as I type these words; the magazines and journals arrive by the carton. The subscriptions are kept up-to-date with the help of a database program; each week I log in the new arrivals. So the clerical chores are a snap. It's the reading itself — the part of the job that involves heart and soul, as well as critical faculties — that demands such special care. How to stay open and receptive to the works before me while still managing to stay abreast of the tide? There are times, I must confess, when reading short stories threatens to become more a discipline than a delight. But then a sentence stops my heart or sets it racing, or a phrase brings me to my knees with its unexpected rightness, or a character announces herself in a voice impossible to ignore, and the delight returns.

The trick, I've learned, is to keep the stories from coming at me too fast. The assembly-line approach doesn't work; nor can I treat the day's quota of short stories like chapters of a novel, reading one after another. Instead, I must allow time for each story to sink in, time for each individual voice to be heard. And so I read a story and get up to make a cup of tea. I read another, then take a walk around the block. Later I read two in quick succession, but fold half a load of laundry in between. My workdays, then, include gallons of tea, lots of walks, lots of unfinished household tasks — all in deference to the stories themselves, which ask to be taken up one at a time and then savored in full, without interruption.

The stories gathered in this volume deserve to be read the same way. Each stands alone, and I encourage you to grant them their independence. Enjoy them one at a time, like chocolate truffles. Read a story, walk the dog, come back later. The stories will keep. Of course, it is our hope that they will also summon you back again and again, hungry for more. And it is our hope too that when the last page has been turned, you will close this book with a greater sense of who we are as a nation of readers and writers as we embark on this new millennium, where we come from and what we care about — for as E. L. Doctorow points out in his introduction to this volume, though we have chosen these twenty-one stories "one at a time, with no thought for their effect overall or their relationship to one another, they turn out to reflect the evolving demographics of our literary republic."

Ursula K. LeGuin suggests that we think of stories as carrier bags. "Like bellies or baskets, like houses or wombs, like the great sac of the cosmos itself," she says, "they are containers for holding something vital." Here then, from the pages of a dozen different publications, both large and small, are the vessels in which this year's writers have put all that is most precious to them. What a pleasure it is to open these disparate containers, to explore their varied contents, to discover new voices and to become reacquainted with familiar ones.

When we invited E. L. Doctorow to serve as guest editor for the eighty-fifth volume of *The Best American Short Stories*, he warned us that his own novel *City of God* would be published just as the deadline approached for his selections for this book. Yet he gamely agreed to combine an intensive period of reading and choosing short stories with his own demanding book tour. So it was that he carried batches of stories with him as he crisscrossed the country. And so it was that he found his own way to give each story its due, reading a bit each day for many days, in airport lounges and hotel rooms, while in temporary exile from his own everyday life. His dedication to the cause was unflagging, his judgment impeccable. In the final winnowing, as we discussed the near-misses by phone, it was clear that he had read all of the stories with utmost care and appreciated each writer's efforts and intentions, even as he made the hard decisions we required of him. We are enormously grateful for his work and for the fine collection he has assembled for the year 2000.

The stories chosen for this anthology were originally published between January 1999 and January 2000. The qualifications for selection are (1) original publication in nationally distributed American or Canadian periodicals; (2) publication in English by writers who are American or Canadian, or who have made the United States or Canada their home; (3) original publication as short stories (excerpts of novels are not knowingly considered). A list of magazines consulted for this volume appears at the back of the book. Editors who wish their short fiction to be considered for next year's edition should send their publications to Katrina Kenison, c/o The Best American Short Stories, Houghton Mifflin Company, 222 Berkeley Street, Boston, MA 02116.

K.K.

Introduction

HERE IN THE YEAR 2000 we lack a proprietary critic of the short story as, for example, Professor Helen Vendler is a proprietary critic of the lyric poem. Given the great story writers — Chekhov, or Joyce, or Hemingway — we might wonder about this, except that Hemingway turned to novels after *In Our Time* just as Joyce did after *Dubliners*. Chekhov in his maturity turned to drama. While there are exceptions — Isaac Babel or Grace Paley, for example, writers-for-life of brilliant, tightly sprung prose designedly inhospitable to the long forms — we may say that short stories are what young writers produce on their way to their first novels, or what older writers produce in between novels. The critic of fiction will hold title to all its estates, and the novel is a major act of the culture.

Apart from that, it may be that the short story, as it has shifted historically from the episodic tale to the compressive illumination, can't sustain that much formal analysis. Some years ago, the late Frank O'Connor published a study of the genre entitled *The Lonely Voice*. O'Connor, himself a masterful writer of short stories, wanted to find some means of distinguishing the form from the novella and the novel. His title suggests the nature of his conclusion: it is not any particular technique of the short story that sets it apart, because as a selective rather than an inclusive art, it can construct itself in an endless number of ways. Nor is its length definitive, for, as he points out, not a few of the great examples of the genre are quite long. What makes the short story a distinct literary form, says O'Connor, is "its intense awareness of human loneliness."

Sprung from Gogol's seminal story "The Overcoat," in which an impoverished clerk in winter manages to buy a warm overcoat only to have it stolen, a disaster that drives him to his death, the modern short story is a genre that deals with members of "submerged population groups," excluded by one means or another from living in the certainties of civilization — people of a minority, outsiders, marginalists, for whom society provides no place or means of self-respect. By contrast, according to O'Connor, the fiction of the novel assumes that man is "an animal who lives in community, as in Jane Austen and Trollope it obviously does."

But one can think immediately of stories rising from non-submerged populations, stories of people centrally located in community — as they are in many of Katherine Mansfield's or Henry James's stories — who are not of the alienated and marginalized, though they may come to be from their own actions.

Perhaps anticipating this problem, O'Connor modifies his thesis to include in his submerged population groups people who are not materially but spiritually isolated — artists, dreamers, idealists, antiheroes, visionaries, and so forth. But then who does not belong to a submerged population group? The lonely voice is a universal chorus, and we are left with the not terribly useful truism that the story as a form deals with the human condition.

Besides which, one is immediately able to cite novels not at all as societally rooted as Austen's or Trollope's: Sartre's *Nausea,* for example, or Richard Wright's *Native Son,* or Samuel Beckett's *Molloy* trilogy, among others. These works bring their awareness of loneliness to a pitch that the word "intense" hardly begins to describe.

So finally O'Connor's attempt to differentiate the short story as a genre by virtue of its sociology doesn't hold up under examination.

On the other hand, if we deny it as a thesis, we can still accept it as an insight. We can acknowledge the tendency of the short story to isolate the individual — paradoxically, perhaps, from the technical factors Frank O'Connor has dismissed. The story as a particular kind of fiction may not be definable by its construction or its length, but what *is* critical is its scale. Smaller in its overall dimensions than the novel, it is a fiction in which society is surmised as the darkness around the narrative circle of light. In other words, the scale of the short story predisposes it to the isolation of the self. And the author's awareness of loneliness is the literary dignity he grants his characters in spite of their circumstances — the same dignity or moral consequence that, according to the critic Walter Benjamin, is granted even to the humblest person on the occasion of his death. We can say, then, that the subjugated population of a short story is likely to be, before anything else, a population of one. And whoever in a short story is deprived of the certainties of civilization may attribute it, among other things, to the author's concise attentions.

It was the Freudian disciple Wilhelm Reich who realized that extensive dream analysis was not necessary to uncover a patient's psyche: anywhere you looked — in actions taken, habits of thought, tone of voice, body language — you would find the typified self. That about describes the working principle of the short story as practiced by James Joyce and Ernest Hemingway.

Joyce, who brought the modern short story to perfection, showed us that its point of entry can be quite close in time to its denouement — in other words, that the story may look in on someone's life as it just happens to reach its moment of inexorable moral definition. Hemingway added to that the technique of composing a story whose suspense derives from the withheld mention of its central problem.

I have read perhaps 140 stories to make this selection of 21 for the year 2000. Here is the news: the writers of today are drifting away from the classic model of the modern short story. They seem more disposed to the episodic than the epiphanic, and so their stories sometimes point to the earlier model of the tale. Stories in this mode tend to be longer, their points of entry can be quite distant from their denouements, and their central problem is made quite explicit.

But if the twenty-one outstanding stories in this volume are an indication, the art of the story hardly seems to have suffered. Oddly, the reader discerns a nice sense of freedom in what has to be thought of as a conservative tendency, one that glances back to the nineteenth century. It's as if some literary shackle has been broken — one made of gold, admittedly, but a shackle nevertheless.

And there is more news: although my coeditor, Katrina Kenison, and I have functioned as plain and modest readers, going from story to story to find the pleasure or excitement or truth in them, and although we have chosen them one at a time with no thought for their effect overall or their relationship to one another, they turn out as a collection to reflect the evolving demographics of our literary republic. Their protagonists are Latino, African American, Chinese, Israeli, Indian, Bosnian, Bengali, Hawaiian, and Trinidadian in greater numbers than they are native white middle-class. This brings us back again to Frank O'Connor's untenable theory but useful insight. I don't mean to suggest that the tones or moods or states of mind of the stories are uniform. Humor, wonder, serenity, horror, sadness, stoicism, and love come off these pages. Geniuses are portrayed, as are the brutally retarded and the Alzheimer-ridden. Parables are given, and stories echo the realism of the front page.

I think it is possible to see in this collection the universality of the literary conscience. You may find proof too of the vibrant, revivified energies given to this country by its immigrant infusions. But above all, here is the felt life conferred by the gifted storyteller . . . who always raises two voices into the lonely universe, the character's and the writer's own.

E. L. Doctorow

The Best
AMERICAN
SHORT
STORIES
2000

GEOFFREY BECKER

Black Elvis

FROM PLOUGHSHARES

AT FIVE P.M. precisely, Black Elvis began to get ready. First, he laid out his clothes, the dark suit, the white dress shirt, the two-tone oxfords. In the bathroom, he used a depilatory powder to remove the stubble from his face, then carefully brushed his teeth and gargled with Lavoris. He applied a light coating of makeup, used a liner to deepen the effect of his eyes. They were big eyes, the color of old ivory, and examining them in the mirror, he had to remind himself once again whose they were.

At the bus stop, his guitar precariously stowed in a chipboard case held together by a bungee cord, he was watched by two shirtless boys on a stoop, drinking sodas. Their young, dark torsos emerged out of enormous dungarees like shoots sprouting.

"Yo," one of them called. "Let me see that."

Black Elvis stayed where he was, but tightened his grip on the case. The boys stood and walked over to him. The sun hung low in the sky, turning the fronts of the row houses golden red.

"Are you a Muslim, brother?" asked the smaller of the two. His hair was cornrowed, and one eye peered unnaturally to the side.

Black Elvis shook his head. He wondered how hot it still was. Eighty, at least.

"He's a preacher," said the other one. "Look at him." This boy, though larger, gave the impression of being less sure of himself. His sneakers were untied and looked expensive and new.

"Singing for Jesus, is that right?"

"No," said Black Elvis.

"For who, then?" said the smaller one.

"For an audience, my man. I have a gig." He knew this boy. Sometimes he drew pictures on the sidewalk with colored chalk.

"Yeah?" The boy trained his one useful eye on the guitar case, the other apparently examining something three feet to the left. "Go on and play something, then."

"I'm a professional. No professional going to play songs at no bus stop."

"When the bus come?"

Black Elvis examined his watch. "Any time now."

"You got time. Play us something."

"Was I talking to this here lamppost? Black Elvis don't play no bus stops."

"Black *what?*" said the bigger of the two boys.

"Elvis."

"Dude is tripping *out.*"

"Yo, Black Elvis. Why don't you help us out with a couple of dollars? Me and my boy here, we need to get some things at the store."

He considered. He had bus fare and another eight dollars on top of that, which he intended to use for beer at Slab's. In case of emergency, there was the ten-dollar bill in his shoe, under the Air-Pillo Insole. He dug into his pocket and pulled out two ones.

"All right, then," he said, and handed them the money.

The smaller one leaned very close as he took it. He was about the same size as Black Elvis, and he smelled strongly of underarm.

"You crazier than shit, ain't you?"

"You take that two dollars," Black Elvis said calmly as the bus pulled in, "go on over to Kroger's, and get yourself some Right Guard."

At Slab's, the smell of grilled meat permeated the walls and the painted windows that advertised ribs, beer, and live music, and extended well out into the parking lot. The dinner rush had already started, and there was a good-sized line of people waiting to place orders. Larry was working the register, grizzled white stubble standing out against his nut-brown skin, grease flames shooting up from the grill behind him as slabs and half slabs were tossed onto the fire. If hell had a front desk, he looked like he was manning it.

Butch, who ran the blues jam, was at his usual front table near the stage, finishing a plate of ribs, beans, and slaw. "Black Elvis," he said, with enthusiasm. He wiped his mouth with a napkin, then smoothed his goatee. His pink face glistened with a thin layer of sweat. "What is up?"

"Oh, you know, same old, same old. You got me?"

"I got you, man, don't worry." He tapped a legal pad with one thick finger. "Wouldn't be the blues jam without Black Elvis."

"I know that's right."

"You heard about Juanita?"

"No."

"Oh, man. She died last night. In her sleep. Put in her regular shift, just sassing people like she always did, you know. Didn't seem like anything was wrong with her at all. But I guess she had a bad ticker. She was a little overweight."

"She was, at that." He thought about Juanita's huge butt and breasts, how she more waddled than walked. But dead? How could that be?

"Yeah, it's a sad thing," said Butch. "Kind of makes you realize how fragile it all is, for all of us."

He watched as the drummer hauled the house snare drum out from the women's bathroom, where it was stored, up next to the stage. The wall behind the stage was painted to look like Stone Mountain, but instead of Confederate generals, the faces looking down at the crowd were those of B. B. King, Muddy Waters, Robert Johnson, and someone else who Black Elvis could never be quite sure about. Whoever had done the painting wasn't much of an artist.

"Hey, you want a beer?" Butch poured the remainder of the pitcher on the table into what looked like a used glass. "Go on, man, on the house."

Black Elvis picked up a napkin and ran it carefully around the rim of the glass. "Thanks," he said.

He found himself a seat next to a table of rich white folks who had been to some movie and were arguing about whether the actress in it had had her breasts enlarged. It had been a long time since Black Elvis had been to the movies, although he sometimes watched the ones they had running back in the video department of the Kroger's, where he cut meat. They mostly looked the same to him, flickering postage stamps of color. They ought never to have gone to color, he thought. A picture ought to be in black and white.

He remembered going to a picture with his father years ago that had pirates in it and Errol Flynn. His father wouldn't buy him popcorn, said it was a waste of money. He must have been about eight. The war was over. There were ships and sword fighting and men with long hair, and suddenly his daddy was pressing a hard-boiled egg into his hand, and saying, "Go on, boy, take it." He ate the egg, shucking it carefully into his hand and placing the shells into the pocket of his shirt, while all around him he smelled the popcorn he really wanted.

He looked up. They'd asked him something, but he could not be sure what.

"Napkins?"

He pushed the dispenser toward them. He'd drifted someplace, it seemed. He took a swallow of beer. He needed something inside him, that was all — some weight to keep him from floating away. He was Black Elvis. He had a show to put on.

He'd been doing the jam now for four years. Everyone knew him. They relied on him. Sometimes he changed his repertoire around a little bit, threw in "Can't Help Falling in Love" or something else unusual — he had a version of "You Were Always on My Mind," but it just never sounded right to him — but for the most part he was a Sun Sessions man. "That's All Right, Mama" for an opener. "Hound Dog." "All Shook Up." "Milkcow Blues Boogie." If there was a band, he'd play with them — he liked that — but it didn't matter, he could do his songs by himself, too. He twisted his lip, stuck out his hip, winked at the ladies. Two years ago, *Creative Loafing* had done an article on Slab's, and his picture appeared next to it, almost as if his face were an addition to the mural, and he kept this taped to the wall next to his bed.

There were moments he'd tucked away in his mind the way people keep photos in their wallets, ones that stood out from the succession of nights of cigarette and pork-grease smell, of cold beers and loud music. The time he'd explained to a fine young blond-haired girl, whose boyfriend had come down to show off his rock-and-roll guitar playing, that it was Elvis who had said, "I'd rather see you dead, little girl, than to be with another man," in "Baby, Let's Play House," and not the Beatles, and the way she'd looked at him then, and said, "You mean they *stole* it?" and he smiled, and said, "That's exactly what I mean." Or the time a young white man in a suit gave him a fifty-dollar tip, and said, "You're the best dang thing I've seen in this whole dang town, and I been here one year exactly come Friday."

He should have been the first one called. That was usual. That was the way things went on blues jam night. But that wasn't what happened. Instead, Butch played a few songs to open — "Let the Good Times Roll" and "Messin' with the Kid" — then stepped to the microphone and looked right past Black Elvis.

"We got a real treat here tonight," he said. "Let's all give it up for Mr. Robert Johnson. I'm serious now, that's his real name. Give him a nice hand."

From somewhere in the back, a person in an old-fashioned-looking suit and fedora worked his way up through the crowded restaurant, holding a black guitar case up high in front of him. Trailing out from the back of the hat was a straight black ponytail. When he reached the stage he opened the case and took out an antique guitar. He turned around and settled into a chair, pulling the boom mike down and into place for him to sing, while Butch arranged another mike for the instrument. Black Elvis just stared.

The man was Chinese.

"Glad to be here," said Robert Johnson. "I only been in Atlanta a week, but I can tell I'm going to like it a lot already." He grinned a big, friendly grin. His voice sounded southern. "Just moved here from Memphis," he said. "First thing I did, I said, 'Man, where am I gonna get me some decent ribs in this town?'" He plucked at the guitar, made a kind of waterfall of notes tumble out of it. "I can tell I'm going to be putting on some weight around here." There was laughter from the crowd.

Black Elvis drank some more beer and listened carefully as Robert Johnson began to play the Delta blues. He was good, this boy. Probably spent years listening to the original recordings, working them out note for note. Either that, or he had a book. Some of those books had it like that, exact translations. But that wasn't important. What was important was on the *inside*. You had to *feel* the music. That just didn't seem likely with a Chinese man, even one that came from Memphis.

He did "Terraplane Blues." He did "Sweet Home Chicago" and "Stones in My Pathway." He played "Love in Vain." Black Elvis felt something dark and opiate creeping through his blood, turning harder and colder as it did so. On the one hand, it should have been him up there, making the crowd love him. But the more he watched, the more he was convinced that he simply could not go on after Robert Johnson. With his pawn shop guitar and clumsy playing, he'd just look like a fool.

He watched Butch's face and saw the enjoyment there. He'd never seen the crowd at Slab's be so quiet or attentive to a performer. Robert Johnson *did* feel the music, even if he was Chinese. It was strange. Black Elvis glanced toward the front door and wondered if there were any way at all he might slip unnoticed through the crowded tables and out.

When Robert Johnson finished his set, people applauded for what seemed like hours. He stood and bowed, antique guitar tucked under one arm. Black Elvis felt he was watching the future, and it was one that did not include him. But that was negative thinking. You couldn't let yourself fall into that. He'd seen it happen to other people his age, the shadows who walked around his neighborhood, vacant-eyed, waiting to die. Esther, who lived in 2C, just below him, who watched television with the volume all the way up and opened the door only once a week for the woman from Catholic Social Services to come deliver her groceries. That woman had stopped up to see Black Elvis, but he'd sent her away. Ain't no Catholic, he'd said. That's not really necessary, she told him. So he told her he carried his own groceries, and got a discount on them, too. And as she was leaving he asked her if she knew what God was, and when she didn't answer, he told her: "The invention of an animal that knows he's going to die."

They were talking to him again, those people at the next table. He shook his head and wondered where he'd gone. His mind was like a bird these days.

"You're up," they told him. "They want you."

He brought his guitar up onto the stage. Robert Johnson had taken a seat with Butch, and they were talking intently about something. Butch had out a datebook and was writing in it. Butch also booked the music for Slab's on the other nights, the ones where the performers got paid. Robert Johnson's Chinese eyes squinted as tight as pistachio nuts when he smiled.

"Black Elvis," someone shouted. He heard laughter.

"I'm going to do something a little different," he said into the microphone. "A good person passed last night. Some of you probably heard about it by now. Juanita —" He struggled to find her last name, then heard himself say "Williams," which he was certain was wrong, but was the only name he could come up with. "Juanita was, you know, family for us here at Slab's, and we loved her. So I'd like to dedicate this song to Juanita. This one for you, baby."

He played a chord and was not surprised when his fourth string snapped like an angry snake striking. Ignoring this, he began to sing.

"Amazing grace, how sweet the sound . . ."

He didn't know if the next chord should be the same, or different, so he just played E again. It wasn't right, but it wasn't that wrong.

"That saved a wretch like me . . ."

He remembered his mother singing this. He could see her on the porch, stroking his sister Mae's head, sitting in the red metal chair with the flaking paint, the smell of chicken cooking in the kitchen flowing out through the patched window screen. His own voice sounded to him like something he was hearing at a great distance.

"I once was lost, but now I'm found . . ."

The people were staring at him. Even Larry had stopped ringing up sales and was watching, the fires continuing to dance behind him.

"Was blind, but now I see."

He lowered his head and hit a few more chords. He felt like he was in church, leading a congregation. He looked up, then nodded somberly and went back to his chair.

"That was beautiful, man," said Butch, coming over to him. "Just fucking beautiful."

Robert Johnson offered to buy him a beer.

"All right," said Black Elvis. "Molson's."

"Molson's, it is." He was gone a few minutes, then returned with a pitcher and two glasses. "I like a beer with flavor," he said. "Microbrews and such."

"I like beer that's cold," said Black Elvis. "I like it even better if it's free."

"Hard to argue with that, my man." He filled the glasses. "I'm sorry to hear about your friend."

Black Elvis stared at him.

"Juanita?"

"That's right. Tragedy. They say she had a bad ticker. She *was* a little overweight, now." He thought again about her. She'd had a lot of facial hair, he remembered that. And she used to wear this chef's hat.

"This is a nice place," said Robert Johnson, looking around. The next group was setting up on stage. "Real homey."

"This is the best place for ribs and blues in Atlanta. Don't let no one tell you different." He peered at Robert Johnson's round, white face. "So, you from Memphis, huh?"

"That's right."

"Memphis, China?"

Robert Johnson laughed. "I'm Korean, not Chinese. Well, my parents are. I was born here. But I've always loved black music. I grew up around it, you know."

"What kind of guitar that is you play?"

"Martin. 1924 00–28 Herringbone. I wish I could tell you I found it in an attic or something, but it's not that good a story. I paid a lot for it. But it's got a nice sound, and it fits with the whole Robert Johnson act, you know?" He adjusted his tie. "I've learned that it's not enough to just be good at what you do, you have to have a marketing angle, too."

"Marketing, you say."

"I've got me a gig here already for next weekend."

Black Elvis was quiet for a moment. "You been to Graceland?"

"Graceland! Well, of course I've been to Graceland. Everyone in Memphis has been to Graceland."

"What's it like?"

"What's it like?" He gave a silver ring on his middle finger a half turn. "Tacky. In some ways, it feels like holy ground, but at the same time, you also feel like you're at an amusement park. The Jungle Room is pretty cool, I guess."

"Sun Studios?"

"They have tours, but I've never done one. If you're so interested, you ought to go."

"You think so?"

"Sure. Why not?"

"You got connections there? Like who could get me a gig?"

Robert Johnson considered this. Black Elvis realized that he'd done exactly what he'd wanted not to do, which was to put this person in a position where he had power over him. But he couldn't get it out of his head that there was something about this meeting that was more than chance. He had a feeling Robert Johnson was someone he was *supposed* to meet, if only he could determine why.

"I don't think so. I mean, if you're going to do an Elvis thing, you're probably better off just about anyplace *but* Memphis. Of course, that's just my opinion."

"I'll bet they don't have no black Elvises."

"Are you kidding? Black, Chinese, Irish, Jewish, you name it. You think fat white men in hairpieces have the market cornered on Elvis impersonation? I know a place where they have a dwarf who sings 'Battle Hymn of the Republic' every evening at ten while two strippers give each other a bath, right onstage."

For a moment, he imagined a big stage — an opera house — with hundreds of Elvises of all shapes and colors pushing and shoving each other to get to the front. The thought made him shiver. "Don't matter. I'm an original."

"No doubt. If you don't mind my asking, what made you decide to start doing this?" He looked at Black Elvis with admiration. "I love your hair, incidentally. I mean, if I looked like you, Jesus. I'd be working all the time. You just have that natural blues man look. You could be John Lee Hooker's cousin or something."

"I don't care much for blues music," said Black Elvis. He sniffed. "Never have."

"Really?"

"I like that rock and roll."

"Well, whatever makes you happy." Robert Johnson made a move to get up.

"No, wait," said Black Elvis, suddenly anxious. "Tell me something. Is that what you think? Have I gotten it wrong all this time? Should I be doing something else? You play good, you sing good, you know about marketing. Just tell me, and I'll listen. I don't have that much time left."

Robert Johnson stood up and adjusted his fedora. He looked slightly embarrassed. "I gotta go talk to a young woman over there," he said. "She's been staring at me ever since I got here. I'm sure you understand." He picked up a napkin and held it out. "You got a little nosebleed going."

Black Elvis took the napkin and held it tight against his nose.

When he got home, Juanita was waiting for him in the living room, wearing her chef's hat and a stained serving apron, her wide body taking up half the sofa.

"You late," she said. "Did you have a good time?"

"Good time?" he said. He thought about this. He didn't really go to the blues jam for a good time. He went because it gave him a purpose, a place to be, and because by now it just seemed that if he *didn't* go, all hell might break loose. The sun might not come up in the morning. "I sang you a song," he said.

"That right? What you sing? One of them Elvis songs?"

"'Amazing Grace.'"

"Well, that's nice. You've got blood on your shirt, you know."

"Mmmm-hmmmm." He pulled up a chair and sat opposite her. He had not turned on any lights, and her figure was shadowy and evanescent, like a glimpse of a fish below the surface of a fast stream. "You supposed to be dead, now."

"Supposed to be."

"Bad ticker, huh?"

"Just stopped on me."

"Hurt?"

"Shit yes. For a second it felt like someone hit me in the chest with a sledgehammer. Now, tell me the truth, how come you singing songs for me? You know I don't care for you much at all. I'd have thought the feeling was mutual."

"Let me turn on a light."

"Don't do that. I like it better in the dark. Come on, now, what's with the song?"

Black Elvis closed his eyes for a moment. "There was a man there, a Chinese man. He took my spot."

"And so you go all churchy? You just nothing but a hypocrite. Just a big old faker."

"I don't believe in you," said Black Elvis. "And I'm turning on the light."

"I don't believe in you, either," said Juanita. "Go ahead."

He cut on the light, and she was gone, as he'd suspected she would be. From the street below, he heard shouting and laughter. He went over to the window and pulled back the curtains just far enough to see.

The two boys he'd seen earlier were out in the middle of the street. One had a spray can of paint and was walking slowly back and forth, while the other, the bigger one, watched and occasionally shouted encouragement. At first, he couldn't tell what the image was, but then the lines began to come together and he realized that it was him the boy was painting, Black Elvis, spray-painted twenty feet high down the center of the street. He watched in amazement as the details took shape, his pompadour, the serious eyes, sideburns, pouting lips.

"Believe in me," he said. "Stupid woman."

AMY BLOOM

The Story

FROM STORY

YOU WOULDN'T have known me a year ago.

A year ago I had a husband, and my best friend was Margeann at the post office. In no time at all my husband got cancer, house prices tumbled in our part of Connecticut, and I got a new best friend. Realtors' signs came and went in front of the house down the road: from the elegant forest green-and-white FOR SALE BY OWNER, nicely handmade to show that they were in no hurry and in no need, to MARTHA BRAE LEWIS AND COMPANY, Realtors who sold only very expensive houses and rode horses in the middle of the day when there was nothing worthwhile on the market and then down, down to the big national relocator company's fiberboard sign practically shouting, "Fire Sale, You Can Have This House for Less Than They Paid for It." My place was nothing special compared to my neighbor's, but it did have the big stained-glass windows Ethan had made, so beautiful, sightseers drove right up our private road, parked by the birches, and begged to come in, just to stand there in the rays of purple and green light, to be charmed by twin redheaded mermaids flanking the front door, to run their fingers over the cobalt blue drops sprayed across the hall, bezel set into the plaster. They stood between the cantering cinnabar legs of the centaur in the middle of the kitchen wall and sighed. After coffee and cookies they would order two windows or six or, one time, wild with real estate money, people from Gramercy Park ordered a dozen botanical panels for their new house in Madison, and Ethan always said, "Why do you do that?" I did it for company and for money, since I needed both and Ethan didn't care. When he asked for the mail, without looking up, or even when he

made the effort to ask about my bad knee, not noticing that we'd
last spoken two full days ago, it was worse than the quiet. If I didn't
ask the New Yorkers for money, he'd shuffle around in his mocca-
sins, picking at his nails until they made an insulting offer or got
back in their cars, baffled and rich.

Six months after Ethan caught cancer like a terrible cold and
died, I went just once to the Unitarian widows group in which all
the late husbands were much nicer than mine had been and even
the angriest woman only said, "Goddamn his smoking," and I
thought, His smoking? Almost all that I liked about Ethan was his
stained glass, his small, wide hands, and the fact that he was willing
to marry Plain Jane me when I thought no one would, and willing
to stay by me when I lost the baby. That was such a bad time I didn't
leave the house for two months and Ethan invited the New Yorkers
in just to get me out of bed. Other than that, I only thought that
if you didn't hate your silent, moody husband after twenty years,
and he didn't seem to hate you and your big blob of despair, you
could call it a good thing, no worse than other marriages. That last
month was like the honeymoon we never took, and when strangers
talk to me now, I sound like a woman who lost her beloved and
grieves still.

I have dead parents — the best kind, I think, at this stage of life
— two sisters, whom I do love at a little distance, a garden that is as
close to God as I need it to be, and a book group I've been in for
fourteen years, which also serves as mastectomy hot line, meno-
pause watch, and PFLAG. I don't mind being alone, having been
raised by hard-drinking, elderly parents, a German and a Swede,
with whom I never had a fight or a moment's pleasure, and I took
off for college at sixteen, with no idea of what to say to these girls
with outerwear for every season (fall coats and spring jackets and
pale blue anoraks) and underwear that was nicer than my church
clothes. Having made my own plain, dark way, and having been
with plain, dark but talented Ethan such a long time, I've been
pleasantly surprised in middle age, to have yoga and gardening for
my soul, and bookkeeping to pay the bills. Clearly, my whole life
was excellent training for money managing of all kinds, and now I
do the books for twenty people like Ethan, gifted and without a
clear thought in their heads about organizing their finances or
feeding their families, if they're lucky enough to have more than a
tiny profit to show for what they do.

I didn't call my new neighbors the Golddust Twins. Margeann, our postmaster, called them that. She nicknamed all the New Yorkers, and preread their magazines and kept the catalogues that most appealed to her. Tallblondgorgeous, she said. And gobs of money, she said. Just gobs of money, and Mr. Golddust had a little sense but she had none and they had a pretty little blond baby who would grow up to be hell on wheels if the mother didn't stop giving her Coca-Cola at nine in the morning and everything else she asked for. And they surely needed a bookkeeper, Margeann said, because Doctor Mrs. Golddust was a psychiatrist and he did something mysterious in the import and export of art. I could tell, just from that, that they would need me, the kind of bookkeeper and accountant and paid liar who could call black white and look you straight in the eye. I put my business card in their mailbox, which they (I assumed she) had covered in bits of fluorescent tile, making a rowdy little work of art, and they called me that night. She invited themselves over for coffee on Sunday morning.

"Oh my God, this house is gorgeous. Completely charming. And that stained glass. You are a genius, Mrs. Baker. Mrs.? Not Ms.? Is Janet all right? This is unbelievable. Oh my God. And your garden. Unbelievable. Miranda, don't touch the art. Let Mommy hold you up to the light. Like a fairy story."

Sam smiled and put out his hand, my favorite kind of male hand, what I would call shapely peasant, auburn hairs on the first joint of each finger and just a little ginger patch on the back. His hands must have been left over from early Irish farmers; the rest of him looked right out of a magazine.

"I know I'm carrying on, but I can't help it. Sam, darlingdarling, please take Miranda so Janet and I can just explore for two minutes."

We walked out to the centauries, and she brushed her long fingers against their drooping blue fringe.

"Can I touch? I'm not much of a gardener. That card of yours was just a gift from God. Not just because of the bookkeeping, but because I wanted to meet you after I saw you in town. I don't think you saw me. At the Dairy Mart."

I had seen her, of course.

"Sam, Janet has forgiven me for being such a loony. Maybe she'll help us out of our financial morass."

Sam smiled and scooped Miranda up just before she smacked

into the coffee table corner. He said he would leave the two of us to it and any help at all would be better than what he had currently. He pressed my hands together in his and put two files between them, hard clear plastic with "MoBay Exports, Incorporated" embossed across the front and a manila folder with stationery from Dr. Sandra Saunders sticking out of it. I sent them away with blueberry jam and a few begonia cuttings. Coming from New York, she thought any simple thing you could do in a garden was wonderful.

Sandra called, "I can tell Miranda's fallen in love with you. Could you possibly watch her tomorrow? Around five? Just for a half hour? Sam has to go to the city."

After two tantrums, juice instead of Coke, stories instead of videos, and no to her organdy dress for playing in the sandbox, it was seven o'clock, then eight. I gave Miranda dinner and a bath. She was, in fact, a very sweet child, and I thought that her mother, like mine, meant well but seemed not to have what was called for. When Sandra came home, Miranda ran to her but looked out between her legs and blew me a kiss.

"Say 'We love you, Janet,'" Sandra said.

"We love you, Jah-net."

"Say 'Please come tomorrow for drinks, Janet.'"

Miranda sighed. "Drinks, Jah-net," she said, indulgently.

I kissed them both good-bye. I had never had such fresh, sweet skin under my lips, Miranda's peach and Sandra's apricots-and-cream moisturizer, and although I wasn't attracted to women or girls, I could see why a person would be.

I planted a small square garden near Sam's studio, sweet William and campanula and Violet Queen asters with a little rosemary bonsai that Miranda could put her pinkie-sized plastic babies around. Sandra was gone more than Sam was. He worked in the converted barn with computers and screens and two faxes and four phone lines, and every time I visited, he brought me a cup of tea and admired our latest accomplishments.

He said, "It's very good of you to do this."

"I don't mind," I said.

"We could always get a sitter," he said, but he knew I knew that wasn't true, because I had done their books.

Can I say that the husband was not any kind of importer? Can I say that he was what he really was, a successful cartoonist? That they lived right behind me, in a house I still find too big and too showy, even now that I am in it?

I haven't even described the boyfriend, the one Sandra went off to canoodle with while I baby-sat. Should I write him as tall and blond when in fact he was dark and muscular, like the husband? It will be too confusing for readers if both men are dark and fit, with long ponytails, but they both were. And they drove the same kind of truck, making for more confusion.

I've given them blandly wholesome, modern names, wishing for the days of Aunt Ada Starkadder and Martin Chuzzlewit and Pompeo Lagunima. Sam's real name conveys more of his rather charming shy stiffness and rectitude, but I keep "Sam," which has the advantage of suggesting an unlikely, misleading blend of Jewish and New England, and I'll call the boyfriend "Joe," suggesting a general good-natured lunkishness. Sandra, as I've named her, actually was a therapist, just as I've written her, but not a psychiatrist, and I disliked her so much, I can't bear to make you think, even in this story, that she had the discipline and drive and intellectual persistence to become a physician. She had nothing but appetite and brass balls, and she was the worst mother I ever saw. Even now, I regard her destruction as a very good thing, which may undermine the necessary fictive texture of deep ambiguity, the roiling ambivalence that gives tension to the narrator's affection.

Sandy pinched her child for not falling asleep quickly enough; she gave her potato chips for breakfast and Slurpees for lunch; she cut her daughter's hair with pinking shears and spent two hundred dollars she didn't have on her own monthly Madison Avenue haircuts. She left that child in more stores than I can remember, cut cocaine on her changing table, and blamed the poor little thing for every disappointment and heartache in her own life, until Miranda's eyes welled up at the sound of her mother calling her name. And if Sandy was not evil, she was worse than foolish, and sick, and, more to the point, incurable. If Sandra were smooshed inside a wrecked car splattered against the inside of a tunnel, I wouldn't feel even so sad for her as I did for Princess Diana, for whom I felt very little indeed.

I think the opening works, and the part about the widows group is true, although I've left out the phone call I got a week after the group met, when the nicest widow, an oversized Stockard

Channing, invited me to a dinner with unmistakable overtones and I didn't go. I wish I had gone; that dinner and its aftermath might make a better story than this one I've been fooling with.

I don't want to leave out the time Sandra got into a fistfight with Joe's previous girlfriend, who knocked Sandra down into the middle of her own potato salad at the Democrats annual picnic, or the time Joe broke into the former marital home after Sandra moved out and threw Sam's library into the fire, not realizing that he was also destroying Sandra's collection of first editions. And when he was done, drunk and sweating, I sat on my porch, watching through my late husband's binoculars ("Ethan" is very much my late husband, a sculptor, not a glassmaker, but correct in the essentials of character; my husband wasn't dead before I met them; he died a year later, and Sam was very kind and Sandra was her usual charming, useless self). I saw Joe trip on little Miranda's Fisher-Price roller skate and slide down the ravine. I went to sleep, and when Sam called me the next day, laughing and angry, watching an ambulance finally come up his long gravel drive and the EMTs put splints all over Joe the Boyfriend, I laughed too and brought over corn chowder and my own rye bread for Sam and Miranda.

I don't have any salt-of-the-earth-type friends like Margeann. Margeanns are almost always crusty and often black and frequently given to pungent phrases and earth wisdom. Sometimes, they're someone's grandmother. In men's stories they're either old and disreputable drinking buddies, someone's tobacco-chewing, trout-fishing grandpaw, or the inexplicably devoted sidekick-of-color, caustic and true.

My friends in real life are two other writers — the movie critic for our nearest daily newspaper and a retired home-and-garden freelancer I've been playing tennis with for twenty years. Estelle, my tennis buddy, has more the character of the narrator than I do, and I thought I could use her experience with Sandra to make a story line. Sandra had sprinkled her psychobabble all over poor Estelle, got her coming three times a week, cash on the table, and had almost persuaded her to leave Dev, her very nice husband, in order to "explore her full potential." Estelle's entire full potential is to be the superb and good-natured tennis partner she is, a gifted gardener (which is where I got all that horticultural detail), and a poor cook and worse housekeeper for an equally easygoing, rosy-cheeked man who inherited two million dollars when he was fifty and about whom I can say nothing worse than at eighty-three Dev's not quite as sharp as he was — although he's nicer. I could not imagine how else Estelle's full potential, at seventy-seven, with cataracts in her left eye, bad hearing, and not the least interest in art, theater, movies, or politics, would express itself. I persuaded Dev to take her on a fancy cruise, two weeks through the canals of France, and when they came back, beaming pinkly, a little chubby, and filled with lively remarks about French bread and French cheese, Estelle said nothing more about her underdeveloped potential and nothing more about meeting with Sandra.

I see that I've made Sam sound more affably dodgy than he really is. He wouldn't have caught my eye in the first place if he was no more than the cardboard charmer I describe, and he was tougher than Joe, in the end. Even if Sandra hadn't been a bad mother, I might have imagined a complex but rosy future with Sam and Miranda, if I was capable of imagining my future.

I don't know what made Sandra think I would be her accomplice. If you are thin and blondly pretty and used to admirers, maybe you see them wherever there are no rivals. But, hell, I read the ladies' magazines and drove all the way to Westport for a new haircut and spent money on clothes, and although she didn't notice that I was coming over in silk knit T-shirts and black jeans, Sam did. When Sandra called me, whispering from Joe's bed, "Ohmigod, make something up, I lost track of time," I didn't. I walked over with dinner for Sam and Miranda, and while Miranda sat in front of her computer, I said, "I'm a bad liar. Sandra called from Joe's. She asked me to make something up, but I can't."

There is no such thing as a good writer and a bad liar.

After she moved out, she called me most mornings, just to report on the night before. She was in heaven. Joe was wonderful in every way but terribly jealous of Sam. Very silly, of course. Very flattering.

I called Joe in the late afternoons. I said, "Oh, Sandy's not there? Oh, of course." Joe was possibly the most easily led person God ever made. I didn't even have to drop a line, I just dangled it loosely and flicked. I said, "She's not at the office. She must be at home. I mean, at Sam's. It's great that they're getting along, for Miranda's sake. Honestly, I think they're better friends now that they're separated."

I did that twice a week, making up different reasons for calling. Joe hit her, once. She told me and I touched the round bruise on her jaw, begging her to press charges, but she didn't.

The part where Joe drove his truck into the back of Sam's house is too good to leave out, and tells funnier than it really was, although the rear end of his pickup sticking out through acres of grape arbor was pretty funny, as was the squish-squish of the grapes as Joe tried to extricate himself, and the smell of something like wine sweeping over us as he drove off, vines twirling around his tires.

I reported Sandy to the ethics committee of the Connecticut Association of Family Counselors. All the things she shouldn't have told me — how she did things in her office, and her financial arrangements with her patients, and the stock tips they gave her, and her insistence on being paid in cash in advance — and the fact that I, who was no kind of therapist at all, knew all these things and all their names, was enough to make them suspend her license for six months.

Sophisticated readers understand that writers work out their anger, their conflicts, their endless grief and rolling list of loss, through their stories. That however mean-spirited or diabolical, it's only a story. That the darkness in the soul is shaped into type and lies there, brooding and inert, black on the page but active, dangerous, only in the reader's mind. Actually, harmless. I am not harmless.

The story I had hoped to write would have skewered her, of course. Anyone who knew her would have read it, known it was her, and thought badly of her while reading. She would have been embarrassed and angry. That really was not what I had in mind. I wanted her skin like a rug on my floor, her slim throat slit, heart still beating behind the newly bricked-up wall. In stories, when someone behaves uncharacteristically, we know a meaningful, even pivotal, moment has come. If we are surprised too often, we either vacillate or just give up and close the book. In real life, when people think they know you, know you well enough not only to say, "It's Tuesday, she must be helping out at the library today," but well enough to have said to the librarian, after you've left the building, "You know, she just loves reading to the four-year-olds. I think it's been such a comfort to her since her little boy died" — when they know you like that, you can do almost any bad, secretive thing and if they hear about it, they will, as readers do, simply disbelieve the narrator.

I find that I have no sympathy with the women who have nannies, on top of baby sitters on top of beepers and pagers and party coordinators, or with the older ones who want to give back their damaged, distressing adopted children, or with the losers who sue to get their children back when they had given them to adequate and loving parents three years before. In my world, none of them would be allowed to be mothers, and if they had slipped through my licensing bureau, their children would be promptly removed and all traces of their maternal claims erased.

As Sandra's dear friend and reliable baby sitter, it was easy to hire Joe to do a little work on my front porch, easy to have him bump into my research assistant, the two of them as much alike as a pair of pretty quarter horses, easy to fuel Sandra's sudden wish to move farther out of town. Easy to send the ethics committee the information they needed to remove her license permanently, easy to suggest she manage Joe's business, easy to suggest that children need quality time not quantity, and that young, handsome lovers need both, easy to wave Sandra and Joe off in their new truck (easy to arrange a ten-thousand-dollar loan when you are such a steady customer of the local bank and own your home outright).

I can't say I didn't intend harm. I did and would not have minded even death, and if death is beyond my psychological reach, then disappearance, which is worse because it's not permanent but better, because there is no body.

And I am like a wife now to this lovely, appreciative man who thinks me devoted and kind, who teases me for trembling at dead robins on the patio, for crying openly at AT&T commercials. And I am like a mother to this girl as rapacious and charming and roughly loving as a lion cub. The whole house creaks with their love, and I walk the floors at night, up and down the handsome distressed pine stairs, in and out of the library and the handmade-in-England kitchen through a family room big enough for anything but contact sports. In the daylight, I make myself garden — fruit trees, flowers, and herbs — and it's no worse than doing the crossword puzzle, as I used to. I have taken a bookkeeping class; we don't need an accountant anymore. I don't write so much as an essay for the library newsletter, although I still volunteer there and at Miranda's school, of course, and I keep our nice house nice. I go to parties where people know not to ask writers how it's going and I still play tennis. Although I feel like a fool and worry that the Tai Chi teacher will sense that I am not like the others, I go twice a week, for whatever balance it will give me.

I slip into the last row and I do not look at the pleasant, dully focused faces of the women on either side of me. *Bear Catching Fish,* she says, and moves her long arms overhead and down, trailing through the imaginary river. *Crane,* and we rise up on one single, shaky leg. At the end of class, we are all sweating lightly, lying in the dusty near-dark of the Lyman School gym. The floor smells of boys and rubber and rosin, and I leave before they rise and bow to each other, hands in front of sternum, ostentatiously relaxed and transcendent.

In the farthest northwest corner of our property, on the far side of the last stand of skinny maples, I put up an arbor and covered it with Markham's Pink clematis and Perle d'Azur. The giant heart-shaped leaves of Dutchman's pipe turn my corner into a secret place. I carried the pieces of a large cedar bench down there one night last fall and assembled it by flashlight.

There is no one in this world now who knew my baby or me, when I was twenty-eight, married four years and living in the graduate student apartments of the University of California at Berkeley. Our apartment was next to a pale, hunched engineer from New Jersey, who lived next to an anguished physicist from Chad and his good-natured Texan wife, baking Derby pie and corn bread for the whole floor, and we were all across from the brilliant Indian brothers, both mathematicians, both with gold-earringed little girls and wives so quick with numbers that when Berkeley's power went out, as it often did during bad weather, the cash registers were replaced by two thin, dark women in fuchsia and turquoise saris rustling over their raw silk *cholis,* adding up the figures without even a pencil. Our babies and toddlers played in the courtyard and the fathers watched and played chess and drank beer and we watched and brushed sand out of the children's hair and smoked Marlboros and were friends in a very particular, young, and hopeful way.

When Eddie died, they all came to the little funeral at the university chapel and filled our apartment with biscuits and samosas and brisket and with their kindness and their own sickening relief. We left the next day, like thieves. I did not finish my Ph.D. in English literature. My husband did not secure a teaching position at the University of San Francisco, and when I meet people who remember Mario Savio's speeches on the steps of Sproul Hall and their cinder-block apartments on Dwight Way, I leave the room. My own self is buried in Altabates Hospital, still between the sheet and the mattress of his peach plastic Isolette, twisted around the tubes that wove in and out of him like translucent vines, trapped inside that giant ventilator, four times Eddie's size without being of any use to him or his little lungs.

I have made the best and happiest ending that I can, in this world, made it out of the flax and netting and leftover trim of someone else's life, I know, but I made it to keep the innocent safe and the guilty punished, and I made it as the world should be and not as I have found it.

MICHAEL BYERS

The Beautiful Days

FROM PLOUGHSHARES

IN THE DAYS of his youth, Aldo often found himself — as many of us did — in a state of grace, and the sensation in his boundless filling heart resembled, to his mind, the transports of love. His Midwestern college, set down in the middle of a cornfield and isolated from any big city by fifty miles of empty, cold-roughened highway, seemed a basin of happiness in which he had been permitted, by some heavenly dispensation, to swim. Elms, dead elsewhere, had somehow survived in this town, pointing their great forked limbs at the sky. The quarry south of campus, hidden in its fringe of college-owned forest, echoed with the autumn shouts of naked swimmers; and in the frigid winters, skaters hiked the long way through the trees and picked their way carefully down to the ice. The rural sky was a comforting black infested with stars, and though he bruised himself when he skated, the cold Ohio air acted as a sort of balm, or at any rate it numbed him until later, when, in the heat of the town's one diner, he could examine his empurpled knees, not without some pride.

Small towns were new to him. The daily goodness of the Ben Franklin on College Street, offering its yarn and Bic lighters and artificial plants to whomever happened to walk through the swinging glass doors, swelled his soul. The tiny bank employed two tellers, both named Marie. The movie theater with its red velvet seats ran only the most second-rate films, and the screen was stained near the upper-left-hand corner; but this became visible only in outdoor scenes, when the stain resembled a small rain cloud. Despite the bad acting and ridiculous, juvenile plots, Aldo usually left the theater in a haze of goodwill, while around him the town disappeared into darkness down its two main streets, streets which carried their heavy freight of brick and ironwork as they had for 160 years. He loved the town and the college, both lit with a stage-set perfection. Naturally, like many other students, he was often tired and fretted over his schoolwork, and his romances were only middlingly satisfying. He was poor, and had grown chubby on dormitory food. But even when he least expected it, he would be visited with a new gust of this unnameable generosity of spirit, when the world seemed nearly platonic in its perfection. At these times he loved the world with such a passion that he worried he would one day lose his way to this grace, that its sources were more mysterious than the town around him: the pharmacy, its valentine hearts illuminated in the window display; the dense tarry air in the army-navy store. The sensation that he was one among many — and yet still one, an individual being set loose on the planet — and that so much beauty abounded, on all sides, in every form, for him to encounter — all this combined to lift his heart above the ordinary, and made him, when it came, inexpressibly joyful. He was not religious, but such moments drove him to believe that something indefinite stood behind the bright curtain of the world — some great moral idea, some brilliant distillation of planetary consciousness that ringed the earth like a second atmosphere — something. It had come on him slowly in his three years here, this feeling, but now he sensed it defined him, and if he lost it, he feared, it would be like dying. Superstitiously he avoided thinking of it, as much as he could. Grace examined was — he suspected — grace denied.

His apartment off-campus Aldo shared with two relative strangers: a woman pianist named Eleanor, who used her long fingers as leverage to open difficult jars; and Bram, a dull, thick-chested economics major. Eleanor the pianist was taller than he, with a great pianist's wingspan, and irritatingly left behind in the shower's drain trap her short brown hairs. Though pretty, she was a poor housekeeper, and her dirtied knives and half-eaten lunches lingered on the brown Formica counters for days. Beneath the window of her long bedroom she kept a sleek Japanese keyboard, futuristically black and technological; wearing headphones, she tamped its keys with great passion. Bram, who had an almost per-

fectly cylindrical head — except for his jutting nose, it looked as
though it had been painstakingly lathed — strenuously lifted bar-
bells in his small room beneath the eaves, filling the hallway with a
sweaty stink. Strutting to the shower after these sessions, he wore
bikini underwear, his blunt uncircumcised penis visible in outline
beneath the fabric. A girlfriend could be heard in his room late at
night, though she never stayed till morning. As for Aldo, he had his
metal shelves and rickety desk, his Greek and Latin dictionaries —
he was a classics major — and his shoeboxes full of vocabulary
flashcards. In the mirror he was a plumpish, curly-headed version
of his father, shorter by three inches and with his mother's large
sorrowful Italian eyes fastened, somewhat incongruously, above his
father's looming, cavernous nose. While not vain exactly, he liked
his own looks, and was bothered only by the troublesome way his
eyebrows met in the middle, giving him a sort of primitive appearance. He had slept with four girls — women — since his freshman
year, when he had lost his virginity to a slim and fragile-feeling
poetess who had since dropped out of school and gone home to
Columbus. Such were the facts of Aldo Gorman's life at twenty:
sexually adequate, though unremarkable; interesting-looking, and
handsome in the manner of most youths; periodically filled with an
inexplicable grace which, when it faded under some daily pressure,
he feared would never come again; and, not unimportantly, devoted to two dead languages, great sloppy tubs of vocabulary and
syntax he hefted alternately — Greek four times a week, Latin five.
And also, that winter, there was a girl he loved who did not love him
back. Her name was Miranda Lowe.

She sat beside him one day in his glaciology class — a gut, to complete his science requirements — and she had forgotten to bring
her book; would he mind if she looked on at his? "Oh — no," he
said, surprised.

"You'd think, with all this snow," she said, almost whispering, "we
wouldn't need a class on glaciers."

"You'd think," he agreed. "I felt like Amundsen this morning."

She smiled. "I know what you mean."

"Without the dogs."

"I don't think he used dogs," she said. "I think he used ponies."

"Oh," he said. "Really? Ponies?"

"One of them did."

"Actual ponies?"

"I think so," she said, glancing at him shyly, "and then I think they ate them."

"Oh," he said again. In the cold classroom full of melting boots and wet wool, she wore only a thin-looking white cotton sweater imprinted with black dots, as though her own heat were enough to keep her warm. Brown hair, brown eyes, pretty, with a fine long nose: in many ways she was a conventional sort of beauty, but what seemed to be shyness — she wouldn't meet his eyes — distinguished her from any of a hundred beautiful girls, as did, seen this close, the ghostly blond mustache on her upper lip, which he imagined another girl might have eradicated in some way. She seemed, like him, mostly innocent, and it was this that twanged at his heart, producing not love but its disreputable cousin, desire. "Okay?" he asked, before turning the page. "Mmm-hmm," she answered. A tiny feather, released from his puffy down jacket, lifted into the air between them.

But she would not have him. She was from New Mexico, and was already engaged — unusual in their generation, but she had the ring to prove it. In the library she held it out, where, under the fluorescent lights, it seemed a pale, fragile thing. "Two years ago," she said.

The news disappointed him, but it wasn't exactly a surprise. "You see him much?"

"At breaks."

"What's his name?"

"Oh . . . I'll tell you, but you can't laugh."

"All right."

"It's *Elmer.* But he's not what you think!" A flush of embarrassment colored her cheeks, and the sight weakened Aldo's heart. "He's very tall, and he doesn't hunt rabbits. And he talks like a normal person."

"He in school?"

"He's doing his residency now."

"He's a doctor?"

"Yes." She hesitated. "Or — almost. He's got a year still."

"And he's back in New Mexico?"

"No," she said. "He's at Harvard."

"Oh."

"He's going back to New Mexico when he finishes, to work on the reservations." She touched his arm, laughing. "He's not at all snobby."

"I didn't say anything."

"The way you said 'Oh.' It was suspicious."

"Elmer."

"Yes: Elmer Grand," Miranda said. And she pronounced the name with such firmness and resolution that Aldo understood at once he had no chance at her. The name as she spoke it seemed a brand of fine paint, or an excellent, old-fashioned toothpaste — something common, decent, thoroughly goodhearted. Like the glue, he thought.

A junior, Aldo was the only student studying Herodotus that year, under the direction of Larry Feingold — a short, skinny man in his seventies whose two front teeth rested endearingly on his lower lip, like a rabbit's. He seemed happy among his decades of books, with the radiator ticking cozily under the snowy window, and despite his age Feingold had a round, childish head and a great shrubbery of curly black hair; settled back in his worn chair, with his tiny brown shoes propped nimbly on the desktop, he looked more like a boy than anything. When Aldo stumbled, Feingold corrected him with a high cackling giggle — it was meant to be encouraging — and then, with a flourish that seemed showy from so small a man, he would lean forward and take over, speaking first one language and then the other, as though playing tennis with a second, equally agile version of himself.

By January they were skipping around in Book Two and had reached the material on Egypt. "When an Egyptian committed a crime," Feingold said, "*adikema*, it was not the custom of Sabacos to punish him with death, *thanatou*, but instead of the death penalty he compelled the offender, see that? Compelled, in the aorist" — he rolled his eyes with the pleasure of it — "to *raise the level of the soil* in the neighborhood, *geitoniai*, dative of location, of his native town, yes, or home, or — well, yes, *native town*, let's say, for simplicity."

"Raise the soil?"

"Yes," said Feingold. "Hmm. I think, in other words, to build a levee. Against the Nile."

This seemed plausible. But down the page, an entire town had somehow been lifted high above the river, houses and all. Had the buildings been somehow propped on jacks, and soil shoveled beneath them? Or were they collapsible structures that one could take down and put up at will, like tents? And where did the extra soil come from? "No," said Feingold, puzzling, "it's just a levee. See? *In the neighborhood* of his native town." He chewed with his rabbity teeth on his lower lip. "But, hmm. The temple stands in the center of the city, *tou polou,* and, since the level of the buildings everywhere else has been raised, *anaskanomai,* one can look down and get a fine view of it from all around. Now that seems to say —"

"But the temple's on the river."

"Oh, that must be it. So, the temple is down *there,* on an island essentially in the middle of the river. The town is up *here* on the riverbanks. They look down on the temple."

"But they did raise the buildings, he says."

"Yes . . . well, fanciful, maybe. It's hearsay, at least. He gets it from the priests, after all. Or maybe he doesn't mean *buildings* really." Feingold read on. "Oh, but look at this, here. The road is lined, *grammatos,* yes, *lined* on both sides with immense trees, so tall that they seem to touch the sky."

"So . . .?"

"Oh, nothing," said Feingold. "Just those trees. Ancient ancient trees that were *there* once, on the road to the temple. Dead twenty-five hundred years, and yet there they stand. God bless the man for that."

Grace was to be found in the library as well, in the long free weekend mornings, when the sun was out over the snowy fields. From the top-floor windows, the little town could be seen huddled under a Saturday morning's icy calm — Aldo might be in the library as early as eight — while light, the cleanest, brightest illumination he had ever seen, poured down from the tiny, wintry sun and, after caroming off the snowy lawns, went flooding back into the empty sky, to fill it more with light. The world, though cold, was illuminated as though by the gods, in a way that seemed somehow removed from time; and the leathery odor of the hundreds of thousands of books — among them his own Greek lexicon, the paper soft with wear — gave even this modern concrete building a gratifying, antique atmosphere, as though he had sat here for a hundred years, and would sit here a hundred more, until the winter's light consumed him.

But he could not forget Miranda Lowe, and she seemed unable, for her part, to leave him alone. Without meaning to, he had become something of a companion to her. They studied together. She was an English major, and he watched as she beat her way faithfully through *Pamela,* the book's polished black cover becoming creased and scuffed and its spine acquiring a series of white cracks. She *used* the book, writing in it heedlessly, while he, beside her, filled notebooks with long columns of writing, leaving his texts clean, unblemished, as though they had never been read at all. Necrophilic, he supposed. Orderly, at any rate. This contrast between them pleased him, though he couldn't say why, exactly. He enjoyed her teasing, maybe. Pacing restlessly the night before an exam she read the dictionary, folding back page after page. "Megrims," she said. And then after a pause, "Mephitic."

Spending so much time with Miranda allowed him to watch her move around in the world. She had long, graceful arms, and though her legs were unremarkable, her feet, when she slid her shoes onto the checkered carpet, were shapely and even-toed. Small, compact breasts. He was not alone in thinking her beautiful. She had dozens and dozens of friends, far more than Aldo, and many of them were admiring men who, after talking with Miranda, would look him over querulously. He permitted himself to feel some pride at such times, though he knew she considered him a sort of eunuch, not to be feared. This was wounding; but there she was, sitting with him, while the other men had to drift away into the stacks. She did talk endlessly about Elmer, which grew tiring; but to her credit she knew it. "I don't want to," she said, "but he's all I think about sometimes."

"It's understandable."

"You'd like him, I think."

"I think maybe I would."

"*Maybe.* Listen to you. He's such a good guy."

"If he's so good, what's he doing away from you?"

"Oh, stop, he is good. He's always talking about *helping* people. Which is, you know — it's good. But he can actually *do* it, and it's what he wants." She touched his books. "Unlike the rest of us. Like me. I'm so *not* good it's not even funny."

He didn't know what to say to this. "You could teach."

"But I don't like kids. I don't know *what* I'll do, I'm so selfish. He's just so *good,* just categorically good. At least in that particular way."

"Good is good."

"But the thing is, he's *too* good sometimes. In that way. *Socially* good. It's like an act sometimes. Especially . . ."

He waited. "Well, badness is good, too, now and then."

"For a change," she said.

"Exactly."

"Mostly he *is* good," she insisted, "and he can't help it. So don't make fun of him."

"I'm not."

"Yes, you are. You always do. It's because of his silly name."

"Like I'm one to talk."

"I like your name. It's exotic. Not like *Elmer.*"

"Forget his name for once."

"But I can't!" she cried. "Elmer Grand!"

Neither had a car, but when a friend of hers drove to Cleveland after Valentine's Day, Aldo came along, squished in the back seat beside Miranda, their arms mashed together and their legs touching from the hip down. For comfort's sake he extended his arm along the back of the seat. They could almost have been a couple. And her beauty, despite his familiarity with it, had not faded. In fact, under the red neon of the Flats bars, he could hardly look at her. But she talked constantly of Elmer, and her frail ring darted in and out of the light. She irritated him. And he wondered what he was doing here, in the racket of the bar — what he hoped for. Nothing, plainly, would come of any of this. It was foolish to think otherwise. She got up to dance, and Aldo, unable to watch, stayed at the table.

But she sat happily beside him on the way back, smelling of cigarettes. "I forgot to tell you," she whispered, her mouth close to his ear. "Elmer's coming to visit."

"Good," he said. "Have a good time." Outside, the flat, frozen landscape sped past in darkness, and the warm air in the car had taken on a beery, hopeless sort of stink. Drunk, he began to feel a little sick. Jacqueline, on the other side of Miranda, slept, her skull rolling against the window.

"I want you to meet him. You've got a lot in common."

At least one thing, he thought. "I'll look forward to it."

"You'd like him."

"Okay."

"You sound reluctant."

"Let me know when he's coming."

"Why? So you can get sick, I guess."

"No, so I can leave town." Daringly he added, "And take you with me."

In the darkness, she said, "Very funny."

"I mean it."

"If you really meant it," she said, "you wouldn't be sitting here."

"I wouldn't?"

"No. You'd be somewhere else. Alone with me."

"I've always figured that was impossible."

"I know you have." She put a hand on his leg. "That's what I like about you."

"No, what you like," he said, "is that I hang around and adore you, and don't make things awkward by making passes at you, which you would be duty-bound to deflect."

"Oh, duty," she said. Spitefully she removed her hand from his thigh. "'New occasions teach new duties.'"

"You can keep that there."

She turned to look at him, her face dark in the darkened car. Her lips were close to his. "I thought I was duty-bound."

"You've always thought so until now."

"How do you know what I've thought?"

"I know what you tell me," he said.

"Oh — you won't get far that way. Being good." She leaned and kissed him carefully, just once, and sat back again, hand on his leg. Then she took her hand back. No one had noticed. The car motored on dumbly into the night.

"I —" he began.

"No, I'm sorry. I won't do that again," she said, her face turned away.

He leaned to kiss her, but caught only the side of her cheek.

"Please don't," she said. "Please."

He tried again.

"Please, Aldo. I'm sorry."

Touching from hip to calf, they rode the rest of the way home in silence. Drunk, he thought. But still, this was unfair. When he climbed alone from the car, the first to get out, he called his good-nights to everyone, but Miranda said nothing: she merely slid over away from Jacqueline, glanced up at him with her apologetic, beautiful eyes, and closed the door.

After this, she stopped returning his calls. When he encountered her by chance in the library, she seemed always to be idling — killing time. She was still as lovely as ever, but she appeared, to his eyes, preoccupied, as though she had been caught in the dragging middle of one of her gigantic novels. He felt he had missed some opportunity — that had he been more forceful earlier, been more daring, he might have won her, and he regretted his weeks of inaction. But he had only been behaving decently, he told himself, and no one could blame him for that. On the other hand, hadn't he been waiting, vulture-like, for the engagement to be miraculously broken off, so he could snatch Miranda before she touched the earth? And how could that be considered decent behavior? In fact, wasn't he both timid and sleazy — and who would ever bother over a man like that?

By the middle of April, the winter had rounded nicely into an early spring, and the elms, so long dormant, had begun again to bud, acquiring a faint green haze. Elmer Grand had come and gone sometime in March, or so Aldo heard: he had fallen that quickly from her circle. He continued to avoid Eleanor and Bram, and in the meantime Cambyses invaded Egypt from Persia, crossing the Arabian desert to engage Psammenitus at the mouth of the Nile. Years after the battle had been fought, Herodotus walked the battlefield, the dry bones of the fallen still divided, as the bodies had been, into Persian and Egyptian camps. "Yes," said Feingold, "the *skulls*, exactly, of the Persians, are so thin that the merest touch, *epaphes*, with a pebble will pierce them, but the skulls of the Egyptians are so tough —"

"That it is hardly possible —"

Feingold put a narrow hand on the back of his head. "Wait," he said. A look of concern crossed his face. "The skulls —"

"That it is hardly possible," Aldo continued, "to break them with a blow from a stone."

"Yes," said Feingold, puzzled.

"Right?"

"Oh — yes," he said again. "Do you know what I was thinking? How much I would like a drink just now."

"Now?"

"And I don't drink," said Feingold. "I haven't for years. I quit twenty years ago, and since then I've been clean. And now suddenly I need a gin and tonic. Out of the blue." He laid his text gently on his desk. "I was a terrible drunk, you know."

"No."

"Oh, I was. Terrible. I stopped because I nearly killed myself. My liver was calcifying, or whatever it is that happens to livers. Lithifying. And I was just careening all over the county." A look of great distance had entered Feingold's eyes. "I never thought I'd get to be this old. I'm seventy-one." He narrowed his expression. "You're a calm boy."

"Calm," said Aldo. "I guess so."

"No, that's good. I don't mean to put you on the spot. I *wasn't* calm, is what I mean."

"But here you are."

Feingold nodded, once. "Yes, here I am. And almost dead, anyway."

"No getting around it."

"No. A cruel thought, but true. Are you a Jew?"

"Me? No," said Aldo. "I'm not."

"No? I thought you and I . . ." Feingold in his sky blue jacket shrugged. "A Christian?"

"No."

"Nothing at all?"

"I guess not," said Aldo.

"Do you believe in an afterlife?"

"Not really."

"But maybe a little bit?"

"I would like to," he said, "but it seems a little delusional."

"Awfully attractive, though, isn't it? Imagine."

Aldo hesitated. "I believe in grace."

"Oh: grace. Are you Catholic?"

"No, just" — it was inexpressible — "happiness."

"Oh. Well, good. Happiness is good."

"But not *only* happiness . . . *grace,*" he said, ferociously. But worryingly he had not felt it in weeks, and it felt like bad luck mentioning it out loud. "It's the only word. When you know your place in the world."

"Yes, I remember the feeling."

"The beauty," said Aldo. "Something about all . . ." He gestured. But it was eluding him. "Everything being *where* it is, in *time,* in the right proportions. *Beauty.* When things are perfect."

"That which is immortal in us."

"Well —"

"That's grace. And then you get to sin: the sullying of that goodness. But to begin with, starting out, *now,* say, for you, that which is immortal is inherently good, by definition."

"But not all goodness is immortal."

Feingold picked up his book again. "I believe in an afterlife," he said, "because it gives me solace, and because so many people have believed in it before me. If it is a delusion, then it is an old and very decent delusion. But people are starting to come back now, with this new technology." He looked away. "That tunnel of light."

"I've heard there's a biological explanation for it."

"Well."

"Dopamine, or something."

"Well, go fuck yourself, Aldo," said Feingold, mildly, "if you can't let an old man believe what he needs to."

"Sorry. That's what I've read. It's all biological."

"Well, go fuck yourself, anyway," said Feingold, with more force. He closed his book. "Just wait till you're my age. Then you'll be happy? I don't think so."

"I'm sorry."

"You should be." Feingold reclined, looked away. "There are other people in the universe, Aldo," he said. "Pay attention."

That afternoon, feeling guilty and ashamed, and sickened by Bram's grunting, Aldo called Miranda. She picked up immediately. "Why, it's Aldo," she said, surprised. "The long-lost stranger."

"Ha," he said.

"Why haven't you been calling me?"

With some irritation he said, "I have been." And he had: once a week at least. Never home. Always got her housemates. "I've left messages."

She sighed. "I don't always check the machine."

"Well, I've been calling."

"I've got something to tell you, actually, Aldo. A little surprise."

"You do?" She'd broken it off, he thought. "What?"

"I think it's better said in person."

"Okay," he said. "There's a movie tonight."

"Fine."

"I won't do anything," he said. "Scout's honor."

"Oh, I wouldn't know a Boy Scout if I stepped on one."

"Really. I won't do anything."

"Fine," she said.

"Just so you know."

"I know, all right?"

"Good."

"So stop talking about it."

"I can't just not bring it up."

"Look," she said, "I'm sorry I didn't call."

"I was wondering about that."

"It was a stupid thing to do," she said. "I mean in the car. But I do like you."

"I know you do."

"Christ almighty," she said, and laughed. "You're so *somber.*"

Though he knew he had no right to be hopeful, he couldn't help it. With great devotion he shaved the smooth planes of his face in the befogged mirror. Flecks of white foam dotted his earlobes. Cowardly, he was. It was cowardly to see Miranda again, rather than forget about her. Or, if not cowardly, then indulgent. He was purposefully fooling himself. Lying.

But he lied all the time. Despite his protestations to Feingold, he did believe — didn't he? — in something like an afterlife; but what an embarrassment to admit to it! Though if he believed in the soul, as he thought he did, then why not? The soul takes nothing with it into the next world, said Plato, except its education and culture. That was a gratifying thought. Silly and unscientific, but gratifying. The springy air puffed through the bathroom window, drying his hair. On the twilit walk across campus through the daffodils, he felt a little shimmering — a faint suggestion of the old feeling — though by the time he met her at the theater it had gone away again. He didn't mind, really. She was lovely, as she always was, waiting for him under the marquee in a yellow dress, holding a magazine, and abruptly he had the sensation that he was exchanging something — trading in, somehow, the ineffable for the tangible. The loose weave of her dress. "This won't be very good," she said.

"I suppose," he said, "we could go elsewhere."

"Like?"

"I don't know. Valentine's? No."

"So, look." She held out a hand. "I have a new ring."

It took a moment to understand. "You're married."

"We did it when he came in March. Downtown."

"Oh. Congratulations." A bitter disappointment rose in him. "That's the surprise."

She smiled. "I didn't want to tell you over the phone."

"He's a lucky man."

"I tell him that, too. We're doing the ceremony this summer, if you'd like to come."

"Maybe I would."

"You and your maybes. *Maybe* you would." They bought tickets.

"It might tear my heart out."

"Oh, Aldo, don't say that."

"You know it would. I don't think that's a secret."

"Well," she said, "I need my friends to be my friends."

"I'll do my best." He followed her down to their seats.

"You did promise."

"I know I did."

Her eyes were weak, and she disliked wearing glasses, so they sat near the front, leaning back in their seats to watch. The movie was bad, and to pass the time Aldo watched the lit-up clock over one of the exits, the second hand patiently sweeping the minutes away. The stain on the screen appeared and disappeared, and he watched it idly. Now and then their arms brushed. Her lovely arms, bare, shone in the white cinematic light. At last, hopelessly, he took her hand. Married, he thought, guiltily. But she allowed it. In the dark he studied the architecture of her fingers. Each one was long and finely articulated — like Eleanor's, he realized. The knuckles were boxy, like dice under the skin. The palm was slender. He heard her breathing beside him, little puffs through her nose. She whispered: "You promised."

"You don't mind," he replied.

"You're being bad."

"Yes I am."

"So am I, I guess."

He clasped her hand more tightly. He touched her wrist: his fingertips against the soft skin.

"I'm married," she told him.

"Big deal." He put his hand on her thigh. "This doesn't count."

"It doesn't?"

"No. We're just friends." He leaned and kissed her ear. "Doesn't count," he said. He had a terrific erection, which pushed uncomfortably against his fly. He kissed her again. "Doesn't count."

"No," she said. She kissed him back, her lips narrow and firm.

When the movie ended they sat together and watched the credits. He counted names: three hundred sixty, and he could stand up and in the darkness rearrange himself without much embarrassment. Then she took his arm and led him through the rear exit, which opened onto the brick-walled alley. Against the wall they began kissing again. That he should be this close to her lovely face — that she should allow it, that she allowed his hands to travel unimpeded over her hips — all this was wonderful to him. At the same time he knew it was a crappy thing to do, and could lead to no good. In fact it was a very bad thing: but he didn't care.

"Miranda —"

"We shouldn't be doing this," she said.

"But you want to," he said, kissing her throat, "and I do, too."

"I almost told him no," she said.

"Don't talk."

"This is why I never called you."

"Good thing I called *you*."

"I can't do this," she said, and kissed him again.

Presently they separated and walked hand in hand down the alley; when they reached the sidewalk they let go and walked hurriedly through town. It was balmy still, and though the sky was clear the horizon flashed with heat lightning, and the elm trees moved their limbs about in the warm wind.

"Come back to my place," he suggested. "It's a nice night."

"I shouldn't." She clasped her bare arms to her sides. "I shouldn't be doing any of this."

"But you want to," he said.

"All right. But we can't do anything."

"Fine," he said, blithely, "we won't."

"We will." She clasped his elbow. "I know we will."

"Not if you don't want to."

"It's not that," she said, "it's not that at all. Obviously."

They kept walking. As they reached the dark side streets, she took his arm again.

"So," he said.

She stopped abruptly. "I left my magazine back there."

"You want to go back?"

"Yes — no," she said. "Never mind."

Three blocks down, they came to his little house sitting on its sloppy lawn. Lights were on inside. "People are home," he said.

She had grown momentarily timid. "That's all right."

He lifted the creaking screen door open. Upstairs, Bram had filled the hall with his sweaty stink, and Eleanor could be heard tamping away at her keyboard. "My housemates," he said, and ducked with her into his bedroom, and locked the door.

"What are their names?"

He told her. "Hear that?" He tipped his head at the wall. "He's lifting weights."

"So neat," she said, glancing around. "It's like a guest room."

"He does it all the time," he said.

"Who?"

"Bram."

"Why doesn't he go to the gym?"

"I don't know. They're actually both sort of gross."

She examined his bookshelf. "That's not very nice of you."

"I mean — I was late with the housing thing. I wouldn't have chosen them."

"That's not very nice, either."

"I'm being bad."

"No," she said, "you're *not* being *nice*. It's different."

He came up behind her and spoke into her ear. "It's not so different," he said. He put his hands on her hips.

"This is the only time this is going to happen," she said, turning to him. "We'll just get it out of our systems."

Bram set down something heavy on the floor. The screws in the bookcase jingled.

She reached behind him to turn out the light. He opened the buttons on the back of her dress: the material was a light cotton, warmed by her skin. He took down her shoulder straps and the dress settled to the carpet. In her white underwear she was much slimmer than he had imagined: the points of her pelvis rose in little knobs. He helped her with his shirt, which slid off him easily, like a jacket off a book. A shaft of orange light from the street entered through the uncurtained window and marked a square on the wall.

"You're so quiet," she said.

"So are you."

"I'm just — I feel like —" She threw out her arms. "Ta-daa." Her little breasts bounced in her brassiere. "Such a performance this is."

"Well."

"So I'm proving something," she whispered, "and I know it, and after this it's forget it, right?" She set her jaw and peered at him. "Right?"

"Right."

Abruptly she reached behind her, unfastened her bra, then stepped out of her underpants. "Okay," she said, and stood naked. "You like this?"

He found it difficult to speak.

"So somber," she said again.

"I," he said.

She took off her ring, set it on the dresser. "Is that better?"

They climbed into bed together. He kissed her and took her breast in one hand, the nipple firm in his palm.

"What if I told you I wasn't married?"

"It wouldn't matter to me." Not true, exactly.

She was disappointed. "Not at all?"

"No. Maybe. I don't think so."

"Isn't it more fun if we're — if I am?"

"We should be quiet," he said, and turned on the radio. "The roommates."

"You care about them?"

"No —"

Her nakedness had surprised him with its loveliness, the sweetness of the curve beneath her little white breasts, the inward dip of her flat, pale stomach, the fine wiry hair in unexpected abundance between her legs and across her lower belly. Beside him it tufted pleasantly against his leg.

"Well," she said, "your move."

"It matters to me that you're married," he said, "because I can't marry you."

"No, you can't."

"But that's all."

"He made me," she said, kissing his throat. "He said he'd leave me if I didn't do it. But this is showing him."

He didn't believe her; it didn't much matter. Still. "Don't do this for me."

"I wouldn't."

"You wouldn't?"

"No. This is for me."

"What if you weren't with — ? Would you — would I —"

"Oh, don't ask me that," she said. "Please."

Hesitantly, he asked, "Do you use any — are you on — ?"

"Yes," she said, blinking. "Yes, yes, yes."

Stupidly he felt as though he might cry; but he stopped it, and turned up the radio, which crackled with the approaching lightning. Shifting his weight, he moved atop her. "Just — ?" he asked.

"Aldo," she said.

His name in her mouth thrilled him. "What?"

"Nothing."

"What?"

"No," she said, "I just wanted to say it."

"Say it again."

She did, and he slid easily into her. Smooth and easy, all the way to the bottom.

"There." She smiled up at him from her tousle of hair. "Feel better?"

"*You* do. Don't lie."

"Yes, I do," she said, *"Aldo."*

"Don't —" He felt himself letting go, pulled back.

"Your own name," she said. "What narcissism."

"Let's not talk."

"My voice?" she asked. "Or is it just your name?"

"No."

"Which one?"

"It's neither."

She laughed. "Aldo!" Loud enough to be heard.

He would make her stop, he thought. "Elmer," he said.

"Okay," she said, wincing. "Don't."

"Don't? Elmer Grand."

"Oh — truce."

"Elmer Grand."

"Truce!"

"Truce," he said.

"You're terrible." She shifted beneath him, locked her legs at the backs of his knees, and pressed upward. "You're so terrible — so bad."

He supposed he was. And if that was what she wanted, then he would say so. "Both of us. You're bad, too," he said. "You're so bad."

"I am?"

"So bad," he said.

"Oh, yes — yes." She grimaced menacingly, eyes shut. "Fuck," she said, "fuck, fuck, fuck —"

Slipping in and out of Miranda he felt — as he had felt before, with other women — that he was exploring a city, an ancient clay-walled town, through the narrow streets, where various flags were hung out . . . She was very firm, and he fit her with a great precision. They sweated a good deal, and their bodies, in the humid room, smacked together like fish hitting a countertop. If it was really to be only one night — and he did not believe this, either — then they were making the most of it. The storm that had stood on the horizon hours ago had come across the countryside and now walked slowly through town, delivering five or six great crashing bolts of lightning which illuminated the room — enough to see Miranda, above him, working in a pose of great determination, gazing down not at his face but at some spot near his sternum. Why, he wondered, had she agreed to this? What did she want to prove? That she was desirable? — but no, that was only too plain. That she was unpredictable? This was closer; but he didn't know, and to his surprise he found he didn't know her well enough to guess.

"Let's do something," she told him, past two, "you've always wanted to do."

"This is about it," he said.

"Something else."

"Oh —"

She propped herself up on an elbow. In the darkness the whites of her eyes flashed. "Think," she said. "Out of our systems."

"Well —"

"That's the deal," she said. "We agreed."

"I know."

She sighed, lay back. "Do you want to tie me up?"

He laughed. "No."

"Do you want me to tie you up?"

"Not really."

"A little bit?"

"No," he said.

"What, then?"

"I don't know."

"I won't tell anyone," she said.

"How about — just —" he motioned, downward.

"Except that," she said.

"Not bad enough?"

"No, it's not bad at all," she said, "I just don't like it."

"Just a little," he said.

"I don't like it."

He said, "You should have said so."

"Maybe."

"Just a little."

She said, "A little."

"Okay, a little."

"Just once," she said.

"Okay."

Grimacing, she made her way down his abdomen. He was sore, slightly, and he flinched when she began, taking him half-erect into her mouth. And he felt it *was* dirty — particularly since she didn't like it. The thought excited him, very suddenly. He held her head. She twisted once, stopped. Quickly he came in her mouth. Extracting himself, he pressed his hand over her lips, over her nose. "Swallow," he said.

She twisted again.

"That's what I want," he said. It was. He knew it as he said it.

She made a sound. Spitting, she bit his hand. "Asshole," she said, hitting him.

"That's what I want."

"Asshole," she repeated. Freeing herself, she spat at him, wiped her mouth on his discarded shirt. "Fucking shithole asshole." Spat again, wiped.

He sat up. "I just thought of it then," he said.

"You incredible fucking asshole." She dressed, retrieved her ring. "Fucking shithole. Jesus."

"I just realized it," he said. What had compelled him? He put on his underwear.

"*Don't* say anything." She pulled her dress over her shoulders. "I can't believe you."

"That was —"

"*Don't* say anything."

"I'm sorry —"

"You're supposed to *know*," she said, "how to *behave*."

"Stay."

"Oh, you fucking asshole," she said, loudly. "You unbelievable fucking asshole."

"Don't — they'll hear —"

"He hates you," she shouted, "he hates you both." She swung, hit him with the sole of her shoe. "Prick," she said. Barefoot, she walked downstairs. The screen door creaked and slammed.

After a moment Bram appeared in the hallway, dressed in his bikini underwear. He filled the corridor, huge.

"Sorry," said Aldo.

"Friend of yours?"

Aldo stepped back into his bedroom, closed the door.

Bram knocked. "Sounded bad," he said, through the door. "Woke me up."

"Sorry."

"Guys were loud."

"What about you and your weights?"

"You should try it. Lose that chub."

"Thanks."

Bram opened the door a crack. "Want to borrow them?"

"Not right this second."

"Whenever," said Bram. "You want a beer?"

"No."

"They're half Eleanor's," he whispered.

"No thanks."

"Say the word."

"Good night," said Aldo.

"Okay," said Bram, "good night."

It was essentially the last he saw of Miranda. He was ashamed of what he had done, and he was happy to avoid her when he could. He caught glimpses of her around campus, but they never spoke. Her friends eyed him unpleasantly. For the second time, she vanished from his life. Embarrassed and contrite, Aldo kept to himself. It was a terrible thing to have done, and he had done it, and couldn't forget it. All the talk about goodness, and *things being right,* and grace, seemed so much crap. And Feingold, though still genial, also withdrew.

After graduation Aldo moved back to Portland, believing he was only taking time off from his studies, that he would return soon enough, but he landed a job teaching Latin at a boys' school in town, and the pleasures of this, and a certain lassitude, kept him from leaving. The corridors smelled of wax and the heated air that came forced through vents in the floor. His classes, full of the sons of the rich and happy, were sedate, and the boys were, as a rule, at least well informed about things, if not always interested or original. When he turned them loose at vacations, Aldo was sorry to see them go. "Good-bye, Fitch," he said, standing at the door, "and Gerard, and Lumber, and Poole, and Regent, and Franklin, and Vinton, and Chillingham," and they would ceremoniously shake his hand as they went out, loosening their ties. He was liked. The custodial staff knew his name, and Mike seemed genuinely affectionate when he arrived in the afternoon to sweep and empty the trash.

"Mr. Gorman."

"Mike."

"Not bad weather."

"Little sun," said Aldo.

"Oh, a little sun, not bad. Not bad at all."

But it was nothing like the grace he had known: no, that had gone, seemingly for good. He was essentially friendless in the dark, gloomy city, and he remembered his college days with a mixture of nostalgia and shame, a complicated shame that had to do with, first, not going on with his education, and second, with the way he had behaved that night with Miranda. He was not civilized, not at heart. No, he was not at heart a good person, and he had proved that. And as if in punishment he had been shunted onto this side track, a track occupied by others like him: Mr. Toobman, who taught history, a sour, balding homosexual who smelled of his lemony soap; Mrs. Graven, the shy, aged mathematics instructor whose throat was peppered with protuberant moles. Even Aldo, old before his time, had grown a gut and developed a persistent phlegmy cough. He was sick all the time. Some weeks he was mostly well, other times the cough racked him, and he would run a fever, which gave him harrowing dreams in which he grew to a terrific size, then shrank away to nothing. His heart raced, then beat lop-sidedly, as though on three legs. Hacking into his handkerchief, he graded his exercises: *That friendly king did not remain there a long time. Our mothers had not understood the nature of that place.* He began to drink more, and thought of Feingold when he did. If this was his punishment, it was not the worst he could imagine; and at any rate he felt he deserved it. And at the same time he knew he was being stupid: that holding on to a little guilt in this way was a waste of time. Forget it, he told himself. But he didn't.

His cough worsened that spring, grew painful, and one week-end the fever knocked him down entirely. In his chilly Saturday apartment he poured sweat terribly into his sheets. From bed he watched the sky change through its stages of gray, one layer of cloud sliding aside sluggishly to reveal another, each darker than the last. It seemed a vision of terrible unhealth, and he grew afraid. Sleep came abruptly around noon, and he woke in darkness, in what felt like the middle of the night, with his heart racing. A gurgling escaped his lungs. He had no one to call. Next door his neighbor was hammering a nail into the plaster. Sitting up in bed he gasped for breath. It was just past dinnertime. Teetering against his dresser, he buttoned his pants with trembling hands. Outside in the parking lot the wind had picked up and blew through his hair, wind that smelled pleasantly of the river. It would not be so bad — he could take a week off. And he was not all that sick, really. But his fingernails on the steering wheel were so purple they looked bruised — and this frightened him — as though he had grasped too eagerly at something, and had it snatched away.

The clinic was empty, and he was seen almost at once by a doctor whose large masculine hands, covered with red hair, pressed the glands in his throat, his armpits, his groin. The doctor looked young, not yet thirty: Dr. Grieve. "Harvard," said Aldo, sighting the diploma.

"Yes."

"What're you doing here?"

"This is where I live." He peered into Aldo's eyes. "Do any drugs?"

"No."

"Drink?"

"Not much."

The doctor sighed. "Why do you ask? You know someone there?"

"Elmer Grand."

"Oh — Elmer Grand," said Dr. Grieve. "I know Elmer Grand."

"Really?"

The doctor peered into his ears. "Friend of yours?"

"No — I don't know him. I used to know his wife."

"Miranda?"

Startled, Aldo croaked, "Yes."

"Miranda. Breathe. In. Now hold it." He applied the stethoscope to Aldo's sternum. "Quite a girl."

He nodded.

"Out." There came a long pause. "Bronchitis," he said at last, "and sounds like pneumonia."

"How is Miranda?"

"Oh, well, fine," said the doctor. "Last I heard."

"No news?"

"Not that I know of. It's only a Christmas-card sort of thing."

"Not — they're still together?"

"They were at Christmas."

"No children?"

"I don't know. I don't think so."

"Well," said Aldo.

Ruefully, Dr. Grieve said, "Elmer was a hound. Anything that walked."

Aldo said, "Really."

"Really. And I imagine she must have known."

"She never — I don't remember her mentioning it," he said.

"You knew her well, then."

"Pretty well. For a while."

"You're pretty sick," said Dr. Grieve. "This cough, how long?"

"I don't know. Months."

"Months? Two? Eight?"

"Six."

"Any blood?"

"No."

"What about your heart?"

"My heart?"

"This kind of long-term infection, it can get lodged in the heart valves. We see that now and then."

"It's been fine," he said.

"No palpitations? No irregularities?"

"Oh —" he said, "no." A current of dread moved through him.

"You're lucky, then."

"Okay," said Aldo. "Good."

"So: Elmer Grand."

"How many —" Aldo stopped. "He did it a lot, then."

"Slept around? Oh, all the time, Jesus. Sleep-deprived and still he'd be after it."

"But —"

"That's what he liked. Likes, still. Probably."

"So," said Aldo.

"You should take a week off. Keep warm. Get these filled. You'll feel better."

He hesitated. "And the heart — ?"

"If anything unusual comes up, come back." He helped Aldo off the table. "Okay? All better."

And he did get better, more quickly than he imagined possible. His lungs cleared. His heart beat normally again, in sequence. His sleep, for the first time in months, was seamless. And by Thursday he was back at school. *"Copia?"* he asked.

"Abundance," said the class.

"Yes. *Ratio?*"

"Judgment," they said.

"Yes. *Duco?*"

"To lead," they said.

Well, it was something, these voices. Always answering. They hardly asked anything of you; and what they did ask, you could give. It was not the life he had wanted; but it was close, in some ways. He had his languages, and he had the afternoons to himself. He thought of Miranda now and then, but less often as time went on. He had lost his way to grace, that was true. Sometimes — driving over a high bridge, say, or waking up early on a bright Saturday — he felt a sort of echo, from what might have been his soul, and then he was sorry for what he had lost. But more often he felt sorry for that old figure of himself, waiting for grace to descend, afraid when it left him. No one could live that way, not forever. It was too much to expect of life. Always waiting. No; but he could work. A cedar tree outside the classroom window broke the sunlight, and the confetti of broken light played on the back wall of the room, where he could watch it in the afternoons. Doors closed, here and there, in the empty cavern of the school. The waxing machines murmured up and down the hallways. When Mike put down the trash can, it made a nice, hollow bonging sound; always he put it down on the wrong side of the door, and Aldo, before he left for the night, would put it back where it belonged.

RON CARLSON

The Ordinary Son

OXFORD AMERICAN

THE STORY of my famous family is a story of genius and its conse-
quences, I suppose, and I am uniquely and particularly suited to
tell the story, since genius avoided me — and I, it. I remain an ordinary man, if there is such a thing, calm in all weathers, aware
of event but uninterested and generally incapable of deciphering
implication. As my genius brother, Garrett, used to say, "Reed,
you're not screwed too tight like the rest of us, but you're still
screwed." Now there's a definition of the common man you can
trust, and further, you can trust me. There's no irony in that or
deep inner meaning or Freudian slips — any kind of slips, really —
simply what it says. My mother told me many times I have a good
heart, and of course she was a genius, and that heart should help
with this story. But a heart, as she said so often, good as it may be, is
always trouble.

Part of the reason this story hasn't come together, the story of
my famous family, is that no one remembers they were related.
They all had their own names. My father was Duncan Landers, the
noted NASA physicist, the man responsible for every facet of the
photography of the first moon landing. There is still camera gear
on the moon inscribed with this name. That is, Landers. He was
born Duncan Lrsdyksz, which was changed when NASA began its
public relations campaigns in the mid-sixties. The space agency
suggested that physicists who worked for NASA should have more
vowels in their names. It didn't want its press releases to seem full
of typographical errors or foreigners. Congress was reading this
stuff. So Lrsdyksz became Landers. (My father's close associate Igor

Oeuroi didn't just get vowels; his name became LeRoy Rodgers. After *le cowboy star*, my mother quipped.)

My mother was Gloria Rainstrap, the poet who spent twenty years fighting for workers' rights from Texas to Alaska. In one string, she gave four thousand lectures, not missing a night as she drove from village to village throughout the country. It still stands as some kind of record.

Wherever she went, she stirred up the best kind of trouble, reading her work and then spending hours in whatever guesthouse or spare bedroom she was given, reading the poems and essays of the people who had come to see her. She was tireless, driven by her overwhelming sense of fairness, and she was certainly the primary idealist to come out of twentieth-century Texas. When she started leaving home for months, and then years, at a time, I was just a lad, but I remember her telling my father, Duncan, one night, "Texas is too small for what I have to do."

This was not around the dinner table. We were a family of geniuses and did not have a dinner table. In fact, the only table we did have was my father's drafting table, which was in the entry so that you had to squeeze sideways to even get into our house. "It sets the tone," Duncan used to say. "I want anyone coming into our home to see my work. That work is the reason we have a roof anyway." He said this one day after my friend Jeff Shreckenbah and I inched past him on the way to my room. "And who are these people coming in the door?"

"It is your son and his friend," I told him.

"Good," he said, his benediction, but he said it deeply into his drawing, which is where he spent his time at home. He wouldn't have known if the Houston Oilers had arrived, because he was about to invent the gravity-free vacuum hinge that is still used today.

Most of my father's, Duncan Landers's, work was classified, top-secret, eyes-only, but it didn't matter. No one except Jeff Shreckenbah came to our house. Other people didn't "come over." We were geniuses. We had no television, and we had no telephone. "What should I do?" my father would say from where he sat in the entry, drawing. "Answer some little buzzing device? Say hello to it?" NASA tried to install phones for us. Duncan took them out. It was a genius household and not to be diminished by primitive electronic foo-fahs.

My older sister was named Christina by my father and given the last name Rossetti by my mother. When she finally fled from MIT at nineteen, she gave herself a new surname: Isotope. There had been some trouble, she told me, personal trouble, and she needed the new name to remind herself she wouldn't last long — and then she asked me how I liked my half-life. I was eleven then, and she laughed and said, "I'm kidding, Reed. You're not a genius; you're going to live forever." I was talking to her on the "hot line," the secret phone that our housekeeper, Clovis Armandy, kept in a kitchen cupboard.

"Where are you going?" I asked her.

"West with Mother," she said. Evidently, Gloria Rainstrap had driven up to Boston to rescue Christina from some sort of meltdown.

"A juncture of some kind," my father told me. "Not to worry."

Christina said, "I'm through with theoretical chemistry, but chemistry isn't through with me. Take care of Dad. See you later."

We three children were eight years apart; that's how geniuses plan their families. Christina had been gone for years, it seemed, from our genius household; she barely knew our baby brother, Garrett.

Garrett and I took everything in stride. We accepted that ours was a family of geniuses and that we had no telephone or refrigerator or proper beds. We thought it was natural to eat crackers and sardines for months on end. We thought the front yard was supposed to be a jungle of overgrown grass, weeds, and whatever reptiles would volunteer to live there. Twice a year the City of Houston street crew came by and mowed it all down, and daylight would pour in for a month or two. We had no cars. My father was always climbing into white Chevrolet station wagons, unmarked, and going off to the Space Center south of town. My mother was always stepping up into orange VW buses driven by other people and driving off to tour. My sister had been the youngest student at MIT. My brother and I did our own laundry for years and walked to school, where, about seventh grade, we began to see the differences between the way ordinary people lived and the way geniuses lived. Other people's lives, we learned, centered fundamentally on two things: television and soft foods rich with all versions of sugar.

By the time I entered junior high school, my mother's travels had kicked into high gear, so she hired a woman we came to know well, Clovis Armandy, to live with us and to assist in our corporeal care. Gloria Rainstrap's parental theory and practice could be summed up by the verse I heard her recite a thousand times before I reached the age of six: "Feed the soul, the body finds a way." And she fed our souls with a groaning banquet of iron ethics at every opportunity. She wasn't interested in sandwiches or casseroles. She was the kind of person who had a moral motive for her every move. We had no refrigerator because it was simply the wrong way to prolong the value of food, which had little value in the first place. We had no real furniture because furniture became the numbing insulation of drones who worked for the economy, an evil in itself. If religion was the opiate of the masses, then home furnishings were the Novocain of the middle class. Any small surfeit of comfort undermined our moral fabric. We live for the work we can do, not for things, she told us. I've met and heard lots of folks who share Gloria's posture toward life on this earth, but I've never found anyone who could put it so well, present her ideas so convincingly, so beautifully, or so insistently. Her words seduced you into wanting to go without. I won't put any of her poems in this story, but they were transcendent. The *Times* called her "Buddha's angry daughter." My mother's response to people who were somewhat shocked at our empty house and its unkempt quality was, "We're ego-distant. These little things," she'd say, waving her hand over the litter of the laundry, discarded draft paper, piles of top-secret documents in the hallway, various toys, the odd empty tin of sardines, "don't bother us in the least. We aren't even here for them." I loved that last part and still use it when a nuisance arises: I'm not even here for it. "Ego-distant," my friend Jeff Schreckenbah used to say, standing in our empty house, "which means your ma doesn't sweat the small stuff."

My mother's quirk, one she fostered, was writing on the bottom of things. She started it because she was always gone, for months at a time, and she wanted us to get her messages throughout her absence and thereby be reminded of making correct decisions and ethical choices. It was not unusual to find ballpoint-pen lettering on the bottoms of our shoes and little marker messages on the bottoms of plates, where she'd written in a tiny script. Anything that you could lift up and look under, she would have left her mark on it. These notes primarily confused me. There I'd be in math class and would cross my legs and see something on the edge of my sneaker, and read, "Your troubles, if you stay alert, will pass very quickly away."

I'm not complaining. I never, except once or twice, felt deprived. I like sardines, still. It was a bit of a pinch when I got to high school and noted with new poignancy that I didn't quite have the wardrobe it took to keep up. Geniuses dress plain and clean but not always as clean as their ordinary counterparts, who have nothing better to do with their lives than buy and sort and wash clothes.

Things were fine. I turned seventeen. I was hanging out sitting around my bare room, reading books — the history of this, the history of that, dry stuff — waiting for my genius to kick in. This is what had happened to Christina. One day when she was ten, she was having a tea party with her dolls, which were two rolled pink towels. The next day she'd catalogued and diagrammed the amino acids, laying the groundwork for two artificial sweeteners and a mood elevator. By the time my mother, Gloria Rainstrap, returned from the Northwest, and my father looked up from his table, the State Department "mentors" had been by, and my sister, Christina, was on her way to the inner sanctums of the Massachusetts Institute of Technology. I remember my mother standing against my father's drafting table, her hands along the top. Her jaw was set, and she said, "This is meaningful work for Christina, her special doorway."

My father dragged his eyes up from his drawings, and said, "Where's Christina now?"

So the day I went into Garrett's room and found him writing equations down a huge scroll of butcher paper on which, until that day, he had drawn battle re-creations of the French and Indian Wars, was a big day for me. I stood there in the gloom, watching him crawl along the paper, reeling out figures of which very few were numbers I recognized, most of the symbols being x's and y's and the little twisted members of the Greek alphabet, and I knew that it had skipped me. Genius had cast its powerful, clear eye on me, and said, "No, thanks." At least I was that smart. I realized that I was not going to get to be a genius.

The message took my body a piece at a time, loosening each

joint and muscle on the way up and then filling my face with a strange warmth, which I knew immediately was relief.

I was free.

I quickly took a job doing landscaping and general cleanup and maintenance at the San Jacinto Resort Motel on the old Hempstead Highway. My friend, Jeff Schreckenbah, worked next door at Alfredo's American Cafe, and he had told me that the last guy doing handiwork at the motel had been fired for making a holy mess of the parking lot with a paintbrush. When I applied, Mr. Rakkerts, the short little guy who owned the place, took me on.

For me, these were the days of the big changes. I bought a car, an act that at one time would have been as alien to me as intergalactic travel or applying to barber college. I bought a car. It was a four-door lime green Plymouth Fury III, low miles. I bought a pair of chinos. These things gave me exquisite pleasure. I was seventeen, and I had not known the tangible pleasure of having things. I bought three new shirts and a wristwatch with a leather strap, and I went driving in the evenings, alone, south from our subdivision of Spring Woods with my arm on the green sill of my lime green Plymouth Fury III through the vast spaghetti bowl of freeways and into the mysterious network of towers that was downtown Houston. It was my dawning.

Late at night, my blood rich with wonder at the possibilities of such a vast material planet, I would return to our tumbledown genius ranch house, my sister off putting new legs on the periodic table, my mother away in Shreveport, showing the workers there the way to political and personal power, my brother in his room, edging closer to new theories of rocket reaction and thrust, my father sitting by the entry, rapt in his schematics. As I'd come in and sidle by his table and the one real light in the whole front part of the house, his pencilings on the space station hinge looking as beautiful and inscrutable to me as a sheet of music, he'd say my name as a simple greeting. "Reed."

"Duncan," I'd say in return.

"How goes the metropolis?" he'd add, not looking up. His breath was faintly reminiscent of sardines; in fact, I still associate that smell, which is not as unpleasant as it might seem, with brilliance. I know he said "metropolis" because he didn't know for a moment which city we were in.

"It teems with industrious citizenry well into the night," I'd answer.

Then he'd say it, "Good," his benediction, as he'd carefully trace his leadholder and its steel-like wafer of 5H pencil-lead along a precise new line deep into the vast white space. "That's good."

The San Jacinto Resort Motel along the Hempstead Highway was exactly what you might expect a twenty-unit motel to be in the year 1966. The many bright new interstates had come racing to Houston and collided downtown in a maze, and the old Hempstead Highway had been supplanted as a major artery into town. There was still a good deal of traffic on the four-lane, and the motel was always about half full — never the same half, as you would expect. There were three permanent occupants, one of them a withered old man named Newcombe Shinetower who was a hundred years old that summer and had no car, just a room full of magazines with red and yellow covers, stacks of these things with titles like *Too Young for Comfort* and *Treasure Chest*. There were other titles. I was in Mr. Shinetower's room on only two occasions. He wore the same flannel shirt every day of his life and was heavily gone to seed. Once or twice a day I would see him shuffling out toward Alfredo's American Cafe where, Jeff told me, he always ate the catfish.

"You want to live to be a hundred," Jeff said, "eat the catfish." I told him I didn't know about a hundred and that I generally preferred smaller fish. I was never sure if Mr. Shinetower saw me or not as I moved through his line of sight. He might have nodded; it was hard to tell. What I felt was that he might exist on another plane, the way rocks are said to; they're in there, but at a rhythm too slow for humans to perceive.

It was in Mr. Shinetower's room, rife with the flaking detritus of the ages, that Jeff tried to help me reckon with the new world.

"You're interested in sex, right?" he asked me one day as I took my break at the counter of Alfredo's. I told him I was, but that wasn't exactly the truth. I was indifferent. I understood how it was being packaged and sold to the American people, but it did not stir me, nor did any of the girls we went to school with, many of whom were outright beauties and not bashful about it. This was Texas in the sixties. Some of these buxom girls would grow up and try to assassinate their daughter's rivals on the cheerleading squad. If sex is the game, some seemed to say, deal me in. And I guess I felt it was a game, too, one I could sit out. I had begun to look a little closer at the ways I was different from my peers, worrying about anything that might be a genius tendency. And I took great comfort in the unmistakable affection I felt for my Plymouth Fury III.

"Good," he said. "If you're interested, then you're safe — you're not a genius. Geniuses" — here he leaned toward me and squinted his eyes to let me know this was a groundbreaking postulate — "have a little trouble in the sex department."

I liked Jeff; he was my first "buddy." I sat on the round red Naugahyde stool at Alfredo's long Formica counter and listened to his speech, including "sex department," and I don't know, it kind of made sense to me. There must have been something on my face, which is a way of saying there must have been nothing on my face, absolutely nothing, a blank blank, because Jeff pulled his apron off his head, and said, "Meet me out back in two minutes." He looked down the counter to where old Mr. Shinetower sucked on his soup. "We got to get you some useful information."

Out back, of course, Jeff led me directly around to the motel and Mr. Shinetower's room, which was not unlocked, but opened when Jeff gave the doorknob a healthy rattle. Inside, in the sour dark, Jeff lit the lamp and picked up one of the old man's periodicals.

Jeff held the magazine and thumbed it like a deck of cards, stopping finally at a full-page photograph, which he presented to me with an odd kind of certainty.

"There," he said. "This is what everybody is trying for. This is the goal." It was a glossy color photograph, and I knew what it was right away, even in the poor light: a shiny shaved pubis, seven or eight times larger than life-size. "This makes the world go round."

I was going along with Jeff all the way on this, but that comment begged for a rebuttal, which I restrained. I could feel my father in me responding about the forces that actually caused and maintained the angular momentum of the earth. Instead, I looked at the picture, which had its own lurid beauty. Of course, what it looked like was a landscape, a barren but promising promontory on not this, but another world, the seam too perfect a fold for anything but ceremony. I imagined landing a small aircraft on the tawny slopes and approaching the entry, stepping lightly with a small party of explorers, alert for the meaning of such a place. The air would be devoid of the usual climatic markers (no clouds or

air pressure), and in the stillness we would be silent and reveren-
tial. The light in the photograph captivated me in that it seemed
to come from everywhere, a flat, even twilight that would indicate
a world with one or maybe two distant polar suns. There was an al-
luring blue shadow that ran along the cleft the way a footprint in
snow holds its own blue glow, and that aberration affected and in-
trigued me.

Jeff had left my side and was at the window, on guard, pleased
that I was involved in my studies.

"So," he said. "It's really something, isn't it?" He came to me,
grabbed the magazine, and took one long look at the page the way
a thirsty man drinks from a jug, then set it back on the stack of Old
Man Shinetower's magazines.

"Yes," I said. "It certainly is." Now that it was gone, I realized I had
memorized the photograph, that place.

"Come on. Let's get out of here before he gets back." Jeff
cracked the door and looked out, both ways. "Whoa," he said, setting the door closed again. "He's coming back. He's on the walk
down about three rooms." Then Jeff did an amazing thing: he
dropped like a rock to all fours, then onto his stomach, and slid under the bed. I'd never seen anyone do that; I've never seen it since.
I heard him hiss, "Do something. Hide."

Again I saw myself arriving in the photograph. Now I was alone.
I landed carefully, and the entire venture was full of care, as if I
didn't want to wake something. I had a case of instruments, and
I wanted to know about that light, that shadow. I could feel my legs
burn as I climbed toward it step by step.

What I did in the room was take two steps back into the corner
and stand behind the lamp. I put my hands at my side and my chin
up. I stood still. At that moment we heard a key in the lock, and
daylight spilled across the ratty shag carpet. Mr. Shinetower came
in. He was wearing the red-and-black-plaid shirt that he wore every
day. It was like a living thing; someday it would go to lunch at
Alfredo's without him.

He walked by me and stopped for a moment in front of the television to drop a handful of change from his pocket into a Mason jar
on top and messed with the television until it lit and focused. Then
he continued into the little green bathroom, and I saw the door
swing halfway closed behind him.

Jeff slid out from the bed, stood hastily, his eyes whirling, and opened the door and went out. He was closing it behind him when I caught the edge and followed him into the spinning daylight. When I pulled the door, he gasped, so I shut it. We heard it register closed, and then we slipped quickly through the arbor to the alley behind the units and ran along the overgrown trail back to the bayou and sat on the weedy slope. Jeff was covered with clots of dust and hairy white goo-gah. It was thick in his hair, and I moved away from him while he swatted at it for a while. Here we could smell the sewer working at the bayou, a rich industrial silage, and the sky was gray, but too bright to look at. I went back to the other world for a moment, the cool, perfect place I'd been touring in Mr. Shinetower's magazine, quiet and still, and offering that light. Jeff was spitting and pulling feathers of dust from his collar and sleeves. I wanted so much to be stirred by what I had seen. I had stared at it and wanted it to stir me, and it had done something. I felt something. I wanted to see that terrain, chart it, understand where the blue glow arose and how it lay along the juncture, and how that light, I was certain, interfered with the ordinary passage of time. Time? I had a faint headache.

"That was close," Jeff said finally. He was still cloaked with flotsam from under Mr. Shinetower's bed. "But it was worth it. Did you get a good look? See what I'm talking about?"

"It was a remarkable photograph," I said.

"Now you know. You've seen it, you know. I've got to get back to work; let's go fishing this weekend." He rose and, still whacking soot and ashes and wicked whatevers from his person, ran off toward Alfredo's.

"I've seen it," I said, and I sat there as the sadness bled through me. Duncan would have appreciated the moment and corrected Jeff the way he corrected me all those years.

"Seeing isn't knowing," he would say. "To see something is only to establish the first terms of your misunderstanding." That I remembered him at such a time, above the effulgent bayou, moments after my flight over the naked photograph, made me sad. I was not a genius, but I would be advised by one forevermore.

Happily, my work at the motel was straightforward, and I enjoyed it very much. I could do most of it with my shirt off, cutting away the tenacious vines from behind each of the rooms so that the air conditioning units would not get strangled, and I sweated profusely in the sweet, humid air. I painted the pool fence and enameled the three metal tables a kind of turquoise blue, a fifties turquoise that has become tony again just this year, a color that calls to the passerby: Holiday! We're on holiday!

Once a week I poured a pernicious quantity of lime into the two manholes above the storm sewer, and it fell like snow on the teeming backs of thousands of albino water bugs and roaches that lived there. This did not daunt them in the least. I am no expert on any of the insect tribes, nor do I fully understand their customs, but my association with those subterranean multitudes suggested to me that they looked forward to this weekly toxic snowfall.

Twice a week I pressed the enormous push broom from one end of the driveway to the other until I had a wheelbarrow full of gravel and the million crushed tickets of litter people threw from their moving vehicles along the Hempstead Highway. It was wonderful work. The broom alone weighed twenty pounds. The sweeping, the painting, and the trimming braced me — work that required simply my back and both my arms and legs, but neither side of my brain.

Mr. Leeland Rakkerts, my boss, lived in a small apartment behind the office and could be summoned by a bell during the night hours. He was sixty that June. His wife had passed away years before, and he'd become a reclusive little gun nut. He had a growing gallery of hardware on a pegboard in his apartment, featuring long-barreled automatic weaponry and at least two dozen huge handguns. But he was fine to me, and he paid me cash every Friday afternoon. When he opened the cash drawer, he always made sure, be you friend or foe, that you saw the .45 pistol that rested there, too. My mother would have abhorred my working for him, a man she would have considered the enemy, and she would have said as much, but I wasn't taking the high road or the low road, just a road. That summer the upkeep of the motel was my job, and I did it as well as I could. I'd taken a summer job and was making money. I didn't weigh things on my scale of ethics every ten minutes, because I wasn't entirely sure I had such a scale. I certainly didn't have one as fully evolved as my mother's.

It was a bit like being in the army: when in doubt, paint something. I remeasured and overpainted the parking lot. The last guy had drunkenly painted a wacky series of parentheses where people were supposed to park, and I did a good job with a big brush and five gallons of high mustard yellow. When I finished, I took the feeling of satisfaction in my chest to be simply that: satisfaction. Even if I was working for the devil, the people who put their cars in his parking lot would be squared away.

Getting into my Plymouth Fury III those days, with a sweaty back and a pocketful of cash, I knew I was no genius, but I felt — is this close? — like a great guy, a person of some command.

That fall my brother, Garrett Lrsdyksz (he'd changed his name back with a legal kit that Baxter, our Secret Service guy, had gotten him through the mail), became the youngest student ever to matriculate at Rice University. He was almost eleven. And he didn't enter as a freshman; he entered as a junior. In physics, of course. There was a little article about it on the wire services, noting that he had, without any assistance, set forward the complete set of equations explaining the relationship between the rotation of the earth and "special atmospheric aberrations most hospitable to exit trajectories of ground-fired propulsion devices." You can look it up, and all you'll find is the title, because the rest, like all the work he did in his cataclysmic year at Rice, is classified, top secret, eyes only. Later, he explained his research this way to me: "There are storms, and then there are storms, Reed. A high-pressure area is only a high-pressure area down here on earth; it has a different pressure on the other side."

I looked at my little brother, a person forever in need of a haircut, and I thought: he's mastered the other side, and I can just barely cope with this one.

That wasn't exactly true, of course, because my Plymouth Fury III and my weekly wages from the San Jacinto Resort Motel allowed me to start having a life, earthbound as it may have been. I started hanging out a little at Jeff Shreckenbah's place, a rambling hacienda out of town with two outbuildings where his dad worked on stock cars. Jeff's mother called me "Ladykiller," which I liked, but which I couldn't hear without imagining my mother's response; my mother, who told me a million times, "Morality commences in the words we use to speak of our next act."

"Hey, Ladykiller," Mrs. Shreckenbah would say to me as we pried open the fridge, looking for whatever we could find. Mr.

Shreckenbah made me call him Jake, saying we'd save the last names for the use of the law-enforcement officials and members of the Supreme Court. They'd let us have Lone Star longnecks, if we were staying, or Coca-Cola, if we were hitting the road. Some nights we'd go out with Jake and hand him wrenches while he worked on his cars. He was always asking me, "What's the plan?" — an opening my mother would have approved of.

"We're going fishing," I told him, because that's what Jeff and I had started doing. I'd greet his parents, pick him up, and then Jeff and I would cruise hard down Interstate 45, fifty miles to Galveston and the coast of the warm Gulf of Mexico, where we'd drink Lone Star and surfcast all night long, hauling in all sorts of mysteries of the deep. I loved it.

Jeff would bring along a pack of Dutch Masters cigars, and I'd stand waist-deep in the warm water, puffing on the cheap cigar, throwing a live shrimp on a hook as far as I could toward the equator, the only light being the stars above us, the gapped two-story skyline of Galveston behind us, and our bonfire on the beach tearing a bright hole in the sky.

When fish struck, they struck hard, waking me from vivid daydreams of Mr. Leeland Rakkerts giving me a bonus for sweeping the driveway so thoroughly, a twenty so crisp it hurt to fold it into my pocket. My dreams were full of crisp twenties. I could see Jeff over there, fifty yards away, the little orange tip of his cigar glowing, starlight on the flash of his line as he cast. I liked having my feet firmly on the bottom of the ocean, standing in the night. My brother and sister and my mother and father could shine their lights into the elemental mysteries of the world; I could stand in the dark and fish. I could feel the muscles in my arm as I cast again; I was stronger than I'd been two months ago. And then I felt the fish strike and begin to run south.

Having relinquished the cerebral (not that I ever had it in my grasp), I was immersing myself in the real world the same way I was stepping deeper and deeper into the Gulf, following the frenzied fish as he tried to take my line. I worked him back, gave him some, worked him back. Though I had no idea what I would do with it, I had decided to make a lot of money, and as the fish drew me up to my armpits and the bottom grew irregular, I thought about the ways it might be achieved. Being no genius, I had few ideas.

I spit out my cigar after the first wavelet broke over my face, and I called to Jeff, "I got one."

He was behind me now, backing toward the fire, and he called, "Bring him up here and let's see."

The top half of my head, including my two hands and the fishing pole, were all that was above sea level when the fish relented, and I began to haul him back. He broke the surface several times as I backed out of the ocean, reeling as I went. Knee-deep, I stopped and lifted the line until a dark form lifted into the air. I ran him up to Jeff by the fire and showed him there, a two-pound catfish. When I held him, I felt the sudden shock of his gaffs going into my finger and palm.

"Ow!" Jeff said. "Who's got who?" He took the fish from me on a gill stick.

I shook my stinging hand.

"It's all right," he assured me, throwing another elbow of driftwood onto the fire and handing me an icy Lone Star. "Let's fry this guy up and eat him right now. I'm serious. This is going to be worth it. We're going to live to be one hundred years, guaranteed."

We'd sit, eat, fish some more, talk, and late late we'd drive back, the dawn light gray across the huge tidal plain, smoking Dutch Masters until I was queasy and quiet, dreaming about my money, however I would make it.

Usually this dream was interrupted by my actual boss, Mr. Leeland Rakkerts, shaking my shoulder as I stood sleeping on my broom in the parking lot of the hot and bothered San Jacinto Resort Motel, saying, "Boy! Hey! Boy! You can take your zombie fits home or get on the stick here." I'd give him the wide-eyed nod and continue sweeping, pushing a thousand pounds of scraggly gravel into a conical pile and hauling it in my wheelbarrow way out back into the thick tropical weeds at the edge of the bayou and dumping it there like a body. It wasn't a crisp twenty-dollar bill he'd given me, but it was a valuable bit of advice for a seventeen-year-old, and I tried to take it as such.

Those Saturdays, after we'd been to the Gulf, beat in my skull like a drum, the Texas sun a thick pressure on my bare back as I moved through the heavy, humid air, skimming and vacuuming the pool and rearranging the pool furniture, though it was never ever moved because no one ever used the pool. People didn't come to the San Jacinto Resort Motel to swim. Then, standing in the slim shade behind the office, trembling under a sheen of sweat, I would suck on a tall bottle of Coca-Cola as if on the very nectar of life, and by midafternoon as I trimmed the hedges along the walks and raked and swept, the day would come back to me, a pure pleasure, my lime green Plymouth Fury III parked on the shady side of Alfredo's American Cafe, standing like a promise of every sweet thing life could offer.

These were the days when my brother, Garrett, was coming home on weekends, dropped at our curb by the maroon Rice University van after a week in the research dorms, where young geniuses from all over the world lived in bare little cubicles, the kind of thing somebody with an IQ of 250 apparently loves. I had been to Garrett's room on campus, and it was perfect for him. There was a kind of pad in one corner surrounded by a little bank of his clothing, and the strip of butcher paper — covered with numbers and letters and tracked thoroughly with the faint gray intersecting grid of sneaker prints — ran the length of the floor. His window looked out onto the pretty, green, grassy quad.

It was the quietest building I have ever been in, and I was almost convinced that Garrett might be the only inmate, but when we left to go down to the cafeteria for a sandwich, I saw the other geniuses in their rooms, lying on their stomachs like kids drawing with crayons on a rainy day. Then I realized that they were kids, and it was a rainy day, and they *were* working with crayons; the only difference was that they were drawing formulas.

Downstairs there was a whole slew of little people in the dining hall, sitting around in the plastic chairs, swinging their feet back and forth six inches off the floor, ignoring their trays of tuna fish sandwiches and tomato soup, staring this way and that as the idea storms in their brains swept through. You could almost see they were thinking by how their hair stood in fierce clusters.

There was one adult present, a guy in a blue sweater-vest who went from table to table urging the children to eat: "Finish that sandwich, drink your milk; go ahead, use your spoon; try the soup, it's good for you." I noticed he was careful to register and gather any of the random jottings the children committed while they sat around doodling in spilled milk. I guess he was a member of the faculty. It would be a shame for some nine-year-old to write the key to universal field theory in peanut butter and jelly and then eat it.

"So, Garrett," I said as we sat down, "how's it going?"

Garrett looked at me, his trance interrupted, and as it melted away and he saw me and the platters of cafeteria food before us, he smiled. There he was, my little brother, a sleepy-looking kid with a spray of freckles up and over his nose like the Crab Nebula and two enthusiastic front teeth that would be keeping his mouth open for decades.

"Reed," he said. "*'How's it going?'* I love that. I've always liked your acute sense of narrative. So linear and right for you." His smile, which took a moment and some force to assemble, was ancient, beneficent, as if he both envied and pitied me for something, and he shook his head softly. "But things here aren't going, kid." He poked a finger into the white bread of his tuna sandwich and studied the indentation like a man finding a footprint on the moon. "Things here are . . . This is it: things . . ." He started again, "Things aren't bad, really. It's kind of a floating circle. That's close. Things aren't going; they float in the circle. Right?"

We were both staring at the sandwich; I think I might have been waiting for it to float, but only for a second. I understood what he was saying. Things existed. I'm not that dumb. Things, whatever they might be — and that was a topic I didn't even want to open — had essence, not process. That's simple, that doesn't take a genius to decipher.

"Great," I said. And then I said what you say to your little brother when he sits there pale and distracted and four years ahead of you in school, "Why don't you eat some of that, and I'll take you out and show you my car."

It wasn't as bad a visit as I'm making it sound. We were brothers; we loved each other. We didn't have to say it. The dining room got to me a little until I realized I needed to stop worrying about these children and whether or not they were happy. Happiness wasn't an issue. The place was clean; the food was fresh. Happiness, in that cafeteria, was simply beside the point.

On the way out, Garrett introduced me to his friend, Donna Li, a ten-year-old from New Orleans, who he said was into programming. She was a tall girl with shiny hair and a ready smile, eating alone by the window. This was 1966, and I was certain she was involved somehow in television. You didn't hear the word "computer" every other sentence back then. When she stood to shake my hand, I had no idea what to say to her, and it came out, "I hope your programming is floating in the circle."

"It is," she said.

"She's written her own language," Garrett assured me, "and now she's on the applications."

It was my turn to speak again, and already I couldn't touch bottom, so I said, "We're going out to see my car. Do you want to see my car?"

Imagine me in the parking lot then with these two little kids. On the way out I'd told Garrett about my job at the motel and that Jeff Shreckenbah and I had been hanging out and fishing on the weekends and that Jeff's dad raced stock cars, and for the first time all day Garrett's face filled with a kind of wonder, as if this were news from another world, which I guess it was. There was a misty rain with a faint petrochemical smell in it, and we approached my car as if it were a sleeping brontosaurus. They were both entranced and moved toward it carefully, finally putting their little hands on the wet fender in unison. "This is your car," Garrett said, and I wasn't sure if it was the *your* or the *car* that had him in awe.

I couldn't figure out what floated in the circle or even where the circle was, but I could rattle my keys and start that Plymouth Fury III and listen to the steady sound of the engine, which I did for them now. They both backed away appreciatively.

"It's a large car," Donna Li said.

"Reed," Garrett said to me. "This is really something. And what's that smell?"

I cocked my head, smelling it, too, a big smell, budging the petrocarbons away, a live, salty smell, and then I remembered: I'd left half a bucket of bait shrimp in the trunk, where they'd been ripening for three days since my last trip to Galveston.

"That's rain in the bayou, Garrett."

"Something organic," Donna Li said, moving toward the rear of the vehicle.

"Here, guys," I said, handing Garrett the bag of candy, sardine tins, and peanut-butter-and-cheese packs I'd brought him. I considered for half a second showing him the pile of rotting crustaceans; it would have been cool, and he was my brother. But I didn't want to give the little geniuses the wrong first impression of the Plymouth.

"Good luck with your programming," I told Donna Li, shaking her hand. "And Garrett, be kind to your rocketry."

Garrett smiled again at that, and said to Donna, "He's my brother."

She added, "And he owns the largest car in Texas."

I felt bad driving my stinking car away from the two young people, but it was that or fess up. I could see them standing in my rearview mirror for a long time. First, they watched me, and then they looked up, both of them, for a long time. They were geniuses looking into the rain. I counted on their being able to find a way out of it.

RAYMOND CARVER

Call If You Need Me

FROM GRANTA

WE HAD BOTH been involved with other people that spring, but when June came and school was out we decided to let our house for the summer and move from Palo Alto to the north coast country of California. Our son, Richard, went to Nancy's grandmother's place in Pasco, Washington, to live for the summer and work toward saving money for college in the fall. His grandmother knew the situation at home and had begun working on getting him up there and locating him a job long before his arrival. She'd talked to a farmer friend of hers and had secured a promise of work for Richard baling hay and building fences. Hard work, but Richard was looking forward to it. He left on the bus in the morning of the day after his high school graduation. I took him to the station and parked and went inside to sit with him until his bus was called. His mother had already held him and cried and kissed him good-bye and given him a long letter that he was to deliver to his grandmother upon his arrival. She was at home now finishing last-minute packing for our own move and waiting for the couple who were to take our house. I bought Richard's ticket, gave it to him, and we sat on one of the benches in the station and waited. We'd talked a little about things on the way to the station.

"Are you and Mom going to get a divorce?" he'd asked. It was Saturday morning, and there weren't many cars.

"Not if we can help it," I said. "We don't want to. That's why we're going away from here and don't expect to see anyone all summer. That's why we've rented our house for the summer and rented the house up in Arcata. Why you're going away, too, I guess. One rea-

son anyway. Not to mention the fact that you'll come home with
your pockets filled with money. We don't want to get a divorce. We
want to be alone for the summer and try to work things out."

"You still love Mom?" he said. "She told me she loves you."

"Of course I do," I said. "You ought to know that by now. We've
just had our share of troubles and heavy responsibilities, like everyone else, and now we need time to be alone and work things out.
But don't worry about us. You just go up there and have a good
summer and work hard and save your money. Consider it a vacation, too. Get in all the fishing you can. There's good fishing
around there."

"Water-skiing, too," he said. "I want to learn to water-ski."

"I've never been water-skiing," I said. "Do some of that for me
too, will you?"

We sat in the bus station. He looked through his yearbook while I
held a newspaper in my lap. Then his bus was called and we stood
up. I embraced him, and said again, "Don't worry, don't worry.
Where's your ticket?"

He patted his coat pocket and then picked up his suitcase. I
walked him over to where the line was forming in the terminal,
then I embraced him again and kissed him on the cheek and said
good-bye.

"Good-bye, Dad," he said, and turned from me so that I wouldn't
see his tears.

I drove home to where our boxes and suitcases were waiting in
the living room. Nancy was in the kitchen drinking coffee with
the young couple she'd found to take our house for the summer.
I'd met the couple, Jerry and Liz, graduate students in math, for
the first time a few days before, but we shook hands again, and
I drank a cup of coffee that Nancy poured. We sat around the table
and drank coffee while Nancy finished her list of things they
should look out for or do at certain times of the month, the first
and last of each month, where they should send any mail, and the
like. Nancy's face was tight. Sun fell through the curtain onto the
table as it got later in the morning.

Finally, things seemed to be in order and I left the three of them
in the kitchen and began loading the car. It was a furnished house
we were going to, furnished right down to plates and cooking uten-
sils, so we wouldn't need to take much with us from this house, only
the essentials.

I'd driven up to Eureka, 350 miles north of Palo Alto, on the north coast of California, three weeks before and rented us the furnished house. I went with Susan, the woman I'd been seeing. We stayed in a motel at the edge of town for three nights while I looked in the newspaper and visited real estate agents. She watched me as I wrote out a check for the three months' rent. Later, back at the motel, in bed, she lay with her hand on her forehead, and said, "I envy your wife. I envy Nancy. You hear people talk about 'the other woman' always and how the incumbent wife has the privileges and the real power, but I never really understood or cared about those things before. Now I see. I envy her. I envy her the life she will have with you in that house this summer. I wish it were me. I wish it were us. Oh, how I wish it were us. I feel so crummy," she said. I stroked her hair.

Nancy was a tall, long-legged woman with brown hair and eyes and a generous spirit. But lately we had been coming up short on generosity and spirit. The man she had been seeing was one of my colleagues, a divorced, dapper, three-piece-suit-and-tie fellow with graying hair who drank too much and whose hands, some of my students told me, sometimes shook in the classroom. He and Nancy had drifted into their affair at a party during the holidays not too long after Nancy had discovered my own affair. It all sounds boring and tacky now — it is boring and tacky — but during that spring it was what it was, and it consumed all of our energies and concentration to the exclusion of everything else. Sometime in late April we began to make plans to rent our house and go away for the summer, just the two of us, and try to put things back together, if they could be put back together. We each agreed we would not call or write or otherwise be in touch with the other parties. So we made arrangements for Richard, found the couple to look after our house, and I had looked at a map and driven north from San Francisco and found Eureka, and an agent who was willing to rent a furnished house to a respectable middle-aged married couple for the summer. I think I even used the phrase second honeymoon to the real estate agent, God forgive me, while Susan smoked a cigarette and read tourist brochures out in the car.

I finished storing the suitcases, bags, and cartons in the trunk and back seat and waited while Nancy said a final good-bye on the porch. She shook hands with each of them and turned and came toward the car. I waved to the couple, and they waved back. Nancy got in and shut the door. "Let's go," she said. I put the car in gear and we headed for the freeway. At the light just before the freeway we saw a car ahead of us come off the freeway trailing a broken muffler, the sparks flying. "Look at that," Nancy said. "It might catch fire." We waited and watched until the car managed to pull off the road and onto the shoulder.

We stopped at a little café off the highway near Sebastopol. EAT AND GAS, the sign read. We laughed at the sign. I pulled up in front of the café and we went inside and took a table near a window in the back of the café. After we had ordered coffee and sandwiches, Nancy touched her forefinger to the table and began tracing lines in the wood. I lit a cigarette and looked outside. I saw rapid movement, and then I realized I was looking at a hummingbird in the bush beside the window. Its wings moved in a blur of motion and it kept dipping its beak into a blossom on the bush.

"Nancy, look," I said. "There's a hummingbird."

But the hummingbird flew at this moment, and Nancy looked, and said, "Where? I don't see it."

"It was just there a minute ago," I said. "Look, there it is. Another one, I think. It's another hummingbird."

We watched the hummingbird until the waitress brought our order and the bird flew at the movement and disappeared around the building.

"Now, that's a good sign, I think," I said. "Hummingbirds. Hummingbirds are supposed to bring luck."

"I've heard that somewhere," she said. "I don't know where I heard that, but I've heard it. Well," she said, "luck is what we could use. Wouldn't you say?"

"They're a good sign," I said. "I'm glad we stopped here."

She nodded. She waited a minute, then she took a bite of her sandwich.

We reached Eureka just before dark. We passed the motel on the highway where Susan and I had stayed and had spent the three nights some weeks before, then turned off the highway and took a road up over a hill overlooking the town. I had the house keys in my pocket. We drove over the hill and for a mile or so until we came to a little intersection with a service station and a grocery store. There were wooded mountains ahead of us in the valley, and pastureland all around. Some cattle were grazing in a field behind the service station. "This is pretty country," Nancy said. "I'm anxious to see the house."

"Almost there," I said. "It's just down this road," I said, "and over that rise." "Here," I said in a minute, and pulled into a long driveway with hedge on either side. "Here it is. What do you think of this?" I'd asked the same question of Susan when she and I had stopped in the driveway.

"It's nice," Nancy said. "It looks fine, it does. Let's get out."

We stood in the front yard a minute and looked around. Then we went up the porch steps and I unlocked the front door and turned on the lights. We went through the house. There were two small bedrooms, a bath, a living room with old furniture and a fireplace, and a big kitchen with a view of the valley.

"Do you like it?" I said.

"I think it's just wonderful," Nancy said. She grinned. "I'm glad you found it. I'm glad we're here." She opened the refrigerator and ran a finger over the counter. "Thank God, it looks clean enough. I won't have to do any cleaning."

"Right down to clean sheets on the beds," I said. "I checked. I made sure. That's the way they're renting it. Pillows even. And pillowcases, too."

"We'll have to buy some firewood," she said. We were standing in the living room. "We'll want to have a fire on nights like this."

"I'll look into firewood tomorrow," I said. "We can go shopping then too and see the town."

She looked at me, and said, "I'm glad we're here."

"So am I," I said. I opened my arms and she moved to me. I held her. I could feel her trembling. I turned her face up and kissed her on either cheek. "Nancy," I said.

"I'm glad we're here," she said.

We spent the next few days settling in, taking trips into Eureka to walk around and look in store windows, and hiking across the pastureland behind the house all the way to the woods. We bought groceries and I found an ad in the newspaper for firewood, called, and a day or so afterward two young men with long hair delivered a pickup truckload of alder and stacked it in the carport. That night we sat in front of the fireplace after dinner and drank coffee and talked about getting a dog.

"I don't want a pup," Nancy said. "Something we have to clean up after or that will chew things up. That we don't need. But I'd like to have a dog, yes. We haven't had a dog in a long time. I think we could handle a dog up here," she said.

"And after we go back, after summer's over?" I said. I rephrased the question. "What about keeping a dog in the city?"

"We'll see. Meanwhile, let's look for a dog. The right kind of dog. I don't know what I want until I see it. We'll read the classifieds and we'll go to the pound, if we have to." But though we went on talking about dogs for several days, and pointed out dogs to each other in people's yards we'd drive past, dogs we said we'd like to have, nothing came of it, we didn't get a dog.

Nancy called her mother and gave her our address and telephone number. Richard was working and seemed happy, her mother said. She herself was fine. I heard Nancy say, "We're fine. This is good medicine."

One day in the middle of July we were driving the highway near the ocean and came over a rise to see some lagoons that were closed off from the ocean by sand spits. There were some people fishing from shore, and two boats out on the water.

I pulled the car off onto the shoulder and stopped. "Let's see what they're fishing for," I said. "Maybe we could get some gear and go ourselves."

"We haven't been fishing in years," Nancy said. "Not since that time Richard was little and we went camping near Mount Shasta. Do you remember that?"

"I remember," I said. "I just remembered too that I've missed fishing. Let's walk down and see what they're fishing for."

"Trout," the man said, when I asked. "Cutthroats and rainbow trout. Even some steelhead and a few salmon. They come in here in the winter when the spit opens and then when it closes in the spring, they're trapped. This is a good time of the year for them. I haven't caught any today, but last Sunday I caught four, about fifteen inches long. Best eating fish in the world, and they put up a hell of a fight. Fellows out in the boats have caught some today, but so far I haven't done anything today."

"What do you use for bait?" Nancy asked.

"Anything," the man said. "Worms, salmon eggs, whole kernel corn. Just get it out there and leave it lay on the bottom. Pull out a little slack and watch your line."

We hung around a little longer and watched the man fish and watched the little boats chat-chat back and forth the length of the lagoon.

"Thanks," I said to the man. "Good luck to you."

"Good luck to you," he said. "Good luck to the both of you."

We stopped at a sporting goods store on the way back to town and bought licenses, inexpensive rods and reels, nylon line, hooks, leaders, sinkers, and a creel. We made plans to go fishing the next morning.

But that night, after we'd eaten dinner and washed the dishes and I had laid a fire in the fireplace, Nancy shook her head and said it wasn't going to work.

"Why do you say that?" I asked. "What is it you mean?"

"I mean it isn't going to work. Let's face it." She shook her head again. "I don't think I want to go fishing in the morning, either, and I don't want a dog. No, no dogs. I think I want to go up and see my mother and Richard. Alone. I want to be alone. I miss Richard," she said, and began to cry. "Richard's my son, my baby," she said, "and he's nearly grown and gone. I miss him."

"And Del, do you miss Del Shraeder, too?" I said. "Your boyfriend. Do you miss him?"

"I miss everybody tonight," she said. "I miss you too. I've missed you for a long time now. I've missed you so much you've gotten lost somehow, I can't explain it. I've lost you. You're not mine any longer."

"Nancy," I said.

"No, no," she said. She shook her head. She sat on the sofa in front of the fire and kept shaking her head. "I want to fly up and see my mother and Richard tomorrow. After I'm gone you can call your girlfriend."

"I won't do that," I said. "I have no intention of doing that."

"You'll call her," she said.

"You'll call Del," I said. I felt rubbishy for saying it.

"You can do what you want," she said, wiping her eyes on her sleeve. "I mean that. I don't want to sound hysterical. But I'm going up to Washington tomorrow. Right now I'm going to go to bed. I'm exhausted. I'm sorry. I'm sorry for both of us, Dan. We're not going to make it. That fisherman today. He wished us good luck." She shook her head. "I wish us good luck too. We're going to need it."

She went into the bathroom, and I heard water running in the tub. I went out and sat on the porch steps and smoked a cigarette. It was dark and quiet outside. I looked toward town and could see a faint glow of lights in the sky and patches of ocean fog drifting in the valley. I began to think of Susan. A little later Nancy came out of the bathroom and I heard the bedroom door close. I went inside and put another block of wood on the grate and waited until the flames began to move up the bark. Then I went into the other bedroom and turned the covers back and stared at the floral design on the sheets. Then I showered, dressed in my pajamas, and went to sit near the fireplace again. The fog was outside the window now. I sat in front of the fire and smoked. When I looked out the window again, something moved in the fog and I saw a horse grazing in the front yard.

I went to the window. The horse looked up at me for a minute, then went back to pulling up grass. Another horse walked past the car into the yard and began to graze. I turned on the porch light and stood at the window and watched them. They were big white horses with long manes. They'd gotten through a fence or an unlocked gate from one of the nearby farms. Somehow they'd wound up in our front yard. They were larking it, enjoying their breakaway immensely. But they were nervous too; I could see the whites of their eyes from where I stood behind the window. Their ears kept rising and falling as they tore out clumps of grass. A third horse wandered into the yard, and then a fourth. It was a herd of white horses, and they were grazing in our front yard.

I went into the bedroom and woke Nancy. Her eyes were red and the skin around the eyes was swollen. She had her hair up in curlers and a suitcase lay open on the floor near the foot of the bed.

"Nancy," I said. "Honey, come and see what's in the front yard. Come and see this. You must see this. You won't believe it. Hurry up."

"What is it?" she said. "Don't hurt me. What is it?"

"Honey, you must see this. I'm not going to hurt you. I'm sorry if I scared you. But you must come out here and see something."

I went back into the other room and stood in front of the window and in a few minutes Nancy came in tying her robe. She looked out the window, and said, "My God, they're beautiful. Where'd they come from, Dan? They're just beautiful."

"They must have gotten loose from around here somewhere," I said. "One of these farm places. I'll call the sheriff's department pretty soon and let them locate the owners. But I wanted you to see this first."

"Will they bite?" she said. "I'd like to pet that one there, that one that just looked at us. I'd like to pat that one's shoulder. But I don't want to get bitten. I'm going outside."

"I don't think they'll bite," I said. "They don't look like the kind of horses that'll bite. But put a coat on if you're going out there; it's cold."

I put my coat on over my pajamas and waited for Nancy. Then I opened the front door and we went outside and walked into the yard with the horses. They all looked up at us. Two of them went back to pulling up grass. One of the other horses snorted and moved back a few steps, and then it too went back to pulling up grass and chewing, head down. I rubbed the forehead of one horse and patted its shoulder. It kept chewing. Nancy put out her hand and began stroking the mane of another horse. "Horsey, where'd you come from?" she said. "Where do you live and why are you out tonight, Horsey?" she said, and kept stroking the horse's mane. The horse looked at her and blew through its lips and dropped its head again. She patted its shoulder.

"I guess I'd better call the sheriff," I said.

"Not yet," she said. "Not for a while yet. We'll never see anything like this again. We'll never, never have horses in our front yard again. Wait a while yet, Dan."

A little later, Nancy was still out there moving from one horse to another, patting their shoulders and stroking their manes, when one of the horses moved from the yard into the driveway and walked around the car and down the driveway toward the road, and I knew I had to call.

In a little while the two sheriff's cars showed up with their red lights flashing in the fog and a few minutes later a fellow with a sheepskin coat driving a pickup with a horse trailer behind it. Now the horses shied and tried to get away, and the man with the horse trailer swore and tried to get a rope around the neck of one horse.

"Don't hurt it!" Nancy said.

We went back in the house and stood behind the window and

watched the deputies and the rancher work on getting the horses rounded up.

"I'm going to make some coffee," I said. "Would you like some coffee, Nancy?"

"I'll tell you what I'd like," she said. "I feel high, Dan. I feel like I'm loaded. I feel like, I don't know, but I like the way I'm feeling. You put on some coffee and I'll find us some music to listen to on the radio and then you can build up the fire again. I'm too excited to sleep."

So we sat in front of the fire and drank coffee and listened to an all-night radio station from Eureka and talked about the horses and then talked about Richard, and Nancy's mother. We danced. We didn't talk about the present situation at all. The fog hung outside the window and we talked and were kind with each other. Toward daylight I turned off the radio and we went to bed and made love.

The next afternoon, after her arrangements were made and her suitcases packed, I drove her to the little airport where she would catch a flight to Portland and then transfer to another airline that would put her in Pasco late that night.

"Tell your mother I said hello. Give Richard a hug for me and tell him I miss him," I said. "Tell him I send love."

"He loves you too," she said. "You know that. In any case, you'll see him in the fall, I'm sure."

I nodded.

"Good-bye," she said, and reached for me. We held each other. "I'm glad for last night," she said. "Those horses. Our talk. Everything. It helps. We won't forget that," she said. She began to cry.

"Write me, will you?" I said. "I didn't think it would happen to us," I said. "All those years. I never thought so for a minute. Not us."

"I'll write," she said. "Some big letters. The biggest you've ever seen since I used to send you letters in high school."

"I'll be looking for them," I said.

Then she looked at me again and touched my face. She turned and moved across the tarmac toward the plane.

Go, dearest one, and God be with you.

She boarded the plane and I stayed around until its jet engines started and, in a minute, the plane began to taxi down the runway. It lifted off over Humboldt Bay and soon became a speck on the horizon.

I drove back to the house and parked in the driveway and looked at the hoofprints of the horses from last night. There were deep impressions in the grass, and gashes, and there were piles of dung. Then I went into the house and, without even taking off my coat, went to the telephone and dialed Susan's number.

KIANA DAVENPORT

Bones of the Inner Ear

FROM STORY

LIGHTNING, and a woman breaks in two. Zigzag of ions, her bone-snap of scream. I remember skies crackling. A roasted peacock falling from a tree. I remember a man's hair turning fright-wig blue. Is what one remembers what really occurred? Uncle Noah said every moment has two truths.

We came from the rough tribes of Wai'anae, wild west coast of the island. Here, native clans spawned outcasts and felons, yet our towns had names like lullabies. Makaha, Ma'ili, Nanakuli, Lualualei. In Nanakuli, a valley slung like a hammock between mountain and sea, I was born in a house known for its damaged men.

Long before my birth time, Grandpa came home from World War I with his nose shot off. Doctors built him a metal nose, which he removed at night before he slept. Folks said that's why Grandma went insane, lying under his empty face. Uncle Ben came back from World War II without an arm. His younger brother, Noah, re-turned from combat in Korea, silent as a grub. In time, my cousin Kimo would come home from Vietnam carrying eighteen ounces of shrapnel that they took from his leg before they amputated it.

When Grandma finally died in the crazy asylum, folks came from everywhere, bringing baskets of food, then sat watching our men like people at a zoo. Grandpa and his boys drank too much, stripped off their clothes, raved and danced with savage grace while light hung in the space of their missing limbs. Their mutila-tions glowed. They wrestled their boar hounds to the ground, played pitch and catch with Grandpa's nose till everyone went home.

After his war, Grandpa worked as a coffin repairman at De-Markles Mortuary, so we grew up on his corpse tales — the terminally infected, the futilely stitched. Women outrunning their stillborns. Bullets outrunning young men. Sometimes while he told his eerie tales, things flew out of the windows of our house. A kitchen knife when our uncles were at it. Bottles aimed at garbage-tipping dogs. Once Kiki flew through a window, thrown by her mother, Aunty Ava, one of Grandpa's daughters.

Five headstrong Hawai'ian beauties, they were famous up and down the coast. Pua, Ginger, and Jade. My mother, Lily. And Ava. She was the one I kept my eye on. Ava and Mama were taxi dancers. Slow-hipped, honey-colored, each night they dressed for the dance halls, Ava rice-powdering her cheeks and arms, trying to make them paler, Mama puckering and rouging her perfect lips. Sometimes in sleep I climb behind my mother's eyes. I slip into her skin. I glide with handsome mix-bloods at the dance halls, legs wrapped around thighs that rudder me round the floor.

Some nights Kiki's father came, a handsome Filipino drummer. He'd close the door to Ava's room. Their singing bedsprings, call-and-response of human moans. Then, the sound of him slapping her, a series of screams. Grandpa aiming his pig-hunting rifle, the drummer running down the road. One night Ava roared up the lane, arms slung around a new man, a surfer on a Harley. Grandpa threw her suitcase in the yard and locked the door. Weeks later, she came begging, and he took her back. She stood in the doorway, flicking ashes, throwing off perfumes. For a while I worshipped her.

One day for no reason, she hit Kiki so hard, the girl flipped sideways, landing on her head. Her eyes rolled backward, showing white, a trick that took my breath. That night it was quiet; I was careful where I looked. Then Grandpa walked up to the chair Ava sat in, lifted her and the chair over his head, and threw them both across the room. She just lay there, her cheekbone's shadow on the floor.

My father was a saxophonist on interisland cruise ships. When he was in port, he liked to surprise Mama by climbing through her window. After he left, she would sleep for days. I would sit outside her door, listening as she snored softly, cousin Kiki beside me. We girls grew so close, we could just look at each other and feel safe.

Life went on in Nanakuli. Shootings. Whirl-kick karate death gangs. Marijuana farmers were hauled off to Halawa prison, while girls gave birth in high-school johns. But there was Nanakuli magic, too. Wild-pig hunting with our uncles, their boar hounds singing up jade mountains. Or torch-fishing nights, elders chanting, bronze muscles flashing, strained by dripping haunches of full nets. In tin-roofed shacks, women swayed, stirring meals at rusty stoves, their shadows epic on the walls.

When all five daughters brought their men home, our house bulged and rocked with human drama. In the mornings while they slept, my cousins and I slicked mulberry juice on our lips, turning them a ghoulish blue, scraped green mold from the walls and smeared it on our eyelids, then pinned plumeria in our hair and slow-danced in couples like the grown-ups.

Then Ava's husband reappeared. The clang of his belt buckle as he draped his pants over the end of their bed. Sounds of passion, then, predictably, her screams. For years, I blamed her temper on that man. Now, I know she was swollen with Grandma's genes. She was blister-tight. She slammed Kiki's head with an iron skillet. Shaved her bald for telling a lie. One day she held Kiki's hand over open flames until Uncle Noah pinned her to the wall.

Year after year, I watched him retreat, observing the world from his window, the windowsill growing shiny through the years of his forearms. He did not remember Korea. When we mentioned that war, Noah frowned, asked if we had made it up. Having dismissed the past, he grew acutely aware of the present, focusing more and more on Ava.

She had grown up wanting to be an Olympic swimmer but then she turned beautiful and the dance halls found her. Folks said she looked like Lena Horne. Ava had a second child. The father, a graceful Chinese famous for his tango, was only five years older than Kiki and me. Grandpa threw Ava out again. She never made it to the clinic. Her baby slid out in the back seat of Nanakuli's only taxi while the driver knelt in the bushes vomiting.

Much later Ava told us how she bit the umbilical cord, swung the baby upside down, slapped it till it screamed, and wrapped it in her skirt. Then she climbed up to the driver's seat, stuffed the man's jacket between her legs, and stole his taxi. For years I pictured her speeding off in a rusty Ford, her newborn yelling itself purple while she shifted gears and struggled with her afterbirth.

She and the tango man hid out in Chinatown, living off the sale of the stripped-down cab. When they were finally arrested, Grandpa posted bail, Ava was put on probation, and he brought her home. The baby, Taxi, was beautiful. But when Kiki bent to lift her little brother, Ava lunged at her.

"Touch him, I break your arm!"

Kiki stood straight, so she and her mother were eye to eye. "Guarantee. I never again come near your little bastard."

It was the first time I saw Kiki's edge. I saw something else that day. Her walk was becoming obvious. For several years now, she had listed slightly, as if her right foot were deprived of a natural heel. Each year the lopsided walk was more pronounced. Grandpa took her to a foot doctor who found nothing, but an ear specialist said her equilibrium was off. Tiny bones of her inner ear were permanently damaged. I thought of Kiki flying headfirst through a window, her mother swinging an iron skillet like a baseball bat. Kiki's flame-scarred hand that took away her lifeline. I crawled into her bed and held her.

That summer was so dry, barking deer stumbled down from the mountains, licking windows of air-conditioned stores. The piss of boar hounds sizzled on tar. Mongooses crawled under our house, coughing and sucking at the pipes. And in the midst of it, my father. A word that always silenced me. He came with his somber eyes and closed the door to my mother's room. I know he loved her at one time. I don't believe he lied. I think that time moved on.

I lifted the window shade, watching moonlight on my feet, imagining my father pacing Mama's room, saying he would not be back. I thought how folks appeared and vanished in our lives, and wondered what controlled them. I pictured a big celestial genie, rubbing whatever makes humans come and go. He left and she played dead as usual. I thought she was playing. Grandpa cried for nights on end, and then we buried her. Shortly after, I slept through a hurricane that lasted three days.

At sixteen Kiki discovered dancing, that when she danced she did not limp. She began to smell of after-shave. Someone was teaching her to tango.

One night she knelt beside my bed. "Ana! I'm in love with Gum. Father of little Taxi."

I sat up, stunned. "You crazy? What about your mama."

"She never loved him. Or anyone."

Gum tried to explain it to Ava; we knew because we heard her screams. We started running up the road, on into the valley, into deep jungle throats that swallowed us. For hours, we shinnied up lava boulders, clinging to roots and knotted vines. Up to our refuge behind a waterfall. Years back when we first braved the falls, we discovered, behind them, an eerie grotto draped in moss, full of scattered bones.

Now, crawling behind those thundering drapes, we fell exhausted into the cave, into man-shaped hollows centuries old. In the dimness, bones glowed green and blue. We lay side by side, feeling warmth from the sun the earth had swallowed. We were children again, cradled in stone.

"Sometimes I see things," Kiki whispered. "I hope they don't see me . . . I hope they don't come after me."

I knew she was afraid she would inherit her mother's temper. "Do you think Grandma did the same thing to your mama?"

"Maybe. Maybe if Mama shaved her head, we'd see the scars."

We stayed behind the falls all night, and in those hours Kiki tried to change her life. Take it off like a coat, leave it behind.

"I'm a woman now. She strike again, I strike back."

Next day we shot out of those falls like bullets, plunging feet-first into thundering foam, down into a swirling river. Grandpa, out searching in his grass rain cape, found us exhausted on the shore. We marched home like woman warriors, full of resolution.

Ava must have sensed it. She never mentioned Gum, but at night she stood in Kiki's room, staring at the empty bed. One day I heard Taxi scream, then muffled silence. Blue moons appeared on his arms and legs, little bruises the size of a pinch. Grandpa saw them too and started throwing chairs again, telling Ava to get out for good, he would raise her kids. She fell to her knees, screaming and pleading.

Grandpa gave in, of course, and Ava stayed. Then our family began to rinse away. One sister stepped into a chauffeured car, was never seen again. Another joined the Catholic order. Third sister married a Samoan who swallowed fire for a living and smelled of gasoline. One-legged Cousin Kimo shocked us all by enrolling at the island's big university. Soon there was just Ava, Noah, and Ben, assorted cousins left with Grandpa.

He began complaining about his nose, and doctors gave him a

new one, an ugly prosthetic that looked eerily real. It had a bitter plastic smell and gave him pain. Then he felt nothing. His nasal passages had gangrened. Grandpa's face was so damaged when he died, we buried him wearing a mask, laid out in his mildewed white linen suit, a ti leaf across his chest for safe journey. Clans came from up and down the coast, leaning into his coffin, trying to see the horror beneath the mask. They twisted in their pews, staring at us like the old days.

I kept my eyes on Ava, still beautiful in a menacing way. Taxi, beside her, five years old, a timid, jumpy little thing, but slender and graceful like his father. Mama had been Grandpa's favorite, but I think Ava loved him best of all. Now she moved to his coffin, her voice growing ugly and amplified.

"Papa! How come all these years you never give me credit? Always yelling how I raise my kids? How come all these years you never *love* me!"

She rocked the coffin back and forth, trying to heave it over. When Father Riley ran down from the altar and tried to pull her back, Ava picked him up and threw him to his knees so hard he skidded. Uncle Ben shouted, reached out with his arm, and knocked her down. In that moment, Kiki moved to little Taxi, took his hand, and quickly led him up the aisle, her walk still lopsided, listing to the right. We buried Grandpa and brought Ava home. She sat in her room, whispering and rocking.

One night she stood in my doorway, then crept close and, with dreamy precision, tapped my hand.

"Your father was real mischief. He once put a lizard in my handbag. Oh, *he* was a dancer!"

I couldn't move. I felt like something with its mouth stitched shut.

She leaned so close, I saw her fillings, blue-black as lava. Strands of saliva clung to the roof of her mouth.

"I had him first, you know. But he was nothing. He just lived. I gave him to your mama."

I looked straight into her eyes. "She killed herself, didn't she?"

"Yes! She was pregnant." She threw back her head and laughed. "Men. They just lay there."

"Maybe they're afraid of you," I said. "Even Kiki's afraid of you. She should hate you . . . all those scars."

Ava laughed again. "Scars make her *interesting*."

Then her skin grew tight, her cheekbones looked whittled down to knuckles. "Where's my boy, Taxi?"

"I won't tell you."

She grabbed my wrist, shook it like a club. "You get him back. Else I burn this house down."

For days, cars dragged up and down our road. One of the boar hounds had dropped a litter, and twelve puppies were for sale. Two were bought by a drag queen out shopping for accessories. She had seen Taxi with Kiki and Gum, practicing at Castro Dance Hall. "Such a little Fred Astaire!"

Hearing that, Ava climbed out of her window and stole the drag queen's truck. She found Taxi asleep in Gum's car beside the dance hall. Nowhere else to run, she drove home and locked the boy in her room with her. At first he screamed, then she calmed him down, holding him, rocking him like a mother. I watched her through the keyhole.

A day and a night we pleaded, banging on the door. Then Ben lowered a bottle of milk on a rope from the second floor down to her window. Ava opened it just enough to grab the bottle. For three days we passed her baskets of food dangled from the rope. She and the child messed in a bucket, which she emptied out the window every night. We heard them laughing. Singing kid songs. When we called Taxi's name, he answered. He and his mama were playing games.

Ben grew impatient. At night while Ava and the boy slept, he tried to wedge her door loose near the hinges. One day, as she reached out the window for their food, Ben tried to break the door in.

Ava went berserk. "You not going take my boy! I warned! I warned!"

Her screams were so awful Kiki dropped to her knees, praying out loud. We called their names for hours, then finished breaking in the door. She lay in the corner with her smothered child. She had slashed her neck to pieces trying to cut her artery. Noah picked up the blood-red boy, carried him outside, and sat in sunlight, hugging him. He opened and closed his mouth like a fish, rocking the body to and fro.

We buried Taxi next to Grandpa, and Ava followed Grandma to Kanehoe State Hospital. Folks drove past our house, taking pictures. I ran out with Grandpa's camera and shot back. But images came after me, tracking me by body heat like morays. I started running in my dreams. One night I boarded a bus, following the ruby-strung arrow of taillights bound for Honolulu.

I learned fast, woman-fast, and in time became a nurse, finding a whole new lineup of humans among the injured and diseased. People who asked nothing of me but comfort. I learned detachment, how to cure, or turn away. I learned you can save a life by lying. And that some folks *need* to die. I hugged the dead even when they'd rigored, in case a soul was hanging back. I held a man's heart outside his chest and found the pulse consoling.

A bifurcated woman. Half of me nursing strangers, the other half nursing drinks at 2 A.M. Stroking slips the color of old peach skin, smelling perfume still clinging to her hairpins. Somewhere, my father had been measured for a hat. Mama had kept that piece of paper with the figures. That's all I was sure of, my mother's slip size, my father's head measurements. Some nights I listened to saxophones. Sometimes at dusk I wept.

Why they released Ava was never clear. Crowded wards. Her age, her edges turning soft and blurred. Uncle Ben signed the release and brought her home, then called me. I stood in that road, beloved slum of potholes, chicken coops, animal fat frying. The house ran out to meet me. Uncle Noah waved, still polishing the windowsill with his forearms. Swimming in the bright aquarium of his thoughts. For years now, he had watched an empty chair rock to and fro, remembering the boy who sat there. That's when I understood how much he had loved little Taxi.

Ava was wearing an ink-colored wig, her forehead pressed to her bedroom wall, telling her confession. Her teeth were gone, eyes empty craters, neck a pearly grid of scars. She turned and ran at me headfirst, then jerked back, like something leaping the length of its chain. She didn't know me. But she had started again on Kiki, whispering outside her door at night. Lurid, obscene things no daughter should have heard. I packed Kiki's bags, planning to take her to Honolulu. But she retreated, up to her elbows in pastries. She had stopped dancing, stopped everything. All she did was eat. Ava kept stalking her, even tried to climb in bed with her.

Uncle Ben shook his head, stroking the shoulder where his arm had been. "Bad thing, I brought her home. She drive dat girl to suicide."

Lightning season came. Air so electric, the fillings in our teeth hummed. Everything we touched just sparked. There were flash floods; the seas gave off a yellow glow. For days lightning zigzagged up the valley. It hit a wild pig that rolled into our yard, completely roasted. Voltaged peacocks fell from trees. One night herringbones of ions, lightning striking everywhere. No one saw Ava leave the house. But then, sky crackling, her awful scream. We found Ben standing over her, his hair electrified a gaseous blue.

She lay facedown, spread out like a pelt. Paramedics said lightning. But her body seemed untouched. Then they said she must have tripped and fallen. The medical examiner found a big crack in the back of her skull from a powerful blow. He thought lightning had hit a branch, which struck her. Folks said Ben struck the blow. Or, Kiki. The skies calmed down. We buried Ava, then sat back, tipping long-necked beers, letting the wounded world become green glass. Those moments were as kind as life would get.

Several years passed before I walked that road again. I stood before the house, completely shocked. Kiki was sitting on the porch, so absolutely huge, she looked like a sofa. She now weighed almost four hundred pounds. She had a heart condition and was deaf in one ear. She was peeling something in a bowl when she looked up. Slowly, almost impossibly, she rose to her feet, which were so swollen, they looked like loaves of bread. She tried to struggle down the steps; I ran forward, flung my arms around her legs, and wept. Kiki bent and stroked my hair.

That night, Ben took me aside, explaining how a year after Gum moved to Seattle, Kiki had tried to hang herself. She thought no one was home. A burglar roaming the house stepped into her room just as she started to kick the chair from under her feet. The man shouted, climbed up beside her on the chair, held her round the waist, and talked to her for hours. Kiki fell in love with the burglar who saved her life.

He moved into the house, and he and Kiki had a child. He sounded like a good man, good to her, but one night he took off down the road forever. Ben said it was Kiki's "fits" that drove him off. They came out of nowhere, like her mother's. Her baby girl was almost two now, a chubby little thing named Lily, for my mother. I found her tethered to a clothesline like a dog. I knelt, looking for bruises, then held her for a while.

I came home again for Uncle Noah. Most of his years had been lived in silence and now, nearing seventy, he was ready to come to a stop. I knelt beside his bed.

"You were always my hero, did you know? I loved how you had all the answers, and kept them to yourself."

He smiled, drifted for a while, then half sat up, pointing to his closet. Inside was something big and round wrapped in moldy cloth. He said two words. "Bury it." That night I unwrapped it in my room. Rusty now, the way iron gets. The weight of the skillet still profound. The back still matted with blood, gray strands of hair, bits of her skull like ice chips. I wiped it clean, buried it with Noah, and went back to Honolulu.

Some nights I sit with patients, placing my hand on their chests to make sure they're still breathing, adjusting my breathing to theirs. Sharing the rhythmic rise and fall, rise and fall. Sometimes the moon-metal blade of a scalpel is like a candle in my face by which I see my life reflected. A careful life, no shocks, no faulty perceptions. A life completely watered-down. Once, I proposed to a man while I emptied his bedpan. I said I liked the way he snored; snores let you know where people are. He thought I was joking. I checked a mirror to see if my face was behaving, then went home and slept for days.

Sometimes I visit Cousin Kimo, a lawyer now, pride of Nanakuli. I watch how gently his son unstraps his father's artificial leg. I stir the ashes of our childhood, wondering why some of us managed to escape that house while others didn't. Kimo says it's in the egg. He says I look like my mother. He says I sleep too much.

Kiki's still living there with Ben's widow and come-and-go cousins. Her heart is worse; medications leave her drowsy. She has forgotten the metaphysics of walking. Her seizures take her unaware. Some days I sit beside her while she naps, her body a breathing mountain. Her features have almost disappeared, but somewhere in that mask of flesh is the girl behind the waterfall: edgy, tough, full of resolution.

One day she wakes and smiles at me. "Even in my sleep, Mama's trying to catch up with me. But, ho! I still outrun her."

I love this woman more and more. Our genes are warped together. Her morphology is mine. And I love her because she's still fighting the hole that wants to suck her in.

Young Lily is eight now. Brown-skinned, lovely. Very bright. Books and toys, a star chart on her ceiling. But something fractured in her eyes. She stands in the kitchen, playing with knobs, watching the slow transformation of electric stove rings turn from gray to orange. She broods in her room full of secrets. One day, I hear her voice, eerie and old. I hear dull thuds and open her door. She's holding a doll I've never seen, an ugly, twisted, broken thing.

"I warned you and warned you," she whispers. "You selfish little bitch." She slaps its face repeatedly. She bangs its head against the floor.

I turn away, keeping myself blind to signals, avoiding the Morse of Lily's steps. That is, I look down when she walks toward me, and when she walks away. I don't want to see that her walk is funny, that she seems to tilt.

But then she comes dragging that ugly, battered doll, its head wrapped in bandages, makeshift Band-Aids on its legs. Lily thrusts herself between my arms, half sitting in my lap, demanding, not asking for, my attention. A quirky and aggressive child. I hug her, pointing to the doll.

"What's all this? I thought you hated her."

She pats its head. "Yeah. But, she needed medical attention."

I laugh. "Well, Lily. Maybe one day you'll be a nurse."

She steps back and studies me. Then adamantly she shakes her head. "No, Aunty! I going be one *doctor.* I going tell folks what to do."

I hug her again, because she is the best of her mother — edgy, full of resolution. She hugs me back with young-girl arms, yet I feel her toughness and her tremor, as if her blood is already marshaling tiny armies that will reinstruct her genes. As if she is already breaking the mold, honoring the daughters born with no clues or codes, and the mothers of those daughters — golden, slow-hipped women who should have been running, not dancing.

Nilda

FROM THE NEW YORKER

NILDA was my brother's girlfriend.

This is how all these stories begin.

She was Dominican from here and had superlong hair, like those Pentecostal girls, and a chest you wouldn't believe — I'm talking world-class. Rafa would sneak her down into our basement bedroom after our mother went to bed and do her to whatever was on the radio right then. The two of them had to let me stay, because if my mother heard me upstairs on the couch everybody's ass would have been fried. And since I wasn't about to spend my night out in the bushes this is how it was.

Rafa didn't make no noise, just a low something that resembled breathing. Nilda was the one. She seemed to be trying to hold back from crying the whole time. It was crazy hearing her like that. The Nilda I'd grown up with was one of the quietest girls you'd ever meet. She let her hair wall away her face and read "The New Mutants," and the only time she looked straight at anything was when she looked out a window.

But that was before she'd gotten that chest, before that slash of black hair had gone from something to pull on the bus to something to stroke in the dark. The new Nilda wore stretch pants and Iron Maiden shirts; she had already run away from her mother's and ended up at a group home; she'd already slept with Toño and Nestor and Little Anthony from Parkwood, older guys. She crashed over at our apartment a lot because she hated her moms, who was the neighborhood borracha. In the morning she slipped out before my mother woke up and found her. Waited for heads at the bus stop, fronted like she'd come from her own place, same clothes as the day before and greasy hair so everybody thought her a skank. Waited for my brother and didn't talk to anybody and nobody talked to her, because she'd always been one of those quiet, semi-retarded girls who you couldn't talk to without being dragged into a whirlpool of dumb stories. If Rafa decided that he wasn't going to school, then she'd wait near our apartment until my mother left for work. Sometimes Rafa let her in right away. Sometimes he slept late and she'd wait across the street, building letters out of pebbles until she saw him crossing the living room.

She had big stupid lips and a sad moonface and the driest skin. Always rubbing lotion on it and cursing the moreno father who'd given it to her.

It seemed like she was always waiting for my brother. Nights, she'd knock and I'd let her in and we'd sit on the couch while Rafa was off at his job at the carpet factory or working out at the gym. I'd show her my newest comics and she'd read them real close, but as soon as Rafa showed up she'd throw them in my lap and jump into his arms.

I missed you, she'd say in a little-girl voice, and Rafa would laugh. You should have seen him in those days: he had the face bones of a saint. Then Mami's door would open and Rafa would detach himself and cowboy-saunter over to Mami, and say, You got something for me to eat, vieja? Claro que sí, Mami'd say, trying to put her glasses on.

He had us all, the way only a pretty nigger can.

Once when Rafa was late from the job and we were alone in the apartment a long time, I asked her about the group home. It was three weeks before the end of the school year and everybody had entered the Do-Nothing Stage. I was fourteen and reading "Dhalgren" for the second time; I had an IQ that would have broken you in two, but I would have traded it in for a halfway decent face in a second.

It was pretty cool up there, she said. She was pulling on the front of her halter top, trying to air her chest out. The food was *bad,* but there were a lot of cute guys in the house with me. They *all* wanted me.

She started chewing on a nail. Even the guys who worked there were calling me after I left, she said.

The only reason Rafa went after her was because his last full-time girlfriend had gone back to Guyana — she was this dougla girl with a single eyebrow and skin to die for — and because Nilda had pushed up to him. She'd been back from the group home only a couple of months, but by then she'd already gotten a rep as a cuero. A lot of the Dominican girls in town were on some serious lockdown — we saw them on the bus and at school and maybe at the Pathmark, but since most families knew exactly what kind of tígueres were roaming the neighborhood these girls weren't allowed to hang out. Nilda was different. She was brown trash. Her moms was a mean-ass drunk and always running around South Amboy with her white boyfriends — which is a long way of saying Nilda could hang and, man, did she ever. Always out in the world, always cars stopping where she was smoking cigarettes. Before I even knew she was back from the group home she got scooped up by this older nigger from the back apartments. He kept her on his dick for almost four months, and I used to see them driving around in his fucked-up rust-eaten Sunbird while I delivered my papers. Motherfucker was like three hundred years old, but because he had a car and a record collection and photo albums from his Vietnam days and because he bought her clothes to replace the old shit she was wearing, Nilda was all lost on him.

I hated this nigger with a passion, but when it came to guys there was no talking to Nilda. I used to ask her, What's up with Wrinkle Dick? And she would get so mad she wouldn't speak to me for days, and then I'd get this note, *I want you to respect my man. Whatever,* I'd write back. Then the old cat bounced, no one knew where, the usual scenario in my neighborhood, and for a couple of months she got tossed by those cats from Parkwood. On Thursdays, which was comic-book day, she'd drop in to see what I'd picked up and she'd talk to me about how unhappy she was. We'd sit together until it got dark and then her beeper would fire up and she'd peer into its display and say, I have to go. Sometimes I could grab her and pull her back on the couch, and we'd stay there a long time, me waiting for her to fall in love with me, her waiting for whatever, but other times she'd be serious. I have to go see my man, she'd say.

One of those comic-book days she saw my brother coming back from his five-mile run. Rafa was still boxing then and he was cut up like crazy, the muscles on his chest and abdomen so striated they looked like something out of a Frazetta drawing. He noticed her because she was wearing these ridiculous shorts and this tank that couldn't have blocked a sneeze and a thin roll of stomach was poking from between the fabrics and he smiled at her and she got real serious and uncomfortable and he told her to fix him some iced tea and she told him to fix it himself. You a guest here, he said. You should be earning your fucking keep. He went into the shower and as soon as he did she was in the kitchen stirring and I told her to leave it, but she said, I might as well. We drank all of it.

I wanted to warn her, tell her he was a monster, but she was already headed for him at the speed of light.

The next day Rafa's car turned up broken — what a coincidence — so he took the bus to school and when he was walking past our seat he took her hand and pulled her to her feet and she said, Get off me. Her eyes were pointed straight at the floor. I just want to show you something, he said. She was pulling with her arm but the rest of her was ready to go. Come on, Rafa said, and finally she went. Save my seat, she said over her shoulder, and I was like, Don't worry about it. Before we even swung onto 516 Nilda was in my brother's lap and he had his hand so far up her skirt it looked like he was performing a surgical procedure. When we were getting off the bus Rafa pulled me aside and held his hand in front of my nose. Smell this, he said. This, he said, is what's wrong with women.

You couldn't get anywhere near Nilda for the rest of the day. She had her hair pulled back and was glorious with victory. Even the white girls knew about my overmuscled about-to-be-a-senior brother and were impressed. And while Nilda sat at the end of our lunch table and whispered to some girls me and my boys ate our crap sandwiches and talked about the X-Men — this was back when the X-Men still made some kind of sense — and even if we didn't want to admit it the truth was now patent and awful: all the real dope girls were headed up to the high school, like moths to a light, and there was nothing any of us younger cats could do about it. My man José Negrón — a.k.a. Joe Black — took Nilda's defection the hardest, since he'd actually imagined he had a chance with her. Right after she got back from the group home he'd held her hand on the bus, and even though she'd gone off with other guys, he'd never forgotten it.

I was in the basement three nights later when they did it. That first time neither of them made a sound.

They went out that whole summer. I don't remember anyone doing anything big. Me and my pathetic little crew hiked over to Morgan

Creek and swam around in water stinking of leachate from the landfill; we were just getting serious about the licks that year and Joe Black was stealing bottles out of his father's stash and we were drinking them down to the corners on the swings behind the apartments. Because of the heat and because of what I felt inside my chest a lot, I often just sat in the crib with my brother and Nilda. Rafa was tired all the time and pale: this had happened in a matter of days. I used to say, Look at you, white boy, and he used to say, Look at you, you black ugly nigger. He didn't feel like doing much, and besides his car had finally broken down for real, so we would all sit in the air-conditioned apartment and watch TV. Rafa had decided he wasn't going back to school for his senior year, and even though my moms was heartbroken and trying to guilt him into it five times a day, this was all he talked about. School had never been his gig, and after my pops left us for his twenty-five-year-old he didn't feel he needed to pretend any longer. I'd like to take a long fucking trip, he told us. See California before it slides into the ocean. California, I said. California, he said. A nigger could make a showing out there.

I'd like to go there, too, Nilda said, but Rafa didn't answer her. He had closed his eyes and you could see he was in pain.

We never talked about our father. I'd asked Rafa once, right at the beginning of the Last Great Absence, where he thought he was, and Rafa said, Like I fucking care.

End of conversation. World without end.

On days niggers were really out of their minds with boredom we trooped down to the pool and got in for free because Rafa was boys with one of the lifeguards. I swam, Nilda went on missions around the pool just so she could show off how tight she looked in her bikini, and Rafa sprawled under the awning and took it all in. Sometimes he called me over and we'd sit together for a while and he'd close his eyes and I'd watch the water dry on my ashy legs and then he'd tell me to go back to the pool. When Nilda finished promenading and came back to where Rafa was chilling she kneeled at his side and he would kiss her real long, his hands playing up and down the length of her back. Ain't nothing like a fifteen-year-old with a banging body, those hands seemed to be saying, at least to me.

Joe Black was always watching them. Man, he muttered, she's so fine I'd lick her asshole *and* tell you niggers about it.

Maybe I would have thought they were cute if I hadn't known Rafa. He might have seemed enamora'o with Nilda but he also had mad girls in orbit. Like this one piece of white trash from Sayreville, and this morena from Amsterdam Village who also slept over and sounded like a freight train when they did it. I don't remember her name, but I do remember how her perm shone in the glow of our night-light.

In August Rafa quit his job at the carpet factory — I'm too fucking tired, he complained, and some mornings his leg bones hurt so much he couldn't get out of bed right away. The Romans used to shatter these with iron clubs, I told him while I massaged his shins. The pain would kill you instantly. Great, he said. Cheer me up some more, you fucking bastard. One day Mami took him to the hospital for a checkup and afterward I found them sitting on the couch, both of them dressed up, watching TV like nothing had happened. They were holding hands and Mami appeared tiny next to him.

Well?

Rafa shrugged. The doc thinks I'm anemic.

Anemic ain't bad.

Yeah, Rafa said, laughing bitterly. God bless Medicaid.

In the light of the TV, he looked terrible.

That was the summer when everything we would become was hovering just over our heads. Girls were starting to take notice of me; I wasn't good-looking but I listened and was sincere and had boxing muscles in my arms. In another universe I probably came out okay, ended up with mad novias and jobs and a sea of love in which to swim, but in this world I had a brother who was dying of cancer and a long dark patch of life like a mile of black ice waiting for me up ahead.

One night, a couple of weeks before school started — they must have thought I was asleep — Nilda started telling Rafa about her plans for the future. I think even she knew what was about to happen. Listening to her imagining herself was about the saddest thing you ever heard. How she wanted to get away from her moms and open up a group home for runaway kids. But this one would be real cool, she said. It would be for normal kids who just got problems. She must have loved him because she went on and on. Plenty of people talk about having a flow, but that night I really heard one, something that was unbroken, that fought itself and worked together all at once. Rafa didn't say nothing. Maybe he had his hands in her hair or maybe he was just like, Fuck you. When she finished he didn't even say wow. I wanted to kill myself with embarrassment. About a half hour later she got up and dressed. She couldn't see me or she would have known that I thought she was beautiful. She stepped into her pants and pulled them up in one motion, sucked in her stomach while she buttoned them. I'll see you later, she said.

Yeah, he said.

After she walked out he put on the radio and started on the speed bag. I stopped pretending I was asleep; I sat up and watched him.

Did you guys have a fight or something?

No, he said.

Why'd she leave?

He sat down on my bed. His chest was sweating. She had to go.

But where's she gonna stay?

I don't know. He put his hand on my face, gently. Why ain't you minding your business?

A week later he was seeing some other girl. She was from Trinidad, a coco pañyol, and she had this phony-as-hell English accent. It was the way we all were back then. None of us wanted to be niggers. Not for nothing.

I guess two years passed. My brother was gone by then, and I was on my way to becoming a nut. I was out of school most of the time and had no friends and I sat inside and watched Univisión or walked down to the dump and smoked the mota I should have been selling until I couldn't see. Nilda didn't fare so well, either. A lot of the things that happened to her, though, had nothing to do with me or my brother. She fell in love a couple more times, really bad with this one moreno truck driver who took her to Manalapan and then abandoned her at the end of the summer. I had to drive over to get her, and the house was one of those tiny box jobs with a fifty-cent lawn and no kind of charm; she was acting like she was some Italian chick and offered me a joint in the car, but I put my hand on hers and told her to stop it. Back home she fell in with more stupid niggers, relocated kids from the City, and they came at her with drama and some of their girls beat her up, a Brick City beat-down, and she lost her bottom front teeth. She was in and out of school and for a while they put her on home instruction, and that was when she finally dropped.

My junior year she started delivering papers so she could make money, and since I was spending a lot of time outside I saw her every now and then. Broke my heart. She wasn't at her lowest yet but she was aiming there and when we passed each other she always smiled and said hi. She was starting to put on weight and she'd cut her hair down to nothing and her moonface was heavy and alone. I always said Wassup and when I had cigarettes I gave them to her. She'd gone to the funeral, along with a couple of his other girls, and what a skirt she'd worn, like maybe she could still convince him of something, and she'd kissed my mother but the vieja hadn't known who she was. I had to tell Mami on the ride home and all she could remember about her was that she was the one who smelled good. It wasn't until Mami said it that I realized it was true.

It was only one summer and she was nobody special, so what's the point of all this? He's gone, he's gone, he's gone. I'm twenty-three and I'm washing my clothes up at the minimall on Ernston Road. She's here with me — she's folding her shit and smiling and showing me her missing teeth and saying, It's been a long time, hasn't it, Yunior?

Years, I say, loading my whites. Outside the sky is clear of gulls, and down at the apartment my moms is waiting for me with dinner. Six months earlier we were sitting in front of the TV and my mother said, Well, I think I'm finally over this place.

Nilda asks, Did you move or something?

I shake my head. Just been working.

God, it's been a long, long time. She's on her clothes like magic, making everything neat, making everything fit. There are four other people at the counters, broke-ass-looking niggers with knee socks and croupier's hats and scars snaking up their arms, and they all seem like sleepwalkers compared with her. She shakes her head, grinning. Your brother, she says.

Rafa.

She points her finger at me like my brother always did.

I miss him sometimes.

She nods. Me, too. He was a good guy to me.

I must have disbelief on my face because she finishes shaking out her towels and then stares straight through me. He treated me the best.

Nilda.

He used to sleep with my hair over his face. He used to say it made him feel safe.

What else can we say? She finishes her stacking, I hold the door open for her. The locals watch us leave. We walk back through the old neighborhood, slowed down by the bulk of our clothes. London Terrace has changed now that the landfill has shut down. Kicked-up rents and mad South Asian people and white folks living in the apartments, but it's our kids you see in the streets and hanging from the porches.

Nilda is watching the ground as though she's afraid she might fall. My heart is beating and I think, We could do anything. We could marry. We could drive off to the West Coast. We could start over. It's all possible but neither of us speaks for a long time and the moment closes and we're back in the world we've always known.

Remember the day we met? she asks.

I nod.

You wanted to play baseball.

It was summer, I say. You were wearing a tank top.

You made me put on a shirt before you'd let me be on your team. Do you remember?

I remember, I say.

We never spoke again. A couple of years later I went away to college and I don't know where the fuck she went.

NATHAN ENGLANDER

The Gilgul of Park Avenue

FROM THE ATLANTIC MONTHLY

THE JEWISH DAY begins in the calm of evening, when it won't shock the system with its arrival. That was when, three stars visible in the Manhattan sky and a new day fallen, Charles Morton Luger understood that he was the bearer of a Jewish soul.

Ping! Like that it came. Like a knife against a glass.

Charles Luger knew, if he knew anything at all, that a Yiddishe *neshama* was functioning inside him.

He was not one to engage taxicab drivers in conversation, but such a thing as this he felt obligated to share. A New York story of the first order, like a woman giving birth in an elevator, or a hot dog vendor performing open-heart surgery with a pocketknife and a Bic pen. Was not this a rebirth in itself? It was something, he was sure. So he leaned forward in his seat, raised a fist, and knocked on the Plexiglas divider.

The driver looked into his rearview mirror.

"Jewish," Charles said. "Jewish, here in the back."

The driver reached up and slid the partition open so that it hit its groove loudly.

"Oddly, it seems that I'm Jewish. Jewish in your cab."

"No problem here. Meter ticks the same for all creeds." The driver pointed at the digital display.

Charles thought about it. A positive experience — or at least benign. Yes, benign. What had he expected?

He looked out the window at Park Avenue, a Jew looking out at the world. Colors were no brighter or darker, though he was, he admitted, already searching for someone with a beanie, a landsman who might look his way, wink, confirm what he already knew.

The cab slowed to a halt outside his building, and Petey, the doorman, stepped toward the curb. Charles removed his money clip and peeled off a fifty. He reached over the seat, holding on to the bill.

"Jewish," Charles said, pressing the fifty into the driver's hand. "Jewish right here in your cab."

Charles hung his coat and placed his briefcase next to the stand filled with ornate canes and umbrellas that Sue — who had carefully scouted them out around the city — would not let him touch. Sue had redone the foyer, the living room, and the dining room all in chintz, an overwhelming number of flora-and-fauna patterns, creating a vast slippery-looking expanse. Charles rushed through it to the kitchen, where Sue was removing dinner from the refrigerator.

She read the note the maid had left, lighting burners and turning dials accordingly. Charles came up behind her. He inhaled the scent of perfume and the faint odor of cigarettes laced underneath. Sue turned, and they kissed, more passionate than friendly, which was neither an everyday occurrence nor altogether rare. She was still wearing her contacts; her eyes were a radiant blue.

"You won't believe it," Charles said, surprised to find himself elated. He was a levelheaded man, not often victim to extremes of mood.

"What won't I believe?" Sue said. She separated herself from him and slipped a pan into the oven.

Sue was the art director of a glossy magazine, her professional life comparatively glamorous. The daily doings of a financial analyst, Charles felt, did not even merit polite attention. He never told her anything she wouldn't believe.

"Well, what is it, Charles?" She held a glass against the recessed ice machine in the refrigerator. "Damn," she said. Charles, at breakfast, had left it set on "crushed."

"You wouldn't believe my taxi ride," he said, suddenly aware that a person disappointed by ice chips wouldn't take well to his discovery.

"Your face," she said, noting his odd expression.

"Nothing — just remembering. A heck of a ride. A maniac. Taxi driver running lights. Up on the sidewalk."

The maid had prepared creamed chicken. When they sat down

to dinner, Charles stared at his plate. Half an hour Jewish and already he felt obliged. He knew there were dietary laws, milk and meat forbidden to touch, but he didn't know if chicken was considered meat and didn't dare ask Sue and chance a confrontation — not until he'd formulated a plan. He would call Dr. Birnbaum, his psychologist, in the morning. Or maybe he'd find a rabbi. Who better to guide him in such matters?

And so, a Marrano in modern times, Charles ate his chicken like a gentile — all the while a Jew in his heart.

At work the next morning Charles got right on it. He pulled out the Yellow Pages, referenced and cross-referenced, following the "see" list throughout the phone book. More than one listing under "Zion" put him in touch with a home for the aged. "Redemption" led him further off course. Finally he came upon an organization that seemed frighteningly appropriate. For one thing, it had a number in Royal Hills, a neighborhood thick with Jews.

The listing was for the Royal Hills Mystical Jewish Reclamation Center, or, as the recorded voice said, "the R-HMJRC" — just like that, with a pause after the first "R." It was a sort of clearinghouse for the Judeo-supernatural: "Press one for messianic time clock, two for dream interpretation and counseling, three for numerology, and four for a retreat schedule." The "and four" took the wind out of his sails. A bad sign. Recordings never said "and four" and then "and five." But the message went on. A small miracle. "For all gilgulim, cases of possible reincarnation, or recovered memory, please call Rabbi Zalman Meintz at the following number."

Charles took it down, elated. This was exactly why he had moved to New York from Idaho so many years before. Exactly the reason. Because you could find anything in the Manhattan Yellow Pages. Anything. A book as thick as a cinder block.

The R-HMJRC was a beautifully renovated Gothic-looking brownstone in the heart of Royal Hills. The front steps had been widened to the width of the building, and the whole façade of the first two floors had been torn off and replaced by a stone arch with a glass wall behind it. The entry hall was marble, and Charles was impressed. There is money in the God business, he told himself, making a mental note.

This is how it went: Standing in the middle of the marble floor, feeling the cold space, the only thing familiar being his unfamiliar self. And then it was back. Ping! Once again, understanding.

Only yesterday his whole life had been his life — familiar, totally his own. Something he lived in like an old wool sweater. Today: Brooklyn, an archway, white marble.

"Over here, over here. Follow my voice. Come to the light."

Charles had taken the stairs until they ended, and he entered what appeared to be an attic, slanted ceilings and dust, overflowing with attic stuff — chairs and a rocking horse, a croquet set, and boxes, everywhere boxes — as if all the remnants of the brownstone's former life had been driven upward.

"Take the path on your right. Make your way. It's possible; I got here." The speech was punctuated with something like laughter. It was vocalized joy, a happy stutter.

The path led to the front of the building and a clearing demarcated by an oriental screen. The rabbi sat in a leather armchair across from a battered couch — both clearly salvaged from the spoils that cluttered the room.

"Zalman," the man said, jumping up and shaking Charles's hand. "Rabbi Zalman Meintz."

"Charles Luger," Charles said, taking off his coat.

The couch, though it had seen brighter days, was clean. Charles had expected dust to rise when he sat. As soon as he touched the fabric, he got depressed. More chintz. Sun-dulled flowers crawled all over it.

"Just moved in," Zalman said. "New space. Much bigger. But haven't organized, as you can see." He pointed at specific things: a mirror, a china hutch. "Please excuse, or forgive — please excuse our appearance. More important matters come first. Very busy lately, very busy." As if to illustrate, a phone perched on a dollhouse set to ringing. "You see," Zalman said. He reached over and shut off the ringer. "Like that all day. At night, too. Busier even at night."

The surroundings didn't inspire confidence, but Zalman did. He couldn't have been much more than thirty, but he looked to Charles like a real Jew: long black beard, black suit, black hat at his side, and a nice big caricaturish nose, like Fagin's but friendlier.

"Well, then, Mr. Luger. What brings you to my lair?"

Charles was unready to talk. He turned his attention to a painted seascape on the wall. "That the Galilee?"

"Oh, no." Zalman laughed and, sitting back, crossed his legs. For the first time Charles noticed that he was sporting heavy wool socks and suede sandals. "That's Bolinas. My old stomping grounds."

"Bolinas?" Charles said. "California?"

"I see what's happening here. Very obvious." Zalman uncrossed his legs, reached out, and put a hand on Charles's knee. "Don't be shy," he said. "You've made it this far. Searched me out in a bright corner of a Brooklyn attic. If such a meeting has been ordained, which by its very nature it has been, then let's make the most of it."

"I'm Jewish," Charles said. He said it with all the force, the excitement, and the relief of any of life's great admissions. Zalman was silent. He was smiling, listening intently, and, apparently, waiting.

"Yes," he said, maintaining the smile. "And?"

"Since yesterday," Charles said. "In a cab."

"Oh," Zalman said. "Oh! Now I get it."

"It just came over me."

"Wild," Zalman said. He clapped his hands together, looked up at the ceiling, and laughed. "Miraculous."

"Unbelievable," Charles added.

"No!" Zalman said, his smile gone, a single finger held up in Charles's face. "No, it's not unbelievable. That it is not. I believe you. Knew before you said — exactly why I didn't respond. A Jew sits in front of me and tells me he's Jewish. This is no surprise. To see a man so Jewish, a person who could be my brother, who *is* my brother, tell me he has only now discovered he's Jewish — that, my friend, that is truly miraculous." During his speech he had slowly moved his finger back; now he thrust it into Charles's face anew. "But not unbelievable. I see cases of this all the time."

"Then it's possible? That it's true?"

"Already so Jewish," Zalman said with a laugh, "asking questions you've already answered. You know the truth better than I do. You're the one who came to the discovery. How do you feel?"

"Fine," Charles said. "Different but fine."

"Well, don't you think you'd be upset if it was wrong what you knew? Don't you think you'd be less than fine if this were a nightmare? Somehow suffering if you'd gone crazy?"

"Who said anything about crazy?" Charles asked. Crazy he was not.

"Did I?" Zalman said. He grabbed at his chest. "An accident, purely. Slip of the tongue. So many who come have trouble with the news at home. Their families doubt."

Charles shifted. "I haven't told her."

Zalman raised an eyebrow, turning his head to favor the accusing eye.

"A wife who doesn't know?"

"That's why I'm here. For guidance." Charles put his feet up on the couch and lay down, as at Dr. Birnbaum's. "I need to tell her, to figure out how. I need also to know what to do. I ate milk and meat last night."

"First, history," Zalman said. He slipped off a sandal. "Your mother's not Jewish?"

"No, no one. Ever. Not that I know."

"This is also possible," Zalman said. "It may be only that your soul was at Sinai. Maybe an Egyptian slave that came along. But once the soul witnessed the miracles at Sinai, accepted there the word, well, it became a Jewish soul. Do you believe in the soul, Mr. Luger?"

"I'm beginning to."

"All I'm saying is, the soul doesn't live or die. It's not an organic thing, like the body. It is there. And it has a history."

"And mine belonged to a Jew?"

"No, no. That's exactly the point. Jew, non-Jew, doesn't matter. The body doesn't matter. It is the soul itself that is Jewish."

They talked for more than an hour. Zalman gave him books: *The Chosen, A Hedge of Roses,* and *The Code of Jewish Law.* Charles agreed to cancel his shrink appointment for the next day; Zalman would come to his office to study with him. A payment would be required, of course: a minor fee, expenses, some for charity and to ensure good luck. The money was not the important thing, Zalman assured him. The crucial thing was having a guide to help him through his transformation. And who better than Zalman, a man who had come to Judaism the same way? Miserable in Bolinas, addicted to sorrow and drugs, he was on the brink when he discovered his Jewish soul.

"And you never needed a formal conversion?" Charles asked, astounded.

"No," Zalman said. "Such things are for others, for the litigious and stiff-minded. Such rituals are not needed for those who are called by their souls."

"Tell me, then," Charles said. He spoke out of the side of his mouth, feeling confident and chummy. "Where'd you get the shtick from? You look Jewish, you talk Jewish — the authentic article. I turn Jewish and get nothing. You come from Bolinas and sound like you've never been out of Brooklyn."

"And if I had discovered I was Italian, I'd play bocce like a pro. Such is my nature, Mr. Luger. I am most open to letting take form that which is truly inside."

This was, of course, a matter of personal experience. Zalman's own. Charles's would inevitably be different. Unique. If the change was slower, then let it be so. After all, Zalman counseled, the laws were not to be devoured like bonbons but to be embraced as he was ready. Hadn't it taken him fifty-five years to learn he was Jewish? Yes, everything in good time.

"Except," Zalman said, standing up, "you must tell your wife first thing. Kosher can wait. Tefillin can wait. But there is one thing the tender soul can't bear — the sacrifice of Jewish pride."

Sue had a root canal after work. She came home late, carrying a pint of ice cream. Charles had already set the table and served dinner, on the off chance she might be able to eat.

"How was it?" he asked. He lit a candle and poured the wine. He did not tease her, did not say a word about her slurred speech or sagging face. He pretended it was a permanent injury, nerve damage, acted as if this were a business dinner and Sue a client with a crippled lip.

She approached the table and lifted the bottle. "Well, you're not leaving me, I can tell that much. You'd never have opened your precious Haut-Brion to tell me you were running off to Greece with your secretary."

"True," he said. "I'd have saved it to drink on our verandah in Mykonos."

"Glad to see," she said, standing on her toes and planting a wet and pitifully slack kiss on his cheek, "that the fantasy has already gotten that far."

"The wine's actually a feeble attempt at topic broaching."

Sue pried the top off her ice cream and placed the carton in the center of her plate. They both sat down.

"Do tell," she said.

"I'm Jewish." That easy. It was not, after all, the first time.

"Is there a punch line?" she asked. "Or am I supposed to supply one?"

He said nothing.

"Okay. Let's try it again. I'll play along. Go — give me your line."

"In the cab yesterday. I just knew. I understood, felt it for real. And —" He looked at her face, contorted, dead with anesthesia. A surreal expression in return for surreal news. "And it hasn't caused me any grief. Except for my fear of telling you. Otherwise, I actually feel sort of good about it. Different. But as if things, big things, were finally right."

"Let's get something out of the way first." She made a face, a horrible face. Charles thought maybe she was trying to bite her lip — or scowl. "Okay?"

"Shoot."

"What you're really trying to tell me is, honey, I'm having a nervous breakdown, and this is the best way to tell you. Correct?" She plunged a spoon into the ice cream and came up with a heaping spoonful. "If it's not a nervous breakdown, I want to know if you feel like you're clinically insane."

"I didn't expect this to go smoothly," Charles said.

"You pretend that you knew I'd react badly." Sue spoke quickly and (Charles tried not to notice) drooled. "Really, though, with your tireless optimism, you thought I would smile and tell you to be Jewish. That's what you thought, Charles." She jammed her spoon back into the carton and left it buried. "Let me tell you, this time you were way off. Wrong in your heart and right in your head. It couldn't have gone smoothly. Do you know why? Do you know?"

"Why?" he asked.

"Because what you're telling me, out of the blue, out of nowhere — because what you're telling me is, inherently, crazy."

Charles nodded his head repeatedly, as if a bitter truth was confirmed. "He said you would say that."

"Who said, Charles?"

"The rabbi."

"You've started with rabbis?" She pressed at her sleeping lip.

"Of course rabbis. Who else gives advice to a Jew?"

Charles read the books at work the next day and filled his legal pad with notes. When his secretary buzzed with Dr. Birnbaum on the line, inquiring about the sudden cancellation, Charles, for the first time since he'd begun his treatment, $15,000 before, did not take the doctor's call. He didn't take any calls; he was absorbed in reading *A Hedge of Roses*, the definitive guide to a healthy marriage through ritual purity, and waiting for Rabbi Zalman.

When Charles heard Zalman outside his office, he buzzed his secretary. This was a first as well. Charles never buzzed her until she had buzzed him first. A protocol governed entry to his office. Visitors should hear buzz and counterbuzz. It set a tone.

"So," Zalman said, seating himself. "Did you tell her?"

Charles placed his fountain pen back in its holder. He straightened the base with two hands. "She sort of half believes me. Enough to worry. Not enough to tear my head off. But she knows I'm not kidding. And she does think I'm crazy."

"And how do you feel?"

"Content." Charles leaned back in his swivel chair, his arms dangling over the sides. "Jewish and content. Excited. Still excited. The whole thing's ludicrous. I was one thing and now I'm another. Neither holds any real meaning. But when I discovered I was Jewish, I think I also discovered God."

"Like Abraham," Zalman said, with a worshipful look at the ceiling. "Now it's time to smash some idols." He pulled out a serious-looking book, leather-bound and gold-embossed. A book full of secrets, Charles was sure. They studied until Charles told Zalman he had to get back to work. "No fifty-minute hour here," Zalman said, blushing and taking a swipe at the psychologist. They agreed to meet daily and shook hands twice before Zalman left.

He wasn't gone long enough to have reached the elevators before Walter, the CEO, barged into Charles's office, stopping immediately inside the door.

"Who's the fiddler on the roof?" Walter said.

"Broker."

"Of what?" Walter tapped his wedding band against the nameplate on the door.

"Commodities," Charles said. "Metals."

"Metals." Another tap of the ring. A knowing wink. "Promise me something, Charley. This guy tries to sell you the steel out of the Brooklyn Bridge, at least bargain with the man."

They had a few nights of relative quiet and a string of dinners with nonconfrontational foods, among them a risotto and then a blackened trout, a spaghetti squash with an eye-watering vegetable marinara, and — in response to a craving of Sue's — a red snapper with tomato and those little bits of caramelized garlic that the maid did so well.

Sue had for all intents and purposes ignored Charles's admission and, mostly, ignored Charles. Charles spent his time in the study, reading the books Zalman had given him. This was how the couple functioned until the day the maid left a pot of boeuf bourguignon.

"The meat isn't kosher, and neither is the wine," Charles said, referring to the wine both in and out of his dinner. "And this bourguignon has a pound of bacon fat in it. I'm not complaining, only letting you know. Really. Bread will do me fine." He reached over and took a few slices from the basket.

Sue glared at him. "You're not complaining?"

"No," he said, and reached for the butter.

"Well, I'm complaining! I'm complaining right now!" She slammed a fist down so hard that her glass tipped over, spilling wine onto the tablecloth she loved. They both watched the tablecloth soak up the wine; the lace and the stitching fattened and swelled, the color spreading along the workmanship as if through a series of veins. Neither moved.

"Sue, your tablecloth."

"Fuck my tablecloth," she said.

"Oh, my." He took a sip of water.

"'Oh, my' is right. You bet, mister." She made a noise that Charles considered to be a growl. His wife of twenty-seven years had growled at him.

"If you think I'll ever forgive you for starting this when I was crippled with Novocain. Attacking me when I could hardly talk. If you think," she said, "if you think I'm going to start paying twelve-fifty for a roast chicken, you are terribly, terribly wrong."

"What is this about chickens?" Charles did not raise his voice.

"The religious lady at work. She puts in orders on Wednesday. Every week she orders the same goddamn meal. A twelve-dollar-

and-fifty-cent roast chicken." Sue shook her head. "You should have married an airline chef if you wanted kosher meals."

"Different fight, Sue. We're due for a fight, but I think you're veering toward the wrong one."

"Why don't you tell me, then?" she said. "Since all has been revealed to you, why don't you enlighten me as to the nature of the conflict?"

"Honestly, I think you're threatened. So I want you to know I still love you. You're still my wife. This should make you happy for me. I've found God."

"Exactly the problem. You didn't find our God. I'd have been good about it if you'd found *our* God — or even a less demanding one." She scanned the table again, as if to find one of his transgressions left out absentmindedly, like house keys. "Today the cheese is gone. You threw out all the cheese, Charles. How could God hate cheese?"

"A woman who thinks peaches are too suggestive for the fruit bowl could give in on a quirk or two."

"You think I don't notice what's going on — that I don't notice you making ablutions in the morning?" She dipped her napkin into her water glass. "I've been waiting for your midlife crisis. But I expected something I could handle — a small test. An imposition. Something to rise above, to prove my love for you in a grand display of resilience. Why couldn't you have turned into a vegan? Or a liberal Democrat? Slept with your secretary for real?" She dabbed at the wine stain. "Any of those, and I would've made do."

Charles scrutinized her. "So essentially you're saying it would be okay if I changed into a West Side Jew. Like if we suddenly lived in the Apthorp."

Sue thought about it. "Well, if you have to be Jewish, why *so* Jewish? Why not like the Browns, in 6K? Their kid goes to Haverford. Why," she said, closing her eyes and pressing two fingers to her temple, "why do people who find religion always have to be so goddamn extreme?"

"Extreme," Charles felt, was too extreme a word considering all he had to learn and all the laws he had yet to implement. He hadn't been to synagogue. He hadn't yet observed the Sabbath. He had only changed his diet and said a few prayers.

For this he'd been driven from his own bedroom.

Occasionally Sue sought him out, always with impeccable timing. She came into the den the first morning he donned prayer shawl and phylacteries, which even to Charles looked especially strange. The leather box and the strap twirled tightly around his arm, another box planted squarely in the center of his head. He was in the midst of the Eighteen Benedictions when Sue entered, and was forced to listen to her tirade in silence.

"My Charley, always topping them all," she said, watching as he rocked back and forth, his lips moving. "I've heard of wolf men and people being possessed. I've even seen modern vampires on TV. Real people who drink blood. But this beats all." She left him and then returned with a mug of coffee in hand.

"I spoke to Dr. Birnbaum. I was going to call him myself, to see how he was dealing with your change." She blew on her coffee. "Guess what, Charley. He calls me first. Apologizes for crossing boundaries, and tells me you've stopped coming, that you won't take his calls. Oh, I say, that's because Charley's Jewish and is very busy meeting with the rabbi. He's good, your shrink. Remains calm. And then, completely deadpan, he asks me — as if it makes any difference — what kind of rabbi. I told him what you told me, word for word. The kind from Bolinas. The kind who doesn't need to be ordained, because he's been a rabbi in his past nine lives. And what, I asked him, does one man, one man himself ten generations a rabbi, what does he need with anyone's diploma?" She put the mug down on a lampstand.

"Dr. Birnbaum's coming to dinner next week. On Monday. I even ordered kosher food, paper plates, the whole deal. You'll be able to eat in your own house like a human being. An evening free of antagonism, when we can discuss this like adults. His idea. He said to order kosher food once before leaving you. So I placed an order." She smoothed down her eyebrows, waiting for a response. "You can stop your praying, Charles." She turned to leave. "Your chickens are on the way."

Charles had no suits left. *Shatnez*, the mixing of linen and wool, is strictly forbidden. On Zalman's recommendation, he sent his wardrobe to Royal Hills for testing and was forced to go to work the next day wearing slacks and suspenders, white shirt and tie. Walter hadn't left him alone since he'd arrived. "It ain't Friday, Charley," he said. "Casual day is only once a week." This he followed with "Why go to so much trouble, Charley? A nicely pressed bathrobe would be fine."

Charles had worked himself into a funk by the time Zalman entered his office. He'd accomplished nothing all morning.

"I am weakening," Charles said. "The revelation lasts about a second, comes and goes, a hot flash in the back of a taxi. But the headache it leaves you with, a whopper of a headache — that persists."

Zalman scratched at his nostril with a pinkie, a sort of refined form of picking. "Were you in a fraternity in college?"

"Of course," Charles said.

"Then consider this pledging. You've been tapped, given a bid, and now is the hard part before all the good stuff. Now's when you buy the letters on the sly and try them on at home in front of the mirror."

"Wonderful, Zalman. Well put. But not so simple. I've got to tell my boss something soon. And tensions have risen at home. We're having dinner on Monday, my wife and my shrink versus me. She's even ordered kosher food, trying to be friendly about it."

"Kosher food." A knee slap, a big laugh. "The first step. Doesn't sound anything but positive to me. By any chance has she gone to the ritual bath yet?"

Charles spun his chair around, looked out the window, and then slowly spun back.

"Zalman," he said, "that's a tough one. And it sort of makes me think you're not following. Sue refuses to go for a couple of reasons. One, because she hates me and our marriage is falling apart. And two, she maintains — and it's a valid point, a fairly good argument — that she's not Jewish."

"I see."

"I want you to come on Monday, Zalman. A voice of reason will come in handy after the weekend. I'm going to keep my first Shabbos. And if Sue remains true to form, I'm in for a doozy."

"Find out where the food is from. If it's really kosher catered, I'll be there."

The clocks had not changed for the season, and Shabbos still came early. Charles put on the one suit jacket that had been deemed kosher and his coat and went home without explanation. He didn't touch the candlesticks on the mantelpiece, didn't risk raising Sue's ire. Instead he dug a pair, dented and tarnished, from a low cabinet in the overstuffed and unused butler's pantry. The maid passed, saying nothing. She took her pocketbook and the day's garbage into the service hall.

In the absence of wife or daughter, the honor of ushering in the Sabbath goes to the lone man. Charles cleared a space on the windowsill in the study and, covering his eyes before the lighted candles, made the blessing. He paused at the place where the woman is permitted to petition the Lord with wishes and private blessings and stood, palms cool against his eyes, picturing Sue.

The candles flickered next to the window, burning lopsided and fast.

Charles extended the footrest on his recliner. He closed his eyes and thought back to his first night away from home, sleeping on a mattress next to his cousin's bed. He was four or five, and his cousin, older, slept with the bedroom door shut tight, not even a crack of light from the hallway. That was the closest to this experience he could think of — the closest he could remember to losing and gaining a world.

The candles were out when Charles heard Sue pass on her way to the bedroom. He tried to come up with a topic of conversation, friendly and day-to-day. He came up with nothing, couldn't remember what they'd talked about over their life together. What had they said to each other when nothing was pressing? What had they chatted about for twenty-seven years?

He got up and went to her.

Sue was sitting at the far window on a petite antique chair that was intended only to be admired. She held a cigarette and flicked ash into a small porcelain dish resting on her knee. In half silhouette against the electric dusk of the city, Sue appeared as relaxed as Charles had seen her since long before his revelation. He could tell, or thought he could, that she was concentrating on ignoring his presence. She would not have her moment of peace compromised.

This was his wife. A woman who, if she preferred, could pretend he was not there. A woman always able to live two realities at once. She could spend a day at work slamming down phones and storming down hallways with layouts she'd torn in half, and then come home to entertain, serve dinner, pass teacups, in a way that hushed a room.

How was he to explain his own lack of versatility? Here was a woman who lived in two realities simultaneously. How was he to make clear his struggle living in one? And how to tell the woman of two lives that he had invited over Zalman, who carried in his soul a full ten?

On Sunday, Charles was reading a copy of Leon Uris's *QB VII* when Sue ran — truly ran — into the study and grabbed him by the arm. He was shocked and made the awkward movements of someone who is both dumbfounded and manhandled at the same time, like a tourist mistakenly seized by the police.

"Sue, what are you doing?"

"I could kill you," she said. Though smaller, she had already pulled him to his feet. He followed her to the foyer.

"What is this?" she yelled, slamming open the door.

"A mezuzah," he said. "If you mean that." He pointed at the small metal casing nailed to the doorpost. "I need it," he said. "I have to kiss it."

"Oh, my God," she said, slamming the door closed, giving the neighbors no more than a taste. "My God!" She steadied herself, putting a hand against the wall. "Well, where did it come from? It's got blue paint on it. Where does one buy a used mezuzah?"

"I don't know where to get one. I pried it off 11D with a letter opener. They don't even use it. Steve Fraiman had me in to see their Christmas tree last year. Their daughter is dating a black man."

"Are you insane? Five years on the waiting list to get into this building, and now you're vandalizing the halls. You think anyone but me will believe your cockamamie story? Oh, I'm not a Nazi, Mrs. Fraiman, just a middle-aged man who woke up a Jew."

"It happened in a cab. I didn't wake up anything."

Sue put her other hand against the wall and let her head hang.

"I've invited the rabbi," Charles said.

"You think that's going to upset me? You think I didn't know you'd drag him into this? Good, bring him. Maybe they have a double open at Bellevue."

"This is very intolerant, Sue." He reached out to touch her.

"Go back to the study," she said. "Go paw one of your books."

They considered the table. Charles and Sue stood at opposite ends, appraising the job the maid had done. It was admirable.

On a paper tablecloth were paper cups and plastic wine glasses with snap-on bases, patterned paper napkins that matched the pattern on the plates, plastic forks and plastic spoons, and a few other things — cheap but not disposable. Knives, for instance. The knives were real, new, wooden-handled steak knives. Sue had even gone to the trouble of finding a decent bottle of kosher wine. One bottle. The other was a blackberry. Charles wondered if the blackberry was a warning of what continued religiosity might do to the refined palate. Screw-top wine. Sugary plonk. He was going to comment, but looking again at the lavish spread, both leaves inserted into the table, the polished silver on the credenza, he reconsidered. This was more than a truce. It was an attempt to be open — or at least a request that the maid make an effort.

"Mortifying," Sue said. "Like a child's birthday party. We've got everything except for a paper donkey tacked to the wall."

"I appreciate it, Sue. I really, really do." He had sweetness in his voice, real love for the first time since he'd made his announcement.

"Eighty-eight dollars' worth of the blandest food you've ever had. The soup is inedible, pure salt. I had a spoonful and needed to take an extra high-blood-pressure pill. I'll probably die before dinner's over, and then we'll have no problems."

"More and more," Charles said, taking a yarmulke from his pocket and fastening it to his head, "more and more, you're the one who sounds like a Jew."

When Charles answered the knock on the study door, he was surprised to find Zalman standing there, surprised that Sue hadn't come to get him.

"She is very nice, your wife," Zalman said. "A sensible woman, it appears."

"Appearances are important," Charles said.

Zalman brightened, and exuded joy as he did. "It will be fine," he said. He hooked Charles's arm into his own and led him down the hall.

Sue and Dr. Birnbaum — sporting a yellow sweater — were already seated. Charles sat at the head of the table, and Zalman stood behind his chair.

The most painful silence Charles had ever experienced ensued. He was aware of his breathing, his pulse and temperature. He could feel the contents of his intestines, the blood in his head, the air settling on his eardrums, lake-smooth without sound.

Zalman spoke. "Is there a place where I can wash?" he asked.

Before eating bread, Charles knew. "Yes," Charles said. "I'll come too."

He looked at Sue as he got up. Charles knew what she was thinking. Say it, he wanted to tell her. Point it out to Dr. Birnbaum. You're right. It's true.

Ablutions.

Ablutions all the time.

Rabbi Zalman made a blessing over the bread, and Dr. Birnbaum muttered, "Amen." Sue just stared. A man with a beard, a long black beard and sidelocks, was sitting in her house. Charles wanted to tell her she was staring, but he stopped himself with "Sue."

"What!" she said. "What, Charles?"

"Shall we eat?"

"Yes," Zalman said, his smile broad, his teeth bright white and Californian. "Let's eat first. We can discuss better on full stomachs." Reaching first one way and then the other, Zalman picked up a bottle and poured himself a brimming glass of blackberry wine.

They ate in a lesser but still oppressive silence. All showed it in their countenances except for Zalman, who was deeply involved in the process of eating and paused only once, to say, "Jewish name — Birnbaum," before going back to his food. The other three took turns looking from one to the other and back to their plates. They stared at Zalman when they could think of nowhere to put their eyes.

"The barley is delicious." Dr. Birnbaum smiled as if Sue had cooked the food.

"Thank you," she said, snatching the empty container from next to Zalman and heading to the kitchen for another. Dr. Birnbaum took that opportunity to broach the topic with Charles.

"I don't think it's unfair to say I was startled by your news."

"Just your everyday revelation, nothing special."

"Even so, I would have hoped you'd feel comfortable discussing it with me. After all this time."

Sue returned with a quart container of barley, the plastic top in her hand. Charles cleared his throat, and no one said a word. Sue cocked her head. A slight tilt, an inquisitive look. Had such silence ever occurred at one of her dinner parties? Had her presence ever brought conversation to an abrupt end?

She slammed the container onto the table, startling Zalman. He looked up at her and removed a bit of barley from his beard.

"I was about to explain my presence," Dr. Birnbaum said. "Let Charles know that I have no secret agenda. This isn't a competency hearing. And I'm not packing a syringe full of Thorazine."

"That was before," Sue said. "Last week, before your patient started pilfering Judaica. Before he started mortifying me in this building. Do you know that on Friday night he rode the elevator up and down like an idiot, waiting for someone to press our floor? Like a retarded child. He gets in the elevator and keeps explaining it to everyone. 'Can't press the button on my Sabbath, ha ha.' He can't ask people outright, because you're only allowed to *hint*."

"Very good," Zalman said. "A fine student."

"You," she said to Zalman. "Interloper!" And then, turning back to Dr. Birnbaum, "I heard it from old Mrs. Dallal. She's the one who pressed the button. Our poor old next-door neighbor, forced to ride the elevator with this maniac. She told me she was talking to Petey, the doorman, and couldn't figure out why the elevator door kept opening and Charley wouldn't come out. She told me that she actually asked him, 'Do you want to come out?' Now, is that insane, Doctor, or is it not? Do sane people need to be invited out of elevators, or do they just get out on their own?"

Charles spoke first. "She turned the light off in the bathroom on Friday night. She knows I can't touch the lights. I had to go in the dark. She's being malicious."

"We are at the table, Charles. Paper plates or not. A man who holds his fork like an animal or not, we shall have some manners."

Zalman laughed out loud at Sue's insult.

"Those are manners — embarrassing a guest?" Now Charles yelled. "And a rabbi, yet."

"He, Charley, is not even Jewish. And neither are you. One need not be polite to the insane. As long as you don't hose them down, all is in good taste."

"She's malicious, Doctor. She brought you here to watch her insult me."

"If I'm supposed to put my two cents in," Dr. Birnbaum said, "I suppose now is the time."

"Two cents?" Zalman said. "What does that come out to for you — a consonant?"

"Thank you," the doctor said. "A perfect example of the inane kind of aggression that can turn a conversation into a brawl."

"It's because you're not wearing a tie," Charles said. "How can you control people without a tie?"

"I'm not trying to control anyone."

"It's true," Zalman said. "I went to a shrink for twelve years. Started in seventh grade. They don't control. They absolve. Like atheist priests. No responsibility for your actions, no one to answer to. Anarchists with advanced degrees." Zalman spoke right to the doctor. "You can't give people permission to ignore God. It is not your right."

"Sir," Dr. Birnbaum said. "Rabbi. I invite you, as Charles's spiritual adviser, to join me in trying to help the situation."

"Exactly why I'm here," Zalman said. He pushed his chair back and rested his elbows on the table. "One way to help would be to give Charles your blessing, or whatever you call it. Shrinks always say it's okay, so tell him it's okay, tell her it's okay, and then all will be better."

"I can't do that — don't, in fact, do that," the doctor said. He addressed his patient. "Should we go into another room and talk?"

"If I wanted that, I'd have come to our sessions. All the therapy in the world could not bring the simple comfort that I've found in worshipping God."

"Listen to this," Sue said. "Do you hear the kind of thing I have to endure? Palaver!" The doctor looked at Sue, raised his hand, and patted the air.

"I'm listening," he said. "I actually *do* want to hear it. But from him. That Charles has gone from Christian nonbeliever to Orthodox Jew is clear. It is also perplexing." He spoke in sensible rhythms. The others listened, all primed to interrupt. "I came to dinner to hear from Charles why he changed."

"Because of his soul," Zalman said, throwing his arms up in frustration. "He's always had this soul. His way of thinking has always been agreeable, but now God has let him know He wasn't pleased with the way Charley was acting."

"It's true," Charles said. "That's how it feels — like it was always in me, but now it's time for me to do God-pleasing work."

Sue didn't speak but clenched her whole body, fists and shoulders and teeth.

"And God-pleasing work is living the life of the Orthodox Jew?" The doctor was all softness. "Are you sure it might not be something else — like gardening or meditation? Have you considered philanthropy, Charley — I mean, as a for-instance?"

"Do you not see what he is doing?" Zalman said. "The sharp tongue of the philosopher." Zalman jumped to his feet, still leaning heavily on the table, which shook under his weight, though silently, devoid of the usual collection of silver and crystal and robbing him of some drama. "Tell him what the king of the Khazars told his own sharp-tongued philosopher five hundred years ago." He pointed an accusing finger. "Thy words are convincing, yet they do not correspond to what I wish to find."

"Just shut up. Would you, please?" Sue said.

"It's all right, Zalman," Charles said. Zalman sat. "That's not how I would have put it," Charles said, "but it's how I feel. You see, Doctor — with your eyes, I mean. You see how I look, how I'm acting. No different from before. Different rituals, maybe. Different foods. But the same man. Only I feel peaceful, fulfilled."

As Charles spoke, Sue slipped from her chair and slid to the floor, as might a drunk. She did not fall over but rested on her knees, interlocking her fingers and bowing her head. She rested in the traditional Christian pose of prayer. His wife, who was mortified by a white purse after Labor Day, was on her knees in front of company.

"Sue, what are you doing? Get up off the floor."

She raised her chin but kept her eyes shut.

"What?" she said. "Do you have a monopoly on God? Are you the only one who can pray?"

"Point taken. Your point is taken."

"I'm making no point," she said. "I understand now. You were as desperate as I've become. God is for the desperate. For when there is nothing left to do."

"There is always something," Zalman said. No one acknowledged him.

"There are options, Sue." Charles was perspiring through his shirt.

Sue opened her eyes and sat leaning on an arm, her legs at her side.

"No," she said. She did not cry, but all could tell that if she hit the wrong note, the wrong word, if she was in any way agitated further, she would lose her composure completely. "You don't seem to understand, Charles. Because you don't want to. But I do not have any idea what to do."

If there was one sacrifice Charles had thought she would not be able to make, it was this — to be open in front of outsiders, to look tired and overworked in front of a table set with paper plates.

"Is that what you want to hear, Charles? I'm not resigned to a goddamn thing. I'm not going to kill you or have you committed or dragged up to the summer house for deprogramming." Charles was at once relieved and frightened — for she had clearly considered her options. "But I will, Charley, be thinking and waiting. You can't stop me from that. I'm going to hope and pray. I'll even pray to your God — beg Him to make you forget Him. To cast you out."

"That's wrong, Sue." It sounded wrong.

"No, Charles. It's fair. More fair than you've been to me. You have an epiphany and want everyone else to have the same one. Well, if we did, even if it was the best, greatest, holiest thing in the world, if every person had the same one, the most you would be left with is a bright idea."

"I don't know if that's theologically sound," Zalman said, twisting the pointed ends of his beard.

"It's wonderful," the doctor said. His face was full of pride.

Charles got down on the floor and sat cross-legged in front of Sue. "What does that mean, Sue? What does it mean for me?"

"It means that your moment of grace has passed. Real or not. It's gone now. You are left with life — daily life. I'm only letting you know that as much as you worry about staying in God's favor, you should worry about staying in mine. It's like taking a new lover, Charles. You're as dizzy as a schoolgirl. But remember which one of us dropped into your life and which of us has been in for the long haul. I *am* going to try and stick it out. But let me warn you: as quickly as God came into your life, I might one day be gone."

"I can't live that way," Charles said.

"That is what I go to sleep hoping."

From the corner of his eye Charles caught Dr. Birnbaum trying to slip out of the room without interrupting the conversation's flow. He watched the doctor recede, backing away with quiet steps, and then turned to Sue. He turned to her and let all the resentment he felt come into his face. He let the muscles go, felt his eyelids drop and harden, spoke to her as intimately as if Zalman were not there.

"The biggest thing that ever happened to me, and you make me feel that I should have kept it to myself."

She considered. "True. It would have been better. I would much rather have found a box after you were gone — prayer books and skullcaps, used needles and women's underwear. At this point, at my age, I'd have had an easier time finding it all after you were gone."

Charles looked to Zalman, who was, like the doctor, slowly making an exit. "You're leaving me too?"

"Not as elegant as the doctor, but not so stupid as to miss when it's time to go."

"One minute," Charles said to his wife. "One minute and I'll be back," he pleaded, untucking his legs. "I'll walk him to the door. Our guest."

Charles followed the rabbi down the front hallway. Zalman put on his coat and tilted his hat forward, an extra edge against the city below.

"This is a crucial time," Charles said.

They were by the umbrella stand. Zalman pulled out a cane. He scratched at his nose with a pinkie. "It's an age-old problem. To all the great ones tests are given. I wouldn't be surprised if the king of the Khazars faced the same one."

"What happened to the king?" Charles asked. "How does it turn out for the great ones?"

Zalman leaned the cane against the wall. "It doesn't matter. The point is they all had God. They knew in their hearts God."

Charles put a hand on Zalman's shoulder. "I'm only asking for you to tell me."

"You already know," Zalman said. The joy drained from his face. "You know but want me to lie."

"Is that so bad?"

The rabbi's face looked long and soft; the rapture did not return. "No hope, Mr. Luger. I tell you this from one Jew to another. There is no hope for the pious."

Charles made his way back to the table only to find Sue gone, the table clean, and the chairs in place. Could more than a minute have passed? He saw the pantry garbage can in the middle of the kitchen, the paper tablecloth sticking out the top. A disposable dinner, the dining room as if untouched.

He started toward the bedroom and stopped at the study door. Sue was standing at the window beside the tarnished candlesticks, which were fused in place where wax had run off the bases. She picked at the hardened formations, forcing her nail underneath and lifting them away from the painted wood of the sill.

"It's not sacrilegious, I hope?" She picked at the wax that ran over the silver necks in braids.

"No," Charles said. "I don't believe it is."

He crossed the room to stand beside Sue. He reached for the hand that scratched at the fine layers of wax on the sill. "So it'll stay there," he said. "So what?"

"It will ruin the paint," she said.

"It will make the window frame look real. Like someone lives in the apartment and uses this room."

Charles looked around the study, at the lamp and the bookcase, and then out the window at the buildings and the sky. He had not read far into the Bible, and still thought that God might orchestrate his rescue.

He took hold of Sue's other hand and held them both in place. He wanted her to understand that a change of magnitude had indeed occurred, but the mark it left was not great. The real difference was contained in his soul, after all.

Sue's gaze fell past him before meeting his eyes.

He tried to appear open before her, to allow Sue to observe him with the profound clarity he had only so recently come to know. Charles was desperate with willingness. He struggled to stand without judgment, to be only for Sue, to be wholly seen, wanting her to love him changed.

PERCIVAL EVERETT

The Fix

FROM NEW YORK STORIES

DOUGLAS LANGLEY owned a little sandwich shop at the intersection of Fourteenth and T streets in the District. Beside his shop was a seldom used alley and above his shop lived a man by the name of Sherman Olney whom Douglas had seen beaten to near extinction one night by a couple of silky-looking men who seemed to know Sherman and wanted something in particular from him. Douglas had been drawn outside from cleaning up the storeroom by a rhythmic thumping sound, like someone dropping a telephone book onto a table over and over. He stepped out into the November chill and discovered that the sound was actually that of the larger man's fists finding again and again the belly of Sherman Olney, who was being kept on his feet by the second assailant. Douglas ran back inside and grabbed the pistol he kept in the rolltop desk in his business office. He returned to the scene with the powerful flashlight his son had given him and shone the light into the faces of the two villains.

The men were not overly impressed by the light, the bigger one saying, "Hey, man, you better get that light out my face!"

They did however show proper respect for the discharging of the .32 by running away. Sherman Olney crumpled to the ground, moaning and clutching at his middle, saying he didn't have it anymore.

"Are you all right?" Douglas asked, realizing how stupid the question was before it was fully out.

But Sherman's response was equally insipid as he said, "Yes."

"Come, let's get you inside." Douglas helped the man to his feet and into the shop. He locked the glass door behind them, then took Sherman over to the counter and helped him onto a stool.

"Thanks," Sherman said.

"You want me to call the cops?" Douglas asked.

Sherman Olney shook his head. "They're long gone by now."

"I'll make you a sandwich," Douglas said, as he stepped behind the counter.

"Really, that's not necessary."

"You'll like it. I don't know first aid, but I can make a sandwich." Douglas made the man a pastrami and Muenster on rye and poured him a glass of barely cold milk, then took him to sit in one of the three booths in the shop. Douglas sat across the table from the man, watched him take a bite of sandwich.

"What did they want?" Douglas put to him.

"To hurt me," Sherman said, his mouth working on the tough bread. He picked a seed from his teeth and put it on his plate. "They wanted to hurt me."

"My name is Douglas Langley."

"Sherman Olney."

"What were they after, Sherman?" Douglas asked, but he didn't get an answer.

As they sat there, the quiet of the room was disturbed by the loud refrigerator motor kicking on. Douglas felt the vibration of it through the soles of his shoes.

"Your compressor is a little shot," Sherman said.

Douglas looked at him, not knowing what he was talking about.

"Your fridge. The compressor is bad."

"Oh, yes," Douglas said. "It's loud."

"I can fix it."

Douglas just looked at him.

"You want me to fix it?"

Douglas didn't know what to say. Certainly he wanted the machine fixed, but what if this man just liked to take things apart? What if he made it worse? Douglas imagined the kitchen floor strewn with refrigerator parts. But he said, "Sure."

With that, Sherman got up and walked back into the kitchen, Douglas on his heels. The skinny man removed the plate from the bottom of the big and embarrassingly old machine and looked around. "Do you have any chewing gum?" Sherman asked.

As it turned out, Douglas had, in his pocket, the last stick of a pack of Juicy Fruit, which he promptly handed over. Sherman unwrapped the stick, folded it in his mouth, then lay there on the floor chewing.

"What are you doing?" Douglas asked.

Sherman paused him with a finger, then as if feeling the texture of the gum with his tongue, he took it from his mouth and stuck it into the workings of the refrigerator. And just like that the machine ran with a quiet steady hum, just like it had when it was new.

"How'd you do that?" Douglas asked.

Sherman, now on his feet, shrugged.

"Thank you, this is terrific. All you used was chewing gum. Can you fix other things?"

Sherman nodded.

"What are you? Are you a repairman or an electrician?" Douglas asked.

"I can fix things."

"Would you like another sandwich?"

Sherman shook his head, and said, "I should be going. Thanks for the food and all your help."

"These men might be waiting for you," Douglas said. He suddenly remembered his pistol. He could feel the weight of it in his pocket. "Just sit in here a while." Douglas felt a great deal of sympathy for the underfed man who had just repaired his refrigerator. "Where do you live? I could drive you."

"Actually, I don't have a place to live." Sherman stared down at the floor.

"Come over here." Douglas led the man to the big metal sink across the kitchen. He turned the ancient lever and the pipes started with a thin whistle and then screeched as the water came out. "Tell me, can you fix that?"

"Do you want me to?"

"Yes." Douglas turned off the water.

"Do you have a wrench?"

Douglas stepped away and into his business office, where he dug through a pile of sweaters and newspapers until he found a twelve-inch crescent wrench and a pipe wrench. He took them back to Sherman. "Will these do?"

"Yes." Sherman took a wrench and got down under the sink.

Douglas bent low to try and see what the man was doing, but before he could figure anything out, Sherman was getting up.

"There you go," Sherman said.

Incredulously, Douglas reached over to the faucet and turned
on the water. The water came out smoothly and quietly. He turned
it off, then tried it again. "You did it. You know, I could really
use somebody like you around here. I mean, do you want a job?
I can't pay much, just minimum wage, but I can let you stay in
the apartment upstairs. Actually, it's just a room. Are you interested?"

"You don't even know me," Sherman said.

Douglas stopped. Of course, the man was right. He didn't know
anything about him. But he had a strong feeling that Sherman
Olney was an honest man. An honest man who could fix things.
"You're right," Douglas admitted. "But I'm a good judge of character."

"I don't know," Sherman said.

"You said you don't have a place to go. You can live here and
work until you find another job." Douglas was unsure why he was
pleading so with the stranger, and, in fact, had a terribly uneasy
feeling about the whole business, but, for some reason, he really
wanted him to stay.

"Okay," Sherman said.

Douglas took the man up the back stairs and showed him the little
room. The single bulb hung from a cord in the middle of the ceiling, and its dim light revealed the single bed made up with a yellow
chenille spread. Douglas had taken many naps there.

"This is it," Douglas said. "The bathroom is down the hall.
There's a narrow shower stall in it."

"I'm sure I'll be comfortable. Thank you."

Douglas stood in awkward silence for a while wondering what
else there was to say. Then he said, "Well, I guess I should go on
home to my wife."

"And I should get some sleep."

Douglas nodded and left the shop.

Douglas's wife said, "Are you crazy?"

Douglas sat at the kitchen table and held his face in his hands.

He could smell the ham, salami, turkey, Muenster, Cheddar, and Swiss from his day's work. He peeked through his fingers and watched his short, plump wife reach over and turn down the volume of the television on the counter. The muted mouths of the news anchors still moved.

"I asked you a question," she said.

"It sounded more like an assertion." He looked at her eyes, which were narrowed and burning into him. "He's a fine fellow. Just a little down on his luck, Sheila."

Sheila laughed, then stopped cold. "And he's in the shop all alone." She shook her head, her lips tightening across her teeth. "You have lost your mind. Now, you go right back down there and you get rid of that guy."

"I don't feel like driving," Douglas said.

"I'll drive you."

He sighed. Sheila was obviously right. Even he hadn't understood his impulse to offer the man a job and invite him to use the room above the shop. So he would let her drive him back down there, and he'd tell Sherman Olney he'd have to go.

So they got into the old, forest green Buick Le Sabre, Sheila behind the wheel and Douglas sunk down into the passenger seat that Sheila's concentrated weight had through the years mashed so flat. He usually hated when she drove, but especially right at that moment, as she was angry and with a mission. She took their corner at Underwood on two wheels and sped through the city and moderately heavy traffic back toward the shop.

"You really should slow down," Douglas said. He watched a man in a blue suit toss his briefcase between two parked cars and dive after it out of the way.

"You're one to give advice. You? An old fool who takes in a stray human being and leaves him alone in his place of business is giving advice? He's probably cleaned us out already."

Douglas considered the situation and felt incredibly stupid. He could not, in fact, assure Sheila that she was wrong. Sherman might be halfway to Philadelphia with twelve pounds of Genoa salami. For all he knew Sherman Olney had turned on the gas of the oven and grilled and blown the restaurant to smithereens. He rolled down his window just a crack and listened for sirens.

"If anything bad has happened, I'm having you committed,"

Sheila said. She let out a brief scream and rattled the steering wheel. "Then I'll sell what little we have left and spend the rest of my life in Bermuda. That's what I'll do."

When Sheila made marks on the street braking to a stop, the store was still there and not ablaze. All the lights were off and the only people on the street were a couple of hookers on the far corner. Douglas unlocked and opened the front door of the shop, then followed Sheila inside. They walked past the tables and counter and into the kitchen where Douglas switched on the bright overhead lights. The fluorescent tubes flickered, then filled the place with a steady buzz.

"Go check the safe," Sheila said.

"There was no money in it," Douglas said. "There never is." She knew that. He had taken the money home and was going to drop it off by the bank on his way to work the next day. He always did that.

"Check it anyway."

He walked into his business office and switched on the standing lamp by the door. He looked across the room to see that the safe was still closed and that the stack of newspapers was still in front of it. "Hasn't been touched," he said.

"What's his name?" Sheila asked.

"Sherman."

"Sherman!" she called up the stairs. "Sherman!"

In short order, Sherman came walking down the stairs in his trousers and sleeveless undershirt. He was rubbing his eyes, trying to adjust to the bright light.

"Sherman," Douglas said, "it's me, Douglas."

"Douglas? What are you doing back?" He stood in front of them in his stocking feet. "By the way, I fixed the toilet and also that funny massager thing."

"You mean my foot massager?" Sheila asked.

"If you say so."

"I told you, Sherman can fix things," Douglas said to Sheila. "That's why I hired him." Sheila had purchased the foot massager from a fancy store in Georgetown. On the days when she worked in the shop she used to disappear every couple of hours for about fifteen minutes and then return happy and refreshed. She would be upstairs in the bathroom, sitting on the closed toilet with her feet stationed on her machine. Then the thing stopped working. Sheila loved the machine.

"The man at the store said my foot massager couldn't be repaired," Sheila said.

Sherman shrugged. "Well, it works now."

"I'll be right back," Sheila said, and she walked away from the men and up the stairs.

Sherman watched her, then turned to Douglas. "Why did you come back?"

"Well, you see, Sheila doesn't think it's a good idea that you stay here. You know, alone and everything. Since we don't know you or anything about you." Douglas blew out a long slow breath. "I'm really sorry."

Upstairs, Sheila screamed, then came running back to the top of the stairs. "It works! It works! He did fix it." She came down, smiling at Sherman. "Thank you so much."

"You're welcome," Sherman said.

"I was just telling Sherman that we're sorry, but he's going to have to leave."

"Don't be silly," Sheila said.

Douglas stared at her and rubbed a hand over his face. He gave Sheila a baffled look.

"No, no, it's certainly all right if Sherman sleeps here. And tomorrow, he can get to work." She grabbed Sherman's arm and turned him toward the stairs. "Now, you get on back up there and get some rest."

Sherman said nothing, but followed her directions. Douglas and Sheila watched him disappear upstairs.

Douglas looked at his wife. "What happened to you?"

"He fixed my foot rubber."

"So that makes him a good guy? Just like that?"

"I don't know," she said, uncertainly. She seemed to reconsider for a second. "I guess. Come on, let's go home."

Two weeks later, Sherman had said nothing more about himself, responding only to trivial questions put to him. He did, however, repair or make better every machine in the restaurant. He had fixed the toaster oven, the gas lines of the big griddle, the dishwasher, the phone, the neon OPEN sign, the electric-eye buzzer on the front door, the meat slicer, the coffee machine, the manual mustard dispenser, and the cash register. Douglas found the man's skills invaluable and wondered how he had ever managed without him. Still, his presence was disconcerting as he never spoke of his past nor family nor friends and he never went out, not even to the store, his food being already there, and so Douglas began to worry that he might be a fugitive from the law.

"He never leaves the shop," Sheila complained. She was sitting in the passenger seat while Douglas drove them to the movie theater.

"That's where he lives," Douglas said. "All the food he needs is right there. I'm hardly paying him anything."

"You pay him plenty. He doesn't have to pay rent and he doesn't have to buy food."

"I don't see what the trouble is," he said. "After all, he's fixed your massage thingamajig. And he fixed your curling iron and your VCR and your watch and he even got the squeak out of your shoes."

"I know. I know." Sheila sighed. "Still, just what do we know about this man?"

"He's honest, I know that. He never even glances at the till. I've never seen anyone who cares less about money." Douglas turned right onto Connecticut.

"That's exactly how a crook wants to come across."

"Well, Sherman's no crook. Why, I'd trust the man with my life. There are very few people I can say that about."

Sheila laughed softly and disbelievingly. "Well, don't you sound melodramatic."

Douglas really couldn't argue with her. Everything she had said was correct and he was at a loss to explain his tenacious defense of a man who was, after all, a relative stranger. He pulled the car into a parallel space and killed the engine.

"The car didn't do that thing," Sheila said. She was referring to the way the car usually refused to shut off, the stubborn engine firing a couple of extra times.

Douglas glanced over at her.

"Sherman," she said.

"This morning. He opened the hood, grabbed this and jiggled that, and then slammed it shut."

The fact of the matter was finally that Sherman hadn't stolen anything and hadn't come across in any way threatening and so Douglas kept his fears and suspicions in check and counted his savings. No more electricians. No more plumbers. No more repairmen of any kind. Sherman's handiness, however, did not remain a secret in spite of Douglas's best efforts.

It began when Sherman offered and then repaired a small radio-controlled automobile owned by a fat boy named Loomis Rump. Fat Loomis Rump and his skinny pals told their friends and they brought in their broken toys. Sherman fixed them. The fat boy's friends told their parents and Douglas found his shop increasingly crowded with customers and their small appliances.

"The Rump boy told me that you fixed his toy car and the Johnson woman told me that you repaired her radio," the short man who wore the waterworks uniform said.

Sherman was wiping down the counter.

"Is that true?"

Sherman nodded.

"Well, you see these cuts on my face?"

Douglas could see the cuts under the man's three-day growth of stubble from the door to the kitchen. Sherman leaned forward and studied the wound.

"They seem to be healing nicely," Sherman said.

"It's this damn razor," the man said, and he pulled the small unit from his trouser pocket. "It cuts me bad every time I try to shave."

"You'd like me to fix your razor?"

"If you wouldn't mind. But I don't have any money."

"That's okay." Sherman took the razor and began taking it apart. Douglas as always moved closer and tried to see. He smiled at the waterworks man, who smiled back. Other people gathered around and watched Sherman's hands. Then they watched him hand the reassembled little machine back to the waterworks man. The man turned on the shaver and put it to his face.

"Hey," he said. "This is wonderful. It works just like it did when it was new. This is wonderful. Thank you. Can I bring you some money tomorrow?"

"Not necessary," Sherman said.

"This is wonderful."

Everyone in the restaurant oohed and aahed.

"Look," the waterworks man said. "I'm not bleeding from my face."

Sherman sat quietly at the end of the counter and fixed whatever was put in front of him. He repaired hair dryers and calculators and watches and cellular phones and carburetors. And while people waited for the repairs to be done, they ate sandwiches, and this appealed to Sherman, though he didn't like his handyman's time so consumed. But the fact of the matter was that there was little more to fix in the shop.

One day a woman who believed her husband was having an affair came in and complained over a turkey and provolone on wheat. Sherman sat next to her at the counter and listened as she finished. ". . . and then he comes home hours after he's gotten off from work, smelling of beer and perfume and he doesn't want to talk or anything and says he has a sinus headache and I'm wondering if I ought to follow him or check the mileage on his car before he leaves in the morning. What should I do?"

"Tell him it's his turn to cook and that you'll be late and don't tell him where you're going," Sherman said.

Everyone in the shop nodded, more in shared confusion than in agreement.

"Where should I go?" the woman asked.

"Go to the library and read about the praying mantis," Sherman said.

Douglas came up to Sherman after the woman had left, and asked, "Do you think that was a good idea?"

Sherman shrugged.

The woman came in the next week, her face full with a smile and announced that her home life was now perfect.

"Everything at home is perfect now," she said. "Thanks to Sherman."

Customers slapped Sherman on the back.

So began a new dimension of fixing in the shop as people brought in with their electric pencil sharpeners, pacemakers and microwaves, their relationship woes and their tax problems. Sherman saved the man who owned the automotive supply business across the street twelve thousand dollars and got him some fifty-seven dollars in refund.

*

One night after the shop was closed, Douglas and Sherman sat at the counter and ate the stale leftover doughnuts and drank coffee. Douglas looked at his handyman and shook his head. "That was really something the way you straightened the Rhinehart boy's teeth."

"Physics," Sherman said.

Douglas washed down a dry bite and set his cup on the counter. "I know I've asked you before, but we've known each other longer now. How did you learn to fix things?"

"Fixing things is easy. You just have to know how things work."

"That's it," Douglas said more than asked.

Sherman nodded.

"Doesn't it make you happy to do it?"

Sherman looked at Douglas, questioning.

"I ask because you never smile."

"Oh," Sherman said, and took another bite of doughnut.

The next day Sherman fixed a chain saw and a laptop computer and thirty-two parking tickets. Sherman, who had always been quiet, became increasingly more so. He would listen, nod, and fix it. That evening, a few minutes before closing, just after Sherman had solved the Morado woman's sexual identity problem, two paramedics came in with a patient on a stretcher.

"This is my wife," the more distressed of the ambulance men said of the supine woman. "She's been hit by a car, and she died in our rig on the way to the hospital," he cried.

Sherman looked at the woman, pulling back the blanket.

"She had massive internal —"

Sherman stopped the man with a raised hand, pulled the blanket off and then over himself and the dead woman. Douglas stepped over to stand with the paramedics.

Sherman worked under the blanket, moving this way and that way, and then he and the woman emerged, alive and well. The paramedic hugged her.

"You're alive," the man said to his wife.

The other paramedic shook Sherman's hand. Douglas just stared at his handyman.

"Thank you, thank you," the husband said, crying.

The woman was confused, but she too offered Sherman thanks.

Sherman nodded and walked quietly away, disappearing into the kitchen.

The paramedics and the restored woman left. Douglas locked the shop and walked into the kitchen, where he found Sherman sitting on the floor with his back against the refrigerator.

"I don't know what to say," Douglas said. His head was swimming. "You just brought that woman back to life."

Sherman's face looked lifeless. He seemed drained of all energy. He lifted his sad face up to look at Douglas.

"How did you do that?" Douglas asked.

Sherman shrugged.

"You just brought a woman back to life and you give me a shrug?" Douglas could hear the fear in his voice. "Who are you? What are you? Are you from outer space or something?"

"No," Sherman said.

"Then what's going on?"

"I can fix things."

"That wasn't a thing," Douglas pointed out. "That was a human being."

"Yeah, I know."

Douglas ran a hand over his face and just stared down at Sherman. "I wonder what Sheila will say."

"Please don't tell anyone about this," Sherman said.

Douglas snorted out a laugh. "Don't tell anyone. I don't have to tell anyone. Everyone probably knows by now. What do you think those paramedics are out there doing right now? They're telling anybody and everybody that there's some freak in Langley's Sandwich Shop who can revive the dead."

Sherman held his face in his hands.

"Who are you?"

News spread. Television news trucks and teams camped outside the front door of the sandwich shop. They were waiting with cameras ready when Douglas showed up to open for business the day following the resurrection.

"Yes, this is my shop," he said. "No, I don't know how it was done," he said. "No, you can't come in just yet," he said.

Sherman was sitting at the counter waiting, his face long, his eyes red as if from crying.

"This is crazy," Douglas said.

Sherman nodded.

"They want to talk to you." Douglas looked closely at Sherman. "Are you all right?"

But Sherman was looking past Douglas and through the front window where the crowd was growing ever larger.

"Are you going to talk to them?" Douglas asked.

Sherman shook his sad face. "I have to run away," he said. "Everyone knows where I am now."

Douglas at first thought Sherman was making cryptic reference to the men who had been beating him that night long ago, but then realized that Sherman meant simply everyone.

Sherman stood and walked into the back of the shop. Douglas followed him, not knowing why, unable to stop himself. He in fact followed the man out of the store and down the alley, away from the shop and the horde of people.

They ran up this street and across that avenue, crossed bridges and scurried through tunnels. Douglas finally asked where they were going and confessed that he was afraid. They were sitting on a bench in the park and it was by now just after sundown.

"You don't have to come with me," Sherman said. "I need only to get away from all of them." He shook his head, and said, more to himself, "I knew this would happen."

"If you knew this would happen, why did you fix all of those things?"

"Because I can. Because I was asked."

Douglas gave nervous glances this way and that across the park. "This has something to do with why the men were beating you that night, doesn't it?"

"They were from the government or some businesses, I'm not completely sure," Sherman said. "They wanted me to fix a bunch of things and I said no."

"But they asked you," Douglas said. "You just told me —"

"You have to be careful about what you fix. If you fix the valves in an engine, but the bearings are shot, you'll get more compression, but the engine will still burn up." Sherman looked at Douglas's puzzled face. "If you irrigate a desert, you might empty a sea. It's a complicated business, fixing things."

Douglas said, "So, what do we do now?"

Sherman was now weeping, tears streaming down his face and curving just under his chin before falling to the open collar of his

light blue shirt. Douglas watched him, not believing that he was
seeing the same man who had fixed so many machines and so
many relationships and so many businesses and concerns and even
fixed a dead woman.

Sherman raised his tear-filled eyes to Douglas. "I am the empty
sea," he said.

Douglas turned to see the night dotted with yellow-orange
torches.

The two men ran, Douglas pushing Sherman, as he was now so
engaged in sobbing that he had trouble keeping his feet. They
made it to the big bridge that crossed the bay and stopped in the
middle, discovering that at either end thousands of people waited.

"Fix us!" they shouted. "Fix us! Fix us!"

Sherman looked down at the peaceful water below. It was a long
drop, which no one could hope to survive. He looked at Douglas.

Douglas nodded.

The masses of people pressed in from either side.

Sherman stepped over the railing and stood on the brink, the
toes of his shoes pushed well over the edge.

"Don't!" they all screamed. "Fix us! Fix us!"

TIM GAUTREAUX

Good for the Soul

FROM STORY

FATHER LEDET took a scorching swallow of brandy and sat in an
iron chair on the brick patio behind the rectory, hemmed in by
walls of Ligustrums stitched through with honeysuckle. His stomach was full from the Ladies' Altar Society supper, where the sweet,
sweet women of the parish had fed him pork roast, potato salad,
and butter beans, filling his plate and making over him as if he
were an old spayed tomcat who kept the cellar free of rats. He was a
big man, white-haired and ruddy, with gray eyes and huge spotted
hands that could make a highball glass disappear. It was Thursday
evening, and not much happened on Thursday evenings. The first
cool front of the fall was nosing through the pecan trees on the
church lot, and nothing is so important in Louisiana as that first release from the sopping, buggy, overheated funk of the atmosphere.
Father Ledet breathed deep in the shadow of a statue of St. Francis.
He took another long swallow, glad that the assistant pastor was on
a visit home in Iowa, and that the deacon wouldn't be around until
the next afternoon. Two pigeons lit on St. Francis's hands as if they
knew who he was. Father Ledet watched the light fade and the
Ligustrums darken, and then he looked a long time at the pint of
brandy before deciding to pour himself another drink.

The phone rang in the rectory, and he got up carefully, moving
inside among the dark wood furnishings and dim holy light. It was
a parishioner, Mrs. Clyde Arceneaux, whose husband was dying of
emphysema.

"We need you for the Anointing of the Sick, Father."

"Um, yes." He tried to say something else, but the words were stuck back in his throat, the way dollar bills sometimes wadded up in the tubular poor box and wouldn't drop down when he opened the bottom.

"Father?"

"Of course. I'll just come right over there."

"I know you've done it for him last week. But this time he might really be going, you know." Mrs. Arceneaux's voice began to shed tears. "He wants you to hear his confession."

"Um." The priest had known Clyde Arceneaux for fifteen years. The old man dressed up on Sunday, came to church, stayed out on the steps during Mass, and smoked with three other men as reverent as himself. As far as he knew, Clyde had never been to confession.

Father Ledet locked the rectory door and went into the garage to start the parish car, a venerable black Lincoln. He backed out onto the street, and when the car stopped, he still floated along in a drifting crescent, and he realized that he'd had maybe an ounce too much of brandy. It occurred to him that he should call the housekeeper to drive him to the hospital. It would take only five minutes for her to get there, but then the old Baptist woman was always figuring him out, and he would have to endure Mrs. Scott's roundabout questions and sniffs of the air. Father Ledet felt his old mossy human side take over, and he began to navigate the streets of the little town on his own, stopping the car too far into the intersection at Jackman Avenue, clipping a curb on a turn at Bourgeois Street. The car had its logical movement, but his head had a motion of its own.

Patrolman Vic Garafola was parked in front of the post office talking to the dispatcher about a cow eating string beans out of Mrs. LeBlanc's garden when he heard a crash in the intersection behind him. In his rearview he saw that a long black sedan had battered the side of a powder blue Ford. He backed his cruiser fifty feet and turned on his flashers. When he got out and saw his own parish priest sitting wide-eyed behind the steering wheel, he ran to the window.

"You all right, Father?"

The priest had a little red mark on his high forehead, but he smiled dumbly and nodded. Patrolman Garafola looked over to the smashed passenger side door of a faded Crown Victoria. A pretty, older woman sat in the middle of the bench seat holding her elbow. He opened the door and saw that Mrs. Mamie Barrilleaux's right arm was obviously broken, her mouth twitching with pain. Vic's face reddened because it made him angry to see nice people get hurt when it wasn't their fault.

"Mrs. Mamie, you hurtin' a lot?" Vic asked. Behind him the priest walked up and put his hand on his shoulder. When the woman saw Father Ledet, her face was transfigured.

"Oh, it's nothing, just a little bump. Father, did I cause the accident?"

The patrolman looked at the priest for the answer.

"Mamie, your arm." He took his hand off the policeman and stepped back. Vic could see that the priest was shocked. He knew that Father Ledet was called out to give last rites to strangers at gory highway wrecks all the time, but this woman was the vice president of the Ladies' Altar Society, the group who polished the old church, put flowers on the altar, knitted afghans to put on his lap in the drafty wooden rectory.

"Father, Mrs. Mamie had the right of way." Vic pointed to the stop sign behind the priest's steaming car.

"I am dreadfully sorry," Father Ledet said. "I was going to the hospital to give the Anointing of the Sick, and I guess my mind was on that."

"Oh," Mrs. Barrilleaux cried. "Who's that ill?"

"Mrs. Arceneaux's husband."

Another cruiser pulled up, its lights sparking the evening. Mrs. Mamie pointed at it. "Vic, can you take him to the hospital and let this other policeman write the report? I know Mrs. Arceneaux's husband, and he needs a priest bad."

Vic looked down at his shoe. He wasn't supposed to do anything like that. "You want to go on to the hospital and then I can bring you back here, Father?"

"Mamie's the one who should go to the hospital."

"Shoo." She waved her good hand at him. "I can hear the ambulance coming now. Go on, I'm not dying."

Vic could see a slight trembling in Mamie's iron gray curls. He put a hand on the priest's arm. "Okay, Father?"

"Okay."

They got into the cruiser and immediately Vic smelled the priest's breath. He drove under the tunnel of oak trees that was Nadine Avenue and actually bit his tongue to keep from asking the inevitable question. When they were in sight of the hospital, Patrolman Garafola could no longer stop himself. "Father, did you have anything to drink today?"

The priest looked at him and blanched. "Why do you ask?"

"It's on your breath. Whiskey."

"Brandy," the priest corrected. "Yes, I had some brandy after supper."

"How much?"

"Not too much. Well, here we are." Father Ledet got out before the patrol car had completely stopped. Vic radioed his location, parked, and went into the modern lobby to find a soft chair.

The priest knew the way to Clyde Arceneaux's room. When he pushed open the door, he saw the old man in his bed, a few strands of smoky hair swept back, his false teeth out, his tobacco-parched tongue wiggling in his mouth like a parrot's. Up close, Father Ledet could hear the hiss of the oxygen through the nose dispenser strapped to the old man's face. He felt his deepest sorrow for the respiratory patients.

"Clyde?"

Mr. Arceneaux opened one eye and looked at the priest's shirt. "The buzzards is circlin'," he rasped.

"How're you feeling?"

"Ah, Padre, I got a elephant standing on my chest." He spoke slowly, more like an air leak than a voice. "Doris, she stepped out a minute to eat." He motioned with his eyes toward the door, and Father Ledet looked at Clyde's hands, which were bound with dark veins flowing under skin as thin as cigarette paper.

"Is there something you'd like to talk about?" The priest heard the faint sound of a siren and wondered if gentle Mrs. Barrilleaux was being brought in to have her arm set.

"I don't need the holy oil no more. You can't grease me so I can slide into heaven." Clyde ate a bite of air. "I got to go to confession."

The priest nodded, removed a broad, ribbonlike vestment from his pocket, kissed it, and hung it around his neck. Mr. Arceneaux couldn't remember the last time he'd been to confession, but he knew that Kennedy had been president then, because it was during the Cuban missile crisis when he thought sure a nuclear strike was coming. He began telling his sins, starting with missing Mass "damn near seven hundred fifty times." Father Ledet was happy that Clyde Arceneaux was coming to God for forgiveness, and in a very detailed way, which showed, after all, a healthy conscience. At one point the old man stopped and began to store up air for what the priest thought would be a new push through his errors, but when he began speaking again, it was to ask a question.

"Sure enough, you think there's a hell?"

Father Ledet knew he had to be careful. Saving a soul sometimes was like catching a dragonfly. You couldn't blunder up to it and trap it with a swipe of the hand. "There's a lot of talk of it in the Bible," he said.

"It's for punishment?"

"That's what it's for."

"But what good would the punishment do?"

The priest sat down. The room did a quarter turn to the left and then stopped. "I don't think hell is about rehabilitation. It's about what someone might deserve." He put his hand over his eyes and squeezed them for a moment. "But you shouldn't worry about that, Clyde, because you're getting the forgiveness you need."

Mr. Arceneaux looked at the ceiling, the corners of his flaccid mouth turning down. "I don't know. There's one thing I ain't told you yet."

"Well, it's now or never." The priest was instantly sorry for saying this, and Clyde gave him a questioning look before glancing at his purple feet.

"I can't hold just one thing back? I'd hate like hell to tell anybody this."

"Clyde, it's God listening, not me."

"Can I just think it to God? I mean, I told you the other stuff. Even about the midget woman."

"If it's a serious sin, you've got to tell me about it. You can generalize a bit."

"This is some of that punishment we were talkin' about earlier. It's what I deserve."

"Let's have it."

"I stole Nelson Lodrigue's car."

Something clicked in the priest's brain. He remembered this himself. Nelson Lodrigue owned an old Toronado parked next to the ditch in front of his house. The car had no mufflers and a huge eight-cylinder engine, and every morning at six sharp Nelson would crank the thing up and race the engine, waking most of his neighbors and all the dogs for blocks around. He did this for about a year, to keep the battery charged, he'd said. When it disappeared, Nelson put a big ad in the paper offering a fifty-dollar reward for information, but no one came forward. The men in the Knights of Columbus talked of it for weeks.

"That was about ten years ago, wasn't it? And isn't Nelson a friend of yours?" Nelson was another Sunday-morning lingerer on the church steps.

Mr. Arceneaux swallowed hard several times and drew in a breath. "Father, honest to God, I ain't never stole nothin' before. My daddy told me thievin' is the worst thing a man can do. I hated to take Nelson's hot rod, but I was fixin' to have a nervous break-down from lack of sleep."

The priest nodded. "It's good to get these things off your chest. Is there anything else?"

Mr. Arceneaux shook his head. "I think we hit the high points. Man, I'm ashamed of that last one."

The priest gave him absolution and a small penance.

Clyde tried to smile, his dark tongue tasting the air. "Ten Hail Marys? That's a bargain, Father."

"If you want to do more, you could call Nelson and tell him what you did."

The old man thought for just a second. "I'll stick with them little prayers for now." Father Ledet got out his missal and read a prayer over Mr. Arceneaux until his words were interrupted by a gentle snoring.

Vic sat in the lobby waiting for the priest. It had been twenty minutes, and he knew the priest's blood alcohol level was ready to peak. He took off his hat and began twirling it in front of him. He wondered what good it would do to charge the priest with drunken driving. Priests had to drink wine every day, and they liked the taste in the evening, too. A ticket wouldn't change his mind for long. On the other hand, Father Ledet had ruined Mrs. Barrilleaux's sedan, which she had pampered like a child for twenty years.

A few minutes earlier, Vic had walked down the corridor and peeked into the room where they were treating her. He hadn't let her see him as he studied her face. Now he sat and twirled his hat, thinking. It would be painful for the priest to have his name in the paper attached to a DUI charge, but it would make him understand the seriousness of what he had done. Patrolman Garafola dealt with too many people who did not understand the seriousness of what they were doing.

The priest came into the lobby and the young policeman stood. "Father, we'll have to take a ride to the station."

"What?"

"I want to run a Breathalyzer test on you."

Father Ledet straightened up, stepped close, and put an arm around the man's shoulders. "Oh, come on. What good would that do?"

The patrolman started to speak, but then he motioned for the priest to follow him. "Let me show you something."

"Where are we going?"

"I want you to see this." They walked down the hall and through double doors to a triage area for emergency cases. There was a narrow window in a wall, and the policeman told the priest to look through it. An oxygen bottle and gauges partially blocked the view. Inside, Mrs. Barrilleaux sat on an examining table, a blue knot swelling on her upper arm. A nurse stood next to her while a doctor worked on her elbow. On the table was a menacing-looking syringe, and Mrs. Barrilleaux was crying, without expression, great patient tears. "Take a long look," Vic said, "and when you get enough, come on with me." The priest turned away from the glass and followed.

"You didn't have to show me that."

"I didn't?"

"That woman is the nicest, the best cook, the best . . ."

"Come on, Father," Vic said, pushing open the door to the parking lot. "I've got a lot of writing to do."

*

Father Ledet's blood alcohol level was twice as much as required for the patrolman to write him up for DUI, to which he added running a stop sign and causing an accident with bodily injury. The traffic court suspended his license, and since he had banged up the Lincoln before, his insurance company dropped his coverage as soon as their computers caught the offenses. A week after the accident, he came into the rectory drinking a glass of tap water, which beaded on his tongue like a nasty oil. The phone rang and the glass jumped in his fingers. It was Mrs. Arceneaux again, who told him she'd been arguing with her husband, who wanted to tell her brother Nelson Lodrigue that he had stolen his car ten years before. "Why'd you tell him to talk to Nelson about the stealing business? It's got him all upset."

The priest did not understand. "What would be the harm in him telling Nelson the truth?"

"Aw, no, Father. Clyde's got so little oxygen in his brain he's not thinking straight. He can't tell Nelson what he did. I don't want him to die with everyone in the neighborhood thinking he's a thief. And Nelson, well, I love my brother, but if he found out my husband stole his old bomb, he'd make Clyde's last days hell. He's just like that, you know?"

"I see. Is there something I can do?" He put down the glass of water on the phone table next to a little white statue of the Blessed Virgin.

"If you would talk to Clyde and let him know it's okay to die without telling Nelson about the car, I'd appreciate it. He already confessed everything anyway, right?"

The priest looked down the hall toward the patio, longing for the openness. "I can't discuss specific matters of confession."

"I know. That's why I gave you all the details again."

"All right, I'll call. Is he awake now?"

"He's here at home. We got him a crank-up bed and a oxygen machine and a nurse sits with him at night. I'll put him on."

Father Ledet leaned against the wall and stared at a crucifix, wondering what Christ had done to deserve his punishment. When he heard the hiss of Clyde Arceneaux's mask come out of the phone, he began to tell him what he should hear, that he was forgiven in God's eyes, that if he wanted to make restitution, he could give money to the poor, or figure out how to leave his brother-in-law something. He hung up and sniffed the waxed smell of the rectory, thinking of the sweet, musky brandy in the kitchen cupboard, and immediately went to find the young priest upstairs to discuss the new Mass schedule.

On Saturday afternoon, Father Ledet was nodding off in the confessional when a woman began to deliver her confession. After she'd mentioned one or two venial sins, she addressed him through the screen. "Father, it's Doris Arceneaux, Clyde's wife."

The priest yawned. "How is Clyde?"

"You remember the car business? Well, something new has come up," she whispered. "Clyde always told me he and the Scadlock kid towed the car off with a rope and when they got it downtown behind the seawall, they pushed it overboard into the bay."

"Yes?"

"There's a new wrinkle."

He put down his missal and removed his glasses to rub his eyes. "What do you mean?"

"Clyde just told me he stored the car. Been paying thirty-five dollars a month to keep it in a little closed bin down at the U-Haul place for the past ten years." She whispered louder, "I don't know how he kept that from me. Makes me wonder about a few other things."

The priest's eyebrows went up. "Now he can give it back, or you can give it back when your husband passes away." As soon as he'd said this, he knew it wouldn't work. It was too logical. If nothing else, his years in the confessional had taught him that people did not run their lives by reason much of the time, but by some inferior motion of the spirit, some pride, some desire that defied the simple beauty of doing the sensible thing.

Mrs. Arceneaux protested that the secret had to be kept. "There's only one way to get Nelson his car back like Clyde wants."

The priest sighed. "How is that?"

Mrs. Arceneaux began to fidget in the dark box. "Well, you the only one besides me who knows what happened. Clyde says the car will still run. He cranks it up once every three weeks so it keeps its battery hot."

The priest put his head down. "And?"

"And you could get up early and drive it back to Nelson's and park it where it was the night Clyde stole it."

"Not no," the priest said, "but hell no!"

"Father!"

"What if I were caught driving this thing? The secret would get out then."

"Father, this is part of a confession. You can't tell."

The priest now sensed a plot. "I'm sorry, I can't help you, Mrs. Arceneaux. Now I'm going to give you a penance of twenty Our Fathers."

"For telling one fib to my daughter-in-law?"

"You want a cut-rate for dishonesty?"

"All right," she said in an unrepentant voice. "And I'll pray for you while I'm at it."

After five o'clock Saturday Mass, Father Ledet felt his soul bang around inside him like a golf ball in a shoebox. He yearned for an inflating swallow of spirits, longed for the afterburn of brandy in his nostrils. He went back into the empty church, a high-ceilinged Gothic building more than a hundred years old, sat in a pew, and steeped himself in the odors of furniture oil, incense, and hot candle wax. He let the insubstantial colors of the windows flow over him, and after a while, these shades and smells began to fill the emptiness he felt. He closed his eyes and imagined the housekeeper's supper, pushing out of mind his need for a drink, replacing the unnecessary with the good. At five to six he walked to the rectory to have his thoughts made into food.

The next evening, after visiting a sick parishioner, he was reading the newspaper in his room when the housekeeper knocked on his door. Mrs. Mamie Barrilleaux was downstairs and would like to speak with him, the housekeeper said.

The first thing Father Ledet noticed when he walked into the study was the white cast on the woman's arm.

"Mamie," he said, sitting next to her on the sofa. "I have to tell you again how sorry I am about your arm."

The woman's face brightened, as though to be apologized to was a privilege. "Oh, don't worry about it, Father. Accidents happen." She was a graying brunette with fair skin, a woman whose cheerfulness made her pretty. One of the best cooks in a town of good cooks, she volunteered for every charity connected with a stove or oven, and her time belonged to anyone who needed it, from her well-fed smirk of a husband to the drug addicts who showed up at the parish shelter. While they talked, the priest's eyes wandered repeatedly to the ugly cast, which ran up nearly to her shoulder. For five minutes he wondered why she had dropped in unannounced. And then she told him.

"Father, I don't know if you understand what good friends Clyde Arceneaux's wife and I are. We went to school together for twelve years."

"Yes. It's a shame her husband's so sick."

Mrs. Barrilleaux fidgeted into the corner of the sofa, put her cast on the armrest, where it glowed under a lamp. "That's sort of why I'm here. Doris told me she asked you to do something for her and Clyde, and you turned her down. I'm not being specific because I know it was a confession thing."

"How much did she tell you?" The priest hoped she wouldn't ask what she was going to ask, because he knew he could not refuse her.

"I don't know even one detail, Father. But I wanted to tell you that if Doris wants it done, then it needs doing. She's a good person, and I'm asking you to help her."

"But you don't know what she wants me to do."

Mrs. Barrilleaux put her good hand on her cast. "I know it's not something bad."

"No, no. It's just . . ." He was going to mention that his driver's license was suspended but realized that he couldn't even tell her that.

Mamie lowered her head and turned her face toward the priest. "Father?"

"Oh, all right."

He visited Mrs. Arceneaux on a Wednesday, got the keys, and late that night he sat on the dark rectory patio for a long time, filling up on the smells of honeysuckle. The young priest finally insisted that he come in out of the mosquitoes and the dampness. Upstairs, he changed into street clothes and lay on the bed like a man waiting for a firing squad. Around midnight his legs began to ache terribly, and the next thing he knew they were carrying him downstairs to the kitchen where the aspirin was kept, and as his hand floated toward the cabinet door to his right, it remembered its accustomed movement to the door on the left where a quart of brandy waited like an airy promise. The mind and the spirit pulled his hand to the right, while the earthly body drew it to the left. He heard somewhere in the air above, the drone of an airplane, and he suddenly thought of an old homily he'd heard, how people were like twin-engine planes, one engine the logical spirit, the other the sensual body, and that when they were not running in concert, the craft ran off course to disaster. The priest supposed he could rev his spirit in some way, but when he thought of driving the stolen car, he opted to throttle up the body. One jigger, he thought, would calm him and give him the courage to do this important and good deed. As he took a drink, he tried to picture how glad Nelson Lodrigue would be to have his old car back. As he took another, he thought of how Mr. Arceneaux could gasp off into the next world with a clear conscience. After several minutes, the starboard engine sputtered and locked up as Father Ledet lurched sideways through the dark house looking for his car keys.

At one o'clock he got into the church's sedan and drove to the edge of town to a row of storage buildings. He woke the manager, a shabby old man living in a trailer next to the gate. Inside the fence, Father Ledet walked along the numbered doors of the storage areas until he found the right one. He had trouble fitting the key into the lock but finally managed to open the door and turn on the light. The Oldsmobile showed a hard shell of rust and dust and resembled a million-year-old museum egg. The door squawked when he pulled on it, and the interior smelled like the closed-in mausoleum at the parish graveyard. He inserted the key, and the motor groaned, then stuttered alive, rumbling and complaining. Shaking his head, the priest thought he'd never be able to drive this car undetected into the quiet neighborhood where Nelson Lodrigue lived. But after he let it idle and warm up, the engine slowed to a breathy subsonic bass, and he put it in reverse for its first trip in ten years.

The plan was to park the car on a patch of grass next to the street in front of Nelson's house, the very spot where it had been stolen. The priest would walk one block to Mrs. Arceneaux's house, and she would return him to his car. He pulled out of the rental place and drove a back road, past tin-roofed shotgun houses and abandoned cars better in appearance than the leprous one that now moved among them. He entered the railroad underpass and emerged in the better part of town, which was moon-washed and asleep. He found that if he kept his foot off the accelerator and just let the car idle along at ten miles an hour, it didn't make much noise, but when he gave the car just a little gas at stop signs, the exhaust sounded like a lion getting ready for mating. The priest was thankful at least for a certain buoyancy of the blood provided by the glasses of brandy, a numbness of spirit that helped him endure. He was still nervous, though, and had trouble managing the touchy accelerator, feeling that the car was trying to bound away in spite of his best efforts to control it. Eventually, he turned onto the main street of Nelson's little subdivision and burbled along slowly until he could see the apron of grass next to the asphalt where he could park. He turned off the car's lights.

One of the town's six policemen had an inflamed gallbladder, and Patrolman Vic Garafola was working his friend's shift, parked in an alley next to the Elks Club, sitting stone-faced with boredom when a shuddering and filthy Toronado crawled past. He would have thought it was just some rough character from the section down by the fish plant, but he got a look at the license plate and saw that it bore a design that hadn't been on any car in at least five years. Vic put his cruiser in gear, left his lights off, and rolled into the town's empty streets, following the Toronado at a block's distance past the furniture store, across the highway, and into little Shade Tree subdivision. He radioed a parish officer he'd seen a few minutes earlier and asked him to park across the entrance, the only way in or out of the neighborhood.

Even in the dark, Vic could see that the car's tires were bagged out and that it was dirty in an unnatural way, pale with dust — the ghost of a car. He closed in as it swayed down Cypress Street. When he saw the driver douse his lights, he thought, Bingo, someone's up to no good, and at once he hit his headlights and flashers, switched on a short burst of the siren. The Toronado suddenly exploded forward in a flatulent rush, red dust and sparks raining from underneath the car as it left the patrolman in twin swirls of tire smoke. Vic started the chase, following but not gaining on the sooty taillights. Shade Tree subdivision was composed of only one long street that ran in an oval like a racetrack. At the first curve, the roaring car fishtailed to the right and Vic followed as best he could, watching as the vehicle pulled away and then turned right again in the distance, heading for the subdivision exit. When Vic went around a curve, he saw a white cruiser blocking the speeding car's escape. The fleeing vehicle then slowed and moved again down Cypress Street toward the middle of the subdivision. Vic watched the grumbling car finally stop in front of Nelson Lodrigue's brick rancher. The patrolman pulled up, opened his door, and pointed his revolver toward the other vehicle.

"Driver, get out," he barked. Slowly, a graying, soft-looking man wearing a dark shirt buttoned to the top slid out of the vehicle, his shaking hands raised high.

"Can you please not yell?" The old man looked around at the drowsing houses.

Vic stared at him, walked close, and looked at his eyes. He holstered his revolver. "Why'd you speed away like that, Father?"

The priest was out of breath. "When you turned on those flashers it frightened me and, well, I guess I pressed the accelerator too hard and this thing took off like a rocket."

Vic looked at the car and back to the priest. "The tag is expired on your vehicle, and it doesn't have an inspection sticker." He went to his patrol car and reached in for his ticket book.

"Could you please turn off those flashers?"

"Have to leave 'em on. Rules, you know," Vic said in a nasty voice. "You want to show me your proof of insurance, driver's license, and pink slip?" He held out a mocking hand.

"You know I don't have any of those."

"Father, what are you doing in this wreck?"

The priest put his hands in front of him, pleading. "I can't say anything. It's related to a confession."

"Oh, is this a good deed or somethin'?"

The priest's face brightened with hope, as though the patrolman understood what this was all about. "Yes, yes."

Vic leaned in and sniffed. "You think it's a good deed to get drunk as a boiled owl and speed around town at night?" he hollered.

"Oh, please, hush."

Vic reached to his gun belt. "Turn around so I can cuff you."

"Have some mercy."

"Them that deserves it gets mercy," Vic told him.

"God would give me mercy," the priest said, turning around and offering his hands at his back.

"Then he's a better man than I am. Spread your legs."

"This won't do anyone any good."

"It'll do me some good." Just then a porch light came on, and a shirtless Nelson Lodrigue padded down the steps to the walk in his bare feet, his moon-shaped belly hanging over the elastic of his pajamas.

"Hey. What's goin' on?"

Other porch lights began to fire up across the street and next door, people coming to the edge of their driveways and looking.

"It's Father Ledet," Vic called out. "He's getting a ticket or two."

Nelson was standing next to the car before his eyes opened fully and his head swung from side to side at the dusty apparition. "What the hell? This here's my old car that got stole."

Vic gave the priest a hard look. "Collections been a little slow, Father?"

"Don't be absurd. I was returning Nelson's car."

"You know who stole my car?" Nelson lumbered around the hood. "You better tell me right now. I didn't sleep for a year after this thing got taken. I always had a feeling it was someone I knew."

"I can't say anything."

"It came out in a confession," Vic explained.

Nelson ran his hand over the chalky paint of the roof. "Well, charge him with auto theft and I'll bet he'll tell us."

Two ladies in curlers and a tall middle-aged man wearing a robe and slippers approached from across the street. "What's going on, Vic?" the man asked. "Hello, Father."

The priest nodded, hiding the handcuffs behind him. "Good evening, Mayor. This isn't what it appears to be."

"I hope not," one of the women said.

Other neighbors began walking into the circle of crackling light cast by the police car's flashers. Then the parish deputy pulled up, his own lights blazing. Vic looked on as the priest tried to explain to everyone that he was doing a good thing, that they couldn't know all the details. The patrolman felt sorry for him, he really did, felt bad as he filled out the tickets, as he pushed the old head under the roof of the patrol car, and later, as he fingerprinted the soft

hands and put the holy body into the cell, taking his belt, his shoe-
laces, and his rosary.

Father Ledet had to journey to Baton Rouge to endure the frowns
and lecturing of the bishop. His parish was taken away for two
months, and he was put into an AA program in his own community where he sat many times in rusty folding chairs along with
fundamentalist garage mechanics, striptease artists, and spoiled
depressed housewives to listen to testimonials, admonitions, con-
fessions without end. He rode cabs to these meetings and in the
evenings no one invited him to the Ladies' Altar Society dinners or
to anyplace else. Mrs. Arceneaux never called to sympathize, and
pretty Mrs. Barrilleaux would not look at him when he waved as she
drove by the rectory in her new, secondhand car. The first day he
was again allowed to put on vestments was a Sunday, and he went in
to say the eleven o'clock Mass. The church was full, and the sun was
bleeding gold streamers of light down through the sacristy windows behind the altar. After the Gloria was sung by the birdlike
voices of a visiting children's choir, the priest stood in the pulpit
and read the gospel, drawing scant solace from the story of Jesus
turning water into wine. The congregation then sat in a rumble of
settling pews and kicked-up kneelers. Father Ledet began to talk
about Christ's first miracle, an old sermon, one he'd given dozens
of times. The elder parishioners in the front pews seemed to regard
him as a stranger, the children were uninterested, and he felt disconnected and sad as he spoke, wondering if he would ever be punished enough for what he had done. He scanned the faces in
the congregation as he preached, looking for forgiveness of any
sort, and fifteen minutes into the sermon, he saw in the fifth pew,
against the wall, something that was better than forgiveness, better
than what he deserved, something that gave sudden light to his
dull voice and turned bored heads up to the freshened preaching.
It was Clyde Arceneaux, a plastic tube creeping from his nose and
taped to his puckered neck. He was asleep, pale, two steps from
death, his head resting against the wall, but at least he had finally
come inside.

ALLAN GURGANUS

He's at the Office

FROM THE NEW YORKER

TILL THE JAPANESE BOMBED Pearl Harbor, most American men wore hats to work. What happened? Did our guys — suddenly scouting overhead for worse Sunday raids — come to fear their hat brims' interference? My unsuspecting father wore his till yesterday. He owned three. A gray, a brown, and a summer straw one, whose maroon-striped rayon band could only have been woven in America in the 1940s.

Last month, I lured him from his self-imposed office hours for a walk around our block. My father insisted on bringing his briefcase. "You never know," he said. We soon passed a huge young hipster, creaking in black leather. The kid's pierced face flashed more silver than most bait shops sell. His jeans, half down, exposed hat racks of white hipbone; the haircut arched high over jug ears. He was scouting Father's shoes. Long before fashion joined him, Dad favored an under-evolved antique form of orthopedic Doc Martens. These impressed a punk now scanning the Sherman tank of a cowhide briefcase with chromium corner braces. The camel-hair overcoat was cut to resemble some boxy-backed 1947 Packard. And, of course, up top sat "the gray."

Pointing to it, the boy smiled. "Way bad look on you, guy."

My father, seeking interpretation, stared at me. I simply shook my head no. I could not explain Dad to himself in terms of tidal fashion trends. All I said was "I think he likes you."

Dad's face folded. "Uh-oh."

By the end, my father, the fifty-two-year veteran of Integrity Office Supplier, Unlimited, had become quite cool again, way.

*

We couldn't vacation for more than three full days. He'd veer our Plymouth toward some way-station pay phone. We soon laughed as Dad, in the glass booth, commenced to wave his arms, shake his head, shift his weight from foot to foot. We knew Miss Green must be telling him of botched orders, delivery mistakes. We were nearly to Gettysburg. I'd been studying battle maps. Now I knew we'd never make it.

My father bounded back to the car and smiled in. "Terrible mixup with the Wilmington school system's carbon paper for next year. Major goof, but typical. Guy's got to do it all himself. Young Green didn't insist I come back, but she sure hinted."

We U-turned southward, and my father briefly became the most charming man on earth. He now seemed to be selling something we needed, whatever we needed. Traveling north into a holiday — the very curse of leisure — he had kept as silent as some fellow with toothaches. Now he was our tour guide, interviewing us, telling and retelling his joke. Passing a cemetery, he said (over his family's dry carbon-paper unison), "I hear they're dying to get in there!" "Look on the bright side," I told myself: "we'll arrive home and escape him as he runs — literally runs — to the office."

Dad was, like me, an early riser. Six days a week, Mom sealed his single-sandwich lunch into its Tupperware jacket; this fit accidentally yet exactly within the lid compartment of his durable briefcase. He would then pull on his overcoat — bulky, war-efficient, strong-seamed, four buttons as big as silver dollars and carved from actual shell. He'd place the cake-sized hat in place, nod in our general direction, and set off hurrying. Dad faced each day as one more worthy enemy. If he had been Dwight Eisenhower saving the Western world, or Jonas Salk freeing kids our age from crutches, okay. But yellow Eagle pencils? Utility paperweights in park-bench green?

Once a year, Mom told my brother and me how much the war had darkened her young husband; he'd enlisted with three other guys from Falls; he alone came back alive with all his limbs. "Before that," she smiled, "your father was funnier, funny. And smarter. Great dancer. You can't blame mustard gas, not this time. It's more what Dick saw. He came home and he was all business. Before that, he'd been mischievous and talkative and strange. He was always playing around with words. Very entertaining. Eyelashes out to here. For years, I figured that in time he'd come back to being whole. But since June of forty-five it's been All Work and No Play Makes Jack."

Mom remembered their fourth anniversary. "I hired an overnight sitter for you two. We drove to an inn near Asheville. It had the state's best restaurant, candlelight, a real string quartet. I'd made myself a green velvet dress. I was twenty-eight and never in my whole life have I ever looked better. You just know it. Dick recognized some man who'd bought two adding machines. Dick invited him to join us. Then I saw how much his work was going to have to mean to him. Don't be too hard on him, please. He feeds us, he puts aside real savings for you boys' college. Dick pays our taxes. Dick has no secrets. He's not hurting anyone." Brother and I gave each other a look Mom recognized and understood but refused to return.

The office seemed to tap some part of him that was either off limits to us or simply did not otherwise exist. My brother and I griped that he'd never attended our Little League games (not that we ever made the starting lineup). He missed our father-son Cub Scout banquet; it conflicted with a major envelope convention in Newport News. Mother neutrally said he loved us as much as he could. She was a funny, energetic person — all that wasted good will. And even as kids, we knew not to blame her.

Ignored, Mom created a small sewing room. Economizing needlessly, she stayed busy stitching all our school clothes, cowboy motifs galore. For a while, each shirt pocket bristled with Mom-designed embroidered cacti. But Simplicity patterns were never going to engage a mind as complex as hers. Soon Mom was spending most mornings playing vicious duplicate bridge. Our toothbrush glasses briefly broke out in rashes of red hearts, black clubs. Mom's new pals were society ladies respectful of her brainy speed, her impenitent wit; she never bothered introducing them to her husband. She laughed more now. She started wearing rouge.

We lived a short walk from both our school and his wholesale office. Dad sometimes left the Plymouth parked all night outside the workplace, his desk lamp the last one burning on the whole third floor. Integrity's president, passing headquarters late, always fell for it. "Dick, what do you do up there all night, son?" My father's shrug became his finest boast. The raises kept pace; Integrity

Office Supplier was still considered quite a comer. And R. Richard Markham, Sr. — as handsome as a collar ad, a hat ad, forever at the office — was the heir apparent.

Dad's was Integrity's flagship office: "Maker of World's Highest Quality Clerical Supplies." No other schoolboys had sturdier pastel subject dividers, more clip-in see-through three-ring pen caddies. The night before school started, Dad would be up late at our kitchen table, swilling coffee, "getting you boys set." Zippered leather cases, English slide rules, folders more suitable for treaties than for book reports (*"Skipper, A Dog of the Pyrenees,* by Marjorie Hopgood Purling"). Our notebooks soon proved too heavy to carry far; we secretly stripped them, swapping gear for lunchbox treats more exotic than Mom's hard-boiled eggs and Sun-Maid raisin packs.

Twenty years ago, Dad's Integrity got bought out by a German firm. The business's vitality proved somewhat hobbled by computers' onslaught. "A fad," my father called computers in 1976. "Let others retool. We'll stand firm with our yellow legals, erasers, Parker ink, fountain pens. Don't worry, our regulars'll come back. True vision always lets you act kind in the end, boys. Remember."

Yeah, right.

My father postponed his retirement. Mom encouraged that and felt relieved; she could not imagine him at home all day. As Integrity's market share dwindled, Dad spent more time at the office, as if to compensate with his own body for the course of modern life.

His secretary, the admired Miss Green, had once been what Pop still called "something of a bombshell." (He stuck with a Second World War terminology that had, like the hat, served him too well ever to leave behind.)

Still favoring shoulder pads, dressed in unyielding woolen Joan Crawford solids, Green wore an auburn pageboy that looked burned by decades of ungrateful dyes. She kicked off her shoes beneath her desk, revealing feet that told the tale of high heels' worthless weekday brutality. She'd quit college to tend an ailing mother, who proved demanding, then immortal. Brother and I teased Mom: poor Green appeared to worship her longtime boss, a guy whose face was as smooth and wedged and classic as his hat. Into Dick Markham's blunted constancy she read actual "moods."

He still viewed Green, now past sixty, as a promising virginal girl. In their small adjoining offices, these two thrived within a fond impersonality that permeated the ads of the period.

Integrity's flagship headquarters remained enameled a flavorless mint green, unaltered for five decades. The dark Mission coatrack was made by Limbert — quite a good piece. One ashtray — upright, floor model, brushed chromium — proved the size and shape of some landlocked torpedo. Moored to walls, dented metal desks were as gray as battleships. A series of forest green filing cabinets seemed banished, as patient as a family of trolls, to one shaming little closet all their own. Dad's office might've been decorated by a firm called Edward Hopper & Sam Spade, Unlimited.

For more than half a century, he walked in each day at seven-oh-nine sharp, as Miss Green forever said, "Morning, Mr. Markham. I left your appointments written on your desk pad, can I get you your coffee? Is now good, sir?" And Dad said, "Yes, why, thanks, Miss Green, how's your mother, don't mind if I do."

Four years ago, I received a panicked phone call: "You the junior to a guy about eighty, guy in a hat?"

"Probably." I was working at home. I pressed my computer's "Save" function. This, I sensed, might take a while. "Save."

"Exit? No? Yes?"

"Yes."

"Mister, your dad thinks we're camped out in his office and he's been banging against our door. He's convinced we've evicted his files and what he calls his Green. 'What have you done with young Green?' Get down here A.S.A.P. Get him out of our hair or it's nine-one-one in three minutes, swear to God."

From my car, I phoned home. Mom must have been off somewhere playing bridge with the mayor's blond wife and his blond ex-wife; they'd sensibly become excellent friends. The best women are the best people on earth; and the worst men the very worst. Mother, overlooked by Dad for years, had continued finding what she called "certain outlets."

When I arrived, Dad was still heaving himself against an office door, deadbolt-locked from within. Since its upper panel was frosted glass, I could make out the colors of the clothes of three or four people pressing from their side. They'd used masking tape to crosshatch the glass, as if bracing for a hurricane. The old man held his briefcase, wore his gray hat, the tan boxy coat.

"Dad?" He stopped with a mechanical cartoon verve, jumped my way, and smiled so hard it warmed my heart and scared me witless. My father had never acted so glad to see me — not when I graduated summa cum laude, not at my wedding, not after the birth of my son — and I felt joy in the presence of such joy from him.

"Reinforcements. Good man. We've got quite a hostage situation here. Let's put our shoulders to it, shall we?"

"Dad?" I grabbed the padded shoulders of his overcoat. These crumpled to reveal a man far sketchier hiding in there somewhere — a guy only twenty years from a hundred, after all.

"Dad? Dad. We have a good-news, bad-news setup here today. It's this. You found the right building, Dad. Wrong floor."

I led him back to the clattering, oil-smelling elevator. I thought to return, tap on the barricaded door, explain. But, in time, hey, they'd peek, they'd figure out the coast was clear. That they hadn't recognized him, after his fifty-two years of long days in this very building, said something. New people, everywhere.

I saw at once that Miss Green had been crying. Her face was caked with so much powder it looked like calamine. "Little mixup," I said.

"Mr. Markham? We got three calls about those gum erasers," she said, faking a frontal normality. "I think they're putting sawdust in them these days, sir. They leave skid marks, apparently. I put the information on your desk. With your day's appointments. Like your coffee? Like it now? Sir?"

I hung his hat on the hat tree; I slid his coat onto its one wooden Deco hanger that could, at any flea market today, bring thirty-five dollars easy, two tones of wood, inlaid.

I wanted to have a heart-to-heart. I was so disoriented as to feel half-sane myself. But I overheard Father already returning his calls. He ignored me, and that seemed, within this radically altered gravitational field, a good sign. I sneaked back to Miss Green's desk, and admitted, "I'll need to call his doctor. I want him seen today, Miss Green. He was up on four, trying to get into that new headhunting service. He told them his name. Mom was out. So they, clever, looked him up in the book and found his junior and phoned me to come help."

She sat forward, strenuously feigning surprise. She looked rigid, chained to this metal desk by both gnarled feet. "How long?" I somehow knew to ask.

Green appeared ecstatic, then relieved, then, suddenly, happily weeping, tears pouring down — small tears, lopsided, mascaraed grit. She blinked up at me with a spaniel's gratitude. Suddenly, if slowly, I began to understand. In mere seconds, she had caved about Dad's years-long caving-in. It was my turn now.

Miss Green now whispered certain of his mistakes. There were forgotten parking tickets by the dozen. There was his attempt to purchase a lake house on land already flooded for a dam. Quietly, she admitted years of covering.

From her purse, she lifted a page covered in Dad's stern Germanic cursive, blue ink fighting to stay isometrically between red lines.

"I found this one last week." Green's voice seemed steadied by the joy of having told. "I fear this is about the worst, to date, we've been."

If they say "Hot enough for you?," it means recent weather. "Yes indeed" still a good comeback. Order forms pink. Requisition yellow. Miss green's birthday June 12. She work with you fifty-one years. Is still unmarried. Mother now dead, since '76, so stop asking about Mother, health of. Home address, 712 Marigold Street: Left at Oak, can always walk there. After last week, never go near car again. Unfair to others. Take second left at biggest tree. Your new Butcher's name is: Al. Wife: Betty. Sons: Matthew and Dick Junior. Grandson Richie (your name with a III added on it). List of credit cards, licnse etc. below in case you lose walet agn, you big dope. Put copies somewhere safe, 3 places, write down, hide many. You are 80, yes, eighty.

And yet, as we now eavesdropped, Dick Markham dealt with a complaining customer. He sounded practiced, jokey, conversant, exact.

"Dad, you have an unexpected doctor's appointment." I handed Dad his hat. I'd phoned our family physician from Miss Green's extension.

For once, they were ready for us. The nurses kept calling him by name, smiling, overinsistent, as if hinting at answers for a kid about to take his make-or-break college exam. I could see they'd always liked him. In a town this small, they'd maybe heard about his trouble earlier today.

As Dad got ushered in for tests, he glowered accusations back at me as if I had just dragged him to a Nazi medical experiment. He finally reemerged, scarily pale, pressing a bit of gauze into the crook of his bare arm, its long veins the exact blue of Parker's washable ink. They directed him toward the lobby bathroom. They gave him a cup for his urine specimen. He held it before him with two hands like some Magus's treasure.

His hat, briefcase, and overcoat remained behind, resting on an orange plastic chair all their own. Toward these I could display a permissible tenderness. I lightly set my hand on each item. Call it superstition. I now lifted the hat and sniffed it. It smelled like Dad. It smelled like rope. Physical intimacy has never been a possibility. My brother and I, half-drunk, once tried to picture the improbable, the sexual conjunction of our parents. Brother said, "Well, he probably pretends he's at the office, unsealing her like a good manila envelope that requires a rubber stamp — legible, yes, keep it legible, *legible,* now speed-mail!"

I had flipped through four stale magazines before I saw the nurses peeking from their crudely cut window. "He has been quite a while, Mr. Markham. Going on thirty minutes."

"Shall I?" I rose and knocked. No answer. "Would you come stand behind me?" Cowardly, I signaled to an older nurse.

The door proved unlocked. I opened it. I saw one old man aimed the other way and trembling with hesitation. Before him, a white toilet, a white sink, and a white enamel trash can, the three aligned — each its own insistent invitation. In one hand, the old man held an empty specimen cup. In the other hand, his dick.

Turning my way, grateful, unashamed to be caught sobbing, he cried, "Which one, son? Fill which one?"

Forcibly retired, my father lived at home in his pajamas. Mom made him wear the slippers and robe to help with his morale. "Think *Thin Man.* Think William Powell." But the poor guy literally hung his head with shame. That phrase took on new meaning now that his routine and dignity proved so reduced. Dad's mopey presence clogged every outlet she'd perfected to avoid him. The two of them were driving each other crazy.

Lacking the cash for live-in help, she was forced to cut way back on her bridge game and female company. She lost ten pounds — it showed in her neck and face — and then she gave up rouge. You could see Mom missed her fancy friends. I soon pitied her nearly as much as I pitied him — no, more. At least he allowed himself to be distracted. She couldn't forget.

Mom kept urging him to get dressed. She said they needed to go to the zoo. She had to get out and "do" something. One morning, she was trying to force Dad into his dress pants when he struck her. She fell right over the back of an armchair. The whole left side of her head stayed a rubber-stamp pad's blue-black for one whole week. Odd, this made it easier for both of them to stay home. Now two people hung their heads in shame.

At a window overlooking the busy street, Dad would stand staring out, one way. On the window glass, his forehead left a persistent oval of human oil. His pajama knees pressed against the radiator. He silently second-guessed parallel parkers. He studied westerly-moving traffic. Sometimes he'd stand guard there for six uninterrupted hours. Did he await some detained patriotic parade? I pictured poor Green on a passing float — hoisting his coffee mug and the black phone receiver, waving him back down to street level, reality, use.

One December morning, Mom — library book in lap, trying to reinterest herself in Daphne du Maurier, in anything — smelled scorching. Like Campbell's mushroom soup left far too long on simmer. Twice she checked their stove and toaster oven. Finally, around his nap time, she pulled Dad away from the radiator: his shins had cooked. "Didn't it hurt you, Dick? Darling, didn't you ever feel anything?"

Next morning at six-thirty, I got her call. Mom's husky tone sounded too jolly for the hour. She described bandaging both legs. "As you kids say, I don't think this is working for us. This might be beyond me. Integrity's fleabag insurance won't provide him with that good a home. We have just enough to go on living here as usual. Now, I'll maybe shock you and you might find me weak or, worse, disloyal. But would you consider someday checking out some nice retreats or facilities in driving distance? Even if it uses up the savings. Your father is the love of my life — one per customer. I just hate to get any more afraid of him!"

I said I'd phone all good local places, adding, giddy, "I hear they're dying to get in there."

This drew a silence as cold as his. "Your dad's been home from the office — what, seven months? Most men lean toward their leisure years, but who ever hated leisure more than Dick? When I think of everything he gave Integrity and how little he's getting back . . . I'm not strong enough to *keep* him, but I can't bear to *put* him anywhere. Still, at this rate, all I'll want for Christmas is a nice white padded cell for two."

I wished my mother belonged to our generation, where the women work. She could've done anything. And now to be saddled with a man who'd known nothing but enslavement to one so-so office. The workaholic, tabled. He still refused to dress; she focused on the sight of his pajamas. My folks now argued with the energy of newlyweds; then she felt ashamed of herself and he forgot to do whatever he'd just promised.

On Christmas Eve, she was determined to put up a tree for him. But Dad, somehow frightened by the ladder and all the unfamiliar boxes everywhere, got her into such a lethal headlock she had to scream for help. Now the neighbors were involved. People I barely knew interrupted my work hours, saying, "Something's got to be done. It took three of us to pull him off of her. He's still strong as a horse. It's getting dangerous over there. He could escape."

Sometimes, at two in the morning, she'd find him standing in their closet, wearing his p.j.s and the season's correct hat. He'd be looking at his business suits. The right hand would be filing, "walking," back and forth across creased pant legs, as if seeking the . . . exact . . . right . . . pair . . . for . . . the office . . . today.

I tried to keep Miss Green informed. She'd sold her duplex and moved into our town's most stylish old-age home. When she swept downstairs to greet me, I didn't recognize her. "God, you look fifteen years younger." I checked her smile for hints of a possible lift.

She just laughed, giving her torso one mild shimmy. "Look, Ma. No shoulder pads."

Her forties hairdo, with its banked, rolled edges, had softened into pretty little curls around her face. She'd let its color go her natural silvery blond. Green gave me a slow look. If I didn't know her better, I'd have sworn she was flirting.

She appeared shorter in flats. I now understood: her toes had been so mangled by wearing those forties Quonset-huts of high heels, ones she'd probably owned since age eighteen. Her feet had grown, but she'd stayed true to the old shoes, part of some illusion she felt my dad required.

Others in the lobby perked up at her fond greeting; I saw she'd already become the belle of this place. She let me admire her updated charms.

"No." She smiled simply. "It's that I tried to keep it all somewhat familiar for him. How I looked and all. We got to where Mr. Markham found any change a kind of danger, so . . . I mean, it wasn't as if a dozen other suitors were beating down my door. What with Mother being moody and sick that long. And so, day to day, well . . ." She shrugged.

Now, in my life I've had very few inspired ideas. Much of me, like Pop, is helplessly a company man. So forgive my boasting of this.

Leaving Miss Green's, I stopped by a huge Salvation Army store. It was a good one. Over the years, I've found a few fine Federal side chairs here and many a great tweed jacket. Browsing through the used-furniture room, I wandered beneath a cardboard placard hand-lettered "The World of Early American." Ladder-back deacon's chairs and plaid upholstered things rested knee to knee, like sad and separate families.

I chanced to notice a homeless man, asleep, a toothless white fellow. His overcoat looked filthy. His belongings were bunched around him in six rubber-banded shoeboxes. His feet, in paint-stained shoes, rested on an ordinary school administrator's putty-colored desk. "The Wonderful World of Work" hung over hand-me-down waiting rooms still waiting. Business furniture sat parlored — forlorn as any gray-green Irish wake. There was something about the sight of this old guy's midday snoring in so safe a fluorescent make-work cubicle.

Mom now used her sewing room only for those few overnight third cousins willing to endure its lumpy foldout couch. The room had become a catchall, cold storage, since about 1970. We waited for Dad's longest nap of the day. Then, in a crazed burst of energy, we cleared her lair, purging it of boxes, photo albums, four unused exercise machines. I paint-rolled its walls in record time, the ugliest latex junior-high-school green that Sherwin-Williams sells (there's still quite a range). The Salvation Army delivers: within two days, I had arranged this new-used-junk to resemble Integrity's work-space, familiarly anonymous. A gray desk nuzzled one wall — the window wasted behind. Three green file cabinets made a glum herd. One swivel wooden chair rode squeaky casters. The hat rack antlered upright over a dented tin wastebasket. The ashtray looked big enough to serve an entire cancer ward. Wire shelves predicted a neutral "in," a far more optimistic "out." I stuffed desk drawers with Parker ink, cheap fountain pens, yellow legal pads, four dozen paper clips. I'd bought a big black rotary phone, and Mom got him his own line.

Against her wishes, I'd saved most of Dad's old account ledgers. Yellowed already, they could've come from a barrister's desk in a Dickens novel. I scattered "1959–62." In one corner I piled all Dad's boxed records, back taxes, old Christmas cards from custom-ers. The man saved everything.

The evening before we planned introducing him to his new quarters, I disarranged the place a bit. I tossed a dozen pages on the floor near his chair. I left the desk lamp lit all night. It gave this small room a strange hot smell, overworked. The lamp was made of nubbly brown cast metal (recast war surplus?), its red button indi-cating "on." Black meant "off."

That morning I was there to help him dress. Mom made us a hearty oatmeal breakfast, packed his lunch, and snapped the Tupperware insert into his briefcase.

"And where am *I* going?" he asked us in a dead voice.

"To the office," I said. "Where else do you go this time of day?"

He appeared sour, puffy, skeptical. Soon as I could, I glanced at Mom. This was not going to be as easy as we'd hoped.

I got Dad's coat and hat. He looked gray and dubious. He would never believe in this new space if I simply squired him down the hall to it. So, after handing him his briefcase, I led Dad back along our corridor and out onto the street.

Some of the old-timers, recognizing him, called, "Looking good, Mr. Markham," or "Cold enough for you?" Arm in arm, we nodded past them.

My grammar school had been one block from his office. Forty years back, we'd set out on foot like this together. The nearer Dad drew to Integrity, the livelier he became; the closer I got to school, the more withdrawn I acted. But today I kept up a mindless overplentiful patter. My tone neither cheered nor deflected him. One block before his office building, I swerved back down an alley toward the house. As we approached, I saw that Mom had been imaginative enough to leave our front door wide open. She'd removed a bird print that had hung in our foyer hall unloved forever. A mere shape, it still always marked this as our hall, our home.

"*Here* we are!" I threw open his office door. I took his hat and placed it on its hook. I helped him free of his coat. Just as his face had grown bored, then irked, and finally enraged at our deception, the phone rang. From where I stood — half in the office, half in the hall — I could see Mom holding the white phone in the kitchen.

My father paused — since when did he answer the phone? — and, finally, flushed, reached for it himself. "Dick?" Mom said. "You'll hate me, I'm getting so absentminded. But you did take your lunch along today, right? I mean, go check. Be patient with me, okay?" Phone cradled between his head and shoulder, he lifted his briefcase and snapped it open — his efficiency still water-clear, and scary. Dad then said to the receiver, "Lunch is definitely here, per usual. But, honey, haven't I told you about these personal calls at the office?"

Then I saw him bend to pick up scattered pages. I saw him touch one yellow legal pad and start to square all desktop pens at sharp right angles. As he pulled the chair two inches forward I slowly shut his door behind me. Then Mother and I, hidden in the kitchen, held each other and, not expecting it, cried, if very, very silently.

When we peeked in two hours later, he was filing.

Every morning, Sundays included, Dad walked to the office. Even our ruse of walking him around the block was relaxed. Mom simply set a straw hat atop him (after Labor Day, she knew to switch to his gray). With his packed lunch, he would stride nine paces from the kitchen table, step in, and pull the door shut, muttering complaints of overwork, no rest ever.

Dad spent a lot of time on the phone. Long-distance directory-assistance charges constituted a large part of his monthly bill. But he "came home" for supper with the weary sense of blurred accomplishment we recalled from olden times.

Once, having dinner with them, I asked Dad how he was. He sighed. "Well, July is peak for getting their school supplies ordered. So the pressure is on. My heart's not what it was, heart's not completely in it lately, I admit. They downsized Green. Terrible loss to me. With its being crunch season, I get a certain shortness of breath. Suppliers aren't where they were, the gear is often second-rate, little of it any longer American-made. But you keep going, because it's what you know and because your clients count on you. I may be beat, but, hey — it's still a job."

"Aha," I said.

Mom received a call on her own line. It was from some kindergarten owner. Dad — plundering his old red address book — had somehow made himself a go-between, arranging sales, but working freelance now. He appeared to be doing it unsalaried, not for whole school systems but for small local outfits like day care centers. This teacher had to let Mom know that he'd sent too much of the paste. No invoice with it, a pallet of free jarred white school paste waiting out under the swing sets. Whom to thank?

Once, I tiptoed in and saw a long list of figures he kept meaning to add up. I noticed that, in his desperate daily fight to keep his desktop clear, he'd placed seven separate five-inch piles of papers at evened intervals along the far wall. I found such ankle-level filing sad till slowly I recognized a pattern — oh, yeah, "The Pile System." It was my own technique for maintaining provisional emergency order, and one which I now rejudged to be quite sane.

Inked directly into the wooden bottom of his top desk drawer was this:

Check Green's sick leave ridic. long. Nazis still soundly defeated. Double enter all new receipts, nincompoop. Yes, you . . . eighty-one. Old Woman roommate is: "Betty."

Mom felt safe holding bridge parties at the house again, telling friends that Dad was in there writing letters and doing paperwork, and who could say he wasn't? Days, Mom could now shop or attend master-point tournaments at good-driving-distance hotels. In her own little kitchen-corner office, she entered bridge chat rooms, Emailing game-theory arcana to well-known French and Russian players. She'd regained some weight and her face was fuller, and prettier for that. She bought herself a bottle-green velvet suit. "It's just a cheap Chanel knockoff, but these ol' legs still ain't that bad, hmm?" She looked more rested than I'd seen her in a year or two.

I cut a mail slot in Dad's office door, and around eleven Mom would slip in his today's *Wall Street Journal*. You'd hear him fall upon it like a zoo animal, fed.

Since Dad had tried to break down the headhunters' door I hadn't dared go on vacation myself. But Mother encouraged me to take my family to Hawaii. She laughed. "Go ahead, enjoy yourself, for Pete's sake. Everything under control. I'm playing what friends swear is my best bridge ever, and Dick's sure working good long hours again. By now I should know the drill, huh?"

I was just getting into my bathing suit when the hotel phone rang. I could see my wife and son down there on the white beach.

"Honey? Me. There's news about your father."

Mom's voice sounded vexed but contained. Her businesslike tone seemed assigned. It let me understand.

"When?"

"This afternoon around six-thirty our time. Maybe it happened earlier, I don't know. I found him. First I convinced myself he was just asleep. But I guess, even earlier, I knew."

I stood here against glass, on holiday. I pictured my father facedown at his desk. The tie still perfectly knotted, his hat yet safe on its hook. I imagined Dad's head at rest atop those forty pages of figures he kept meaning to add up.

I told Mom I was sorry; I said we'd fly right back.

"No, please," she said. "I've put everything off till next week. It's just us now. Why hurry? And, son? Along with the bad news, I think there's something good. He died at the office."

Blind Jozef Pronek

FROM THE NEW YORKER

FROM THE AIR, Chicago in the snow looked like a frosted computer-chip board, the cars moving serenely across it like bytes between chips. As the plane was circling, it hit some turbulence, and the orange juice Pronek had been drinking jumped out of its plastic cup and landed on his beige pants. Only once he'd landed and unbuckled his seat belt did Pronek realize that the juice had left behind a stain with the subtle hue of urine. Andrea was waiting for him at the exit. He pointed to the stain and made a joke about his bladder and the wretched refuse it contained. Andrea didn't laugh. She offered him her right cheek and the upper body attached to it, while keeping her lower body a couple of feet away, as if she were worried about what might happen if their pelvises made contact.

They stood on the moving walkway, gliding through a dark tunnel as a synthetic female voice warbled a warning against leaving baggage unattended.

Pronek tried to be charming. "If the thing that takes you up is escalator, is this levelator?" he asked.

"Yeah, right," Andrea said, digging through her purse and excavating a banana.

Pronek had met her the summer before, in Ukraine. It was 1991, and they had roamed through Kiev together, flirting during the putsch. They had held hands in front of the Ukrainian Parliament as it declared independence, while everyone around them waved flags and blushed with patriotic excitement. Andrea had had a British boyfriend, who wore a pink headband at all times and spent every night optimistically scouring Kiev for a rave — and never finding one. He worked as a cameraman for the BBC, and on the day independence was declared he was — bless his heart — very busy. So Andrea and Pronek walked to the Dnieper and, for a couple of dollars, bought a Red Army officer's hat and a nicked leather belt. They ate a Frisbee-sized pizza with carrot-and-beet topping and watched the river glittering with the scattered stars of dead fish. Pronek explored the inside of Andrea's thighs, never getting past the panty line, as the tips of their tongues collided clumsily. In a fit of inexplicable giddiness, Pronek panted a Sinatra song in her ear: *"Eye praktis ehvree day to faind sum klehvr lains to say, too maik da meenin cum truh . . ."* It was one of the songs that his blues band, Blind Jozef Pronek & Dead Souls, played in Sarajevo, where — he claimed — they were popular. Miraculously, she found it endearing. But the next day she left for Kharkiv with the cameraman.

After Pronek returned to Sarajevo, he wrote her love letters that were full of auburn autumn leaves and reminiscences about the time (a total of fifty-three hours) they had spent together. In reply, she said that she missed him and wanted to see him again — a desire that was driven, Pronek thought, by the unlikelihood of its being fulfilled. They began to rewrite the time they had spent together: she remembered drinking sweet wine, although in Kiev they had drunk only infernal vodka. He recalled her fragrant perfume, although they had both been in a perpetual sweat in a city where the water pressure was perennially too low to bathe. With titillating intensity, they remembered dancing cheek to cheek, when in reality they had trotted idiotically to the rhythm of anachronistic German disco, as hirsute Ukrainian men swarmed around Andrea and tried to rub their perspiring bodies against hers. Once they had forged a sufficient number of counterfeit memories, she invited him to Chicago, perhaps prompted by a news report about the war in Croatia and "tensions" in Bosnia. It had been a generous invitation, and neither of them had imagined that Pronek would ever be able to accept it. But then he received an official invitation to visit the United States in the capacity of a freedom-loving writer, and he added Chicago to his itinerary.

She looked different from how he remembered her: she was paler, her hair was shorter and darker, and she wore a silver nose ring. But he still longed to touch her.

As they approached the city, the skyline was flat against the blank sky, like the bottom of a Tetris screen. Andrea drove through what she called the Loop, pointing at each skyscraper and announcing its function. It was all gibberish to Pronek: the Board of Trade, the tallest building in the world, the biggest something, the busiest something else. He rolled down the window and looked up, but he couldn't see the tops of the buildings.

"This is how cockroach sees furniture in apartment," he said.

"I'm sure," Andrea said, turning on the radio.

She unlocked her apartment door (a sign on it read "VIOLA-TORS WILL BE TOWED"), and a pungent wave of smoke and French fries filled Pronek's nostrils.

"My roommate is a slob," she said. Pronek panned the room: a sofa with stuffing hatching from its cushions, a stereo, and a TV stacked with CDs and videos. There was a small table, its surface buried under McDonald's bags, crushed cigarette packages, and ashtrays brimming with butts and ashes. The window looked out on a brick wall. A porcine black cat glanced at Pronek and then turned away. On the kitchen table was a throng of beer bottles with their labels torn off, huddled together as if awaiting execution. The sink was filled with dishes submerged in a murky liquid.

"Who is your roommate?" Pronek asked.

"He's my boyfriend," Andrea said. "But we have separate bed-rooms."

"How long have you been together?"

"On and off, about ten years. But I hate the fucker. I think I wanna break up."

"He knows about me?"

"Oh yeah, sure. I told him you were coming. He doesn't give a fuck."

She handed him a cup of coffee across the table covered with greasy film. He wanted to touch her cheeks, and the shimmering gossamer on the nape of her neck. He was mesmerized by her lips, which barely touched each other as she uttered her *b*'s and *m*'s, and her teeth flashing as she formed her fricatives. Then he carried his two suitcases to her bedroom, where her bras hung, like rabbit skins, from doorknobs.

That night, they made love. Before they did, Andrea unrolled a scroll of condoms and made him wear one. "This is the nineties," she said. "People can only touch each other if they wear rubber gloves." As they ground the sheets and the bed creaked enthusiastically, Andrea kept asking, "Isn't this good? Do you like this? Isn't this great?" Then she went to the bathroom. Her silhouette against the light, Pronek realized, was gorgeous.

When she came back in, smelling of banana shampoo, he disrobed his penis, got up, and kissed her wet hair on his way out of the room, the condom dangling from his hand. But as he was about to enter the bathroom the door opened and a man came out. Pronek stood there, in front of him, nude and suddenly very aware of his hairless chest.

"Hi," Pronek said.

"How're you doing?" the man answered.

"Good."

"Good."

Silence.

"Who are you?"

"I am Andrea's friend."

"I'm Carwin," he said. He was fashionably unshaved and had unruly hair. He wore an unbuttoned flannel shirt and a T-shirt with a picture of a crucified blond angel on it. "Are you Russian?"

Pronek's feet were cold, so he put his left sole on his right calf, and stood there like a Masai warrior — except that he was holding a used condom instead of a spear.

"No, I'm from Sarajevo, Bosnia," he said. "But we met in Ukraine."

"Well, it's nice to meet you," he said. "I hope I never see your fucking face again." Then he yelled toward Andrea's room, "Now you bring in fucking foreigners. American dick isn't good enough for you, you fucking bitch."

"Fuck you, you fucking Anglo asshole!" she yelled back.

Pronek finally slipped into the bathroom. He dropped the condom into the toilet, but every time he flushed it came back up, bobbing defiantly. He looked in the mirror and saw vermillion pimples on his face, sallow teeth, and a square Slavic head with greasy hair that stuck to his low forehead. He recognized himself as a foreigner — an unseemly, uncouth body with nowhere to go. Then he shaved and washed, as if celebrating his new identity.

Andrea was an artist. She showed Pronek her most recent painting, a self-portrait with a hog and a sow, entitled "Home." In the painting, Andrea's arms were slung around the hams of both pigs. All three figures were staring at Pronek. The pigs were adamantly pink, and the sow had swollen teats. Andrea told him that she'd painted it two years before and hadn't done anything since. "There are things I need to understand about myself before I can share them with other people," she said.

Andrea worked in the gift shop at the Art Institute of Chicago. Every morning, she would lurch upright in bed — the way women in horror movies wake from a nightmare just before the killer comes in to slash them — then light a cigarette. She smoked with a curious intensity: she'd inhale with small, furious gasps and exhale with a low, burdened sigh, while keeping her right elbow wedged into the palm of her left hand, the cigarette always in close proximity to her mouth. Then she would whistle. Pronek, half-asleep, would hear the bustle of her picking through the wardrobe and the rustle of her rolling stockings. He'd try to recognize the song she was whistling, but would sink back into sleep before he could.

When Pronek finally got up, a couple of hours later, he'd follow her scent to the bathroom, where the bathtub still displayed the curled vestiges of her hair. Having performed his toilet duties, he'd salvage a plate from the dish swamp and eat some limp mozzarella with crackers. He'd sip coffee from a cup that had lipstick scars on the brim and he'd try to write to his parents in Sarajevo. He could never get beyond the place and date — which seemed, to him, self-explanatory. He wanted to call them instead, but he had no money to pay for a call. On the news, he saw barricades, people running in panic, and white armored vehicles parked in the middle of a Sarajevo street.

Most days, he met Andrea for lunch, walking to the museum along the Magnificent Mile — which made him think of *The Magnificent Seven,* then of *The Seven Samurai,* though there was nothing magnificent about the morguelike buildings and the lugubrious mile or about the marble-faced people who walked along it, clutching their purses and briefcases. As he trudged through the April slush, he realized just how superfluous he was, how everything would be exactly the same if the space his body occupied at that moment were empty. When he later shared this thought with Andrea, she said, with a nasty giggle, "The land of the free, the home of the brave."

Pronek would wait for Andrea to take her lunch break, then

they'd drift together through the museum, following a battalion of high school kids, predominantly blond and obese ("Corn-fed," Andrea whispered), who heehawed in front of naked-lady pictures. Pronek tried to sound cultured and civilized and made the most of the two hours he had once spent in the Louvre, much of it lost in a nightmarish eighteenth-century wing.

Andrea's favorite painting was huge and completely black — black wrinkles, black smudges, black puckered paint. Pronek didn't know why he liked it, but he did. They'd gawk at it for a while, then Andrea would say, "Who are we in the hands of an angry God?"

One afternoon, Andrea accompanied Pronek to the coat check. "How can you ever know that you're getting right coat?" he asked.

"Because you have a number," Andrea said.

"But I think maybe they're going through your pockets, photographing what's in there, making copies of keys, and changing everything, so when you get out and put your coat on your memories don't look right."

Andrea shrugged. "You Eastern Europeans are weird," she said.

When Pronek got home, Carwin was there, watching television. He leaped off the couch — probably interrupted while masturbating — and headed for his room. Pronek changed the channel from "The Dukes of Hazzard" to CNN and saw a crowd of people in front of the Parliament building in Sarajevo, cowering or running for cover. There was a quick shot of two feet, one with a sneaker, one bare, both twitching. The rest of the body was obscured by people trying to help, some of them crying and wiping their cheeks with bloody hands.

Pronek decided that he would stay in the United States, possibly for the rest of his life, on a snowy night, after Carwin had dropped a pot of spaghetti sauce on the floor and yelled "Fuck!" Pronek woke up from a nightmare with his heart pounding. Through the open door, he could see that Carwin was trying to clean up the sauce but was instead spreading it, like red paint, all over the floor. It looked like blood, and Pronek imagined himself lying on that floor, with his brains slowly leaking out, feeling nothing but a tingling dizziness. Carwin, having pensively scratched his crotch, decided to abandon the cleanup effort, said "Fuck!" again to seal the decision, then stomped off to the couch to watch TV.

The next morning, Pronek woke up ill, with his forehead and the nape of his neck throbbing. Andrea was gone. He heard the TV but couldn't get up, so he closed his eyes again and floated in and out of listless dreams. Andrea came home after work, made some tea, gave him a bowl of Wheaties floating in glistening milk, kissed his hot forehead, and then went off to a gallery opening. She didn't come back that night, and Pronek was still sweating when he woke up the next morning, the sheets stuck to his febrile body. He didn't know how long he stayed in bed — intermittent kisses, tepid cups of tea, and waking up in cold, damp sheets all merged into one long repetitive action, like a busy signal. He did remember the wind banging impatiently at the window and a choir of electronic voices shrieking "Touchdown!" And he had a dim recollection of calling his parents: his father telling him that it would be unwise to come home now and his mother saying that there had been less shooting today than yesterday.

Eventually, he gathered his energy and found Carwin and his buddies gathered around the TV, which was showing a porn movie. Pronek took a while to recognize a gaping vagina. But they weren't watching it; they were engaged in a game that involved throwing a hackysack at a revolving ceiling fan. Andrea needed a break, Carwin said, and had gone to De Kalb for a couple of weeks. After the porn movie had ended in a moment of collective ecstasy, Pronek took hold of the remote and found "Headline News." Paramilitary units had entered Bosnia from Serbia, it said, and had "committed atrocities."

"What's with you people?" a guy in a Bears hat asked. "Why can't you just chill out?"

"Aren't you going back?" Carwin asked.

"I'm supposed to go back in couple of weeks," Pronek said.

"Why don't you stay here?" the guy with the hat asked.

"What can I do here?" Pronek said. "My parents are there."

"Man, I hope I never see my fuckin' parents again," Carwin said.

"You should stay and get your family out and let those fuckers kill each other if they want," the Bears man said. "I mean, fuck, war is good. If we didn't have war, there would be way too many people, man. It's like natural selection, like free market. The best get on top, the shit sinks. I don't know much about you, Ruskie, but if you got here you must be worth something. It's like those immigrants, man. They were shit at home, they got here, they became fucking millionaires. That's why we're the toughest motherfucking country in the world. Because only the fittest survive here."

Carwin was sucking on a McDonald's straw, watching the news about the Bulls. "Man," he said, "we're gonna kick ass again this year."

Andrea returned from De Kalb refreshed, and informed Pronek that they were going to her parents' house for dinner. She whistled "Dear Prudence" on the way there, and after they had listened to a news break about the imminent war in Bosnia, she said, "You should stay, you know."

"I know," Pronek said.

The streetlights were glaringly bright in the frigid northern wind. They drove past the dark castles of the University of Chicago and entered a maze of identical red brick buildings.

Andrea's father shook Pronek's hand vigorously, and her mother said, "We've heard so much about you." They introduced him to an old woman, bent over a walker, gripping its handles as if she were delivering a speech from a pulpit.

"Nana," Andrea's mother said, "this is Andrea's friend from Bosnia."

"I never was in Boston," Nana said.

"Bosnia, Nana, Bosnia. Near Czechoslovakia," Andrea's mother said, shaking her head and waving her hands as if pushing away a basketball. In a moment of confusion, Pronek took off his shoes. Andrea's mother glanced at his feet, and said, "We don't take our shoes off here, but it's all right," then pointed left, and said, "Let's move to the salon."

They sat at a round table, and Andrea's father filled their wineglasses. He loomed over Pronek with the green bottle in his hand, waiting for him to try the wine. Pronek sipped cautiously, and the glass clinked against his teeth. He said, "It's good. Little sweet."

"Well, it's a Chardonnay," Andrea's father said, delighted.

"I want some wine," Nana said.

"You know it's not good for you, Nana," Andrea's mother said.

"What kind of wine do you have back home?" Andrea's father asked, tilting his head to the left to signal intense interest.

"I don't know," Pronek said. "Local kinds."

"Andrea told us you were a writer," Andrea's mother said. She had glasses and a pearl choker and her teeth were white and orderly.

"I was," Pronek said.

"We like good writing," Andrea's mother said.

"Have you ever read Richard Ford?" Andrea's father asked.

"Sensitive middle-class macho shit," Andrea snapped.

"Very well written," Andrea's father said, shaking his head. "Very well written."

Andrea's mother served a sequence of foods unknown to Pronek, ending with blackberry nonfat cheesecake with low-fat kiwi frozen yogurt and French hazelnut-vanilla decaf coffee. Pronek sensed that his feet were about to begin exuding a stench, so he covered his left toes with his right foot. He was convinced that he should move as little as possible, lest unnecessary motion release molecules of body odor. Nana sat across the table from him, smacking her lips and wiggling her jaw, and they could all hear her dentures clacking. She loaded her mouth and chewed patiently, looking around with weary uninterest. Her face was a map of valleys and furrows, cheekbones protruding like mountains. She had a dim blue number tattooed on her right arm.

"What's going on in Czechoslovakia?" Andrea's mother asked.

"Yugoslavia, Mom, Yugoslavia," Andrea said.

"I read about it. I tried to understand it, but I simply can't," Andrea's father said. "Thousands of years of hatred, I guess."

"It's a sad saga," Andrea's mother said.

"Mind-boggling," Andrea's father said. "I hope it'll be over before we have to get involved."

"Where is Bruno?" Nana hollered suddenly. "Bruno, come here!"

"Calm down, Nana. Bruno's gone," Andrea's mother said.

"Come here, Bruno!" Nana yelled toward the kitchen. "Eat with us! We have everything now!"

"Calm down, Nana, or you'll have to go to your room," Andrea's father said sternly and turned to Pronek. "She can be rather obstreperous sometimes."

Pronek didn't know what "obstreperous" meant. "It's okay," he said. "No problem."

While Pronek was putting on his shoes, Andrea's father held out his coat.

"You should dry-clean it," he said.

Andrea's mother pressed her cheek, soft and redolent of coconut, against Pronek's cheek and kissed the air around his ear.

"Are you going to see Bruno?" Nana asked.

"No, Nana," Pronek said. "I am sorry."

"It was nice having you," Andrea's father said, shaking his hand. "I'm sure you'll do fine if you stay here. This is the greatest country in the world. You just have to work hard."

Pronek hated hard work, but he needed a job. He got up and put on his best attire: a gray silk shirt, smuggled from China by a family friend, which had an amoeba-shaped grease spot just above the left nipple; his stained beige pants; a tie with a Mickey Mouse pattern that belonged to Carwin; and an orange jacket, also lent by Carwin, who hadn't worn it in years, one size too small.

The streets in downtown Chicago were named after deceased presidents, and Pronek imagined the presidents building the city, gathered around a Monopoly board in Heaven (or Hell). He headed east down Jackson, then north toward Madison, until he reached the Boudin Sourdough Bakery.

A woman, labeled Dawn Wyman by a steel nametag, was waiting for him. Her eyelids were efficiently blue and she had earrings shaped like eyeballs, glaring at him.

"Where are you from?" Dawn asked.

"Bosnia," Pronek said.

"That's in Russia, right?"

"It was in Yugoslavia."

"Right. Well, tell me why you'd like to work for us."

A man in a white cowboy hat was sitting in a corner spooning brown sludge into his mouth, under a picture of the first Boudin Bakery, established in San Francisco in the black-and-white era.

"I like European touch here," Pronek said.

"Right," Dawn said, and smiled. There was a trace of lipstick on her white teeth. "We like to provide something different for the customer with sophisticated taste and international experience."

"Right," Pronek said.

"What do you think you can offer to the Boudin Sourdough Bakery?"

"I am hard worker and I like to work with people. I used to be journalist and communicated very much. I can offer life experience," he said.

"Right," Dawn said, and yawned, looking at the application. "What do you expect your wage to be?"

"I don't know. Ten dollars for hour."

"We can offer you five, and maybe you can work your way up. Here everyone has a fair chance."

"Right," Pronek said.

On his first day, he cut open croissants, spread Dijon mustard inside them, and then slid them over to the sandwich person. ("This is the sandwich person. This is the kitchen help" was how Dawn introduced them.) He nearly sliced off his left thumb and passed along a sequence of blood-soaked croissants. Then he cut tomatoes into thin slices for the sandwich person to insert into the abdomens of the croissants. He sprinkled cheese crumbles over a platoon of mini-pizzas and filled plastic-foam bowls with reduced-sodium, fat-free Cajun gumbo soup and passed them to the soup person. ("Small bowl — large gumbo. Big bowl — jumbo gumbo" was how Dawn explained the gumbo situation.) He cut the tops off sourdough loaves and disemboweled them, throwing the soft, yeast-smelling viscera into a garbage can before filling the hollow with reduced-fat chili. The first day, he ate a lot of dough instead of throwing it out and suffered gut-wrenching cramps as a punishment.

The first time he went to the large, safelike refrigerator to get a head of lettuce, the door slowly closed behind him, and he found himself alone in an immutable frozen hum lit by a solitary dim bulb. He started pounding on the door, yelling for help, but no one heard him. He pressed his head against the door in desperation and his forehead stuck to the icy surface. He tried to peel it off but it was too painful and he was overcome by fatalistic resignation. When Dawn opened the door, he stumbled out, pulled forward by the door, and then stood in front of her with a red mark across his forehead.

"What are you doing?" she asked.

"I was closed there," Pronek said.

"You can open the door from the inside — you just have to push it a little," she said.

"Oh, I know," Pronek said.

By the end of the first week, Pronek was in charge of garbage disposal. He emptied abandoned trays with hollowed-out loaves, mauled croissants, and desiccated bowls, and then pulled out the loaded garbage bags and dragged them off, like corpses, to a nook in the kitchen.

Pronek rode the El back to Andrea's apartment in a car full of exhausted, sweaty people bunched together like asparagus stalks. Andrea had gone to Ukraine — "I need some space to think," she had told Pronek, "but you can stay here" — and the apartment was being renovated, so that Andrea's parents could sell it. Carwin had moved out and was living in Lincoln Park, so when Pronek came home there were only four Polish construction workers waiting for him, stripping paint off walls, ripping out doorposts, and digging up floor tiles. There was a nylon path leading to Andrea's room, held down by paint cans and obscure tools.

The bedroom looked like a monk's cell: a bed and a little tower of books, his empty suitcases, the TV, and a mound of dirty, decaying clothes. Pronek entered it as if boarding a submarine that would carry him to a placid ocean floor, glimmering plankton and evanescent protozoa floating slowly past his window in mesmerizing silence. He lay there until the workers were gone, and then slurped tomato soup in bed, watching "Headline News": Sarajevo was besieged, there was a severe shortage of food, and there were rumors of Serb death camps. He watched to see if he could recognize anyone. Once he thought he saw his father running down Sniper's Alley, covering his head with a newspaper.

The day Pronek got fired, he saw a picture on the cover of *Time* of a man in a Serb death camp: the man was standing behind three lines of barbed wire — his skin stretched across his rib cage — and he was careful not to look directly at the camera, as if he didn't know whether it would save his life or get him killed. Pronek mumbled his way to his locker at the Boudin Bakery, a surge of heat pressing up behind his eyes. He put on his cherry-red Boudin Bakery apron and beret and went to empty the trays.

As he was piling them on top of the trash can, he was beckoned by a man wearing a grass green shirt with a little golfer swinging a golf club over his heart.

Pronek walked over to the man's table and stood there. The man had immaculately combed blond hair and a monstrous gold ring on his pinkie. He pointed at the croissant on his plate.

"I wanted romaine lettuce on my Turkey Dijon. This is iceberg lettuce." Pronek said nothing. "Well, what do you have to say about that?"

Pronek was about to go tell the sandwich person about the problem, but for some reason he stopped. He said, "Nothing."

"I'd like my Turkey Dijon with romaine lettuce, please," the man said.

"What's difference?" Pronek said.

"Excuse me?" the man raised his voice, his double chin corrugated in disbelief.

"Romaine lettuce, iceberg lettuce, what's difference?" Pronek said.

"May I talk to someone who can speak English, please?" the man said, and pushed his tray away with resolve. Pronek felt pain climbing up his calves, passing through his pelvis, and settling in his stomach as a cramp. He wanted to say something, something clever and devastating, but could not think of any English words that would convey the magnitude of the absurdity, other than "Romaine lettuce, iceberg lettuce, what's difference?" He kept muttering it and wobbled away in the vain hope that the man might just give up. But the man did not give up, and when Dawn walked over to him with the man in tow Pronek had to listen while he ranted. When he finally stopped, Pronek whimpered, "Romaine, iceberg, all same."

"I'm sorry," Dawn said. "But we have to let you go."

"I go," Pronek said. "No problem. I go."

In the spring of 1993, Pronek discovered, after a complicated series of transactions, involving a Red Cross worker in Sarajevo, a radio operator, a cousin living in France, and Zbisiek, one of the Polish construction workers, who happened to answer the phone, that his parents were on the list for a convoy that would soon leave the city.

"When?" Pronek asked Zbisiek, whose blue eyes, framed by ruptured blood vessels, were moist with Slavic compassion.

"He didn't said it," Zbisiek said.

It was only then that Pronek began to fear for his parents' lives. Suddenly he realized that death was the cessation of life. He watched CNN and saw people with familiar faces crawling in their own blood, begging the camera for help, their stumps spurting.

Sometimes, the people who were trying to help them were cut down by sniper fire. Pronek understood that what those people had been doing before that moment — whatever it was — would never continue. Even their suffering would end.

He devoured Snickers and Baby Ruths, followed by bags of Cheerios and Doritos, and he gained weight. He panicked as he walked down the street and realized that he didn't know the names of the trees and flowers around him — they were blank pages in a photo album from which the pictures had been removed. He forced himself to look down at the ground instead: concrete cracks, flat cigarette butts, broken twigs. He wished he were blind. He suffered through an interminable sinus infection. He started mumbling to himself, giggling and growling in response to his own inaudible discourse.

He slept among paint cans, in a noxious mist. The Poles seemed to think he had lost his mind and gave him thirty-three dollars they had collected among themselves. He worked as a parking assistant in a lot near Wrigley Field, revolving his arm like a windmill on game days, until he had a painful epiphany about the absurdity of the job and quit. He began to think of himself as someone else entirely — a cartoon character, a dog, a detective. He stopped desiring women and devoted his sexual life to detached masturbation, not even bothering to fantasize. Afterward, he took long showers, trying to clean himself, then ended them suddenly when he remembered the water shortages in Sarajevo. He was convinced that he stank and that people walked around him on the street and avoided sitting next to him on the El.

In September, Andrea's father appeared and solemnly informed Pronek that he would soon have to leave the apartment because it had been sold to a distinguished Realtor and they had to finish it as soon as possible. Pronek watched the Poles shrugging their shoulders benevolently behind Andrea's father's back and, numb with despair, announced that he was currently unemployed. Andrea's father told him that his wife ran a cleaning agency called Home Clean Home and offered to help him find a job there.

Pronek had a delightful interview with Andrea's mother. "I know you're a hard worker," she said. "It is people like you who built this great country for us." She patted him on the back and sent him off to the agency supervisor, Stephen Rhee, an ex-marine who promptly informed Pronek that there would be no screwing around with him. He had a crewcut and a bushy mole on his cheek that looked from afar like a tiny bullet wound.

"Dust is our mortal enemy, vacuum cleaners are our AK-47s," Rhee announced as he showed Pronek his locker, which smelled of someone else's sweat.

As a novice, Pronek became a bathroom cleaner, "the shit boy." He cleaned slowly, mercilessly effacing all trace of human life. He grew to like doing it; it stopped him from thinking. He focused instead on stains and hairs, enjoying their steady and inevitable disappearance. His world was reduced to a pimple-pus speck on a mirror which could be quickly wiped away. When he had finished cleaning, he'd emerge from the sparkling bathroom purified, as if his self had changed profoundly while it was away from him.

In this manner, he became a true professional, and his wage rose from $6.oo an hour to $6.50. He had soon earned enough to move to a furnitureless studio apartment in West Rogers Park. Pronek went through all this in an aching daze, occasionally interrupted by involuntary memories. The smell of chlorine brought back his days of cleaning toilets in the army. When he scrubbed burned grease off a stove, he'd recall walking through Bascarsija, where kebab shops spewed barbecue smoke. Breathing the dust raised by his vacuum cleaner, he remembered how, on Saturday mornings, his mother would make him crawl under the bed to reach the clusters of lint that had gathered against the wall. The lead-and-wood scent of pencil shavings in a wastebasket reminded him of the pencils he had shared with Mirza, his best friend in grammar school.

Eventually, Rhee allowed him to go on solo missions, cleaning Lincoln Park or Gold Coast condos by himself. He liked entering those apartments, where the scent of shower gel and deodorant lingered, and dusting the Ansel Adams photographs of vapid gray deserts and the family pictures on the piano, vacuuming the rugs that stretched across floors like lazy cats, and browsing through the bookshelves filled with titles like *Seven Spiritual Laws of Growth, What's Inside — A User's Guide to the Soul, Investing Today,* and *The Client.* He developed a healthy stable of steady customers, who never saw him but regularly left tips for him under the fruit bowl or on the coffee table.

Sometimes after he had finished cleaning, Pronek would sit in an armchair and imagine his life in that particular condo. He saw himself walking through the door, checking the abundant stack of mail; he'd head for the tall bottle of Scotch and pour himself a generous drink; he'd check the messages — "Hi! Um, this is Andrea, returning your call. . . . Um, I guess I can squeeze you in next Tuesday. . . . I kind of like Italian food, I guess." He'd saunter to the closet, still sipping his drink, and hang up his navy blue jacket; he'd turn on the TV and watch the end of a Bulls game before deciding to drive up to White Pigeon, Michigan, to visit his parents, who he knew would just annoy the hell out of him; then he'd put on some blues ("I'd Rather Go Blind Than See You Walk Away from Me") and slowly drink until he passed out.

Each morning, Pronek would sit on the only chair he owned and eat cereal out of a bowl on his knees while watching a sunbeam climb through the window like a curious squirrel. Every day, he would leave for work at the same time, with a Wonder-bread-and-bologna sandwich, then ride the same clattering train home. Every evening, he'd enter his apartment and wait for a moment before turning on the light, giving the cockroaches a chance to reach a dark corner. He'd check the roach motel, where yesterday's dried-up roach hung from the ceiling and today's was still alive, stuck in sweet glue. "Honey," he'd say, "I'm home."

For months, he watched the same images, which alternated with optimistic car commercials: shots of Karadzic and Milosevic shaking hands; of men with shaved heads walking in long sad columns, escorted by men wearing black ski masks and carrying rifles; of a man waving at a bus, while a woman leaning on the bus's filthy window waved back. Eventually, Pronek would turn off the TV and lie staring at the ceiling fan as it revolved slowly, like an exhausted dragonfly.

And as long as each day was like any other day his life had not ceased. His parents were still alive; they were waiting to get on the convoy, which would leave the city soon and move forward without stopping, until it reached its destination.

KATHLEEN HILL

The Anointed

FROM DOUBLETAKE

My harp is turned to mourning.
And my flute to the voice of those who weep.
   — Job 30:31

One

IN MISS HUGHES'S seventh-grade music class, we were expected
to sit without moving finger or foot while she played for us what she
called "the music of the anointed." At a moment known only to
herself, Miss Hughes opened the album of records ready at her elbow and, tipping her head from side to side, cautiously turned the
leaves as if they had been the pages of a precious book. When she
had found the seventy-eight she was looking for, she drew it from its
jacket and placed it on the spinning turntable. But before lowering
the needle she took a moment to see that we were sitting as she had
instructed: backs straight, feet on the floor, hands resting on our
darkly initialed wooden desktops.

While the record was playing, Miss Hughes's face fell into a
mask, her mouth drooping at the corners. A small woman in high
heels, she stood at attention, hands clasped at her waist, shiny
red nails bright against her knuckles. She wasn't young, but we
couldn't see that she was in any way old. The dress she wore was
close-fitting. Often it was adorned by a scarf, but not the haphazard
affair some of our teachers attempted. Miss Hughes's scarf was chosen with care, a splash of blue or vermilion to enliven a somber day,

and was generous enough to allow for a large, elegant loop tied between her breasts.

Most of us had turned twelve that year and were newly assembled at the high school. The spring before we had graduated from one or another of our town's four elementary schools, where we had stooped to water fountains and drawn time charts on brown paper. Now we watched with furtive interest while the juniors and seniors parked their cars with a single deft twist of the steering wheel. This was the grown-up world we had been waiting for, fervently and secretly, but once here most of us knew we had still a long way to travel. Our limbs were ungainly, ridiculous. We twitched in our seats; our elbows and knees, scratched and scabbed, behaved like children's. We knew we couldn't lounge at our lockers with the proper air of unconcern, nor did we suppose we could sit upright and motionless for the duration of the "Hallelujah Chorus" from Handel's *Messiah* or a Beethoven sonata. Yet under Miss Hughes's surveillance, we learned to do so. If the grind of a chair's legs or a sigh reached her ears, Miss Hughes carefully lifted the needle from the spinning record and, staring vaguely into space, showing no sign that she recognized the source of the disturbance, waited until the room was silent before beginning again.

In other classes we doodled in our notebooks, drawing caricatures of our teachers, words streaming from their mouths in balloons. Small pink erasers flew through the air. On the Monday morning following a stormy bout with us on Friday, Mrs. Trevelyan, our math teacher, was tearful. "My weekend was ruined," she told us. "It troubles me very much when we don't get along together. Surely we can do better, can't we? If we make a little effort?" We looked at her with stony eyes. To our social studies teacher, Miss Guthrie, we were deliberately cruel. Her voice was high, her mouth was tense, and often when she spoke a tiny thread of spittle hung between her lips. If someone answered a question in a strangled voice, mimicking her, she pretended not to notice.

Miss Hughes neither cajoled nor ignored us. Instead she made us her confidants. Music class met on Friday afternoons and through the windows the dusty autumn sunlight fell in long strips across our backs and onto the wooden floor. Behind us, flecked with high points of light, trees lined one end of the playing field. It was hard to tell, turning to look after a record had wound to its

end, if the sun were striking to gold a cluster of leaves still green
and summery or if a nighttime chill had done it.

The class always followed the same turn: first, Miss Hughes dictated to us what she called "background," pausing long enough for
us to take down what she said in the notebooks we kept specially for
her class, or for her to write on the blackboard a word we might not
know how to spell. *To what class of stringed instruments does the pianoforte belong?* we wrote. *The pianoforte belongs to the dulcimer class of
stringed instruments.* Or: *Name several forerunners of the pianoforte. Several forerunners of the pianoforte are the clavichord, the virginal, the harpsichord, the spinet.* If giggles rose involuntarily in our throats at the
word "virginal," we managed to suppress them.

Following dictation, which she delivered without comment or
explanation, she would ask us to assume our "postures." We had already written down the name of the piece we were about to hear, its
composer, and usually some fact having to do with its performance
— on *the harpsichord, the third movement of Mozart's Sonata in A Major,
otherwise known as the "Turkish March," played by Wanda Landowska.*
After Miss Hughes had set the needle on its course, we were for the
moment alone with ourselves, a fact we were given to understand
by the face wiped clean of all expression she held before us. We
were then free to think of whatever we liked: a nightmare we had
almost forgotten from the night before; a dog shaking water from
its back, the drops flying everywhere like rain; a plan we had made
with a friend for the weekend. Or we were free simply to watch the
dust floating in the shafts of sunlight, to follow a path the sounds
led us up and down.

We marveled that Miss Hughes always knew exactly when to turn
and lift the needle, that she knew without looking when the record
was almost over. After she had replaced the arm in its clasp, she
turned her full attention to us. "You have just heard, boys and girls,
in the 'Turkish March,' a great virtuoso performance. What do I
mean by 'virtuoso'? A virtuoso performance is one executed by an
instrumentalist highly skilled in the practice of his art, one who
is able to bring to our ears music that we would otherwise go to
our graves without hearing. The first great virtuosi pianists were
Liszt and the incomparable Chopin, both of whom you will meet in
due course.

"In fact, boys and girls," she said, lowering her voice a little so that we had to lean forward to hear, "we have our own virtuosi pianists, ones who regularly perform close by in New York City, only a half hour's ride away on the train. You have heard the name Artur Rubinstein, perhaps? You have heard the name Myra Hess? These are artists whose work you must do everything in your power to appreciate firsthand. We go to sleep at night, we wake in the morning, we blink twice and our lives are over. But what do we know if we do not attend?"

Miss Hughes suddenly held up her two hands in front of us, red fingernails flashing. "You will see, boys and girls, I have a fine breadth of palm. My fingers are not as long as they might be, but I am able to span more than an octave with ease. Perhaps you do not find that remarkable. But I assure you that for a woman a palm of this breadth is rare. I had once a great desire to become a concert pianist myself. A very great desire. And I had been admitted to study at Juilliard with a teacher of renown. A teacher, Carl Freidburg, who in his youth in Frankfurt had been the student of Clara Schumann. Who had heard Liszt interpret his own compositions. When I went for my audition, when I entered the room where the piano was waiting and Mr. Freidburg was sitting nearby, I was afraid. I do not hide that from you, boys and girls. I was very much afraid. But as soon as I began to play Chopin's Polonaise in A-flat, a piece that requires much busy fingerwork by the left hand and a strong command of chords, I was so carried away by the fire of the music that I forgot the teacher. I forgot the audition. I forgot everything except the fact that I was now the servant of something larger than myself. When I reached the end and looked up — and I was in a bit of a daze, I may tell you — the great teacher's eyes were closed. He bowed his head once, very simply. That was all. I left the room. Soon afterward I received a letter assuring me that he would be proud to have me for his student."

Miss Hughes's face had registered the sweep of feelings she was recounting to us. Her eyes had narrowed with her great desire to be a pianist; entering the audition room, her jaw had grown rigid with fear; and while the great teacher had sat listening to her play, her face had assumed the look we were familiar with, the mask. Now her dark eyes took on a dreamy expression we had not yet seen. She seemed to be looking for words in a place that absorbed all her attention, over our heads, out the window, beyond.

"It was that winter, boys and girls, that my destiny revealed itself to me. If it were not too dramatic to put it this way, I would say that my fate was sealed. Everything I had hoped for, worked for, practicing seven hours each day after I had finished giving lessons — everything was snatched away in a single instant. I will tell you how it happened. Because someday in your own lives you may wake to a new world in which you feel a stranger. And you will know, if by chance you remember our conversation here today, that someone — no, my dear boys and girls, many others, a host of others, have also risen to a dark morning.

"A friend, a friend whom I loved, had asked if I would accompany him on a skiing trip to Vermont. Of course I said yes. Why should I not? We were to spend a day on the slopes. I was a great skier — my father had taught me when I was a child — and I looked forward to this holiday with the greatest excitement. I had been working hard that winter, too hard. It may have been my fatigue that in the end brought about my ruin. Because taking a curve that at any other time I might have managed with ease, my legs shot out from beneath me, and in an attempt to catch myself I let go of my pole and put out my hand, as any good skier knows not to do. Instead of fracturing a leg or a hip, both of which I might easily have spared, I injured my left hand, breaking three fingers that never properly healed."

This time Miss Hughes raised her left hand alone. She must have been about to point out to us the fatally injured fingers when the bell rang and she immediately dropped her arm. "To each of you a pleasant weekend, boys and girls," she said, turning to replace her records in their sleeves.

By class the following Friday we had other things to think about, and perhaps she did as well. We had just listened to Bach's Fugue in G Minor, for the purpose of learning to recognize the sound of the oboe — and the room for once had an air not of enforced constraint but of calm — when Miss Hughes lifted her head and, looking out the window, told us that there was one of us, sitting now in our midst, who listened to music in a manner quite unlike the rest. "He listens as if for his life, boys and girls, and it is in this manner that the music of the anointed was written. For the composer, the sounds struggling in his imagination are a matter of life and death. They are as necessary to him as the air he breathes."

She kept us in no more suspense, but allowed her gaze to rest on a boy who always sat, no matter the classroom, at the end of a row. We had scarcely noticed him at all, those of us who had not gone to elementary school with him. But there he sat — at this moment, blushing. His hair was sandy, his face was freckled, and he wore glasses with clear, faintly pinkish rims. His name was Norman de Carteret, a name that in a room full of Daves and Mikes and Steves we found impossible to pronounce without lifting our eyebrows. During the first week of September, Miss Hughes had asked him how he would like us to say his last name, and he had answered quietly, so quietly we could scarcely hear him, that it was Carteret, pronouncing the last syllable as if it were the first letter of the alphabet. The "de" he swallowed entirely.

"Then," Miss Hughes had said, "your father or his father must have come from France, the country that gave us Rameau, that invaluable spirit who for the first time set down the rules of harmony. The country to which we are indebted as well for Debussy, who accomplished what might have been thought impossible: he permitted us to hear the sound of moonlight."

I knew something about Norman the others didn't.

My mother had lived in our town as a child and occasionally met on the street someone she would later explain was once a friend of her mother's, dead long ago. Hilda Kelleher was one of these friends, even a cousin of sorts, and lived in a large, brown-shingled Victorian house, not far from the station. A wide porch, in summer strewn with wicker rocking chairs, ran along the front and disappeared around one side. The other end of the house was flanked by tall pines that in winter received the snow. Hilda was of an uncertain age — older than my mother, but maybe not a full generation older. Her hair was dyed bright yellow, and when she smiled her mouth twitched up at one corner uncovering teeth on which lipstick had left traces. Hilda had never married, but there was nothing strange in that. The town was full of old houses in which single women who had grown up in them lived on with their aging mothers, going "to business," teaching in the schools, supplementing their incomes in whatever ways they could. I supposed that they, too, had been girls, just as I was then, walking on summer nights beneath streetlights that threw leafy shadows on the sidewalks, that they, too, had listened to the murmur of voices drifting from screened porches, had heard the clatter of passing trains and dreamed of what would happen to them next. But life had passed them by, that was clear.

Hilda had dealt with the problem of dwindling resources by taking in boarders. An aunt of my mother's, a retired art teacher who, as my mother liked to say, "had no one in the world," was looking for a place to live. One afternoon in late summer, just before school opened, my mother visited Hilda to inquire about arrangements, and I went with her. While they sat talking in rocking chairs on the front porch I discovered around to the side a swing hanging from four chains. It was easy to imagine sitting there on summer nights behind a screen of vines, morning glories closed to the full moon, listening to the cicadas. Swinging back and forth I could hear their voices, my mother's telling Hilda how Aunt Ruth had lived in Mrs. Hollingsworth's house in Tarrytown, how this arrangement would seem familiar to her. I heard Hilda saying how glad she was that a room was available, that we would look at it in a moment. She went on to say that one boarder, who had been with her a year, had moved out of the room into a smaller one that better suited his means. Did my mother know a Mr. de Carteret? He had a son who was going to the high school, she thought, in the fall. The son lived with the mother but came to visit the father on Saturdays. The terrible thing was that when he came the father wouldn't open the door of his room to him.

Her voice sank so low that I got out of the swing and stood along the wall to listen. "The poor child," she said in a loud whisper. "He knocks, and when his father won't let him in he sits outside the door in the hall. Saturday after Saturday he comes to the house and waits outside his father's room and still his father won't see him. Sometimes — oh, the poor child, I wish I knew what to do — he is there all afternoon."

I was back in the swing by the time they called me to look at the vacated room. We followed Hilda up a staircase of wide oak steps and along a hall, passing mahogany doors on either side. At last she threw one open on a room that had a neat bed covered with a white spread, a desk, and a chest of drawers. The afternoon sun was sifting through the pines and falling on the bed. My mother said she couldn't imagine that her aunt wouldn't be happy here; the room seemed to breathe tranquillity. We closed the door, then went down the hallway to the staircase and out of the house.

I had been wondering whether or not I should whisper to my closest friends what I had heard Hilda say about Norman, but after Miss Hughes had asked us to notice his perfect attention it seemed to me I should not. Why not, I couldn't be sure, except it seemed that if he were listening "as if for his life," he had heard something in the music that I hadn't, and I didn't think the others had either. I felt out of my depth. And soon enough, by saying nothing, by keeping to myself what I took to be his secret, I came to feel that some understanding had sprung up between us, that we shared a knowledge hidden from the others.

Then, very soon, our paths crossed.

Two

In our old school there had been a classroom filled with books which we called the library. Twice a week we sat in a circle around Miss Kendall, the librarian, while she read to us, turning the book around from time to time to show us the pictures. I knew the books I wanted to read in that library; they were not the history books urged on us by our teachers, or the books about boys running away to sea, or even the large and lavishly illustrated volumes of myths and fairy tales. It was stories about girls I wanted, mostly orphan girls, or at least girls, like Sarah Crewe, whose mothers were dead and who had been left to the care of cruel adults to whom they refused to be grateful — to whom, in moments of passion, they poured out their long-suppressed feelings of outrage.

I had tried to explain all this to the older girl in the high school library who was supposed to show us around, and she had said I might like to read *Jane Eyre*, pointing to shelves lodged in a corner. I should look under the B's, she said, but I ended up nearby, facing shelves where all the books were written by people whose names began with a C. I was stopped by a title: *Lucy Gayheart*, a book about a girl, and perhaps even the kind I had in mind. It was written by Willa Cather, a name I had never heard, and I quickly looked around for a place to read.

This library was much larger than our old one, and instead of a little table where books were set on their ends for display — picture books and books for older children with such titles as *The Story of Electricity* and *Abigail Adams: A Girl of Colonial Days* — here there were unadorned long tables stretching the width of the room, with chairs tucked in on either side. High windows filled one end, and beneath them the librarian sat at her desk, ink pad and rubber date stamps poised at her elbow. I had sat down and opened the dark blue cover of the book to the first page when I looked up and saw Norman de Carteret sitting across the table, poring over an immense open volume. One foot was drawn up to rest on the seat of his chair, and as he read he leaned his face against his knee. It was a book about ships, I could see that; there was a full-scale picture of a sloop, or a schooner, with all its sails unfurled. There was writing on the different parts of the ship and on the sails, too, probably to let you know what they were called. Norman was absorbed, and I began to read:

> In Haverford on the Platte the townspeople still talk of Lucy Gayheart. They do not talk of her a great deal, to be sure; life goes on and we live in the present. But when they do mention her name it is with a gentle glow in the face or the voice, a confidential glance which says: "Yes, you, too, remember?" They still see her as a slight figure always in motion; dancing or skating, or walking swiftly with intense direction, like a bird flying home.

Lucy was one of the vivid creatures I wanted to read about, that was clear, but there was something that seemed not quite right, some note I had not yet heard. The story was already over and she lived on the first page not as a living person but as a memory.

I read on and to my surprise saw that Lucy, like Miss Hughes, wanted to be a pianist. She had been giving lessons to beginners from the time she was in tenth grade and had left Haverford to study music with a teacher in Chicago. Now she had come home for the Christmas holidays and had gone skating with her friends on the Platte. A young man, Harry, had joined them, and at sunset Lucy and he had sat together

> on a bleached cottonwood log, where the black willow thicket behind them made a screen. The interlacing twigs threw off red light like incandescent wires, and the snow underneath was rose-colour. . . . The round red sun was falling like a heavy weight; it touched the horizon line and sent quivering fans of red and gold over the wide country. . . . In an in-

stant the light was gone. . . . Wherever one looked there was nothing but flat country and low hills, all violet and grey.

These words, too, seemed remarkable, because I thought I recognized the place. In our town, if you followed the railroad tracks over the bridge that looked down on Main Street, on past the redbrick factory and Catholic church, you came to a reservoir that in spring was overhung with Japanese cherry trees, their branches weeping pink blossoms into the black water. During the winter months, when the reservoir had frozen over, we skated there. No prairie surrounded the water, only rocks and frozen grass and crouching woods; but the sky loomed wide overhead, and on winter afternoons the red sun was caught for a moment in the drooping silver branches of the cherry trees. I thought I knew how the Platte would look, the sun going down on it, thought I knew how afterward everything would turn ordinary and flat.

Norman was still contemplating the picture of the sailing ship. I could glimpse him sitting there as I lowered my head to continue reading. Now Lucy and Harry were settled in a sleigh that was, I read,

a tiny moving spot on that still white country settling into shadow and silence. Suddenly Lucy started and struggled under the tight blankets. In the darkening sky she had seen the first star come out; it brought her heart into her throat. That point of silver light spoke to her like a signal, released another kind of life and feeling which did not belong here.

I closed the book, deciding for today to forget *Jane Eyre*. I knew I had never read a book like this one. I had been expecting someone else to come along, or for Lucy and Harry to say something surprising or romantic to each other — something to happen besides the round red sun falling on the prairie and the star speaking to Lucy like a signal. And yet I felt that in this book these were enough. The pages I had read threw open the strange possibility that looking at things, feeling them, were also things that happened to you, just as much as meeting someone or going on a trip. What you thought and felt when you were alone or silently in the presence of someone else also made a story.

I looked up to see that Norman seemed to have fallen asleep on his book. His glasses were standing on their lenses beside him on the table and his face was in his arms. When the bell shrilled through the room, his shoulders twitched and he raised his head from the picture of the boat with all its sails. Looking up, still half asleep, his shortsighted blue eyes came to rest on mine. Another time I might have looked away. But as I, too, was half asleep, entertaining visions of quivering fans of red and gold playing on the prairie, turning over my new thoughts, I realized only after a moment that Norman had smiled at me as if he were still dreaming, as if he had been alone and, suddenly seized by a happy idea, were smiling at himself in a mirror.

Three

One Friday afternoon in October we filed into Miss Hughes's classroom to find her standing beside the day's album of records, dressed entirely in white. Her dress, made of soft white wool, fell just below her knees. There was no crimson or purple scarf tied round her neck; instead, a long necklace of pearls hung between her breasts.

"You will be wondering, boys and girls," she said to us as soon as we were seated, "why you find me today dressed as you see. I am in mourning, but a mourning turned to joy. White is the color of sorrow, as it is of radiance. And today I am going to play for you a piece of music that throughout your lives you will return to again and again. If ever you must make a decision, if ever you find yourselves tossing on a stormy sea — and life will not spare you, boys and girls; it spares no one — I beg you to do as I say. Find a spot where no living soul will disturb you, not even your dearest friend, and in the silent reaches of your soul listen to the music you are about to hear. Today we shall have no dictation, because it is my idea that Mozart's Requiem is best introduced without preliminaries. A requiem, you must know, is a prayer for the dead. Today we shall hear the opening section of this great work. One day — we shall see when — I shall play for you another."

Miss Hughes lowered the needle to the record that was already in place and spinning on the turntable. For a few moments a mournful sound filled the room, something that seemed to move forward, as if people were walking — a rhythmic, purposeful sound, with an echo for every step — when suddenly, without any warning, a blare of trumpets and kettledrums broke it all up, a frightening, violent blast that made us jump in our seats. Then, into the clamor, a chorus of men's voices forced their way, low, solemn, moving forward as before, but confident, as if they were sure of what they were saying. We were just getting used to the chorus when high above all the rest floated a single woman's voice, a voice raised high above the world but sliding down to meet it, and so calm, so full of understanding, I could have cried.

Miss Hughes lifted the needle and allowed her face to keep the expression of the mask for a few moments longer than usual. Then she drew a deep breath. "To comment on this music, boys and girls, would be an impertinence. We must let it rest in us where it will. Rest: a word, as it is used in music, to mean the absence of sound, a silence, sometimes short and sometimes long, when we hear only the vibrations of what has come before and prepare for those that will follow. You will understand what I mean if you think of a wave, the kind you see in a Japanese painting, caught in that moment just before it breaks."

The record had remained spinning on the turntable, its black surface crossed by a silver streak of light. Now Miss Hughes bent down, turned the knob, and the record slowly wound to a halt. Then she again stood upright, facing us. "The word 'requiem' — a Latin word you of course already know — might best be translated by several words in English: may he find rest at last, the one who has died. But my own prayer, I shall tell you now, is that we, the living, may find rest within the span of our own lives. I mean that rest we know only when we are most awake to sorrow and to joy, when we find we can no longer tell the difference. Then we are living outside of time, as we are when we are listening to music such as that we have just heard. In such an instance, death is only something that happens to us, like being born or growing old, but is of less consequence than the many deaths we sustain in life. I mean the deaths, my friends, when our dearest hopes are blasted."

Miss Hughes had been speaking slowly, meditatively, choosing her words with care. Her eyes had gone from one of us to the other. Now she assumed the dreamy look we had seen once before. She looked beyond us, through the clear panes of the window, into the distance. "Because, boys and girls, death may come to us in many disguises. You see, I, too, have gone down into the waters.

"I think I have told you already that my great desire in life was to have become a pianist, to play for myself one of the late piano concerti of Chopin, let us say, or of Schubert's impromptus. To that end I was living in Paris, studying with a teacher who was drawing from me all those feelings that I had supposed — young as I was — must remain outside music, separate from it. I had embraced discipline, and practicing for hours and hours everyday was the only way I knew to approach a sonata or prelude. It was this teacher who showed me that music is composed by a spirit alive to suffering and to joy and must be played by another such spirit. That it was only by bringing every moment of my life to the music that I could hope to draw from it what the composer had put in."

For a moment Miss Hughes seemed to wake from a sleep and looked at us alertly. "As indeed, boys and girls, in this room we must bring every moment of our lives to the music as we listen."

I wondered, while she stared from face to face, if her damaged hand had healed by the time she arrived in Paris, or if all this had taken place sometime before the skiing accident. But I would no more have thought to question her than to question whether or not Lucy Gayheart had taken the train back to Chicago the night after she had sat on the log and seen the round red sun falling like a weight into the prairie. The facts, the before and after of events, had their own logic by which, trusting the source, I supposed they must take their place in some pattern hidden from me.

Miss Hughes was playing with her pearls, winding them around her fingers. Again her gaze had retired to a place beyond the window.

"The city of light, boys and girls; that's what you will hear Paris called. But it is also, I will tell you, the city of darkness. If you cross the Pont des Arts one day, you will see the Île de la Cité, that great barge of an island, drifting up the river — the river Seine, I'm sure you know. And on that island, as you make your way across the bridge, you will see swing slowly into view a spectacle that has greeted the eyes of bewildered humanity for almost eight hundred years, the great square towers of Notre Dame. I say 'slowly,' you will notice, because like the opening of the requiem we have just heard, like Bach's Fugue that stirred our souls a few weeks ago, that's how many of the best things come to us. The catastrophes stop us in our tracks. I know, my friends, because I came to a halt on the bridge that day; I was unable to continue my walk. I had a letter with me that I had only just received and that had thrown me into a state of the most painful confusion."

In the silence that followed these words we could hear the excited cawing of crows on the playing field behind us.

"The letter was from a close friend at home relating the pitiable state into which my father had fallen. A debilitating illness from which he could not recover. The friend, who was old himself, did not ask me to return. But how could I think of anything else? Who would care for my father if I did not? I was all he had in the world, and it was to him that I owed my early life in music, he who had given me my first lessons on the piano. Of course I must return to look after him.

"And yet — and here, my dear boys and girls, I do not seek an answer — how would that be possible? To leave Paris, to leave the city in which I had been so happy! To leave all those feelings I had begun to put into my music! In short, to leave my teacher! It was not to be thought of. I leaned out over the edge of the bridge and looked down into the river flowing beneath. I could not see my way. I tasted the bitter waters of defeat. Oh, I was tempted! Finally, scarcely knowing how I got there, I found myself in my room, and after closing the door and pulling the shutters, I listened to Mozart's Requiem. By the time it had concluded I knew my way."

Miss Hughes, standing immobile in white, continued to gaze out the window. Surely the class would be over in a minute or two, but she didn't seem to recollect our presence. I stealthily turned my head to see sleek black crows lifting out of the trees and lighting back into them, their outspread wings glinting in the afternoon light, the branches with all their yellow leaves tossing up and down.

Four

In the days that followed, I decided that Miss Hughes had been in love with her teacher. She must have been, I thought, because I had now followed Lucy Gayheart to Chicago, where she lived alone in a room at the top of a stairs. A room, perhaps, like the room in Paris to which Miss Hughes had stumbled and had drawn shutters on a bright day. Lucy Gayheart was not in love with her teacher, but her teacher had urged her to attend a concert given by a celebrated singer named Clement Sebastian who, although he lived in France, was spending the winter in Chicago. "Yes, a great artist should look like that," she had thought the moment he had walked onto the stage. And then he had sung a Schubert song.

> The song was sung as a religious observance in the classical spirit, a rite more than a prayer. . . . *In your light I stand without fear, O august stars! I salute your eternity.* . . . Lucy had never heard anything sung with such elevation of style. In its calmness and serenity there was a kind of large enlightenment, like daybreak.

I remembered that Lucy had struggled up in Harry's sleigh when she had seen the first star flashing to her on the wide prairie, and I thought perhaps this was what Miss Hughes had meant about listening for your life: what you heard in the music was something exalted that you already knew, but weren't aware that you did — something you had blindly felt or heard or seen.

But then, reading on, I learned that Lucy's mood had quickly changed. There was to be no more serenity and calm. She listened to Sebastian sing five more Schubert songs, all of them melancholy, and felt that

> there was something profoundly tragic about this man. . . . She was struggling with something she had never felt before. A new conception of art? It came closer than that. A new kind of personality? But it was much more. It was a discovery about life, a revelation of love as a tragic force, not a melting mood, of passion that drowns like black water.

Although I didn't understand exactly how the music had led to this discovery, I knew that in this book, called by her name, I was not reading about Lucy alone. The lines that came next made it clear she was merely one member of a select company, a company set apart — as Miss Hughes had set Norman apart — by a destiny determined from within: "Some peoples' lives are affected by what happens to their person or their property; but for others fate is what happens to their feelings and their thoughts — that and nothing more."

Five

One Saturday afternoon in late October my mother asked if I would take Hilda and Aunt Ruth a lemon poppyseed cake she had made for them. It was not only Aunt Ruth she felt had no one in the world, but Hilda as well. "Poor souls," she said. "To be all alone like that." I put the cake, wrapped in wax paper, in the straw basket that hung from the handlebars of my bike. The leaves were now almost gone from the trees, but the day was clear and warm, like a day in early September. In less than a week it would be Halloween, and although we now thought it childish to go out begging, it was nice to think about walking from house to house, the night with its bare branches stark against a sky filled with spirits riding the air. I was in no rush to arrive at Hilda's because Aunt Ruth made me uneasy. When she came to our house she would give paper and colored pencils to my sisters and me and tell us to let our imaginations run wild. Then she would look at our efforts and to mine she would say, "D minus." Just as she might say the same if one of us carried her a cup of coffee that was not hot enough. But how could you obey a direction to let your imagination run wild? It was like someone wishing you sweet dreams.

By the time Hilda's house came into view I was riding my bike in loops, swerving sharply toward one curb, then the other, doubling back. In the middle of the street I made a circle three times. I knew now it was not so much Aunt Ruth I was afraid of running into; it was Norman de Carteret. Suppose he was sitting in the dark hall outside his father's door? Or suppose I met him coming out of the house as I was going in?

And then, my bike making wider and wider loops both toward and away, going over in my mind what I would say to Norman if we happened to meet, I finally dared to look up and saw him there on the porch at the side of the house, sitting on the swing that hung from the four chains. The morning glory vines were bare, and he was sitting with his feet against the porch railing, pushing himself back and forth. I could see, too, that when he saw me he flinched and lowered his head to hide his face. But then, as I was about to ride by, pretending I hadn't seen him, he looked up and — as he had done in the library — smiled. I parked my bike at the bottom of the steps, removed the cake from the basket, and went around the corner of the porch to where he was sitting.

"Hi," he said. His brown high-top sneakers were resting on the porch railing. Behind his glasses his blue eyes floated a little.

"Hi," I said. There was a long pause before I thought of something to say. "My aunt lives here."

"I know." His voice was high and childish. "So does my father."

I sat down on the railing not far from his feet, swung my legs up, and leaned back against one of the round white pillars. It seemed surprising that Norman spoke of his father. Had he knocked on his door this morning and, like all the other times, been greeted with silence? Had he been waiting in the hall for hours, not knowing what to do, and finally come down to sit on the swing?

"Did you come here to see him?" I asked, both fearful and eager that he say more.

"Yes," he answered, looking straight ahead, out between the vines that in August had made a screen from the sun. Now a few shriveled leaves hung in the warm afternoon. Just as at school, Norman was wearing corduroy trousers a little too big for him, and a plaid flannel shirt buttoned at the neck. The sleeves came down almost to his knuckles. "I'm waiting till he wakes up. He told me not to go away. He wants me to wait for him here."

"Oh," I said, and came to a stop. His voice had something in it I thought I recognized. It was in Miss Hughes's voice when she stared out the window while the crows were squawking and flapping in the trees. But Miss Hughes, as she stood there with her hands clasped at her waist, seemed to be communing with something only she could see. Norman's face, on the other hand, had lost its dreamy quality: his freckles stood out while he spoke; his eyes looked sharp and aware. He was looking at me as if he had made a point that he expected me to respond to.

Suddenly overcome with anxiety, not knowing what to answer, wanting only to erase the look in his eyes that made me afraid, I started unwrapping the cake. "Want some?" I asked.

"Sure," he said, and when I broke off a large chunk and held it out to him he leaned forward in the swing and took it in a hand I could see was trembling. I broke off another chunk for myself. At first we ate demurely, silently, spilling a few crumbs around us and brushing them away. I would find a way later on, I thought, to explain to my mother about the cake. Then I swallowed a piece that was too big for me and choked and sputtered, and then, on purpose this time, crammed a fistful in my mouth, pretending to frown at him disapprovingly, as if he were the one stuffing his mouth, until suddenly I was aping convulsions, bent double, holding my side, almost falling off the railing. Norman at first looked on, snorting with laughter. Then he, too, snatched a handful of cake and shoved it in his mouth, and soon we were both grabbing for more, exploding in high giggles, looking at each other cross-eyed, holding our sides, pretending to be on the point of collapse, pretending to be falling and dying, until the cake had disappeared, lying around us in half-eaten pieces.

Gradually we subsided, our shoulders stopped shaking, and we could breathe without gasping for air. The afternoon grew quiet around us. We could hear children playing up the block and the sound of someone raking leaves. Inside the house someone began to play the piano, some song from a time before we were born, something the grown-ups had sung when they were young. On the other side of the hedge, the late sun struck a large window into a flaming pool of orange. We avoided each other's eyes as if we had shared a secret we were ashamed of. After a while whoever was playing the piano broke off abruptly in the middle of a song and closed the cover with a bang. The sun slipped from the window, the branches of the trees reached ragged above our heads. When I finally got to my feet, taking leave of Norman without saying a word, it was almost dark.

For a few days afterward I tried falling in love with Norman de Carteret. I passed him in the halls sometimes, and once caught sight of him at his locker, turning his combination lock. But since our afternoon on Hilda's porch we were shy with each other, lowering our eyes when we met. Once, in music class, when Miss Hughes was playing a Brahms quintet for clarinet and strings, I tried to imagine how he might be listening, perhaps in the way Lucy had listened to Sebastian sing the Schubert songs. He was seated behind me, at the end of the row, and when I turned my head very slightly I could see him sitting there, his eyes sharp and aware, as they had been when he talked about his father. But at the end of the class when he walked through the door, his corduroy pants hanging from his hips, I could see he was only a child like myself.

Six

During the following weeks I pursued the story of Lucy Gayheart in fits and starts. I read with a sense of exaltation and impending doom, dipping back from time to time, for reassurance, into the

world of Sara Crewe and Anne of Green Gables. There was some
new strain in the voice telling the story, something I had not encountered in any other book. It ran along beneath the words like a
stream beneath a smooth surface of ice, some undertone murmur-
ing, "This is the way life is, this is the way life is." It was a voice —
dispassionate, stern — I listened for with joy, as if it brought news
from a country for which I had long been homesick. And yet my
nightly dreams told me, too, it was a country where terror and brutality might strike out of a benign blue sky. It seemed not so much
that my child life was fading into the past. It was more that my entire future life was rising before me, as if it were already known to
me, as if it had already happened long ago and was waiting to be remembered.

Despite my fitful reading, Lucy's story was quickly running
its course. She had already become Clement Sebastian's piano accompanist, already fallen in love with him. He was Europe, the
wide world, the life of feelings, unabashed and unashamed, not
cramped or peevish as in Haverford. He was a singer, an artist. And
although he was married, he had fallen in love with Lucy, with her
youth, her enthusiasm, perhaps with her rapturous admiration of
himself, he who was disillusioned and tired of the world. And so
when Harry came to see her in Chicago, to take her to a week of
operas and to propose marriage, she told him desperately that she
couldn't marry him, that she was in love with someone else.

None of this seemed surprising. The undertone I listened for,
I knew, had something to do with desire, with wanting someone
who wasn't there. Or maybe someone who was there but whom
you couldn't reach out and touch. It had to do with feelings that
couldn't be spoken and yet had to be spoken, the space between.

But now Lucy's story was taking an unexpected turn, was moving
in directions my daytime self would not have thought possible. In
response to what Lucy told him, Harry, in a fit of pique, married a
woman lacking in that quick responsiveness he had loved in Lucy,
and regretted the marriage immediately. Sebastian left Chicago for
a summer concert tour in Europe and met a sudden death. In despair, Lucy returned to Haverford, to a "long blue-and-gold autumn in the Platte valley."

Then January came and "the town and all the country round
were the colour of cement." Lucy left the house one afternoon to

skate on the river, just as we would soon be skating on our reservoir with its weeping cherry trees. What she didn't know was that the bed had shifted, that what once had been only a narrow arm of the river had become the swift-flowing river itself. She skated straight out onto the ice, large cracks spreading all around her. For a moment she was waist deep in icy water, her arms resting on a block of ice. Then "the ice cake slipped from under her arms and let her down."

I was incredulous. Despite the opening sentences of the book, I thought I hadn't understood and read the passage over and over, looking for some hint, some odd word or phrase, that would change its meaning. And yet, even while searching, even while trying to reassure myself that I must have missed something, I was aware — by some inner quaking that echoed the sound of splintering ice — I had understood very well. Harry is left to take up a life wracked with remorse that only time will soften, and Lucy slips into the regions of the remembered. It was as the undertone running beneath the story had assured all along: Lucy's response to Sebastian's songs, her bleak sense of foreboding, would be fulfilled. An early death — anticipated by the intense life of feelings — had been her destiny, and at the appointed time her death had risen to meet her. This, I supposed, was what people called tragedy.

Seven

Because of Haverford, whose sidewalks Lucy had walked in the long autumn of her return, the houses and streets of our town looked different, the late gardens of chrysanthemums and Michaelmas daisies, the silver moon rising above them. In the November afternoons we ran up and down the hockey field in back of the school, and even at 4:00 the red bayberries flickered in the twilight. Walking home, thinking of Lucy, I noticed the cracks in the sidewalks, the way the roots of trees had splintered them. Beneath the sidewalks ran a river of fast-flowing roots that could throw slabs of cement into the air, make a graveyard of the smooth planes where we used to roller-skate and sit playing jacks. From the end of one street I could see the train station, its roof black against the orange sky, and could imagine the tracks running over the bridge and past the reservoir into the city. Even now Myra Hess might be practicing the Chopin she would play tonight to a crowd at Carnegie Hall. Perhaps Miss Hughes was sitting on the train that would take her to the concert; perhaps she would return late at night to a room in a big house like Hilda's, a room that looked on pines.

For Thanksgiving my mother invited Hilda and Aunt Ruth, who must not be left alone. Hilda's lipstick, a wan hope, had left traces on her teeth, I took note as she leaned across the table to ask if I had met Norman de Carteret in any of my classes. Before answering I vowed I would not, cost what it might, be trapped as she had been, would not become an old woman in a town where life was one long wait. Hilda went on to recount to the table at large that Mr. de Carteret, who had scarcely stirred from his room for months, had been busy during the last days buying a turkey to cook for his son. He had bought cranberry sauce and sweet potatoes, she told us, and a bag of walnuts. It was all assembled on the table in the kitchen, and she herself had contributed two bottles of ginger ale. She had helped him put the turkey in the oven several hours before and at this moment it must almost be done. She hoped he wouldn't leave it in so long that it dried out. She hoped, too, that he remembered to turn off the oven once he took it out, because something might catch fire. She wondered if she should telephone him now to warn him but was persuaded by my father that a fire was unlikely.

On Monday we were back in school. I didn't see Norman that day, or the next, or the next, not until Friday, when, passing in the hall, I caught sight of him standing at his locker. He was standing idly there, staring into it in his usual absentminded way, not looking for anything in particular, it seemed. That was in the morning. By lunch a rumor had run through the school like fire through grass. One friend whispered it, and then another. Had I heard? Norman de Carteret's father had killed himself. Yes, it was true. He had drowned himself in the reservoir on Saturday. He'd done it by putting stones in his pockets. Someone's father had been there, had been part of the group that had pulled him from the water on Saturday night. That's why Norman hadn't been in school. All the teachers had been sent a notice, but Norman was in school today. Had I seen him? I had? What did he look like? Was he crying?

I absorbed the news as if it were of someone I knew nothing about, someone I had to strain to place or remember, someone whose name I barely recognized. Norman had again become a stranger, someone wrapped in an appalling story. My exchanges with him had separated me from the group; for a while I had shared his isolation and in drawing near him had drawn closer to my dreaming self, my reading self. Now I wanted nothing more to do with him. I was terrified that recalling our shared silences might draw me into some vortex of catastrophe. My fear was akin to what I had felt when, reaching the end of Lucy's story, I had looked frantically for something to tell me that I had not understood, that the words printed so boldly in black on the white page spelled out a meaning I had not grasped.

All day there had been the promise of snow in the air, and when we filed into Miss Hughes's room a few stray flakes had begun to fall. They were there in the window, the first of the season. Norman was already sitting in his place at the end of a row and the snow was falling behind him. He was sitting bolt upright in his seat, staring straight ahead, the corners of his mouth twisted up into something like a grin. But we only glanced at him, we didn't stare, sitting down as quickly as we could in our own places to get him out of our sight. We were overwhelmed with curiosity but also repelled. It would have been better if he hadn't been there at all, if we could have gone over the story, embellishing it with each retelling, without having to look at him, without having to sit with him in the same room.

Miss Hughes was, as usual, standing in her place beside the phonograph, the album on the table beside her. She was wearing a dark gray dress with a scarf that shimmered blue one moment, green the next. We had not met for two weeks because of the Thanksgiving vacation, but she had told us the last time we had seen her that she would welcome us back by introducing us to that consummate artist, Chopin. Now, rather brusquely, without the preliminary remarks with which she usually asked us "to silently invite our souls in order to prepare for the journey ahead," she asked us to open our notebooks and she began to dictate. "For Chopin," she pronounced, "the keyboard was a lyric instrument. He told his students, 'Everything must be made to sing.'"

For a few moments there were the sounds of papers rustling and of pencil cases coming unzipped. Then we settled to writing down her words.

"Chopin was a romantic in his impulse to render passing moods, but he was a classicist in his search for purity of form. His work is not given to digression. The Preludes are visionary sketches, none of them longer than a page or two. 'In each piece,' Schumann said, 'we find in his own hand, "Frederic Chopin wrote it!" He is the boldest, the proudest poet of his time.'"

We wrote laboriously, stopping as Miss Hughes carefully wrote on the board the words "classicist," "digression," "visionary." She made sure we had written quotation marks around Schumann's words, the exclamation point where it belonged. Out of the corner of my eye I saw that Norman was hunched over his notebook, writing.

Miss Hughes had turned to the album. "Now, boys and girls, we shall listen to one of Chopin's Preludes, the fourth, in E minor. It is very brief."

She drew a record out of its sleeve and placed it on the spinning turntable. After three months' training, we knew to assume our postures, so she had only to glance quickly around the room before lowering the needle. We heard the chords, the chords going deeper and deeper, and I pictured pine trees pointing to the sky at sunset; a darkness was about to overwhelm them, but for the moment they were lit by the setting sun. Everything was disappearing, the chords were telling us; a deep shadow was falling over the side of the mountain, yet the melody was singing of the last golden light thrown up from behind the rim.

"Do you hear it, boys and girls?" Miss Hughes asked us as she lifted the needle from the record. "Do you hear there the voice of desire? Not for one thing or another, not for a person or a place, but desire detached from any object. What we have heard in this fourth Prelude is the voice of longing when it breaks through into the regions of poetry, into the regions of whatever lives closest to us and furthest away."

Miss Hughes's scarf flashed blue, then green, against her gray dress, against the dark square of the blackboard behind her. Her eyes assumed the dreamy look we had seen before. "It was for this I had hopes of becoming a pianist," she told us, looking out the window. "To coax that voice from the instrument, to allow others to hear it in the way that I did." She was gazing into the snowflakes, it seemed, into the bare, black branches through which they were falling in the waning afternoon. She was watching them spill from the gray sky; in a trance she was following their white tumble. But all at once, as if she, too, were falling from some high place, as if she, too, were whirling through deep silent spaces, she seemed to catch herself. I had turned in my seat to look at the snow but also to catch a glimpse of Norman. He was sitting now with his face buried in his arms, as he had sat that day in the library.

Miss Hughes looked around her sleepily, and for the first time we saw her face, without the prompting of music, assume the mask. For a long moment she stood before us, impassive, mouth pulled down at the corners, eyes closed. When she opened them, they rested darkly on Norman's lowered head. She allowed them to remain there a few seconds, taking her time, as if she were inviting us to consider with her which words she might choose.

"Is there anything we can do for you, Norman?" she asked at last.

There was silence in the room. I thought of the snow hitting the ground and wondered whether it had already begun to cover the brown grass beneath the trees, thought of Norman's father lying somewhere in the earth, his body in its coffin perhaps already beginning to rot, his grave still raw and exposed. The snow would hide all that, the dirt piled on top, and if Norman went to look where his father was, he would see an even cover of white.

"Because," Miss Hughes continued, "we would like you to know that you are sitting in the company of friends."

She brooded, frowning, while we sat rigidly in our seats. Then she turned her eyes from Norman to us. "You are perhaps not aware, boys and girls, that Mozart was Chopin's favorite composer. I shall now tell you a story. When Chopin died at the age of thirty-nine, in Paris, his funeral was held at the Madeleine, a church of that city. Afterward he was buried in a cemetery called Père-Lachaise, where you may someday wish to visit his grave. But at his funeral, it was Mozart's Requiem that the gathered mourners were given to hear. I once told you that before long we would listen together to another section of it. Today we shall hear the Lacrimosa. The word means 'full of tears.'"

We waited while she returned the record we had heard to its sleeve and drew out another.

She brooded over us now as a moment ago she had brooded over

Norman. "We cannot see into the mysteries of another person's life, dear boys and girls. We have no way of knowing what deaths a soul has sustained before the final one. It is for this reason that we must never presume to judge or to speak in careless ways about lives of which we understand nothing. I tell you this so that you may not forget it. We may honor many things in life. But for someone else's sorrow we must reserve our deepest bow."

Miss Hughes had placed the record on the turntable and now paused before lowering the needle. "You will hear in the music that I am about to play for you a prayer for the dead, a prayer that they may at last find the peace that so often escapes us in life. Because, boys and girls, in praying for the dead we are praying for ourselves in that hour when we, too, far away as that hour might seem to us now, shall join their ranks. But even more — and you will understand me in time — we are honoring the suffering in our own lives, those of us who barely know how we shall survive the day. If you listen closely I know you cannot fail to hear something else: the tale of how our grief, the desire for what we do not have, the desire for what is forever denied us, may at length — when embraced as our destiny — become indistinguishable from our joy. Indistinguishable, you will understand, my dear friends, in that moment when time, as in the most sublime music, has ceased to be.

"When the record comes to an end I ask that you gather your things and silently take your leave. I shall look forward, in a week's time, to the return of your company."

We heard strings draw out one note and then two more, a little higher, the same pattern repeated three times, very sweet, very light, as if we might all float on these blithe strains forever. Into this — not denying but blending — broke a chorus of plaintive voices repeating something twice, voices asking, imploring, like a wind that moans in the night; then quickly gaining strength and conviction, they began an ascent, a climb, in which they mounted higher and higher, at each step becoming bolder, a procession like the first section we had heard weeks before. But now the voices surged as if straining toward something nobody had ever reached, up and up, the procession climbing higher and higher, the kettledrums pounding, the trumpets blaring, the echo falling in the wake of each step, until they could mount no higher and then — with utter simplicity, with utter calm — the voices returned to the point from which they had begun and pronounced their words in an ordinary manner, foot to earth.

When the record had spun to its end, when there was nothing more to listen for, we slowly picked up our books and filed out of the room. At the door I turned to look back and saw Miss Hughes still standing at attention before the phonograph, her hands together in front of her. Norman had not moved; his face was hidden in his arms. It was early December and already the room was filling with shadows, but the snow swirling at the window cast a restless light, the flickering light of water, over Miss Hughes's frozen mask, over Norman bowed at his desk. For the moment Miss Hughes was standing watch. But soon Norman would raise from his arms the face we had not yet seen and that would be his until, in life or in death, he opened his eyes on eternity.

HA JIN

The Bridegroom

FROM HARPER'S MAGAZINE

BEFORE BEINA'S FATHER DIED, I promised him that I'd take care of his daughter. He and I had been close friends for twenty years. He left his only child with me because my wife and I had no children of our own. It was easy to keep my word when Beina was still a teenager. As she grew older, it became more difficult, not because she was willful or troublesome but because no man was interested in her, a short, homely girl. When she turned twenty-three and still had no boyfriend, I began to worry. Where could I find her a husband? Timid and quiet, she didn't know how to get close to a man. I was afraid she'd become an old maid.

Then out of the blue Baowen Huang proposed to her. I found myself at a loss, because they'd hardly known each other. How could he be serious about his offer? I feared he might make a fool of Beina, so I insisted they get engaged if he meant business. He came to my home with two trussed-up capons, four cartons of Ginseng cigarettes, two bottles of Five Grains' Sap, and one tall tin of oolong tea. I was pleased, though not very impressed by his gifts.

Two months later they got married. My colleagues congratulated me, saying, "That was fast, Old Cheng."

What a relief to me. But to many young women in our sewing-machine factory, Beina's marriage was a slap in the face. They'd say, "A hen cooped up a peacock." Or, "A fool always lands in the arms of fortune." True, Baowen had been one of the most handsome unmarried men in the factory, and nobody had expected that Beina, stocky and stout, would win him. What's more, Baowen was good-natured and well educated — a middle-school graduate — and he didn't smoke or drink or gamble. He had fine manners and often smiled politely, showing his bright, straight teeth. In a way he resembled a woman, delicate, clear-skinned, and soft-spoken; he even could knit things out of wool. But no men dared bully him because he was skilled at martial arts. Three times in a row he had won the first prize for kung fu at our factory's annual sports meet. He was very good at the long sword and freestyle boxing. When he was in middle school, bigger boys had often picked on him, so his stepfather had sent him to the martial arts school in their hometown. A year later nobody would ever bug him again.

Sometimes I couldn't help wondering why Baowen had chosen Beina. What in her had caught his heart? Did he really like her fleshy face, which often reminded me of a globefish? Although we had our doubts, my wife and I couldn't say anything negative about the marriage. Our only concern was that Baowen might be too good for our nominal daughter. Whenever I heard that somebody had divorced, I'd feel a sudden flutter of panic.

As the head of the Security Section in the factory, I had some pull and did what I could to help the young couple. Soon after their wedding I secured them a brand-new two-bedroom apartment, which angered some people waiting in line for housing. I wasn't daunted by their criticism. I'd do almost anything to make Beina's marriage stable, because I believed that if it survived the first two years, it might last decades — once Baowen became a father, it would be difficult for him to break loose.

But after they'd been married for eight months, Beina still wasn't pregnant. I was afraid that Baowen would soon grow tired of her and run after another woman, since many young women in the factory were still attracted to him. A brazen one even declared that she'd leave her door open for him all night long. Some of them frequently offered him movie tickets and meat coupons. It seemed that they were determined to wreck Beina's marriage. I hated them, and just the thought of them would give me an earache or a sour stomach. Fortunately, Baowen hadn't yet done anything outside the bounds of a decent husband.

One morning in early November, Beina stepped into my office. "Uncle," she said in a tearful voice, "Baowen didn't come home last night."

I tried to remain calm, though my head began to swim. "Do you know where he's been?" I asked.

"I don't know. I looked for him everywhere." She licked her

cracked lips and took off her green work cap, her hair in a huge bun.

"When did you see him last?"

"At dinner yesterday evening. He said he was going to see somebody. He has lots of buddies in town."

"Is that so?" I didn't know he had many friends. "Don't worry. Go back to your workshop and don't tell anybody about this. I'll call around and find him."

She dragged herself out of my office. She must have gained at least a dozen pounds since the wedding. Her blue dungarees had become so tight that they seemed about to burst. Viewed from behind, she looked like a giant turnip.

I called the Rainbow Movie Theater, Victory Park, and a few restaurants in town. They all said they had not seen anyone matching Baowen's description. Before I could phone the city library, where Baowen sometimes spent his weekends, a call came in. It was from the city's Public Security Bureau. The man on the phone said they'd detained a worker of ours named Baowen Huang. He wouldn't tell me what had happened. He just said, "Indecent activity. Come as soon as you can."

It was a cold day. As I cycled toward downtown, the shrill north wind kept flipping up the front ends of my overcoat. My knees were sore, and I couldn't help shivering. Soon my asthma tightened my throat and I began moaning. I couldn't stop cursing Baowen. "I knew it. I just knew it," I said to myself. I had sensed that sooner or later he'd seek pleasure with another woman. Now he was in the police's hands, and the whole factory would talk about him. How could Beina take this blow?

At the Public Security Bureau I was surprised to see that about a dozen officials from other factories, schools, and companies were already there. I knew most of them, who were in charge of security affairs at their workplaces. A policewoman conducted us into a conference room upstairs, where green silk curtains hung in the windows. We sat down around a long mahogany table and waited to be briefed about the case. The glass tabletop was brand-new, its edge still sharp. I saw worry and confusion on the other men's faces. I figured Baowen must have been involved in an organized crime — either an orgy or a gang rape. On second thought I felt he couldn't have been a rapist; by nature he was kindhearted, very

gentle. I hoped this was not a political case, which would be absolutely unpardonable. Six or seven years ago a half-wit and a high
school graduate had started an association in our city, named the
China Liberation Party, which had later recruited nine members.
Although the sparrow is small it has a complete set of organs —
their party elected a chairman, a secretary, and even a prime minister. But before they could print their manifesto, which expressed
their intention to overthrow the government, the police rounded
them up. Two of the top leaders were executed, and the rest of the
members were jailed.

As I was wondering about the nature of Baowen's crime, a middle-aged man came in. He had a solemn face, and his eyes were half
closed. He took off his dark blue tunic, hung it on the back of a
chair, and sat down at the end of the table. I recognized him; he
was Chief Miao of the Investigation Department. Wearing a sheepskin jerkin, he somehow reminded me of Genghis Khan, thick-
boned and round-faced. His hooded eyes were shrewd, though
they looked sleepy. Without any opening remarks he declared that
we had a case of homosexuality on our hands. At that, the room
turned noisy. We'd heard of the term but didn't know what it
meant exactly. Seeing many of us puzzled, Chief Miao explained,
"It's a social disease, like gambling, or prostitution, or syphilis." He
kept on squirming as if itchy with hemorrhoids.

A young man from the city's Fifth Middle School raised his hand.
He asked, "What do homosexuals do?"

Miao smiled and his eyes almost disappeared. He said, "People
of the same sex have a sexual relationship."

"Sodomy!" cried someone.

The room turned quiet for at least ten seconds. Then somebody
asked what kind of crime this was.

Chief Miao explained, "Homosexuality originated from Western
capitalism and bourgeois lifestyle. According to our law it's dealt
with as a kind of hooliganism. Therefore, every one of the men we
arrested will serve a sentence, from six months to five years, de-
pending on the severity of his crime and his attitude toward it."

A truck blew its horn on the street and made my heart twinge. If
Baowen went to prison, Beina would live like a widow, unless she divorced him. Why had he married her to begin with? Why did he
ruin her this way?

What had happened was that a group of men, mostly clerks, artists, and schoolteachers, had formed a club called Men's World, a
salon of sorts. Every Thursday evening they'd met in a large room
on the third floor of the office building of the Forestry Institute.
Since the club admitted only men, the police suspected that it
might be a secret association with a leaning toward violence, so
they assigned two detectives to mix with the group. True, some of
the men appeared to be intimate with each other in the club, but
most of the time they talked about movies, books, and current
events. Occasionally music was played, and they danced together.
According to the detectives' account, it was a bizarre, emotional
scene. A few men appeared in pairs, unashamed of necking and
cuddling in the presence of others, and some would say with tears,
"At last we men have a place for ourselves." A middle-aged painter
wearing earrings exclaimed, "Now I feel alive! Only in here can I
stop living in hypocrisy." Every week two or three new faces would
show up. When the club grew close to the size of thirty men, the police took action and arrested them all.

After Chief Miao's briefing, we were allowed to meet with the
criminals for fifteen minutes. A policeman led me into a small
room in the basement and let me read Baowen's confession while
he went to fetch him. I glanced through the four pages of interro-
gation notes, which stated that Baowen had been new to the club
and that he'd joined them only twice, mainly because he was interested in their talks. Yet he didn't deny that he was a homosexual.

The room smelled of urine, since it was next to a bathroom. The
policeman took Baowen in and ordered him to sit opposite me at
the table. Baowen, in handcuffs, avoided looking at me. His face
was bloated, covered with bruises. A broad welt left by a baton,
about four inches long, slanted across his forehead. The collar of
his jacket was torn open. Yet he didn't appear frightened. His calm
manner angered me, though I felt sorry for him.

I kept a hard face, and said, "Baowen, do you know you committed a crime?"

"I didn't do anything. I just went there to listen to them talk."

"You mean you didn't do that thing with any man?" I wanted to
make sure so that I could help him.

He looked at me, then lowered his eyes, saying, "I might've done
something, to be honest, but I didn't."

"What's that supposed to mean?"

"I — I liked a man in the club, a lot. If he'd asked me, I might've agreed." His lips curled upward as if he prided himself on what he had said.

"You're sick!" I struck the table with my knuckles.

To my surprise, he said, "So? I'm a sick man. You think I don't know that?"

I was bewildered. He went on, "Years ago I tried everything to cure myself. I took a lot of herbs and boluses, and even ate baked scorpions, lizards, and toads. Nothing helped me. Still I'm fond of men. I don't know why I'm not interested in women. Whenever I'm with a woman my heart is as calm as a stone."

Outraged by his confession, I asked, "Then why did you marry my Beina? To make fun of her, eh? To throw mud in my face?"

"How could I be that mean? Before we got married, I told her I didn't like women and might not give her a baby."

"She believed you?"

"Yes. She said she wouldn't mind. She just wanted a husband."

"She's an idiot!" I unfolded my hanky and blew my clogged nose into it, then asked, "Why did you choose her if you had no feelings for her at all?"

"What was the difference? For me she was similar to other women."

"You're a scoundrel!"

"If I didn't marry her, who would? The marriage helped us both, covering me and saving face for her. Besides, we could have a good apartment — a home. You see, I tried living like a normal man. I've never been mean to Beina."

"But the marriage is a fake! You lied to your mother too, didn't you?"

"She wanted me to marry."

The policeman signaled that our meeting was over. In spite of my anger, I told Baowen that I'd see what I could do, and that he'd better cooperate with the police and show a sincere attitude.

What should I do? I was sick of him, but he belonged to my family, at least in name, and I was obligated to help him.

On the way home I pedaled slowly, my mind heavy with thoughts. Gradually I realized that I might be able to do something to prevent him from going to jail. There were two steps I could take: first, I would maintain that he had done nothing in the club, so as to isolate him from those real criminals; second, I would present him as a sick man, so that he might receive medical treatment instead of a prison term. Once he became a criminal, he'd be marked forever as an enemy of society, no longer redeemable. Even his children might suffer. I ought to save him.

Fortunately both the party secretary and the director of our factory were willing to accept Baowen as a sick man, particularly Secretary Zhu, who liked Baowen's kung-fu style and had once let him teach his youngest son how to use a three-section cudgel. Zhu suggested we make an effort to rescue Baowen from the police. He said to me in the men's room inside our office building, "Old Cheng, we must not let Baowen end up in prison." I was grateful for his words.

All of a sudden homosexuality became a popular topic in the factory. A few old workers said that some actors of the Beijing opera had slept together as lovers in the old days, because no women were allowed to perform in any troupe and the actors could spend time with men only. Secretary Zhu, who was well read, said that some emperors in the Han Dynasty had owned male lovers in addition to their large harems. Director Liu had heard that the last emperor, Puyi, had often ordered his eunuchs to suck his penis and caress his testicles. Someone even claimed that homosexuality was an upper-class thing, not something for ordinary people. All the talk sickened me. I felt ashamed of my nominal son-in-law. I wouldn't join them in talking and just listened, pretending I wasn't bothered.

As I expected, rumors went wild in the factory, especially in the foundry shop. Some people said Baowen was impotent. Some believed he was a hermaphrodite, otherwise his wife would've been pregnant long ago.

To console Beina, I went to see her one evening. She had a pleasant home, in which everything was in order. Two bookcases, filled with industrial manuals, biographies, novels, and medical books, stood against the whitewashed wall, on either side of the window. In one corner of the living room was a coat tree on which hung the red feather parka Baowen had bought her before their wedding, and in another corner sat a floor lamp. At the opposite end of the room two pots of blooming flowers, one of cyclamens and the other of Bengal roses, were placed on a pair of low stools kept at an equal distance from each other and from the walls on both sides.

Near the inner wall, beside a yellow enamel spittoon, was a large sofa upholstered in orange imitation leather. A black-and-white TV perched on an oak chest against the outer wall.

I was impressed, especially by the floor inlaid with bricks and coated with bright red paint. Even my wife couldn't keep a home so neat. No doubt it was Baowen's work, because Beina couldn't be so tidy. Already the room showed the trace of her sloppy habits — in a corner were scattered an empty flour sack and a pile of soiled laundry. Sipping the tea she had poured me, I said, "Beina, I'm sorry about Baowen. I didn't know he was so bad."

"No, he's a good man." Her round eyes looked at me with a steady light.

"Why do you say that?"

"He's been good to me."

"But he can't be a good husband, can he?"

"What do you mean?"

I said bluntly, "He didn't go to bed with you very often, did he?"

"Oh, he can't do that because he practices kung fu. He said if he slept with a woman, all his many years' work would be gone. From the very beginning his master told him to avoid women."

"So you don't mind?" I was puzzled, saying to myself, What a stupid girl.

"Not really."

"But you two must've shared the bed a couple of times, haven't you?"

"No, we haven't."

"Really? Not even once?"

"No." She blushed a little and looked away, twisting her earlobe with her fingertips.

My head was reeling. After eight months' marriage she was still a virgin! And she didn't mind! I lifted the cup and took a large gulp of the jasmine tea.

A lull settled in. We both turned to watch the evening news; my numb mind couldn't take in what the anchorwoman said about a border skirmish between Vietnamese and Chinese troops.

A moment later I told Beina, "I'm sorry he has such a problem. If only we had known."

"Don't feel so bad, Uncle. In fact he's better than a normal man."

"How so?"

"Most men can't stay away from pretty women, but Baowen just likes to have a few buddies. What's wrong with that? It's better this way, 'cause I don't have to worry about those shameless bitches in our factory. He won't bother to give them a look. He'll never have a lifestyle problem."

I almost laughed, wondering how I should explain to her that he could have a sexual relationship with a man and that he'd been detained precisely because of a lifestyle problem. On second thought I realized it might be better for her to continue to think that way. She didn't need more stress at the moment.

Then we talked about how to help Baowen. I told her to write a report, emphasizing what a good, considerate husband he'd been. Of course she must not mention his celibacy in their marriage. Also, from now on, however vicious her fellow workers' remarks were, she should ignore them and never talk back, as if she'd heard nothing.

That night when I told my wife about Beina's silly notions, she smiled, saying, "Compared with most men, Baowen isn't too bad. Beina's not a fool."

I begged Chief Miao and a high-ranking officer to treat Baowen leniently and even gave each of them two bottles of brandy and a coupon for a Butterfly sewing machine. They seemed willing to help but wouldn't promise me anything. For days I was so anxious that my wife was afraid my ulcer might recur.

One morning the Public Security Bureau called, saying they had accepted our factory's proposal and would have Baowen transferred to the mental hospital in a western suburb, provided our factory agreed to pay for his hospitalization. I accepted the offer readily, feeling relieved. Later, I learned that there wasn't enough space in the city's prison for twenty-seven gay men, who couldn't be mixed with other inmates and had to be put in solitary cells. So only four of them were jailed; the rest were either hospitalized (if their work units agreed to pay for the medical expenses) or sent to some labor farms to be reformed. The two party members among them didn't go to jail, though they were expelled from the party, a very severe punishment that ended their political lives.

The moment I put down the phone, I hurried to the assembly

shop and found Beina. She broke into tears at the good news. She ran back home and filled a duffel bag with Baowen's clothes. We met at my office, then together set out for the Public Security Bureau. I rode my bicycle while she sat behind me, embracing the duffel as if it were a baby. With a strong tailwind, the cycling was easy and fast, so we arrived before Baowen left for the hospital. He was waiting for a van in front of the police station, accompanied by two policemen.

The bruises on his face had healed, so he looked handsome again. He smiled at us, and said rather secretively, "I want to ask you a favor." He rolled his eyes as the dark green van rounded the street corner, coming toward us.

"What?" I said.

"Don't let my mother know the truth. She's too old to take it. Don't tell her, please!"

"What should we say to her, then?" I asked.

"Just say I have a temporary mental disorder."

Beina couldn't hold back her tears anymore, saying loudly, "Don't worry. We won't let her know. Take care of yourself and come back soon." She handed him the duffel, which he took without a word.

I nodded to assure him that I wouldn't reveal the truth. He smiled at her, then at me. For some reason his face turned rather sweet — charming and enticing, as though it were a mysterious female face. I blinked my eyes and wondered if he was really a man. It flashed through my mind that if he were a woman he could've been a beauty — tall, slim, muscular, and slightly languid.

My thoughts were cut short by a metallic screech as the van stopped in front of us. Baowen climbed into it; so did the policemen. I walked around the van, and shook his hand, saying that I'd visit him the next week and that meanwhile, if he needed anything, just to give me a ring.

We waved good-bye as the van drew away, its tire chains clattering and flinging up bits of snow. After a blasting toot, it turned left and disappeared from the icy street. I got on my bicycle as a gust of wind blew up and almost threw me down. Beina followed me for about twenty yards, then leaped on the carrier, and together we headed home. She was so heavy. Thank heaven, I was riding a Great Golden Deer, one of the sturdiest makes.

*

During the following week I heard from Baowen once. He said on the phone that he felt better now and less agitated. Indeed his voice sounded calm and smooth. He asked me to bring him a few books when I came, specifically his *Dictionary of Universal Knowledge,* which was a hefty, rare book translated from the Russian in the late fifties. I had no idea how he had come by it.

I went to see him on Thursday morning. The hospital was on a mountain, six miles southwest of Muji City. As I was cycling on the asphalt road, a few tall smokestacks fumed lazily beyond the larch woods in the west. To my right the power lines along the roadside curved, heavy with fluffy snow, which would drop in little chunks whenever the wind blew across them. Now and then I overtook a horse cart loaded with earless sheaves of wheat, followed by one or two foals. After I pedaled across a stone bridge and turned into the mouth of a valley, a group of brick buildings emerged on a gentle slope, connected with one another by straight cement paths. Farther up the hill, past the buildings, there was a cow pen, in which about two dozen milk cows were grazing on dry grass while a few others huddled together to keep warm.

It was so peaceful here that if you hadn't known this was a mental hospital, you might have imagined it was a sanatorium for ranking officials. Entering Building 9, I was stopped by a guard, who then took me to Baowen's room on the ground floor. It happened that the doctor on duty, a tall fortyish man with tapering fingers, was making the morning rounds and examining Baowen. He shook hands with me and said that my son-in-law was doing fine. His surname was Mai; his whiskered face looked very intelligent. When he turned to give a male nurse instructions about Baowen's treatment, I noticed an enormous wart in his ear almost blocking the ear hole like a hearing aid. In a way he looked like a foreigner. I wondered if he had some Mongolian or Tibetan blood.

"We give him the electric bath," Doctor Mai said to me a moment later.

"What?" I asked, wincing.

"We treat him with the electric bath."

I turned to Baowen. "How is it?"

"It's good, really soothing." He smiled, but there was a churlish look in his eyes, and his mouth tightened.

The nurse was ready to take him for the treatment. Never having heard of such a bath, I asked Doctor Mai, "Can I see how it works?"

"All right, you may go with them."

Together we climbed the stairs to the second floor. There was another reason for me to join them. I wanted to find out whether Baowen was a normal man. The rumors in our factory had gotten on my nerves, particularly the one that said he had no penis — that was why he had always avoided bathing in the workers' bathhouse.

After taking off our shoes and putting on plastic slippers, we entered a small room that had pea green walls and a parquet floor. At its center lay a porcelain bathtub, as ghastly as an apparatus of torture. Affixed along the interior wall of the tub were rectangles of black perforated metal. Three thick rubber cords connected them to a tall machine standing by the wall. A control board full of buttons, gauges, and switches slanted atop the machine. The young nurse, burly and square-faced, turned on the faucet; steaming water began to tumble into the tub. Then he went over to operate the machine. He seemed good-natured; his name was Fuhai Dong. He said he came from the countryside, apparently of peasant stock, and had graduated from Jilin Nursing School.

Baowen smiled at me while unbuttoning his zebra-striped hospital robe. He looked fine now — all the bruises had disappeared from his face, which had become pinkish and smooth. I was scared by the tub. It seemed suitable for electrocuting a criminal. However sick I was, I wouldn't lie in it with my back resting against that metal groove. What if there was an electricity leak?

"Does it hurt?" I asked Baowen.

"No."

He went behind a khaki screen in a corner and began taking off his clothes. When the water half filled the tub, the nurse took a small bag of white powder out of a drawer, cut it open with scissors, and poured the stuff into the water. It must have been salt. He tucked up his shirtsleeves and bent double to agitate the solution with both hands, which were large and sinewy.

To my dismay, Baowen came out in a clean pair of shorts. Without hesitation he got into the tub and lay down, just as one would enter a lukewarm bathing pool. I was amazed. "Have you given him electricity yet?" I asked Nurse Dong.

"Yes, a little. I'll increase it by and by." He turned to the machine and adjusted a few buttons.

"You know," he said to me, "your son-in-law is a very good patient, always cooperative."

"He should be."

"That's why we give him the bath. Other patients get electric cuffs around their limbs or electric rods on their bodies. Some of them scream like animals every time. We have to tie them up."

"When will he be cured?"

"I'm not sure."

Baowen was noiseless in the electrified water, with his eyes shut and his head resting on a black rubber pad at the end of the tub. He looked fine, rather relaxed.

I drew up a chair and sat down. Baowen seemed reluctant to talk, concentrating on the treatment, so I remained silent, observing him. His body was wiry, his legs hairless, and the front of his shorts bulged quite a bit. He looked all right physically. Once in a while he breathed a feeble sigh.

As the nurse increased the electric current, Baowen began to squirm in the tub as if smarting from something. "Are you all right?" I asked, and dared not touch him.

"Yeah."

He kept his eyes shut. Glistening beads of sweat gathered on his forehead. He looked pale, his lips curling now and again as though he were thirsty.

Then the nurse gave him more electricity. Baowen began writhing and moaning a little. Obviously he was suffering. This bath couldn't be as soothing as he'd claimed. With a white towel Nurse Dong wiped the sweat off Baowen's face, and whispered, "I'll turn it down in a few minutes."

"No, give me more!" Baowen said resolutely without opening his eyes, his face twisted.

I felt as though he was ashamed of himself. Perhaps my presence made this section of the treatment more uncomfortable to him. His hands gripped the rim of the tub, the arched wrists trembling. For a good three minutes nobody said a word; the room was so quiet that its walls seemed to be ringing.

As the nurse gradually reduced the electricity, Baowen calmed down. His toes stopped wiggling.

Not wanting to bother him further with my presence, I went out to look for Doctor Mai, to thank him and find out when Baowen could be cured. The doctor was not in his office, so I walked out of the building for a breath of air. The sun was high and the snow blazingly white. Once outside, I had to close my eyes for a minute to adjust them. I then sat down on a bench and lit a cigarette. A young woman in an ermine hat and army mittens passed by, holding an empty milk pail and humming the song "Comrade, Please Have a Cup of Tea." She looked handsome, and her crisp voice pleased me. I gazed at the pair of thick braids behind her, which swayed a little in the wind.

My heart was full of pity for Baowen. He was such a fine young man that he ought to be able to love a woman, have a family, and enjoy a normal life.

Twenty minutes later I rejoined him in his room. He looked tired, still shivering a little. He told me that as the electric currents increased, his skin had begun prickling as though stung by hundreds of mosquitoes. That was why he couldn't stay in the tub for longer than half an hour.

I felt for him, and said, "I'll tell our leaders how sincere your attitude is and how cooperative you are."

"Oh sure." He tilted his damp head. "Thanks for bringing the books."

"Do you need something else?"

"No." He sounded sad.

"Baowen, I hope you can come home before the New Year. Beina needs you."

"I know. I don't want to be locked up here forever."

I told him that Beina had written to his mother, saying he'd been away on a business trip. Then the bell for lunch rang in the building, and outside the loudspeaker began broadcasting the fiery music of "March of the Volunteers." Nurse Dong walked in with a pair of chopsticks and a plate containing two corn buns. He said cheerily to Baowen, "I'll bring you the dish in a minute. We have tofu stewed with sauerkraut today, also bean sprout soup."

I stood up and took my leave.

When I reported Baowen's condition to the factory leaders, they seemed impressed. The term "electric bath" must have given their imagination free rein. Secretary Zhu kept shaking his head, and said, "I'm sorry Baowen has to go through such a thing."

I didn't explain that the electric bath was a treatment less severe than the other kinds, nor did I describe what the bath was like. I just said, "They steep him in electrified water every day." Let the terror seize their brains, I thought, so that they might be more sympathetic to Baowen when he is discharged from the hospital.

It was mid-December, and Baowen had been in the hospital for a month already. For days Beina went on saying that she wanted to see how her husband was doing; she was eager to take him home before the New Year. Among her fellow workers rumors persisted. One said the electric bath had blistered Baowen; another claimed that his genitals had been shriveled up by the treatment; another added that he had become a vegetarian, nauseated at the mere sight of meat. The young woman who had once declared she'd leave her door open for him had just married and proudly told everybody she was pregnant. People began to be kind and considerate to Beina, treating her like an abused wife. The leaders of the assembly shop assigned her only the daytime shift. I was pleased that Finance still paid Baowen his wages as though he were on sick leave. Perhaps they did this because they didn't want to upset me.

On Saturday Beina and I went to the mental hospital. She couldn't pedal, and it was too far for me to carry her on my bicycle, so we took the bus. She had been there by herself two weeks ago to deliver some socks and a pair of woolen pajamas she'd knitted for Baowen.

We arrived at the hospital early in the afternoon. Baowen looked healthy, in good spirits. It seemed that the bath had helped him. He was happy to see Beina and even cuddled her in my presence. He gave her two toffees; knowing I disliked candies, he didn't give me one. He poured a large mug of malted milk for both of us, since there was only one mug in the room. I didn't touch the milk, unsure whether homosexuality was communicable. I was glad to see that he treated his wife well. He took a genuine interest in what she said about their comrades in our factory, and now and then laughed heartily. What a wonderful husband he could have been if he were not sick.

Having sat with the couple for a few minutes, I left so that they could be alone. I went to the nurses' office upstairs and found Fuhai Dong writing at a desk. The door was open, and I knocked on its frame. Startled, he closed his brown notebook and stood up.

"I didn't mean to scare you," I said.

"No, Uncle, I just didn't expect anyone to come up here."

I took a carton of Peony cigarettes out of my bag and put it on the desk, saying, "I won't take too much of your time, young man. Please keep this as a token of my regards." I didn't mean to bribe him. I was sincerely grateful to him for treating Baowen well.

"Oh, don't give me this, please."

"You don't smoke?"

"I do. Tell you what, give it to Doctor Mai. He'll help Baowen more."

I was puzzled. Why didn't he want the top-quality cigarettes if he smoked? Seeing that I was confused, he went on, "I'll be nice to Baowen without any gift from you. He's a good man. It's the doctor's wheels that you should grease."

"I have another carton for him."

"One carton's nothing here. You should give him at least two."

I was moved by his words, thanked him, and said good-bye.

Doctor Mai happened to be in his office. When I walked in, he was reading the current issue of *Women's Life,* whose back cover carried a large photo of Madame Mao on trial — she wore black and stood, handcuffed, between two young policewomen. Doctor Mai put the magazine aside and asked me to sit down. In the room, tall shelves, loaded with books and files, lined the walls. A smell of rotten fruit hung in there. He seemed pleased to see me.

After we exchanged a few words, I took out both cartons of cigarettes and handed them to him. "This is just a small token of my gratitude, for the New Year," I said.

He took the cigarettes and put them away under his desk. "Thanks a lot," he whispered.

"Doctor Mai, do you think Baowen will be cured before the holiday?" I asked.

"What did you say? Cured?" He looked surprised.

"Yes."

He shook his head slowly, then turned to check that the door was shut. He motioned me to move closer. I pulled the chair forward a little and rested my forearms on the edge of his Bakelite desktop.

"To be honest, there's no cure," he said.

"What?"

"Homosexuality isn't an illness, so it has no cure. Don't tell anyone I said this."

"Then why torture Baowen like that?"

"The police sent him here and we couldn't refuse. Besides, we ought to make him feel better and hopeful."

"So it isn't a disease?"

"Unfortunately no. Let me say this again: there's no cure for your son-in-law, Old Cheng. It's not a disease. It's just a sexual preference; it may be congenital, like being left-handed. Got it?"

"Then why give him the electric bath?" Still I wasn't convinced.

"Electrotherapy is prescribed by the book — a standard treatment required by the Department of Public Health. I have no choice but to follow the regulations. That's why I didn't give him any of those harsher treatments. The bath is very mild by comparison. You see, I've done everything in my power to help him. Let me tell you another fact: according to the statistics, so far electrotherapy has cured only one out of a thousand homosexuals. I bet cod liver oil, or chocolate, or fried pork, anything, could produce a better result. All right, enough of this. I've talked too much."

At last his words sank in. For a good while I sat there motionless with a numb mind. A flock of sparrows were flitting about in the naked branches outside the window, chasing the one that held a tiny ear of millet in its bill. Another of them dragged a yellow string tied around its leg, unable to fly as nimbly as the others. I rose to my feet and thanked the doctor for his candid words. He stubbed out his cigarette in the ashtray on the windowsill, and said, "I'll take special care of your son-in-law. Don't worry."

I rejoined Beina downstairs. Baowen looked quite cheerful, and it seemed they'd had a good time. He said to me, "If I can't come home soon, don't try too hard to get me out. They won't keep me here forever."

"I'll see what I can do."

In my heart I was exasperated, because if Doctor Mai's words were true, there'd be little I could do for Baowen. If homosexuality wasn't a disease, why had he felt sick and tried to have himself cured? Had he been shamming? It was unlikely.

Beina had been busy cleaning their home since her last visit to the hospital. She bought two young drakes and planned to make drunk duck, a dish she said Baowen liked best. My heart was heavy. On the one hand, I'd have loved to have him back for the holiday;

on the other hand, I was unsure what would happen if his condition hadn't improved. I dared not reveal my thoughts to anybody, not even to my wife, who had a big mouth. Because of her, the whole factory knew that Beina was still a virgin, and some people called her the Virgin Bride.

For days I pondered what to do. I was confused. Everybody thought homosexuality was a disease except for Doctor Mai, whose opinion I dared not mention to others. The factory leaders would be mad at me if they knew there was no cure for homosexuality. We had already spent over three thousand yuan on Baowen. I kept questioning in my mind, If homosexuality is a natural thing, then why are there men and women? Why can't two men get married and make a baby? Why didn't nature give men another hole? I was beset by doubts. If only I could have seen a trustworthy doctor for a second opinion. If only there were a knowledgeable, honest friend I could have talked with.

I hadn't yet made up my mind about what to do when Chief Miao called from the Public Security Bureau five days before the holiday. He informed me that Baowen had repeated his crime, so the police had taken him out of the hospital and sent him to the prison in Tangyuan County. "This time he did it," said the chief.

"Impossible!" I cried.

"We have evidence and witnesses. He doesn't deny it himself."

"Oh." I didn't know how to continue.

"He has to be incarcerated now."

"Are you sure he's not a hermaphrodite?" I mentioned that as a last resort.

Miao chuckled dryly. "No, he's not. We had him checked. Physically he's a man, healthy and normal. Obviously it's a mental, moral disease, like an addiction to opium."

Putting down the phone, I felt dizzy, cursing Baowen for having totally ruined himself. What had happened was that he and Fuhai Dong had developed a relationship secretly. The nurse often gave him a double amount of meat or fish at dinner. Baowen, in return, unraveled his woolen pajamas and knitted Dong a pullover with the wool. One evening when they were lying in each other's arms in the nurses' office, an old cleaner passed by in the corridor and coughed. Fuhai Dong was terrified and convinced that the man had seen what they had been doing. For days, however hard Baowen tried to talk him out of his conviction, Dong wouldn't change his mind, blaming Baowen for having misled him. He said that the old cleaner often smiled at him meaningfully and would definitely turn them in. Finally Fuhai Dong went to the hospital leaders and confessed everything. So, unlike Baowen, who got three and a half years in jail, Nurse Dong was merely put on probation; if he worked harder and criticized himself well, he might keep his current job.

That evening I went to tell Beina about the new development. As I was talking, she sobbed continually. Although she'd been cleaning the apartment for several days, her home was in shambles, most of the flowers half-dead, and dishes and pots piled in the sink. Mopping her face with a pink towel, she asked me, "What should I tell my mother-in-law?"

"Tell her the truth."

She made no response. I said again, "You should consider a divorce."

"No!" Her sobbing turned into wailing. "He — he's my husband and I'm his wife. If I die my soul belongs to him. We've sworn never to leave each other. Let others say whatever they want, I know he's a good man."

"Then why did he go to bed with a guy?"

"He just wanted to have a good time. That was all. It's nothing like adultery or bigamy, is it?"

"But it's a crime that got him into jail," I said. Although in my heart I admitted that Baowen in every way was a good fellow except for his fondness for men, I had to be adamant about my position. I was in charge of security for our factory; if I had a criminal son-in-law, who would listen to me? Wouldn't I be removed from my office soon? If I lost my job, who could protect Beina? Sooner or later she would be laid off, since a criminal's wife was not supposed to have the same opportunities for employment as others. Beina remained silent; I asked again, "What are you going to do?"

"Wait for him."

I took a few spiced pumpkin seeds from a bowl, stood up, and went over to the window. Under the sill the radiator was hissing softly with a tiny steam leak. Outside, in the distance, firecrackers one after another scattered clusters of sparks into the indigo dusk.

I turned around, and said, "He's not worth waiting for. You must divorce him."

"No, I won't," she moaned.

"Well, it's impossible for me to have a criminal as my son-in-law. I've been humiliated enough. If you want to wait for him, don't come to see me again." I put the pumpkin seeds back into the bowl, picked up my fur hat, and dragged myself out the door.

MARILYN KRYSL

The Thing Around Them

FROM NOTRE DAME REVIEW

IT WAS because of the boy dragged behind the jeep that Vasuki gave Nadesan the money to buy the ticket. When she went to her brother with the bills tucked into her sari, she did not speak the language of the master countries, nor did she know anyone who had traveled there. She was aware that at some point the island had been occupied by foreign powers, but she was not sure which powers, or when. That the Portuguese had stayed until driven out by the Dutch; that the Dutch were driven out by the British; that the British had granted the island its independence when the Crown's hand had been forced by its other colonies — these were facts she had never been told by anyone. Or if she had been told these things by a teacher or heard them referred to by a politician campaigning for a seat in Parliament, they were not facts that had seemed important. What she remembered about the master countries was that there was abundance in such degree that even the few poor were well enough off. People lived together peacefully and moved about the streets of the cities and the roads between towns without fear. She'd watched her son's face that same afternoon, how it had become lit when she gave him grain to feed the chickens. She'd taken pleasure in seeing her son's pleasure, and then she had thought of the boy behind the jeep.

Vasuki knew the boy's mother. She'd seen this boy on the school playground with the older boys, a cricket bat in his hands. Afterward, at the funeral, Vasuki had approached this boy's mother, touched her papery hand. Vasuki had felt the live dampness of that other mother's hand, and in those moments it had become clear to

Vasuki who she herself was: she was Mannika's mother, Poniah's mother. She had a girl, she had a boy, and her boy would grow to the same age as that schoolboy. A boy with shy eyes, a smile like the quick flash of a parrot bursting from its perch amid banana leaves — but the soldiers insisted this boy spied for the insurgents.

She imagined the scene in a kind of haze, its outline vibratory in the way that memories of childhood shimmer and have no edge. The boy's mother had had to watch the soldiers. They'd thrown her son down, tied one foot to the back fender of their jeep. One foot, tied at the ankle. Then they had climbed into the jeep and driven off, shouting in that language no one could understand.

When Vasuki thought of her childhood, what she remembered was herself inside a damp, shimmering sphere, a globe of green air. Her body had been itself a small globe, tenuous and full and open, merging with the air, the foliage, the waters of the lagoon, the other bodies, moving with them in the green light, the air. Her parents had rocked her in their body life the way a boat is rocked by water, and it had been as though all of them and all that was around them were the body of a single animal, sliding from the bank into the water, moving with the lagoon's lapping, which moved with the sea and with the larger currents of the air.

Vasuki and Sri had run back and forth in that green light with their brothers. Nadesan was the second son. He was their clown, sensing the ridiculous in adults, miming it. Sometimes he mimed Vasuki, her dreaminess and awe. Then she threw handfuls of sand at him. He ran, ducking, protesting. He would cover his head with his hands in mock distress, until finally she too was laughing.

She loved Nadesan for his merriment. With Sinniah, the eldest, she felt like his cherished child. She heard him shout her name: Vasuki! The tenor of his voice made it sound as if her name were made of gold. He took charge, planning expeditions to the flame trees' shade, instructing them to pack up food in banana leaves, their school thermoses. When Vasuki and Sri quarreled, he calmed them. "Don't pull your sister's hair. Be nice to each other." He taught them the names of birds, the properties of the alari. They could gather the yellow blossoms, but they should never touch the poisonous seeds.

Vasuki observed Sinniah leaning over his books in an ardor of concentration. He would take care of them all, he said, when their parents were old. "I'll find handsome husbands for you both," he told his sisters. "I'll work to make your dowries big."

In school there were clear rules, a single language. Vasuki did not understand that this was not the language of the more numerous group of people on the island. She imagined it was the universal language spoken by people everywhere, and she went on imagining this, until the army set up headquarters in the town. The army had come to protect people from the insurgents, her parents said. Though the soldiers spoke a language no one could understand, the mayor said they were friendly. Neither Vasuki's mother nor father had actually seen the soldiers, though Sinniah had looked into the back of a lorry turning a corner. One lorry held many men standing close, in dark green uniforms, each with his own rifle. Nadesan had run with his friends to the cricket field, which the soldiers had commandeered. He'd watched them marching in formation. Or was this an exercise he'd seen on the TV at the electronics shop? Nadesan's tales they didn't always believe. Still, when he mimed the soldiers' drill, their abrupt, mechanical movements, even their mother and father laughed.

Evenings were a span of blue light in which the air softened as blue sank toward black. That evening their father had just pulled Sri down onto his lap and kissed her cheek. Sri laughed with the pleasure of being at that moment the center of his attentive affection. There had been the smell of limes, the heated damp in which geckoes lived their shy lives and brilliant birds called out their daily ecstasy. Then there were soldiers — how many? — bunched in the doorway.

One of the soldiers spoke to their father in that other language. He gestured for their father to follow. Their father moved Sri from his lap and stood. Vasuki understood that somehow he had made these men angry. She felt ashamed. Her father must have done something shameful. But she was also afraid for him. It was as though some foreign thing had entered the compound, something dark and shifting that none of them, not even the soldiers, could see. She tried to look for this thing, to find its shape in the air, but the soldiers had burst through the green shimmering, ripping it. That same soldier who'd spoken now spat out an order. Two others moved forward, took hold of their father, and swept him through the doorway, down the path, into their jeep.

To have a person snatched away, just like that, as though a slit had been cut in the green air and he had been pulled through! That same night two others who cut timber with Vasuki's father were also arrested. No insurgents had appeared where they were cutting, and none of them had imagined that working in the forest where the insurgents were said to roam might cast suspicion on them. It was true that the insurgents, who had first built their camps in the north, had later built camps here, but these were inland, away from the town. They collected taxes, but after all, they had to. They were fighting for Eelam, that heaven on earth where the people would be safe. The fighters visited schools in the town and villages, recruiting young boys. Sometimes they wanted your firewood or one of your bags of rice, but usually they paid. Once, when Vasuki was in fourth grade, three young men in spotted uniforms had come, asking for petrol. When Vasuki's mother said they had none, the three had gone on.

"Who were they, in those funny clothes?" Vasuki had asked.

"Just some men needing petrol," her mother said. "Bring me a bucket of water from the well."

Each time Vasuki's mother and the other wives inquired at the army camp, the sergeant was courteous. He spoke their language, and he invited them to sit down. He listened while they repeated their petitions. Then he said he was very sorry to tell them the army knew nothing about the whereabouts of their husbands. Still, he assured them the army cared for their welfare. Inquiries would be made.

Vasuki's mother had heard there were men in the north who, like her husband, had been taken away. Some had returned and some had not. But she had not credited these rumors. Even when her husband was taken, she continued to believe he was not one of those who would not be released. There had been some mistake, and she believed the sergeant would find it. While she waited, the army set up more camps south of the town.

Then the police arrested six fishermen. The next day four were released. The other two they gave to the army for questioning. When another man arrested by the army in a northern town turned out to be her husband's cousin, Vasuki's mother did not tell her children. She told them this cousin had gone to the capital to take a plane to the Middle East, where he had found work. Vasuki listened. Her mother did not seem especially pleased by this news, but since her father had been arrested, a certain anxiousness had become the horizon note in her mother's being.

One afternoon when her mother had gone to the sergeant's office, Vasuki came home from school and began to eat a bowl of pittu. Her mother came through the gate, entered, and sat down at the table. On the way in, she had picked an alari blossom. Now she placed it before her on the table, near the bowl of bananas. Slanted sunlight fell across the flower. Her mother's face was as though fallen in.

"What is it?" Vasuki said. "Did someone hit you?"

"No," her mother said. "No one hit me." Vasuki had begun to listen more carefully to what people said. She thought of the Catholic priest who, though her family was not Catholic, had volunteered to intercede for them with the sergeant. He had used an expression Vasuki had not heard before: the disappeared.

Through the doorway Vasuki could see, on the lagoon, a single boat, bobbing. Though she could see nothing out of the ordinary, it seemed to her that this boat, which seemed to sit innocently on the water, was in danger. Something could rip the boat from the water, and, in a moment, splinter it. The light across the table had moved over the alari blossom. Now the blossom lay in shadow. Her mother looked at the blossom. Then she raised her eyes. Her mother's face was an opening into a vast place where anyone might quickly be lost.

Vasuki lifted her new son, Poniah, from the bath and held him above her. Droplets shimmered from his skin. Her daughter, Mannika, sat in the tin tub of water and chattered. Vasuki could hear the clink of pans, her mother moving about the kitchen. Two golden shower trees across the road floated in yellow haze, and the flame trees in back sent up their red fires. The lagoon at midday burned too fiercely to look at. It would have been like looking into the sun.

Each morning she watched her husband, Raj, ride toward the bridge on his bicycle. He worked at the pharmacy his family owned. She'd heard Nadesan and Sinniah leave in the early morning. For three weeks they'd worked construction. Raj had helped them get the jobs by speaking to the foreman, a friend of his father's. The pay was good, and they gave their wages for household expenses. Sinniah wanted to go to university but hadn't qualified. Today he was excused from work to take the entrance exam again. She'd recognized Nadesan's voice wishing Sinniah good luck.

Vasuki seldom thought of her father. Though the family lived in the ancestral house that was now hers, though this was the house where her father had lived with them, even her mother rarely spoke of him. The army had pulled out, moving its troops north, Vasuki and Raj had married, and children had taken up the foreground. Then the family had had to see to a dowry house for Sri. Nadesan and Sinniah had built Sri's house on a piece of land Raj purchased. Both sisters and their mother enmeshed themselves in the net of leaf, mist, birdcry. The emblems of their lives were the shredding of coconut meat, the whimper of a child in the hour before dawn, the lagoon riffled with tiny waves when a breeze swept across it.

But now the army had appeared again. Soldiers had set up a camp. They'd set up checkpoints with bunkers at either end of the bridge leading into the town. When women went to the market, the soldiers made them line up, show their ID cards, open their bags.

The soldiers had been sent to protect the people from the fighters, but this was the insurgent's home turf, and they spoke the local language. You could see how nervous the soldiers were. At night a few insurgents might enter the town to get food, or petrol. Once in a while one of them threw a grenade into an army bunker. And among the civilians the soldiers were supposed to protect, there were bound to be some who sympathized with the insurgents' cause. The soldiers were especially suspicious of young men. Young men might be fighters out of uniform, come into the town to buy food. Even if they weren't, they might help the fighters get petrol or repair a vehicle.

Families had been broken into pieces and one or two of those pieces dragged off. Sometimes the soldiers let the young man go the next morning. Sometimes they kept him a few days, then transferred him to the civil prison. Often they maintained they knew nothing of his whereabouts. It was thought important that the young man's family go to the army camp as quickly after an arrest as possible. Getting there quickly might make a difference. Once a father and two uncles had gone immediately, taking a lawyer with them, and the son had been released. If a way seemed to work, others tried it. Always they tried to find someone of stature to speak for them. Sometimes they offered the sergeant what money they had.

One young man who'd been kept almost a year had come back. His story was not a good one. Things had been done to him, things with electricity. Things with water. And yet the moon rose and set, moving the ocean's ablutions. The green curtain rippled when a breeze blew over the lagoon. Birds sang out their vibratory calls before dawn, urging the sun onto its arc. The air tasted sweet. Light laid on its hands.

Poniah made the soft sounds of a baby. Vasuki kissed him on both cheeks, blew air against the skin of his belly. His arms waved. He reminded her of a fat insect turned onto its back. She kissed Mannika's shoulder, then eased the dress over her daughter's head. While Mannika ate, Vasuki fed Poniah bites of milk-rice. Her mother went into the yard to take down laundry. Mannika examined her plastic wristwatch, playing at telling time. Now Poniah closed his lips against the bite she offered. He blew air through pursed lips and arched his back. He wanted down.

The alari bloomed beside the gate. Her mother stood there, speaking to someone. Vasuki recognized Nadesan's voice. Then her mother's voice, not speech, but a cry. She lurched across the sand, toward the house, arms around a sheaf of clothes.

"Sinniah!" Their mother sank to her knees, threw herself over the heap of laundry. "Get Raj to come with us. Vasuki! Go ask him!"

Nadesan knelt beside his mother. "I'll go for Raj," he said. He looked at Vasuki. "Yesterday four soldiers were shot. In a jeep, not far from the university, where the coconut trees are. Today the army closed the campus. They rounded up the men students, seventy of them. Seventy, Vasuki. They made them stand against a wall. Then they took them away in lorries."

"They'll let some of them go," their mother said. "There's no reason to keep Sinniah. He's not a student."

"When has reason mattered?" Nadesan said. "Four soldiers were shot."

Poniah had been wiggling in his chair. Now he sat, watching them, sensing urgency. The color of his eyes reminded Vasuki of the polished stones along the lagoon's edge, if these stones were to come alive.

Poniah learned to walk. He toddled after his father each morning, stood at the gate and watched his father wheel away. He picked alari flowers and took them to Mannika. He liked Mannika to sing to him. They played in the sand, building mounds and basins. Sometimes Sri brought her baby girl and sat in the shade with the children while Vasuki took their mother to the market.

In midday heat Poniah fell asleep against Vasuki's breast. Above the cadjan fence she could see the lagoon. The water seemed a thing alive, part of the sea's body that had flowed inland, shimmering like thousands of floating coins. People had got together a citizens' committee. This committee kept records of those who were arrested and passed on this information to the member of Parliament from their district. Still Sinniah hadn't been released. Nor did the army admit to having taken him.

At night now they heard firing in the distance. Sometimes they saw the faint flash of mortars. People talked about the thing around them, how you couldn't see how big it might be, how you couldn't tell when it would come. Even the son of the barrister, on the train to the capital, had been caught in the insurgents' ambush. The doctor's daughter walked partway home from school with her friends, waved to them, went on alone. The girls had followed this pattern every day. One day this daughter hadn't come home.

A lime green parrot squawked and flew across the compound. Vasuki carried Poniah inside, laid him on the mat, lay down beside him. Mannika napped next to her grandmother. The fighters had blown up a cargo ship in the harbor of the capital on the west side of the island. Here they'd set mines south of town where a convoy had to pass. When the mine exploded, nine soldiers died. Afterward the army burned a village in the interior.

"The army has come here to kill us," Vasuki's neighbor said.

No one said much about the fighters. Their struggle was for the people, but though they usually paid for what they took, their taxes were in addition to the government's taxes. Still the sons of some fishermen and shopkeepers had left home and joined them. Some

girls had joined too. Some of these boys and girls had been killed
in scrimmages with the army. One girl from the town who'd joined
and then been murdered was hailed by the insurgents as a mar-
tyred hero. Vasuki had seen her photograph tacked to a lamppost.

There were also boys in the town who'd trained with the fighters,
then become disillusioned. Once they deserted, they were wary of
the fighters. Most of them wanted to buy a ticket out of the country.
Sometimes two or three went from house to house, demanding
money. They threatened to identify a son or daughter to the army
as a supporter of the fighters if the family didn't pay. When one of
them went with the soldiers to the bridge to act as informer, the soldiers covered his head with a black hood so that no one could identify him. The ones he pointed to were taken away.

Vasuki turned onto her side so that she could look at Poniah
while he slept. His breath was sweet. She had learned that most
people on the island spoke the army's language. It was the language of the group from which the prime minister and most members of Parliament had been elected. It was not her language, but it
hadn't mattered. There was a member of Parliament from her district, and there were TV programs in her language. Just last week a
policeman from the group whose language Vasuki spoke and a policewoman from the larger group had celebrated their wedding at
a local hotel.

Some people also spoke the language of the master countries.
Now Vasuki knew that when the British left, the larger group on
the island had dominated Parliament. They'd declared their language the official language. Suddenly people who spoke Vasuki's
language couldn't do business, couldn't get a job. In the next generation the two groups managed to renegotiate the issue of language. For a while both languages on the island and the master language too became official languages, and the master language was
taught in schools. Then the government began to promote the
idea that native languages were superior, and the master language
was dropped from the schools' curriculum. Lately, though, it had
been reinstated. Now Mannika was learning songs in this language.
There were television programs in this language. Businessmen who
had come to set up factories spoke this language.

Vasuki had heard there was war in the master countries too,
small bits of fighting that took place in fragments: groups of boys in

gangs, policemen attacking a man with dark skin, a crowd in one city burning shops owned by Koreans. And war within families: sons killing a father, a father raping a daughter, a husband killing his adulterous wife. Vasuki thought these stories were probably exaggerated. Anyway, those things were not war. And besides, mostly people said that those who learned the master language and went to one of the master countries became very wealthy. It would be to Poniah's advantage, she thought, if he could learn the language of the more numerous group and a bit of the master language too.

The green curtain tore. Soldiers cut the coconut trees to use the trunks for bunkers. It felt as though angry speech had shot out across the air, cursing whatever lovely thing was in its path. Orchard after orchard all the way back to that first generation fell in this cutting. Even the orchards that belonged to the Catholic priests were cut without a single piece of paper granting official dispensation. The stumps were white, shocking. Afterward the undergrowth died. An acreage of sand lay flat beneath the sun. You didn't want to walk there. There was too much sadness in those places.

For the second year there was drought. People had to carry water from the few wells in the town deep enough to reach what was left. Sometimes the wind picked up a sheet of sand and blew it against the houses. Drought leached color from leaves. The sky was dun.

Vasuki paid attention to news. The papers reported both good things and bad things. A new five-star hotel opened in the capital. Nine village boys were picked up by soldiers, kept for a day, then delivered to the civil prison. There was a new TV program in which the women looked like women from the master countries. Nineteen boys were lured away by videos the fighters had shown at the high school. A new fertilizer plant opened in a city to the south, which would employ three thousand people. Thirty-six boys gathered for a sports match were rounded up and taken away.

Then the fighters blew up two oil storage tanks on the outskirts of the capital. Quickly the police went through the capital's neighborhoods, calling in for questioning young men whose names and language identified them as belonging to the smaller group. Some of these young men were let go. Others were held but not charged. On the eighth day after the oil fires, twenty-three bodies were found floating in a lake twenty miles from the capital. The young men's hands had been tied behind their backs.

Vasuki stood mixing pittu with her hands. The lagoon swayed in its shallow basin, its surface silver riffles. It was said there were fish in the middle of the lagoon, fish which at midnight on the night of the full moon would begin to sing. You could hear them, the singing fish, if you took a boat to the middle of the water. But no one now took a boat out after dark.

A boy appeared at the window. He wore a knife strapped to his belt, and a T-shirt. The lettering on the T-shirt was in the master language. He was one of those boys who'd left the fighters, she thought, and now wanted money.

"Go," Vasuki said. "I have nothing for you."

"Give me something."

"I can give you a packet of food."

"Hurry up, then," he said. He watched her spoon rice and curry into a banana leaf. She offered the packet. He took it and walked to where the chickens pecked at their grain. He knelt. A curious hen eyed him. When the hen came close, he grabbed her by the legs and carried her, squawking, through the gate.

Raj was tall. Height singled him out. People turned their bodies toward him. Because he inspired trust, he'd been asked to join the Citizens' Committee. Though he left for the pharmacy each morning, the effect of his height lingered in the compound. He was there, or nearby. He was going, or coming. The sun climbed its arc, leveled, slid slowly down the sky. He returned before the advent of twilight.

He returned to Vasuki where she stood in the doorway. She was the color red, its heated pulse. Now the family had a man to tend its flame. When Mannika was born, Vasuki became the mother of the family. She assumed the mother's place in her mother's ancestral house. Raj was the priest, holding aloft the burning camphor, approaching the inner room of the temple. There at the center stood Vasuki, the flaming mouth.

On the afternoon Raj was stopped on the bridge, Mannika had come out of school carrying the drawing she'd made of an umbrella. The fighters had recently acquired new weapons, and when three air force planes had flown over one of the insurgents' camps, the fighters were able to shoot all three down. Everyone knew there would be reprisals. Though Mannika was seven and could walk to school by herself, Vasuki had begun to accompany her. She left Poniah at Sri's house and picked him up on the way back. There was wind that day. Though usually Vasuki welcomed its wildness, that day it stung. She put her arm around Mannika to shield her. Mannika told her mother how first she'd chosen red for the umbrella, then blue, then changed her mind a third time to yellow. Finally she'd decided to make each panel of the umbrella a different color. When she'd done that, there were still colors she hadn't used. So many colors, and they all deserved to be seen. What was one to do?

Vasuki had thought ahead to Raj's arrival. She would repeat Mannika's story. He would be amused. When they'd picked up Poniah, Vasuki carried him, trying to protect him from the wind's whipping. Mannika complained that she too needed to be carried. At their gate the wind had blown down a scatter of alari blossoms. Vasuki brought the children inside to play.

A little later the wind stopped. The quiet seemed pristine. Like a god stepping down, it announced itself. Then Nadesan was at the gate.

"Raj," he said. "At the bridge."

Later, after she and Nadesan had left the sergeant's office, she remembered a thing she'd noticed that afternoon while Mannika and Poniah played on the floor. Wind had roughed up the lagoon's surface. The ripples had seemed to her as though beaten with a whip, as though the wind were flaying a skin.

Inside herself Vasuki constructed a pyre like the one on which the family would have cremated Raj's body. She would not be like those other women, helpless in their waiting. She would not soften like a ripe fruit left to rot. She would not wait. She would not hope. She was the mother, and now she stood up inside this presence. She would become even more fiercely the mother.

She lit the pyre and the sticks caught. Flame after flame rose up, combining in conflagration. She imagined this heat destroying all hurt, redeeming Raj from the pain he had surely suffered. Each time she felt herself beginning to long for him, she went back to the smoking pyre. She fed the flame sticks. She gave it food. She gave it flowers. She went back again. She stood watch over this burning.

Mannika was at the top of her class. She would flit quickly from one part of the house to another, so that in these quick movements she seemed to be sparkling. She liked teaching Poniah songs in the master language. Sometimes she sat him on her lap and read to him. He gazed into the distance, eagerly and with a small frown, imagining the events Mannika described. Afterward, while Mannika helped him perform his chore, stacking palm branches the wind had blown down, she would sing a line, and Poniah would sing it after her.

You couldn't get widow's compensation without a death certificate, and you couldn't get a death certificate for a person unless you could prove he had died. Her mother's health began to fail, and there were medical expenses. Her mother left the house to help care for Sri's second daughter, but Vasuki had to help Sri and her husband pay for their mother's treatment. Nadesan gave Vasuki almost all his salary for her household expenses, but the drought drove up prices. Raj's younger brother took over the pharmacy, but he was able to give Vasuki only a little.

Still she began to set aside little bits of money. Raj had put away money against emergencies, and when she could she added to this. That year Nadesan was approached with marriage proposals from four families. There were fewer young men now, and more women had to go without husbands. Nadesan was handsome, and his mischievousness had matured into an attractive cheerfulness. He chose a girl whose family were cashew growers. When he moved into his wife's ancestral house, he continued to give Vasuki money.

Vasuki went to the temple to pray for her children's safety. She had taken a vow, asked the goddess to protect them. To perform the vow, she had walked the fire with the other women, carrying Poniah in her arms. She tried to live simply, to treat others with generosity. But sometimes a searing fear shot through her. A slit in the air: you couldn't see it, but suddenly someone who'd been right beside you was pulled out.

Sons more than daughters. Though more and more it seemed what was around them might devour a daughter as easily as a son. The soldiers picked up girls at random, kept them a few days, dropped them by the side of the road. Some lay in the ditch and did not move. Others managed to walk back to their houses. One lay in bed two months, then died. Some came back to their parents' houses, then swallowed the poisonous seeds of the alari.

Vasuki's mother caught pneumonia. Two days later she died. After the funeral Vasuki asked Nadesan to put a little money aside for her. He asked why. When she told him, he shook his head. He had heard that in one of those countries some Turks, refugees, he said, had been sleeping, and their hostel had been set on fire by a crowd. The crowd watched the fire rise up and cheered. Those who ran out were caught and beaten by people in the crowd.

Vasuki listened with impatience. There may have been some incident where one or two people got hurt, but everyone knew people in the master countries were rich, and there was no war. People there wanted to adopt foreign children, so why would they beat up foreigners? There any child could learn to become a doctor or scientist or the head of a manufacturing firm. There were washing machines, vacuum cleaners, a VCR. Everyone owned a car. Children were driven to school in these cars and picked up when school let out.

Nadesan, she thought, was playing the part of family patriarch. He and his wife were expecting a baby, and he was proud in that strutting way of a rooster. He would become a father. Ensconced in this dispensation, he spoke with confidence.

"Things are going to be better here," he said. "You'll see."

Many mango trees died from the drought. The army banned fishing because fighters had come into the town and thrown grenades over the fence near the brigadier's headquarters. There was not much fish in the market, and vegetables were expensive. Vasuki stood in the queue for water. The women waiting talked. America had sent Green Berets to help train the soldiers. The generals expected that with the Americans would come better, more expensive equipment, which would enable them to rout the insurgents. Young men who had previously shunned the army's ranks were signing up. They wanted to be near these foreign soldiers who wore their tall, powerful bodies like a uniform and looked as though nothing at all could stand against them.

Soon after the Green Berets arrived, the army announced the

north had been "cleared." The generals sent more troops east.
Suddenly there were many more soldiers in the town. When their
lorries weren't enough, they commandeered public buses. One
woman said she'd set off to attend a funeral, but there had been no
bus. At checkpoints the soldiers ran their bayonets through the
women's cloth bags of rice. It was only a matter of time, the women
agreed, before the fighters killed some of these new soldiers. Then
there would be a very bad incident, perhaps several. Young men
would be rounded up, or the soldiers might set a village afire, or
they might arrest fishermen because their work in the sun made
their skins very dark, like the skins of the fighters who lived in the
open.

"The best thing," one of the women said, "would be if a big
bomb came and killed all of us at once."

At the end of the second day of the army's assault, Nadesan's wife
went into labor. The fighters had attacked an army camp near the
town, killed fifty-two soldiers, and set three tents on fire. Soldiers
shot farmers in their fields, burned houses. In the town no queues
formed. No buses ran. Shops closed. People went into their houses
and shut the doors. Now something was wrong with Nadesan's wife.
The labor went on longer than it should have. When the midwife
pulled the baby out, the little boy was dead.

That same day soldiers tied the boy's foot to the bumper of their
jeep. The boy's mother told Vasuki that the jeep had come back.
The driver had halted on the main street. She'd hurried to meet it,
stood a little away, watched one of the soldiers step down. If he noticed her, he'd paid no attention. He'd taken a knife from his belt
and cut the rope.

The next day Vasuki gave Nadesan the money. She took the children to the lagoon. Poniah reminded his mother of one of the tiny
chittering frogs that appeared in the mud after a rain. He squatted
and set his paper boat onto the swaying water. He watched the boat
rocking on the waves and sang one of the songs Mannika had
taught him.

"Look!" he said, pointing up. Five gulls wheeled over the water.

"You're going to fly like one of those gulls," Vasuki said. She explained he would travel in a very big airplane to a new country
where there were no soldiers and children ran about freely. On the

plane, there would be a kind auntie who would give him sweets and a toy plane to play with while the big plane flew through the sky.

He would be the first to see the new country. She and Mannika would come a little later. The gulls flew toward the sea. Mannika frowned. Would Sri and their cousins come too? Their uncle Nadesan? Vasuki nodded.

"Poniah's too little to go alone," Mannika said. "I should go with him."

"You would leave your mother alone?" Vasuki teased.

"Of course not," Mannika said. "We would send for you as soon as we got there."

The neighbor's bitch, a small terrier, had come in heat. Her suitors came three nights, baying in the moonlight, sprinting up and down along the fence. The third night Vasuki got up, filled a bucket with the bad well water, and threw it on them. In the ensuing quiet she slept without dreams. She woke early and went through the gate into the lane. To the west the full moon stood just above the horizon. To the east the sun was appearing over the water. She stood exactly between these poles. Encompassed by the timed motion of these bodies, she felt her decision confirmed.

But could she manage the pain of ripping Poniah from her? That morning she got a small suitcase ready. In it she put new clothes, small toys. A statue of the goddess. She'd bought a book, the book Mannika was reading to Poniah in the master language. She pictured Poniah holding his little bag, stepping down from the plane. There below, smiling, the kind parents, ready to love him, the mother bending over, ready to take his miniature body into her arms. Though perhaps an official would meet him, take him somewhere else to meet the parents? Either way, his mother would be blond. Vasuki imagined the little ways in which this new woman would cherish his perfect body. And the father, a tall man, like one of those Green Berets, would be kind. She imagined his approval, his head nodding. He would be proud of this good son.

Green parrots squawked and dove in and out of the banana leaves. The flame trees put forth their fiery petals. When she'd finished her morning chores, she took Poniah to the lagoon. Two butterflies near a margosa swooped in elliptical arcs around each other. A fisherman repairing his boat agreed to give Poniah a ride.

They stayed close to shore, and when the fisherman steered the boat in, Poniah climbed out, splashing and smiling.

"Has Mannika been in a boat?" he said. "I don't think so."

At dusk Vasuki let him feed the chickens. They clucked excitedly, running to where his arm flung the grain. Poniah came back to the house suffused with accomplishment. The moon rose over the lagoon. Stars glittered above the sand. Mannika helped Poniah finish filling the suitcase. He put in a toy truck and a small doll Mannika gave him. Then he brought his favorite sheet from the clothesline.

"It has dried in the moonlight," he announced. He laid the sheet across the doll. Then he ran outside, plucked three alari blossoms and laid them on top.

Earth and air conspired in the darkness, and sweet rain fell in abundance. The golden shower trees across the lane and the flame trees in back were drunk with it. Tiny birds perched, ruffling their feathers. Rain dripped from their tails. The sand was pounded, washed clean.

Vasuki lay beside Poniah. When the rain ceased, she was able to sleep. Later, when the alarm woke her, the moon was just going down. She woke Poniah, bathed and dressed him. While he ate, Nadesan arrived, hearty and joking. He would take Poniah to the capital. He'd arranged for another passenger, a distant cousin of his wife's, to look out for Poniah on the flight. He admired his nephew's suitcase. He tapped Poniah on the shoulder and winked.

"You and I are going off to adventure. The others are not brave enough, and so must stay here where nothing happens."

It was light enough to see. Mannika still slept, and Poniah went to her and kissed her cheek. He walked with his mother and uncle to the gate. Vasuki kissed him, then stood back. She watched Poniah take his uncle's hand. They stepped through the gate. Poniah turned and waved. Vasuki waved back. She stood in the lane until they turned the corner.

She walked to the house through the cries of parrots. Each morning she heard their raucous calls, like bolts of color shot through the highest branches. This morning each cry sounded like the glint of a blade.

The flame trees held out their handfuls of hot petals. A breeze riffled the fronds of the neighbor's banana trees. Mannika was gay, getting dressed. She chattered about what Poniah might be doing at this moment. Vasuki hoped Poniah wouldn't become homesick before the plane took off. Her grief hovered on that nebulous, shifting division between bearable and unbearable. She would be like Sri, with a daughter, without a boy. She would live around Mannika's needs. She would join the Citizens' Committee. And she resolved to learn a little of the language Mannika was becoming so good at, the language that was going to become Poniah's language.

On the walk to school Mannika made up a list of things she and her mother would do together. A lark swooped down before them, its glide a soft whistle, then turned its trajectory up and away. Vasuki was relieved that Mannika didn't seem to miss Poniah too much, at least not yet. She noticed the shape of a blossom fallen in the road beside the school gate. The lilt and rush of excitement in Mannika's good-bye seemed to Vasuki new language the universe was just now creating, language she was barely beginning to hear.

She walked back through the pattern of light and shade spread on the sand. In the compound a yellow bird flitted down to peck grain the chickens missed. It was necessary to boil more drinking water. She set about this task and began to weep. She wept, and the heat built its esplanade across the day. Geckoes slid off into shade. The lagoon lay flat, as though there were no disturbance anywhere in the world, as though whole things could not be broken.

When she sat to drink a glass of water, the heat felt like a familiar body, someone she slept next to. But this world beyond her body seemed strange now. It was as though a strange new color had been loosed into the world. She could not decide whether this color was beautiful.

A haze of yellow butterflies flitted above the alari, and on the fence perched two tiny birds whose heads were azure. Vasuki stepped into the lane, closed the gate. Usually the lane was empty. Now five soldiers came striding toward her. One of them glanced at her, then away. Vasuki stepped aside to let them pass.

Soldiers did not come here. They stayed on the other side of the bridge. She walked to where the lane met the main road. Now there were many soldiers, spreading out from lorries. Those near glanced at her and moved on. Four and five at a time were going door to door, knocking, shouting for the occupants. In one doorway a young man appeared in his sarong, his eyes nervously darting among the soldiers' faces.

What had happened to make the soldiers come here? It must have been something bigger than a mine. There was the smell of smoke, of someone cooking. Or was it a cooking fire kicked apart by a soldier? Lucky that Nadesan had gone to the capital, lucky that Sri's husband wouldn't have come home yet. Vasuki hurried toward the school. The lagoon water was as smooth and perfect as a mirror. She tried to calm herself, to become still, swaying only a little, like water. But her body refused this counsel. How slow and soft the air around her, and how nervously she was rushing through it. Then the school was before her, two hibiscus at the gate, their flowers hot orange. The playground was deserted. The principal, a stately woman who always wore a sari, let Vasuki in. Other mothers were gathered just inside the entrance.

"What's happened?" Vasuki asked. The principal shook her head.

"Who can say? Best to wait here until the soldiers go back across the bridge. We'll all wait together."

Mannika saw Vasuki and ran to her, waving a piece of paper.

"This is our house, at night. You can't see us because you and Daddy and I and Poniah are sleeping, but all the trees are there, and I've put in a moon."

Vasuki knelt and hugged her. She looked at Mannika's drawing.

"Soldiers!" a boy called. Vasuki stood. Through the open casement she saw them. Seven soldiers. They'd come through the gate and now stood, waiting. Behind them, one at a time, more soldiers were coming through the gate. All of them wore the same black-laced boots.

They spread out in a line facing the school's entrance. The children hushed. In the quiet the children's white uniforms seemed very bright. Vasuki closed her eyes, let them rest for a moment on blankness. When she opened them, she saw a child tugging his mother's sari, pleading to be picked up. His mother lifted him, and he clutched her waist with his legs.

The soldiers stood close enough that Vasuki could see their faces. She saw how different each face was, one handsome, the next with pocked skin, one fierce, another bewildered, nervous. They were young, hardly more than schoolboys. Beyond them the hibiscus put forth its blooms. Vasuki wanted to call out to the soldiers, ask their names, the names of their parents. But none of the soldiers looked at her. The line curved and kept curving until it circled the school. Then one of the soldiers shouted in Vasuki's language.

"Out!" he shouted. "Everyone come out."

The principal stepped forward.

"Don't go," one mother said. "Don't open the door."

The principal frowned. She held herself proudly. "I must talk to them," she said. "It may be that they only want the building."

Mannika tugged at Vasuki's sari. Vasuki spoke the appropriate, calming words, but as soon as she'd spoken, she could not remember what she'd said. She thought how the green still held in some places. So many rips, so much tearing, and yet a mango was still perfectly what it was. No matter how many soldiers died, you could take a bath, feel the water's sacral pouring. And children kept coming into the world, running from shade to sunlit sand, their voices calling each other the way gulls called out from their wheeling.

Something hidden and hot swelled in Vasuki then, like a flag grandly unfurling from its pole. She'd acted in time. She'd outsmarted these soldiers. Poniah was on his way to a country where kind and wealthy people wanted foreign children. She'd thought ahead, she'd done the right thing. She'd sent her son out of the country of death to another country where he would be safe.

She tried to focus on the face of the nearest soldier, but her vision wavered as though she were seeing through scrim. Mannika's body pressed against her hip. Vasuki looked down at Mannika's hand, holding the drawing. Such a small hand, a hand that had gripped a green crayon, had moved it decisively across paper. She saw her own hand, gathering in Mannika's shoulder. She looked at her own long fingers.

This was not a hand that could save anyone. It was good only for brushing away flies, for mixing pittu. Then, for a moment, this hand seemed not her own but the hand of a stranger. It occurred to her that there was a thing this hand might do, a thing she had not thought of until now. If the soldiers let them go home, this hand could do it, as she and Mannika entered the compound. She imagined this hand reaching out to the alari. She imagined its fingers gathering the alari's seeds.

JHUMPA LAHIRI

The Third and Final Continent

FROM THE NEW YORKER

I LEFT INDIA in 1964 with a certificate in commerce and the equivalent, in those days, of ten dollars to my name. For three weeks I sailed on the S.S. *Roma,* an Italian cargo vessel, in a cabin next to the ship's engine, across the Arabian Sea, the Red Sea, the Mediterranean, and finally to England. I lived in London, in Finsbury Park, in a house occupied entirely by penniless Bengali bachelors like myself, at least a dozen and sometimes more, all struggling to educate and establish ourselves abroad.

I attended lectures at LSE and worked at the university library to get by. We lived three or four to a room, shared a single, icy toilet, and took turns cooking pots of egg curry, which we ate with our hands on a table covered with newspapers. Apart from our jobs we had few responsibilities. On weekends we lounged barefoot in drawstring pajamas, drinking tea and smoking Rothmans, or set out to watch cricket at Lord's. Some weekends the house was crammed with still more Bengalis, to whom we had introduced ourselves at the greengrocer, or on the Tube, and we made yet more egg curry, and played Mukesh on a Grundig reel-to-reel, and soaked our dirty dishes in the bathtub. Every now and then someone in the house moved out, to live with a woman whom his family back in Calcutta had determined he was to wed. In 1969, when I was thirty-six years old, my own marriage was arranged. Around the same time, I was offered a full-time job in America, in the processing department of a library at MIT. The salary was generous enough to support a wife, and I was honored to be hired by a world-famous university, and so I obtained a green card, and prepared to travel farther still.

By then I had enough money to go by plane. I flew first to Calcutta, to attend my wedding, and a week later to Boston, to begin my new job. During the flight I read "The Student Guide to North America," for although I was no longer a student, I was on a budget all the same. I learned that Americans drove on the right side of the road, not the left, and that they called a lift an elevator and an engaged phone busy. "The pace of life in North America is different from Britain, as you will soon discover," the guidebook informed me. "Everybody feels he must get to the top. Don't expect an English cup of tea." As the plane began its descent over Boston Harbor, the pilot announced the weather and the time, and that President Nixon had declared a national holiday: two American men had landed on the moon. Several passengers cheered. "God bless America!" one of them hollered. Across the aisle, I saw a woman praying.

I spent my first night at the YMCA in Central Square, Cambridge, an inexpensive accommodation recommended by my guidebook which was within walking distance of MIT. The room contained a cot, a desk, and a small wooden cross on one wall. A sign on the door said that cooking was strictly forbidden. A bare window overlooked Massachusetts Avenue. Car horns, shrill and prolonged, blared one after another. Sirens and flashing lights heralded endless emergencies, and a succession of buses rumbled past, their doors opening and closing with a powerful hiss, throughout the night. The noise was constantly distracting, at times suffocating. I felt it deep in my ribs, just as I had felt the furious drone of the engine on the S.S. *Roma*. But there was no ship's deck to escape to, no glittering ocean to thrill my soul, no breeze to cool my face, no one to talk to. I was too tired to pace the gloomy corridors of the YMCA in my pajamas. Instead I sat at the desk and stared out the window. In the morning I reported to my job at the Dewey Library, a beige fortlike building by Memorial Drive. I also opened a bank account, rented a post office box, and bought a plastic bowl and a spoon. I went to a supermarket called Purity Supreme, wandering up and down the aisles, comparing prices with those in England. In the end I bought a carton of milk and a box of cornflakes. This was my first meal in America. Even the simple chore of buying milk was new to me; in London we'd had bottles delivered each morning to our door.

*

In a week I had adjusted, more or less. I ate cornflakes and milk morning and night, and bought some bananas for variety, slicing them into the bowl with the edge of my spoon. I left my carton of milk on the shaded part of the windowsill, as I had seen other residents at the YMCA do. To pass the time in the evenings I read the *Boston Globe* downstairs, in a spacious room with stained-glass windows. I read every article and advertisement, so that I would grow familiar with things, and when my eyes grew tired I slept. Only I did not sleep well. Each night I had to keep the window wide open; it was the only source of air in the stifling room, and the noise was intolerable. I would lie on the cot with my fingers pressed into my ears, but when I drifted off to sleep my hands fell away, and the noise of the traffic would wake me up again. Pigeon feathers drifted onto the windowsill, and one evening, when I poured milk over my cornflakes, I saw that it had soured. Nevertheless I resolved to stay at the YMCA for six weeks, until my wife's passport and green card were ready. Once she arrived I would have to rent a proper apartment, and from time to time I studied the classified section of the newspaper, or stopped in at the housing office at MIT during my lunch break to see what was available. It was in this manner that I discovered a room for immediate occupancy, in a house on a quiet street, the listing said, for $8 per week. I dialed the number from a pay telephone, sorting through the coins, with which I was still unfamiliar, smaller and lighter than shillings, heavier and brighter than paisas.

"Who is speaking?" a woman demanded. Her voice was bold and clamorous.

"Yes, good afternoon, Madam. I am calling about the room for rent."

"Harvard or Tech?"

"I beg your pardon?"

"Are you from Harvard or Tech?"

Gathering that Tech referred to the Massachusetts Institute of Technology, I replied, "I work at Dewey Library," adding tentatively, "at Tech."

"I only rent rooms to boys from Harvard or Tech!"

"Yes, Madam."

I was given an address and an appointment for seven o'clock that evening. Thirty minutes before the hour I set out, my guidebook in my pocket, my breath fresh with Listerine. I turned down a street shaded with trees, perpendicular to Massachusetts Avenue. In spite of the heat I wore a coat and tie, regarding the event as I would any other interview; I had never lived in the home of a person who was not Indian. The house, surrounded by a chain-link fence, was off-white with dark brown trim, with a tangle of forsythia bushes plastered against its front and sides. When I pressed the bell, the woman with whom I had spoken on the phone hollered from what seemed to be just the other side of the door, "One minute, please!"

Several minutes later the door was opened by a tiny, extremely old woman. A mass of snowy hair was arranged like a small sack on top of her head. As I stepped into the house she sat down on a wooden bench positioned at the bottom of a narrow carpeted staircase. Once she was settled on the bench, in a small pool of light, she peered up at me, giving me her undivided attention. She wore a long black skirt that spread like a stiff tent to the floor, and a starched white shirt edged with ruffles at the throat and cuffs. Her hands, folded together in her lap, had long pallid fingers, with swollen knuckles and tough yellow nails. Age had battered her features so that she almost resembled a man, with sharp, shrunken eyes and prominent creases on either side of her nose. Her lips, chapped and faded, had nearly disappeared, and her eyebrows were missing altogether. Nevertheless she looked fierce.

"Lock up!" she commanded. She shouted even though I stood only a few feet away. "Fasten the chain and firmly press that button on the knob! This is the first thing you shall do when you enter, is that clear?"

I locked the door as directed and examined the house. Next to the bench was a small round table, its legs fully concealed, much like the woman's, by a skirt of lace. The table held a lamp, a transistor radio, a leather change purse with a silver clasp, and a telephone. A thick wooden cane was propped against one side. There was a parlor to my right, lined with bookcases and filled with shabby claw-footed furniture. In the corner of the parlor I saw a grand piano with its top down, piled with papers. The piano's bench was missing; it seemed to be the one on which the woman was sitting. Somewhere in the house a clock chimed seven times.

"You're punctual!" the woman proclaimed. "I expect you shall be so with the rent!"

"I have a letter, Madam." In my jacket pocket was a letter from

MIT confirming my employment, which I had brought along to prove that I was indeed from Tech.

She stared at the letter, then handed it back to me carefully, gripping it with her fingers as if it were a plate heaped with food. She did not wear glasses, and I wondered if she'd read a word of it. "The last boy was always late! Still owes me eight dollars! Harvard boys aren't what they used to be! Only Harvard and Tech in this house! How's Tech, boy?"

"It is very well."

"You checked the lock?"

"Yes, Madam."

She unclasped her fingers, slapped the space beside her on the bench with one hand, and told me to sit down. For a moment she was silent. Then she intoned, as if she alone possessed this knowledge:

"There is an American flag on the moon!"

"Yes, Madam." Until then I had not thought very much about the moon shot. It was in the newspaper, of course, article upon article. The astronauts had landed on the shores of the Sea of Tranquillity, I had read, traveling farther than anyone in the history of civilization. For a few hours they explored the moon's surface. They gathered rocks in their pockets, described their surroundings (a magnificent desolation, according to one astronaut), spoke by phone to the president, and planted a flag in lunar soil. The voyage was hailed as man's most awesome achievement.

The woman bellowed, "A flag on the moon, boy! I heard it on the radio! Isn't that splendid?"

"Yes, Madam."

But she was not satisfied with my reply. Instead she commanded, "Say 'Splendid!'"

I was both baffled and somewhat insulted by the request. It reminded me of the way I was taught multiplication tables as a child, repeating after the master, sitting cross-legged on the floor of my one-room Tollygunge school. It also reminded me of my wedding, when I had repeated endless Sanskrit verses after the priest, verses I barely understood, which joined me to my wife. I said nothing.

"Say 'Splendid!'" the woman bellowed once again.

"Splendid," I murmured. I had to repeat the word a second time at the top of my lungs, so she could hear. I was reluctant to raise my voice to an elderly woman, but she did not appear to be offended. If anything the reply pleased her, because her next command was:

"Go see the room!"

I rose from the bench and mounted the narrow staircase. There were five doors, two on either side of an equally narrow hallway, and one at the opposite end. Only one door was open. The room contained a twin bed under a sloping ceiling, a brown oval rug, a basin with an exposed pipe, and a chest of drawers. One door led to a closet, another to a toilet and a tub. The window was open; net curtains stirred in the breeze. I lifted them away and inspected the view: a small back yard, with a few fruit trees and an empty clothesline. I was satisfied.

When I returned to the foyer the woman picked up the leather change purse on the table, opened the clasp, fished about with her fingers, and produced a key on a thin wire hoop. She informed me that there was a kitchen at the back of the house, accessible through the parlor. I was welcome to use the stove as long as I left it as I found it. Sheets and towels were provided, but keeping them clean was my own responsibility. The rent was due Friday mornings on the ledge above the piano keys. "And no lady visitors!"

"I am a married man, Madam." It was the first time I had announced this fact to anyone.

But she had not heard. "No lady visitors!" she insisted. She introduced herself as Mrs. Croft.

My wife's name was Mala. The marriage had been arranged by my older brother and his wife. I regarded the proposition with neither objection nor enthusiasm. It was a duty expected of me, as it was expected of every man. She was the daughter of a schoolteacher in Beleghata. I was told that she could cook, knit, embroider, sketch landscapes, and recite poems by Tagore, but these talents could not make up for the fact that she did not possess a fair complexion, and so a string of men had rejected her to her face. She was twenty-seven, an age when her parents had begun to fear that she would never marry, and so they were willing to ship their only child halfway across the world in order to save her from spinsterhood.

For five nights we shared a bed. Each of those nights, after applying cold cream and braiding her hair, she turned from me and wept; she missed her parents. Although I would be leaving the country in a few days, custom dictated that she was now a part of my household, and for the next six weeks she was to live with my brother and his wife, cooking, cleaning, serving tea and sweets to guests. I did nothing to console her. I lay on my own side of the bed, reading my guidebook by flashlight. At times I thought of the tiny room on the other side of the wall which had belonged to my mother. Now the room was practically empty; the wooden pallet on which she'd once slept was piled with trunks and old bedding. Nearly six years ago, before leaving for London, I had watched her die on that bed, had found her playing with her excrement in her final days. Before we cremated her I had cleaned each of her fingernails with a hairpin, and then, because my brother could not bear it, I had assumed the role of eldest son, and had touched the flame to her temple, to release her tormented soul to heaven.

The next morning I moved into Mrs. Croft's house. When I unlocked the door I saw that she was sitting on the piano bench, on the same side as the previous evening. She wore the same black skirt, the same starched white blouse, and had her hands folded together the same way in her lap. She looked so much the same that I wondered if she'd spent the whole night on the bench. I put my suitcase upstairs and then headed off to work. That evening when I came home from the university, she was still there.

"Sit down, boy!" She slapped the space beside her.

I perched on the bench. I had a bag of groceries with me — more milk, more cornflakes, and more bananas, for my inspection of the kitchen earlier in the day had revealed no spare pots or pans. There were only two saucepans in the refrigerator, both containing some orange broth, and a copper kettle on the stove.

"Good evening, Madam."

She asked me if I had checked the lock. I told her I had.

For a moment she was silent. Then suddenly she declared, with the equal measures of disbelief and delight as the night before, "There's an American flag on the moon, boy!"

"Yes, Madam."

"A flag on the moon! Isn't that splendid?"

I nodded, dreading what I knew was coming. "Yes, Madam."

"Say 'Splendid!'"

This time I paused, looking to either side in case anyone was there to overhear me, though I knew perfectly well that the house was empty. I felt like an idiot. But it was a small enough thing to ask. "Splendid!" I cried out.

Within days it became our routine. In the mornings when I left for the library Mrs. Croft was either hidden away in her bedroom, on the other side of the staircase, or sitting on the bench, oblivious of my presence, listening to the news or classical music on the radio. But each evening when I returned the same thing happened: she slapped the bench, ordered me to sit down, declared that there was a flag on the moon, and declared that it was splendid. I said it was splendid, too, and then we sat in silence. As awkward as it was, and as endless as it felt to me then, the nightly encounter lasted only about ten minutes; inevitably she would drift off to sleep, her head falling abruptly toward her chest, leaving me free to retire to my room. By then, of course, there was no flag standing on the moon. The astronauts, I read in the paper, had seen it fall before they flew back to Earth. But I did not have the heart to tell her.

Friday morning, when my first week's rent was due, I went to the piano in the parlor to place my money on the ledge. The piano keys were dull and discolored. When I pressed one, it made no sound at all. I had put eight dollar bills in an envelope and written Mrs. Croft's name on the front of it. I was not in the habit of leaving money unmarked and unattended. From where I stood I could see the profile of her tent-shaped skirt in the hall. It seemed unnecessary to make her get up and walk all the way to the piano. I never saw her walking about, and assumed, from the cane propped against the round table, that she did so with difficulty. When I approached the bench she peered up at me and demanded:

"What is your business?"

"The rent, Madam."

"On the ledge above the piano keys!"

"I have it here." I extended the envelope toward her, but her fingers, folded together in her lap, did not budge. I bowed slightly and lowered the envelope, so that it hovered just above her hands. After a moment she accepted it, and nodded her head.

That night when I came home, she did not slap the bench, but out of habit I sat beside her as usual. She asked me if I had checked the lock, but she mentioned nothing about the flag on the moon. Instead she said:

"It was very kind of you!"

"I beg your pardon, Madam?"

"Very kind of you!"

She was still holding the envelope in her hands.

On Sunday there was a knock on my door. An elderly woman introduced herself: she was Mrs. Croft's daughter, Helen. She walked
into the room and looked at each of the walls as if for signs of
change, glancing at the shirts that hung in the closet, the neckties
draped over the doorknob, the box of cornflakes on the chest of
drawers, the dirty bowl and spoon in the basin. She was short and
thick-waisted, with cropped silver hair and bright pink lipstick. She
wore a sleeveless summer dress, a necklace of white plastic beads,
and spectacles on a chain that hung like a swing against her chest.
The backs of her legs were mapped with dark blue veins, and her
upper arms sagged like the flesh of a roasted eggplant. She told me
she lived in Arlington, a town farther up Massachusetts Avenue. "I
come once a week to bring Mother groceries. Has she sent you
packing yet?"

"It is very well, Madam."

"Some of the boys run screaming. But I think she likes you.
You're the first boarder she's ever referred to as a gentleman."

She looked at me, noticing my bare feet. (I still felt strange wearing shoes indoors, and always removed them before entering my
room.) "Are you new to Boston?"

"New to America, Madam."

"From?" She raised her eyebrows.

"I am from Calcutta, India."

"Is that right? We had a Brazilian fellow, about a year ago. You'll
find Cambridge a very international city."

I nodded, and began to wonder how long our conversation
would last. But at that moment we heard Mrs. Croft's electrifying
voice rising up the stairs.

"You are to come downstairs immediately!"

"What is it?" Helen cried back.

"Immediately!"

I put on my shoes. Helen sighed.

I followed Helen down the staircase. She seemed to be in no
hurry, and complained at one point that she had a bad knee. "Have
you been walking without your cane?" Helen called out. "You know

you're not supposed to walk without that cane." She paused, resting her hand on the banister, and looked back at me. "She slips sometimes."

For the first time Mrs. Croft seemed vulnerable. I pictured her on the floor in front of the bench, flat on her back, staring at the ceiling, her feet pointing in opposite directions. But when we reached the bottom of the staircase she was sitting there as usual, her hands folded together in her lap. Two grocery bags were at her feet. She did not slap the bench, or ask us to sit down. She glared.

"What is it, Mother?"

"It's improper!"

"What's improper?"

"It is improper for a lady and gentleman who are not married to one another to hold a private conversation without a chaperone!"

Helen said she was sixty-eight years old, old enough to be my mother, but Mrs. Croft insisted that Helen and I speak to each other downstairs, in the parlor. She added that it was also improper for a lady of Helen's station to reveal her age, and to wear a dress so high above the ankle.

"For your information, Mother, it's 1969. What would you do if you actually left the house one day and saw a girl in a miniskirt?"

Mrs. Croft sniffed. "I'd have her arrested."

Helen shook her head and picked up one of the grocery bags. I picked up the other one, and followed her through the parlor and into the kitchen. The bags were filled with cans of soup, which Helen opened up one by one with a few cranks of a can opener. She tossed the old soup into the sink, rinsed the saucepans under the tap, filled them with soup from the newly opened cans, and put them back in the refrigerator. "A few years ago she could still open the cans herself," Helen said. "She hates that I do it for her now. But the piano killed her hands." She put on her spectacles, glanced at the cupboards, and spotted my tea bags. "Shall we have a cup?"

I filled the kettle on the stove. "I beg your pardon, Madam. The piano?"

"She used to give lessons. For forty years. It was how she raised us after my father died." Helen put her hands on her hips, staring at the open refrigerator. She reached into the back, pulled out a wrapped stick of butter, frowned, and tossed it into the garbage. "That ought to do it," she said, and put the unopened cans of soup in the cupboard. I sat at the table and watched as Helen washed the dirty dishes, tied up the garbage bag, and poured boiling water into two cups. She handed one to me without milk, and sat down at the table.

"Excuse me, Madam, but is it enough?"

Helen took a sip of her tea. Her lipstick left a smiling pink stain on the rim of the cup. "Is what enough?"

"The soup in the pans. Is it enough food for Mrs. Croft?"

"She won't eat anything else. She stopped eating solids after she turned one hundred. That was, let's see, three years ago.

I was mortified. I had assumed Mrs. Croft was in her eighties, perhaps as old as ninety. I had never known a person who had lived for over a century. That this person was a widow who lived alone mortified me further still. Widowhood had driven my own mother insane. My father, who worked as a clerk at the General Post Office of Calcutta, died of encephalitis when I was sixteen. My mother refused to adjust to life without him; instead she sank deeper into a world of darkness from which neither I, nor my brother, nor concerned relatives, nor psychiatric clinics on Rash Behari Avenue could save her. What pained me most was to see her so unguarded, to hear her burp after meals or expel gas in front of company without the slightest embarrassment. After my father's death, my brother abandoned his schooling and began to work in the jute mill he would eventually manage, in order to keep the household running. And so it was my job to sit by my mother's feet and study for my exams as she counted and recounted the bracelets on her arm as if they were the beads of an abacus. We tried to keep an eye on her. Once she had wandered half-naked to the tram depot before we were able to bring her inside again.

"I am happy to warm Mrs. Croft's soup in the evenings," I suggested. "It is no trouble."

Helen looked at her watch, stood up, and poured the rest of her tea into the sink. "I wouldn't if I were you. That's the sort of thing that would kill her altogether."

That evening, when Helen had gone and Mrs. Croft and I were alone again, I began to worry. Now that I knew how very old she was, I worried that something would happen to her in the middle of the night, or when I was out during the day. As vigorous as her voice was, and as imperious as she seemed, I knew that even a scratch or a cough could kill a person that old; each day she lived, I knew, was something of a miracle. Helen didn't seem concerned. She came and went, bringing soup for Mrs. Croft, one Sunday after the next.

In this manner the six weeks of that summer passed. I came home each evening, after my hours at the library, and spent a few minutes on the piano bench with Mrs. Croft. Some evenings I sat beside her long after she had drifted off to sleep, still in awe of how many years she had spent on this earth. At times I tried to picture the world she had been born into, in 1866 — a world, I imagined, filled with women in long black skirts, and chaste conversations in the parlor. Now, when I looked at her hands with their swollen knuckles folded together in her lap, I imagined them smooth and slim, striking the piano keys. At times I came downstairs before going to sleep, to make sure she was sitting upright on the bench, or was safe in her bedroom. On Fridays I put the rent in her hands. There was nothing I could do for her beyond these simple gestures. I was not her son, and, apart from those eight dollars, I owed her nothing.

At the end of August, Mala's passport and green card were ready. I received a telegram with her flight information; my brother's house in Calcutta had no telephone. Around that time I also received a letter from her, written only a few days after we had parted. There was no salutation; addressing me by name would have assumed an intimacy we had not yet discovered. It contained only a few lines. "I write in English in preparation for the journey. Here I am very much lonely. Is it very cold there. Is there snow. Yours, Mala."

I was not touched by her words. We had spent only a handful of days in each other's company. And yet we were bound together; for six weeks she had worn an iron bangle on her wrist, and applied vermilion powder to the part in her hair, to signify to the world that she was a bride. In those six weeks I regarded her arrival as I would the arrival of a coming month, or season — something inevitable, but meaningless at the time. So little did I know her that, while details of her face sometimes rose to my memory, I could not conjure up the whole of it.

A few days after receiving the letter, as I was walking to work in the morning, I saw an Indian woman on Massachusetts Avenue, wearing a sari with its free end nearly dragging on the footpath, and pushing a child in a stroller. An American woman with a small black dog on a leash was walking to one side of her. Suddenly the dog began barking. I watched as the Indian woman, startled, stopped in her path, at which point the dog leaped up and seized the end of the sari between its teeth. The American woman scolded the dog, appeared to apologize, and walked quickly away, leaving the Indian woman to fix her sari, and quiet her crying child. She did not see me standing there, and eventually she continued on her way. Such a mishap, I realized that morning, would soon be my concern. It was my duty to take care of Mala, to welcome her and protect her. I would have to buy her her first pair of snow boots, her first winter coat. I would have to tell her which streets to avoid, which way the traffic came, tell her to wear her sari so that the free end did not drag on the footpath. A five-mile separation from her parents, I recalled with some irritation, had caused her to weep.

Unlike Mala, I was used to it all by then: used to cornflakes and milk, used to Helen's visits, used to sitting on the bench with Mrs. Croft. The only thing I was not used to was Mala. Nevertheless, I did what I had to do. I went to the housing office at MIT and found a furnished apartment a few blocks away, with a double bed and a private kitchen and bath, for $40 a week. One last Friday I handed Mrs. Croft eight dollar bills in an envelope, brought my suitcase downstairs, and informed her that I was moving. She put my key into her change purse. The last thing she asked me to do was hand her the cane propped against the table, so that she could walk to the door and lock it behind me. "Good-bye, then," she said, and retreated back into the house. I did not expect any display of emotion, but I was disappointed all the same. I was only a boarder, a man who paid her a bit of money and passed in and out of her home for six weeks. Compared with a century, it was no time at all.

At the airport I recognized Mala immediately. The free end of her sari did not drag on the floor, but was draped in a sign of bridal modesty over her head, just as it had draped my mother until the day my father died. Her thin brown arms were stacked with gold bracelets, a small red circle was painted on her forehead, and the edges of her feet were tinted with a decorative red dye. I did not embrace her, or kiss her, or take her hand. Instead I asked her, speaking Bengali for the first time in America, if she was hungry.

She hesitated, then nodded yes.

I told her I had prepared some egg curry at home. "What did they give you to eat on the plane?"

"I didn't eat."

"All the way from Calcutta?"

"The menu said oxtail soup."

"But surely there were other items."

"The thought of eating an ox's tail made me lose my appetite."

When we arrived home, Mala opened up one of her suitcases, and presented me with two pullover sweaters, both made with bright blue wool, which she had knitted in the course of our separation, one with a V-neck, the other covered with cables. I tried them on; both were tight under the arms. She had also brought me two new pairs of drawstring pajamas, a letter from my brother, and a packet of loose Darjeeling tea. I had no present for her apart from the egg curry. We sat at a bare table, staring at our plates. We ate with our hands, another thing I had not yet done in America.

"The house is nice," she said. "Also the egg curry." With her left hand she held the end of her sari to her chest, so it would not slip off her head.

"I don't know many recipes."

She nodded, peeling the skin off each of her potatoes before eating them. At one point the sari slipped to her shoulders. She readjusted it at once.

"There is no need to cover your head," I said. "I don't mind. It doesn't matter here."

She kept it covered anyway.

I waited to get used to her, to her presence at my side, at my table and in my bed, but a week later we were still strangers. I still was not used to coming home to an apartment that smelled of steamed rice, and finding that the basin in the bathroom was always wiped clean, our two toothbrushes lying side by side, a cake of Pears soap residing in the soap dish. I was not used to the fragrance of the co- conut oil she rubbed every other night into her scalp, or the deli- cate sound her bracelets made as she moved about the apartment. In the mornings she was always awake before I was. The first morning when I came into the kitchen she had heated up the leftovers and set a plate with a spoonful of salt on its edge, assuming I would eat rice for breakfast, as most Bengali husbands did. I told her cereal would do, and the next morning when I came into the kitchen she had already poured the cornflakes into my bowl. One morning she walked with me to MIT, where I gave her a short tour of the campus. The next morning before I left for work she asked me for a few dollars. I parted with them reluctantly, but I knew that this, too, was now normal. When I came home from work there was a potato peeler in the kitchen drawer, and a tablecloth on the table, and chicken curry made with fresh garlic and ginger on the stove. After dinner I read the newspaper, while Mala sat at the kitchen table, working on a cardigan for herself with more of the blue wool, or writing letters home.

On Friday, I suggested going out. Mala set down her knitting and disappeared into the bathroom. When she emerged I regretted the suggestion; she had put on a silk sari and extra bracelets, and coiled her hair with a flattering side part on top of her head. She was prepared as if for a party, or at the very least for the cinema, but I had no such destination in mind. The evening was balmy. We walked several blocks down Massachusetts Avenue, looking into the windows of restaurants and shops. Then, without thinking, I led her down the quiet street where for so many nights I had walked alone.

"This is where I lived before you came," I said, stopping at Mrs. Croft's chain-link fence.

"In such a big house?"

"I had a small room upstairs. At the back."

"Who else lives there?"

"A very old woman."

"With her family?"

"Alone."

"But who takes care of her?"

I opened the gate. "For the most part she takes care of herself."

I wondered if Mrs. Croft would remember me; I wondered if she had a new boarder to sit with her each evening. When I pressed the bell I expected the same long wait as that day of our first meeting, when I did not have a key. But this time the door was opened almost immediately, by Helen. Mrs. Croft was not sitting on the bench. The bench was gone.

"Hello there," Helen said, smiling with her bright pink lips at Mala. "Mother's in the parlor. Will you be visiting awhile?"

"As you wish, Madam."

"Then I think I'll run to the store, if you don't mind. She had a little accident. We can't leave her alone these days, not even for a minute."

I locked the door after Helen and walked into the parlor. Mrs. Croft was lying flat on her back, her head on a peach-colored cushion, a thin white quilt spread over her body. Her hands were folded together on her chest. When she saw me she pointed at the sofa, and told me to sit down. I took my place as directed, but Mala wandered over to the piano and sat on the bench, which was now positioned where it belonged.

"I broke my hip!" Mrs. Croft announced, as if no time had passed.

"Oh dear, Madam."

"I fell off the bench!"

"I am so sorry, Madam."

"It was the middle of the night! Do you know what I did, boy?"

I shook my head.

"I called the police!"

She stared up at the ceiling and grinned sedately, exposing a crowded row of long gray teeth. "What do you say to that, boy?"

As stunned as I was, I knew what I had to say. With no hesitation at all, I cried out, "Splendid!"

Mala laughed then. Her voice was full of kindness, her eyes bright with amusement. I had never heard her laugh before, and it was loud enough so that Mrs. Croft heard, too. She turned to Mala and glared.

"Who is she, boy?"

"She is my wife, Madam."

Mrs. Croft pressed her head at an angle against the cushion to get a better look. "Can you play the piano?"

"No, Madam," Mala replied.

"Then stand up!"

Mala rose to her feet, adjusting the end of her sari over her head and holding it to her chest, and, for the first time since her arrival, I felt sympathy. I remembered my first days in London, learning how to take the Tube to Russell Square, riding an escalator for the first time, unable to understand that when the man cried "piper" it

meant "paper," unable to decipher, for a whole year, that the conductor said "Mind the gap" as the train entered each station. Like
me, Mala had traveled far from home, not knowing where she was
going, or what she would find, for no reason other than to be my
wife. As strange as it seemed, I knew in my heart that one day her
death would affect me, and stranger still, that mine would affect
her. I wanted somehow to explain this to Mrs. Croft, who was still
scrutinizing Mala from top to toe with what seemed to be placid
disdain. I wondered if Mrs. Croft had ever seen a woman in a sari,
with a dot painted on her forehead and bracelets stacked on her
wrists. I wondered what she would object to. I wondered if she
could see the red dye still vivid on Mala's feet, all but obscured by
the bottom edge of her sari. At last Mrs. Croft declared, with the
equal measures of disbelief and delight I knew well:

"She is a perfect lady!"

Now it was I who laughed. I did so quietly, and Mrs. Croft did not
hear me. But Mala had heard, and, for the first time, we looked at
each other and smiled.

I like to think of that moment in Mrs. Croft's parlor as the moment
when the distance between Mala and me began to lessen. Although
we were not yet fully in love, I like to think of the months that followed as a honeymoon of sorts. Together we explored the city and
met other Bengalis, some of whom are still friends today. We discovered that a man named Bill sold fresh fish on Prospect Street,
and that a shop in Harvard Square called Cardullo's sold bay leaves
and cloves. In the evenings we walked to the Charles River to watch
sailboats drift across the water, or had ice cream cones in Harvard
Yard. We bought a camera with which to document our life together, and I took pictures of her posing in front of the Prudential
building, so that she could send them to her parents. At night we
kissed, shy at first but quickly bold, and discovered pleasure and solace in each other's arms. I told her about my voyage on the S.S.
Roma, and about Finsbury Park and the YMCA, and my evenings
on the bench with Mrs. Croft. When I told her stories about my
mother, she wept. It was Mala who consoled me when, reading the
Globe one evening, I came across Mrs. Croft's obituary. I had not
thought of her in several months — by then those six weeks of the
summer were already a remote interlude in my past — but when I
learned of her death I was stricken, so much so that when Mala

looked up from her knitting she found me staring at the wall, unable to speak. Mrs. Croft's was the first death I mourned in America, for hers was the first life I had admired; she had left this world at last, ancient and alone, never to return.

As for me, I have not strayed much farther. Mala and I live in a town about twenty miles from Boston, on a tree-lined street much like Mrs. Croft's, in a house we own, with room for guests, and a garden that saves us from buying tomatoes in summer. We are American citizens now, so that we can collect Social Security when it is time. Though we visit Calcutta every few years, we have decided to grow old here. I work in a small college library. We have a son who attends Harvard University. Mala no longer drapes the end of her sari over her head, or weeps at night for her parents, but occasionally she weeps for our son. So we drive to Cambridge to visit him, or bring him home for a weekend, so that he can eat rice with us with his hands, and speak in Bengali, things we sometimes worry he will no longer do after we die.

Whenever we make that drive, I always take Massachusetts Avenue, in spite of the traffic. I barely recognize the buildings now, but each time I am there I return instantly to those six weeks as if they were only the other day, and I slow down and point to Mrs. Croft's street, saying to my son, Here was my first home in America, where I lived with a woman who was 103. "Remember?" Mala says, and smiles, amazed, as I am, that there was ever a time that we were strangers. My son always expresses his astonishment, not at Mrs. Croft's age but at how little I paid in rent, a fact nearly as inconceivable to him as a flag on the moon was to a woman born in 1866. In my son's eyes I see the ambition that had first hurled me across the world. In a few years he will graduate and pave his own way, alone and unprotected. But I remind myself that he has a father who is still living, a mother who is happy and strong. Whenever he is discouraged, I tell him that if I can survive on three continents, then there is no obstacle he cannot conquer. While the astronauts, heroes forever, spent mere hours on the moon, I have remained in this new world for nearly thirty years. I know that my achievement is quite ordinary. I am not the only man to seek his fortune far from home, and certainly I am not the first. Still, there are times I am bewildered by each mile I have traveled, each meal I have eaten, each person I have known, each room in which I have slept. As ordinary as it all appears, there are times when it is beyond my imagination.

WALTER MOSLEY

Pet Fly

FROM THE NEW YORKER

I HAD BEEN SEEING Mona Donelli around the building since my first day working in interoffice mail. Mona laughing, Mona complaining about her stiff new shoes or the air conditioning or her boyfriend refusing to take her where she wanted to go. She's very pretty. Mona wears short skirts and giggles a lot. She's not serious at all. When silly Mona comes in she says hello and asks how you are, but before you get a chance to answer she's busy talking about what she saw on TV last night or something funny that happened on the ferry from Staten Island that morning.

I would see Mona almost every day on my delivery route — at the coffee-break room on the fifth floor or in a hallway, never at a desk. So when I made a rare delivery to the third-floor mortgage department and saw her sitting there, wearing a conservative sweater buttoned all the way up to her throat, I was surprised. She was so subdued, not sad but peaceful, looking at the wall in front of her and holding a yellow pencil with the eraser against her chin.

"Air conditioning too high again?" I asked, just so she'd know that I paid attention to the nonsense she babbled about.

She looked at me and I got a chill, because it didn't feel like the same person I saw flitting around the office. She gave me a silent and friendly smile, even though her eyes seemed to be wondering what my question meant.

I put down the big brown envelope addressed to her department and left without saying anything else.

Back in the basement, I asked my boss, Ernie, what was wrong with Mona.

"Nothing," he said. "I think she busted up with some guy or something. No, no, I'm a liar. She went out with her boyfriend's best friend without telling him. Now she doesn't get why the boyfriend's mad. That's what she said. Bitch. What she think?"

Ernie didn't suffer fools, as my mother would say. He was an older black man who had moved to New York from Georgia thirty-three years ago. He had come to work at Carter's Home Insurance three days after he arrived. "I would have been here on day one," he told me, "but my bus got in on Friday afternoon."

I'd been there for only three weeks. After I graduated from Hunter College, I didn't know what to do. I had a B.A. in poli sci, but I didn't really have any skills. Couldn't type or work a computer. I wrote all my papers in longhand and used a typing service. I didn't know what I wanted to do, but I had to pay the rent. When I applied for a professional-trainee position that Carter's Home had advertised at Hunter, the personnel officer told me that there was nothing available, but maybe if I took the mailroom position something might open up.

"They hired two white P.T.s the day after you came," Ernie told me at the end of the first week. I decided to ignore that. Maybe those people had applied before me, or maybe they had skills with computers or something.

I didn't mind my job. Big Linda Washington and Little Linda Brown worked with me. The Lindas had earphones and listened to music while they wheeled around their canvas mail carts. Big Linda liked rap and Little Linda liked R & B. Neither one talked to me much.

My only friend at work was Ernie. He was the interoffice mail director. He and I would sit in the basement and talk for hours sometimes. Ernie was proud of his years at Carter's Home. He liked the job and the company, but he had no patience for most of the bosses.

"Workin' for white people is always the same thing," Ernie would say.

"But Mr. Drew's black," I said the first time I heard his perennial complaint. Drew was the supervisor for all postal and interoffice communication. He was a small man with hard eyes and breath that smelled of vitamins.

"Used to be," Ernie said. "Used to be. But ever since he got pro-

moted he forgot all about that. Used to be he'd come down here
and we'd talk like you 'n' me doin'. But now he just stands at the
door and grins and nods. Now he's so scared I'm gonna pull him
down that he won't even sit for a minute."

"I don't get it," I once said to Ernie. "How can you like the job
and the company if you don't like the people you work for?"

"It's a talent," he replied.

Why 'on't you tuck in your shirt?" Big Linda Washington said,
sneering at me on the afternoon after I had seen Mona Donelli at
her third-floor desk. "You look like some kinda fool, hangin' out all
over the place."

Big Linda was taller than I, broader, too, and I'm pretty big. Her
hair was straightened and frosted in gold. She wore dresses in primary colors, as a rule. Her skin was berry black. Her face, unless it
was contorted from appraising me, was pretty.

We were in the service elevator, going up to the fifth floor. I
tucked the white shirttails into my black jeans.

"At least you could make it even so the buttons go straight
down," she remarked. "Just 'cause you light-skinned you can't go
'round lookin' like a mess."

I would have had to open up my pants to do it right, and I didn't
want Big Linda to get any more upset than she already was.

She grunted and sucked a tooth.

The elevator opened, and she rolled out her cart. We had parallel routes, but I went in the opposite direction, deciding to take
mail from the bottom of the stack rather than let her humiliate me.

The first person I ran into was Mona. Now she was wearing a one-
piece deep red dress held up by spaghetti straps. Her breasts were
free under the thin fabric, and her legs were bare. Mona was short,
with thick black hair and green eyes. Her skin had a hint of olive
but not so deep as what you think of as a Sicilian complexion.

"I can see why you were wearing that sweater at your desk," I said.

"What?" she replied, in a very unfriendly tone.

"That white sweater you were wearing," I said.

"What's wrong with you? I don't even own a white sweater."

She turned abruptly and clicked away on her red high heels. I
wondered what had happened. I kept thinking that it was because
of my twisted-up shirt. Maybe that's what made people treat me
badly, maybe it was my appearance.

I continued along my route, pulling files from the bottom and placing them in the right "in" boxes.

"If the boxes ain't side by side, just drop it anywhere and pick up whatever you want to," Ernie had told me on my first day. "That's what I do. Mr. Averill put down the rules thirteen years ago, just before they kicked him upstairs."

Bernard Averill was the vice president in charge of all non-professional employees. He administered the cafeteria workers, the maintenance staff, secretarial services, and both the inter-office and postal mail departments. He was Ernie's hero because he was the only V.P. who had worked his way up from an entry-level position.

When I'd finished the route, I went through the exit door at the far end of the hall to get a drink of water. I planned to wait there long enough for Big Linda to have gone back down. While I was at the water fountain, a fly buzzed by my head. It caught my attention because not many flies made it into the air-conditioned buildings around Wall Street, even in summer.

The fly landed on my hand, then flew to the cold aluminum bowl of the water fountain. He didn't have enough time to drink before zooming up to the ceiling. From there he lit on the doorknob, then landed on the baby finger of my left hand. After that he buzzed down to the floor. He took no more than a second to enjoy each perch.

"You sure jumpy, Mr. Fly," I said, as I might have when I was a child. "But you might be a Miss Fly, huh?"

The idea that the neurotic fly could be a female brought Mona to mind. I hustled my cart toward the elevator, passing Big Linda on the way. She was standing in the hall, talking to another young black woman.

"I got to wait for a special delivery from, um, investigations," Big Linda explained.

"I got to go see a friend on three," I replied.

"Oh." Big Linda seemed relieved.

I realized that she was afraid I'd tell Ernie that she was idling with her friends. Somehow that stung more than her sneers.

She was still wearing the beaded sweater, but instead of the eraser she had a tiny Wite-Out brush in her hand, half an inch from a sheet of paper on her violet blotter.

"I bet that blotter used to be blue, huh?"

"What?" She frowned at me.

"That blotter — it looks violet, purple, but that's because it used to be blue but the sun shined on it, from the window."

She turned her upper torso to look out the window. I could see the soft contours of her small breasts against the white fabric.

"Oh," she said, turning back to me. "I guess."

"Yeah," I said. "I notice things like that. My mother says that's why I never finish anything. She says I get distracted all the time and don't keep my eye on the job."

"Do you have more mail for me?"

"No, uh-uh, I was just thinking."

She looked at the drying Wite-Out brush and then jammed it back into the small bottle that was in her other hand.

"I was thinking about when I saw you this morning," I continued. "About when I saw you and asked about the air conditioning and your sweater and you looked at me like I was crazy."

"Yes," she said, "why did you ask that?"

"Because I thought you were Mona Donelli," I said triumphantly.

"Oh." She sounded disappointed. "Most people figure out that I'm not Mona because my nameplate says Lana Donelli."

"Oh," I said, suddenly crushed. I could notice a blotter turning violet, but I couldn't read a nameplate.

Lana was amused.

"Don't look so sad," she said. "I mean, even when they see the name some people still call me Mona."

"They do?"

"Yeah. It's a problem having an identical twin. They see the name and think that Mona's a nickname or something. Isn't that dumb?"

"I didn't know you had a sister, but I saw Mona on the fifth floor in a red dress, and then I saw a fly that couldn't sit still, and then I knew that you had to be somebody else," I said.

"You're funny," Lana said, crinkling up her nose, as if she were trying to identify a scent. "What's your name?"

"Rufus Coombs."

"Hi, Rufus," she said.

"Hey," I said.

*

My apartment is on 168th Street, in Washington Heights. It's pretty much a Spanish-speaking neighborhood. I don't know many people there, but the rent is all I can afford. My apartment — living room with a kitchen alcove, a small bedroom, and a toilet with a shower — is on the eighth floor and looks out over the Hudson. The $458 a month includes heat and gas, but I pay my own electric. I took it because of the view. There was a cheaper unit on the second floor, but it had windows that look out on a brick wall and I was afraid I'd be burglarized.

"Do you own a TV or a stereo?" my mother asked when I was trying to decide which apartment to take.

"You know I don't."

"Then you ain't got nuthin' to burgle," she said. I had called her in California, where she lives with my uncle.

"But they don't know that," I said. "I might have a color TV with VCR and a bad sound system."

"Lord," my mother prayed.

I didn't own much; she was right about that. Single mattress on the floor, an old oak chair that I found on the street, and kitchen shelving that I bought from a liquidator, for bookshelves, propped up in the corner. I also have a rice pot, a frying pan, and a kettle, with cutlery and enough plates for two.

I have Rachel, an ex-girlfriend living in the East Village, who will call me back at work if I don't call her too often. My two other friends are Eric Chen and Willy Jones. They both live in Brooklyn and still go to school.

That evening, I climbed the seven flights up to my apartment. The elevator had stopped working a month ago. I sat in my chair and looked at the water. It was peaceful and relaxing. A fly was buzzing against the glass, trying to get out.

I got up to kill him. But up close I hesitated. His coloring was unusual, a metallic green. The dull red eyes seemed too large for the body, as though he were an intelligent mutant fly from some far-flung future on late-night television.

He buzzed against the pane, trying to get away from me. When I returned to my chair, he settled. The red sun was hovering above the cliffs of New Jersey. The green fly watched. I thought of the fly I'd seen at work. That bug had been black and fairly small by fly standards. Then I thought about Mona and then Lana. The smallest nudge of an erection stirred. I thought of calling Rachel, but I didn't have the heart to walk the three blocks to a phone booth. So I watched the sunset gleaming around the fly, who was now just a black spot on the window. I fell asleep in the chair.

At three A.M. I woke up and made macaroni and cheese from a mix. The fly came into the cooking alcove, where I stood eating my meal. He lit on the big spoon I'd used to stir the dinner and joined me for supper.

Ernie told me that mortgaging didn't get much interoffice mail.

"Most of their correspondence comes by regular mail," he explained.

"Aren't they on the newsletter list?"

"She a white girl?"

"So?"

"Nuthin'. But I want you to tell me what it's like if you get it."

I didn't answer him.

I began delivering invitations to office parties, sales force newsletters, and productivity tips penned by Mr. Averill to Lana Donelli. We made small talk for thirty seconds or so, then she'd pick up the phone to make a call. I always looked back as I rounded the corner to make sure she really had a call to make. She always did.

The following Monday, I bought a glass paperweight with the image of a smiling Buddha's face etched in the bottom. When I got to Lana's desk, she wasn't there. I waited around for a while but she didn't appear, so I wrote her a note that said "From Rufus to Lana" and put the leaded-glass weight on it.

I went away excited and half scared. What if she didn't see my note? What if she did and thought it was stupid? I was so nervous that I didn't go back to her desk that day.

"I really shouldn't have left it," I said that night to the green fly. He was perched peacefully on the rim of a small saucer. I had filled the inner depression with a honey-and-water solution. I was eating a triple cheeseburger with bacon and fries from Wendy's. My pet fly seemed happy with his honey water and buzzed my sandwich only a few times before settling down to drink.

"Maybe she doesn't like me," I said. "Maybe it's just that she was nice to me because she feels sorry for me. But how will I know if I don't try and see if she likes me?"

*

"Hi," I said to Lana the next morning. She was wearing a jean jacket over a white T-shirt. She smiled and nodded. I handed her Mr. Averill's productivity tips newsletter.

"Did you see the paperweight?"

"Oh, yeah," she said without looking me in the eye. "Thanks." Then she picked up the phone and began pressing buttons. "Hi, Tristan? Lana. I wanted to know if . . ." She put her hand over the receiver and looked at me. "Can I do something else for you?"

"Oh," I said. "No. No," and I wheeled away in a kind of euphoria.

It's only now, when I look back on that moment, that I can see the averted eyes, the quick call, and the rude dismissal for what they were. All I heard then was "Thanks." I even remember a smile. Maybe she did smile for a brief moment, maybe not.

On Tuesday and Wednesday, I left three presents for her. I left them when she was away from her desk. I got her a small box of four Godiva chocolates, a silk rose, and a jar of fancy rose-petal jelly. I didn't leave any more notes. I was sure that she'd know who it was.

On Thursday evening, I went to a nursery on the East Side, just south of Harlem proper. There I bought a bonsai, a crab apple tree, for $347.52. I figured I'd leave it during Lana's Friday lunch break, and then she'd be so happy that on Monday she'd have to have lunch with me, no matter what.

I suspected that something was wrong when my pet fly went missing. He didn't even show up when I started eating a Beef Burrito Supreme from Taco Bell. I checked the big spiderweb near the bathroom window, but there were no little bundles that I could see.

That evening I was on edge, thinking I saw flies flitting into every corner.

"What's that?" Ernie asked me the next morning when I came in with the tiny crab apple tree.

"It's a tree."

"Tree for what?"

"My friend Willy wanted me to pick it up for him. He wants it for his new apartment, and the only place he could get it is up near me. I'm gonna meet him at lunch and give it to him."

"Uh-huh," Ernie said.

"You got my cart loaded?" I asked him.

Just then the Lindas came out of the service elevator. Big Linda looked at me and shook her head, managing to express contempt and pity at the same time.

"There's your carts," Ernie said to them.

They attached their earphones and rolled back to the service elevator. Little Linda was looking me in the eye as the slatted doors closed. She was still looking at me as the lift rose.

"What about me?"

"That's all I got right now. Why don't you sit here with me?"

"Okay." I sat down, expecting Ernie to bring up one of his regular topics, either something about Georgia, white bosses, or the horse races, which he followed but never wagered on. But instead of saying anything he just started reading the *Post.*

After a few minutes I was going to say something, but the big swinging door opened. Our boss, Mr. Drew, leaned in. He smiled and nodded at Ernie and then pointed at me.

"Rufus Coombs?"

"Yeah?"

"Come with me."

I followed the dapper little man through the messy service hall to the passenger elevator, which the couriers rarely took. It was a two-man elevator, so Drew and I had to stand very close to each other. He wore too much cologne, but otherwise he was perfect for his supervisory job, wearing a light gray suit with a shirt that hinted at yellow. I knew that he must have been in his forties, but he could have passed for a graduate student. He was light-skinned, like me, with what my mother called good hair. There were freckles around his eyes. I could see all of that because Mr. Drew avoided my gaze. He wouldn't engage me in any way.

We got out on the second floor and went to his office, which was at the far end of the mail-sorting room.

I looked around the room as Drew was entering his office. I saw Mona looking at me from the crevice of a doorway. I knew it was Mona because she was wearing a skimpy dress that could have been worn on a hot date. I got only a glimpse of her before she ducked away.

"Come on in, Coombs," Drew said.

The office was tiny. Drew actually had to stand on the tips of his toes and hug the wall to get behind his desk. There was a stool in front of the desk, not a chair.

By the time he said, "Sit down," I had lost my nervousness. I gauged the power of Mr. Leonard Drew by the size of his office.

"You're in trouble, Rufus," he said, looking as somber as he could.

"I am?"

He lifted a pink sheet of paper and shook it at me.

"Do you recognize this?" he asked.

"No."

"This is a sexual-harassment complaint form."

"Yeah?"

"It names you on the complaint."

"I don't get it."

"Lana Donelli . . ." He went on to explain everything that I had been doing and feeling for the last week as if they were crimes. Going to Lana's desk, talking to her, leaving gifts. Even remarking on her clothes had been construed as if there was a sexual innuendo attached. By the time he was finished, I was worried that the police might be called in.

"Lana says that she's afraid to come in to work," Drew said, his freckles disappearing into angry lines around his eyes.

I wanted to say that I didn't mean to scare her, but I could see that my intentions didn't matter, that a small woman like Lana would be afraid of a big, sloppy mail clerk hovering over her and leaving notes and presents.

"I'm sorry," I said.

"Sorry doesn't mean much when it's got to this point," he said. "If it was up to me, I'd send you home right now. But Mr. Averill says he wants to talk to you."

"Aren't you supposed to give me a warning?" I asked.

Drew twisted up his lips, as if he had tasted something so foul that he just had to spit it out. "You haven't been here a month. You're on probation."

"Oh," I said.

"Well?" he asked after a few moments.

"What?"

"Go back to the mailroom and stay down there. Tell Ernie that I don't want you in the halls. You're supposed to meet Mr. Averill at one-forty-five, in his office. I've given him my recommendation to let you go. After something like this, there's really no place for you here. But he can still refer the matter to the police. Lana might want a restraining order."

I wanted to tell him that a restraining order was ridiculous. I wanted to go to Lana and tell her the same thing. I wanted to tell her that I bought her a rose because she wore rose toilet water, that I bought her the tree because the sun on her blotter could support a plant. I really liked her. But even while I was imagining what I could say, I knew that it didn't matter.

"Well?" Drew said. "Go."

Ernie made busywork for us that morning. He told me that he was upset about what had happened, that he'd told Drew to go easy.

"You know if you was white this wouldn't never have happened," Ernie said. "That girl just scared you some Mandingo gonna rape her. You know that's a shame."

I went up to the third floor a little before twelve. Lana was sitting at her desk, writing on a yellow legal pad. I walked right up to her and started talking so she couldn't ignore what I had to say.

"I just wanted to tell you that I'm sorry if you think I was harassing you. I didn't mean it, but I can see how you might have thought I was . . ."

Lana's face got hard.

". . . but I'm gonna get fired right after lunch and I just wanted to ask you one thing."

She didn't say anything, so I said, "Is it because I'm black that you're so scared'a me?"

"You're black?" she said. "I thought you were Puerto Rican or Spanish or something. I didn't know you were black. My boyfriend is black. You just give me the creeps. That's why I complained. I didn't think they were going to fire you."

She didn't care if I lived or died. She wasn't even scared, just disgusted. I thought I was in love, and I was about to be fired, and she'd never even looked close enough to see me.

I was so embarrassed that I went away without saying another word. I went down to the mailroom and sorted rubber bands until one-thirty-five.

Vice President Bernard Averill's office was on the forty-eighth floor of the Carter's Home Building. His secretary's office was larger by far than Mr. Drew's cubbyhole. The smiling blonde led

me into Averill's airy room. Behind him was a giant window looking out over Battery Park, Ellis Island, and the Statue of Liberty. I
would have been impressed if I wasn't empty inside.

Averill was on the phone.

"Sorry, Nick," he said into the receiver. "My one-forty-five is
here."

He stood up, tall and thin. His gray suit looked expensive. His
white shirt was crisp and bright under a rainbow tie. His gray
hair was combed back, and his mustache was sharp enough to cut
bread, as my mother is known to say.

"Sit down, Mr. Coombs."

He sat also. In front of him were two sheets of paper. At his left
hand was the pink harassment form, at his right was a white form.
Outside, the Budweiser blimp hovered next to Lady Liberty.

Averill brought his fingertips to just under his nose and gazed at
a spot above my head.

"How's Ernie?" he asked.

"He's good," I said. "He's a great boss."

"He's a good man. He likes you."

I didn't know what to say to that.

Averill looked down at his desk. "This does not compute."

"What?"

He patted the white page. "This says that you're a college graduate, magna cum laude in political science, that you came here to be
a professional trainee." He patted the pink sheet. "This says that
you're an interoffice-mail courier who harasses secretaries in the
mortgage department."

Averill reached into his vest pocket and came out with an open
package of cigarettes. At orientation they'd told us that there was
absolutely no smoking anywhere in the building, but he took one
out anyway. He lit up and took a deep drag, holding the smoke in
his lungs for a long time before exhaling.

"Is there something wrong with you?" he asked.

"I don't think so," I said, swallowing hard.

Averill examined me through the tobacco haze. He seemed disgusted.

Staring directly into my eyes, he said, "Do you see this desk?"

The question petrified me, but I couldn't say why. Maybe it was
the intensity of his gaze.

"I could call five or six women into this office right now and have them right here on this desk. Right here." He jabbed the desk with his middle finger.

My heart was racing. I had to open my mouth to get enough air.

"They're not going to fill out any pink slips," he said. "Do you know why?"

I shook my head.

"Because I'm a man. I don't go running around leaving choco-lates on empty desks like bait. I don't fake reasons to come skulking around with newsletters."

Averill seemed angry as well as offended. I wondered if he knew Lana, or maybe her family. Maybe he wanted to fight me. I wanted to quit right then, to stand up and walk out before anything else happened. I was already thinking of where I could apply for an-other job when Averill sat back and smiled.

"Why are you in the interoffice-mail room?" he asked, suddenly much friendlier.

"No P.T. positions were open when I applied," I said.

"Nonsense. We don't have a limit on P.T.s."

"But Ms. Worth said —"

"Oh." Averill held up his hand. "Reena. You know, Ernie helped me out when I got here, twenty-three years ago. I was just a little older than you. They didn't have the P.T. program back then, just a few guys like Ernie. He never even finished high school, but he showed me the ropes."

Averill drummed the fingers of his free hand between the two forms that represented me.

"I know this Lana's sister," he said. "Always wearing those cocktail dresses in to work. Her boss is afraid to say anything, otherwise he might get a pink slip, too." He paused to ponder some more. "How would you like to be a P.T. floater?"

"What's that?" I asked.

"Bumps you up to a grade seven and lets you move around in the different departments until you find a fit."

I was a grade B1.

"I thought you were going to fire me."

"That's what Drew suggested, but Ernie says that it's just a mixup. What if I talked to Lana? What if I asked her to hold this back, to give you a second chance?"

"I'd like that," I said. "Thanks."

"Probably be better if I let Drew fire you, you know," he said, standing up. I stood, too. "I mean if you fuck up once you'll probably just do it again, right?"

He held out his hand.

Watching the forbidden smoke curl around his head, I imagined that Averill was some kind of devil. When I thanked him and shook his hand, something inside me wanted to scream.

I found six unused crack vials a block from the subway stop near my apartment. I knew they were unused because they still had the little plastic stoppers in them.

When I got upstairs, I spent hours searching my place. I looked under the mattress and behind the toilet, under the radiator, and even down under the burners on the stove. Finally, after midnight, I decided to open the windows.

The fly had crawled down into the crack between the window frame and the sill in my bedroom. His green body had dried out, which made his eyes even bigger. He'd gone down there to die, or maybe, I thought, he was trying to get away from me. Maybe I had killed him. Later, I found out that flies have a very short life span. He probably died of old age.

I took his small, dried-out corpse and put it in one of the crack vials. I stoppered him in the tiny glass coffin and buried him among the roots of the bonsai crab apple.

"So you finally bought something nice for your house," my mother said after I told her about the changes in my life. "Maybe next you'll get a real bed."

ZZ PACKER

Brownies

FROM HARPER'S MAGAZINE

BY THE END of our first day at Camp Crescendo, the girls in my Brownie troop had decided to kick the asses of each and every girl in Brownie Troop 909. Troop 909 was doomed from the first day of camp; they were white girls, their complexions like a blend of ice cream: strawberry, vanilla. They turtled out from their bus in pairs, their rolled-up sleeping bags chromatized with Disney characters — Sleeping Beauty, Snow White, Mickey Mouse — or the generic ones cheap parents bought — washed-out rainbows, unicorns, curly-eyelashed frogs. Some clutched Igloo coolers and still others held on to stuffed toys like pacifiers, looking all around them like tourists determined to be dazzled.

Our troop wended its way past their bus, past the ranger station, past the colorful trail guide drawn like a treasure map, locked behind glass.

"Man, did you smell them?" Arnetta said, giving the girls a slow once-over. "They smell like Chihuahuas. *Wet* Chihuahuas." Although we had passed their troop by yards, Arnetta raised her nose in the air and grimaced.

Arnetta said this from the very rear of the line, far away from Mrs. Margolin, who strung our troop behind her like a brood of obedient ducklings. Mrs. Margolin even looked like a mother duck — she had hair cropped close to a small ball of a head, almost no neck, and huge, miraculous breasts. She wore enormous belts that looked like the kind weight lifters wear, except hers were cheap metallic gold or rabbit fur or covered with gigantic fake sunflowers. Often these belts would become nature lessons in and of themselves. "See," Mrs. Margolin once said to us, pointing to her belt. "This one's made entirely from the feathers of baby pigeons."

The belt layered with feathers was uncanny enough, but I was more disturbed by the realization that I had never actually *seen* a baby pigeon. I searched for weeks for one, in vain — scampering after pigeons whenever I was downtown with my father.

But nature lessons were not Mrs. Margolin's top priority. She saw the position of troop leader as an evangelical post. Back at the A.M.E. church where our Brownie meetings were held, she was especially fond of imparting religious aphorisms by means of acrostics — Satan was the "Serpent Always Tempting And Noisome"; she'd refer to the Bible as "Basic Instructions Before Leaving Earth." Whenever she occasionally quizzed us on these at the beginning of the Brownie meeting, expecting to hear the acrostics parroted back to her, only Arnetta's correct replies soared over our vague mumblings. "Jesus?" Mrs. Margolin might ask expectantly, and Arnetta alone would dutifully answer, "Jehovah's Example, Saving Us Sinners."

Arnetta made a point of listening to Mrs. Margolin's religious talk and giving her what she wanted to hear. Because of this, Arnetta could have blared through a megaphone that the white girls of Troop 909 were "wet Chihuahuas" without arousing so much as a blink from Mrs. Margolin. Once Arnetta killed the troop goldfish by feeding it a French fry covered in ketchup, and when Mrs. Margolin demanded an explanation, Arnetta claimed that the goldfish had been eyeing her meal for *hours*, until — giving in to temptation — it had leapt up and snatched the whole golden fry from her fingertips.

"*Serious* Chihuahua," Octavia added — though neither Arnetta nor Octavia could *spell* "Chihuahua" or had ever *seen* a Chihuahua. Trisyllabic words had gained a sort of exoticism within our fourth-grade set at Woodrow Wilson Elementary. Arnetta and Octavia, compelled to outdo each other, would flip through the dictionary, determined to work the vulgar-sounding ones like "Djibouti" and "asinine" into conversation.

"*Caucasian* Chihuahuas," Arnetta said.

That did it. Drema and Elise doubled up on each other like inextricably entwined kites; Octavia slapped the skin of her belly; Janice jumped straight up in the air, then did it again, just as hard, as if to slam-dunk her own head. No one had laughed so hard since a boy named Martez had stuck his pencil in the electric socket and spent the whole day with a strange grin on his face.

"Girls, girls," said our parent helper, Mrs. Hedy. Mrs. Hedy was Octavia's mother. She wagged her index finger perfunctorily, like a windshield wiper. "Stop it now. Be good." She said this loudly enough to be heard, but lazily, nasally, bereft of any feeling or indication that she meant to be obeyed, as though she would say these words again at the exact same pitch if a button somewhere on her were pressed.

But the girls didn't stop laughing; they only laughed louder. It was the word "Caucasian" that had got them all going. One day at school, about a month before the Brownie camping trip, Arnetta had turned to a boy wearing impossibly high-ankled floodwater jeans, and said "What are *you? Caucasian?*" The word took off from there, and soon everything was Caucasian. If you ate too fast, you ate like a Caucasian; if you ate too slow, you ate like a Caucasian. The biggest feat anyone at Woodrow Wilson could do was to jump off the swing in midair, at the highest point in its arc, and if you fell (like I had, more than once) instead of landing on your feet, knees bent Olympic-gymnast-style, Arnetta and Octavia were prepared to comment. They'd look at each other with the silence of passengers who'd narrowly escaped an accident, then nod their heads, and whisper with solemn horror and haughtiness, *"Caucasian."*

Even the only white kid in our school, Dennis, got in on the Caucasian act. That time when Martez stuck the pencil in the socket, Dennis had pointed, and yelled, "That was *so* Caucasian!"

Living in the south suburbs of Atlanta, it was easy to forget about whites. Whites were like those baby pigeons: real and existing, but rarely thought about. Everyone had been to Rich's to go clothes shopping, everyone had seen white girls and their mothers coocooing over dresses; everyone had gone to the downtown library and seen white businessmen swish by importantly, wrists flexed in front of them to check the time on their watches as though they would change from Clark Kent into Superman any second. But those images were as fleeting as cards shuffled in a deck, whereas the ten white girls behind us — *invaders,* Arnetta would later call them — were instantly real and memorable, with their long shampoo-commercial hair, as straight as spaghetti from the box. This alone was reason for envy and hatred. The only black girl most of us had ever seen with hair that long was Octavia, whose hair hung past her butt like a Hawaiian hula dancer's. The sight of Octavia's mane prompted other girls to listen to her reverentially, as though whatever she had to say would somehow activate their own follicles. For example, when, on the first day of camp, Octavia made as if to speak, a silence began. "Nobody," Octavia said, "calls us niggers."

At the end of that first day, when half of our troop made its way back to the cabin after tag-team restroom visits, Arnetta said she'd heard one of the girls in Troop 909 call Daphne a nigger. The other half of the girls and I were helping Mrs. Margolin clean up the pots and pans from the ravioli dinner. When we made our way to the restrooms to wash up and brush our teeth, we met up with Arnetta midway.

"Man, I completely heard the girl," Arnetta reported. "Right, Daphne?"

Daphne hardly ever spoke, but when she did her voice was petite and tinkly, the voice one might expect from a shiny new earring. She'd written a poem once, for Langston Hughes Day, a poem brimming with all the teacher-winning ingredients — trees and oceans, sunsets and moons — but what cinched the poem for the grown-ups, snatching the win from Octavia's musical ode to Grand-master Flash and the Furious Five, were Daphne's last lines:

> You are my father, the veteran
> When you cry in the dark
> It rains and rains and rains in my heart

She'd worn clean, though faded, jumpers and dresses when Chic jeans were the fashion, but when she went up to the dais to receive her prize journal, pages trimmed in gold, she wore a new dress with a velveteen bodice and a taffeta skirt as wide as an umbrella. All the kids clapped, though none of them understood the poem. I'd read encyclopedias the way others read comics, and I didn't get it. But those last lines pricked me, they were so eerie, and as my father and I ate cereal, I'd whisper over my Froot Loops, like a mantra, *"You are my father, the veteran. You are my father, the veteran, the veteran, the veteran,"* until my father, who acted in plays as Caliban and Othello and was not a veteran, marched me up to my teacher one morning, and said, "Can you tell me what the hell's wrong with this kid?"

I had thought Daphne and I might become friends, but she

seemed to grow spooked by me whispering those lines to her, begging her to tell me what they meant, and I had soon understood that two quiet people like us were better off quiet alone.

"Daphne? Didn't you hear them call you a nigger?" Arnetta asked, giving Daphne a nudge.

The sun was setting through the trees, and their leafy tops formed a canopy of black lace for the flame of the sun to pass through. Daphne shrugged her shoulders at first, then slowly nodded her head when Arnetta gave her a hard look.

Twenty minutes later, when my restroom group returned to the cabin, Arnetta was still talking about Troop 909. My restroom group had passed by some of the 909 girls. For the most part, they had deferred to us, waving us into the restrooms, letting us go even though they'd gotten there first.

We'd seen them, but from afar, never within their orbit enough to see whether their faces were the way all white girls appeared on TV — ponytailed and full of energy, bubbling over with love and money. All I could see was that some rapidly fanned their faces with their hands, though the heat of the day had long passed. A few seemed to be lolling their heads in slow circles, half-purposefully, as if exercising the muscles of their necks, half-ecstatically, rolling their heads about like Stevie Wonder.

"We can't let them get away with that," Arnetta said, dropping her voice to a laryngitic whisper. "We can't let them get away with calling us niggers. I say we teach them a lesson." She sat down cross-legged on a sleeping bag, an embittered Buddha, eyes glimmering acrylic black. "We can't go telling Mrs. Margolin, either. Mrs. Margolin'll say something about doing unto others and the path of righteousness and all. Forget that shit." She let her eyes flutter irreverently till they half closed, as though ignoring an insult not worth returning. We could all hear Mrs. Margolin outside, gathering the last of the metal campware.

Nobody said anything for a while. Arnetta's tone had an upholstered confidence that was somehow both regal and vulgar at once. It demanded a few moments of silence in its wake, like the ringing of a church bell or the playing of taps. Sometimes Octavia would ditto or dissent whatever Arnetta had said, and this was the signal that others could speak. But this time Octavia just swirled a long cord of hair into pretzel shapes.

"*Well?*" Arnetta said. She looked as if she had discerned the hidden severity of the situation and was waiting for the rest of us to catch up. Everyone looked from Arnetta to Daphne. It was, after all, Daphne who had supposedly been called the name, but Daphne sat on the bare cabin floor, flipping through the pages of the Girl Scout handbook, eyebrows arched in mock wonder, as if the handbook were a catalogue full of bright and startling foreign costumes. Janice broke the silence. She clapped her hands to broach her idea of a plan.

"They gone be sleeping," she whispered conspiratorially, "then we gone sneak into they cabin, then we gone put daddy longlegs in they sleeping bags. Then they'll wake up. Then we gone beat 'em up till they flat as frying pans!" She jammed her fist into the palm of her hand, then made a sizzling sound.

Janice's country accent was laughable, her looks homely, her jumpy acrobatics embarrassing to behold. Arnetta and Octavia volleyed amused, arrogant smiles whenever Janice opened her mouth, but Janice never caught the hint, spoke whenever she wanted, fluttered around Arnetta and Octavia futilely offering her opinions to their departing backs. Whenever Arnetta and Octavia shooed her away, Janice loitered until the two would finally sigh, "What *is* it, Miss Caucasoid? What do you want?"

"Oh shut up, Janice," Octavia said, letting a fingered loop of hair fall to her waist as though just the sound of Janice's voice had ruined the fun of her hair twisting.

"All right," Arnetta said, standing up. "We're going to have a secret meeting and talk about what we're going to do."

The word "secret" had a built-in importance. Everyone gravely nodded her head. The modifier form of the word had more clout than the noun. A secret meant nothing; it was like gossip: just a bit of unpleasant knowledge about someone who happened to be someone other than yourself. A secret *meeting*, or a secret *club*, was entirely different.

That was when Arnetta turned to me, as though she knew doing so was both a compliment and a charity.

"Snot, you're not going to be a bitch and tell Mrs. Margolin, are you?"

I had been called "Snot" ever since first grade, when I'd sneezed in class and two long ropes of mucus had splattered a nearby girl.

"Hey," I said. "Maybe you didn't hear them right — I mean —"

"Are you gonna tell on us or not?" was all Arnetta wanted to know, and by the time the question was asked, the rest of our Brownie troop looked at me as though they'd already decided their course of action, me being the only impediment. As though it were all a simple matter of patriotism.

Camp Crescendo used to double as a high school band and field hockey camp until an arching field hockey ball landed on the clasp of a girl's metal barrette, knifing a skull nerve, paralyzing the right side of her body. The camp closed down for a few years, and the girl's teammates built a memorial, filling the spot on which the girl fell with hockey balls, upon which they had painted — all in nail polish — get-well tidings, flowers, and hearts. The balls were still stacked there, like a shrine of ostrich eggs embedded in the ground.

On the second day of camp, Troop 909 was dancing around the mound of nail polish–decorated hockey balls, their limbs jangling awkwardly, their cries like the constant summer squeal of an amusement park. There was a stream that bordered the field hockey lawn, and the girls from my troop settled next to it, scarfing down the last of lunch: sandwiches made from salami and slices of tomato that had gotten waterlogged from the melting ice in the cooler. From the stream bank, Arnetta eyed the Troop 909 girls, scrutinizing their movements to glean inspiration for battle.

"Man," Arnetta said, "we could bum-rush them right now if that damn lady would *leave*."

The 909 troop leader was a white woman with the severe pageboy hairdo of an ancient Egyptian. She lay sprawled on a picnic blanket, Sphinxlike, eating a banana, sometimes holding it out in front of her like a microphone. Beside her sat a girl slowly flapping one hand like a bird with a broken wing. Occasionally, the leader would call out the names of girls who'd attempted leapfrogs and flips, or of girls who yelled too loudly or strayed far from the circle.

"I'm just glad Big Fat Mama's not following us here," Octavia said. "At least we don't have to worry about her." Mrs. Margolin, Octavia assured us, was having her Afternoon Devotional, shrouded in mosquito netting, in a clearing she'd found. Mrs. Hedy was cleaning mud from her espadrilles in the cabin.

"I handled them." Arnetta sucked on her teeth and proudly grinned. "I told her we was going to gather leaves."

"Gather leaves," Octavia said, nodding respectfully. "That's a good one. They're so mad-crazy about this camping thing." She looked from ground to sky, sky to ground. Her hair hung down her back in two braids like a squaw's. "I mean, I really don't know why it's even called *camping*— all we ever do with Nature is find some twigs and say something like, 'Wow, this fell from a tree.'" She then studied her sandwich. With two disdainful fingers, she picked out a slice of dripping tomato, the sections congealed with red slime. She pitched it into the stream embrowned with dead leaves and the murky effigies of other dead things, but in the opaque water a group of small silver-brown fish appeared. They surrounded the tomato and nibbled.

"Look!" Janice cried. "Fishes! Fishes!" As she scrambled to the edge of the stream to watch, a covey of insects threw up tantrums from the wheatgrass and nettle, a throng of tiny electric machines, all going at once. Octavia snuck up behind Janice as if to push her in. Daphne and I exchanged terrified looks. It seemed as though only we knew that Octavia was close enough — and bold enough — to actually push Janice into the stream. Janice turned around quickly, but Octavia was already staring serenely into the still water as though she were gathering some sort of courage from it. "What's so funny?" Janice said, eyeing them all suspiciously.

Elise began humming the tune to "Karma Chameleon," all the girls joining in, their hums light and facile. Janice began to hum, against everyone else, the high-octane opening chords of "Beat It."

"I love me some Michael Jackson," Janice said when she'd finished humming, smacking her lips as though Michael Jackson were a favorite meal. "I will marry Michael Jackson."

Before anyone had a chance to impress upon Janice the impossibility of this, Arnetta suddenly rose, made a sun visor of her hand, and watched Troop 909 leave the field hockey lawn.

"Dammit!" she said. "We've got to get them *alone*."

"They won't ever be alone," I said. All the rest of the girls looked at me. If I spoke even a word, I could count on someone calling me Snot, but everyone seemed to think that we could beat up these girls; no one entertained the thought that they might fight *back*. "The only time they'll be unsupervised is in the bathroom."

"Oh shut up, Snot," Octavia said.

But Arnetta slowly nodded her head. "The bathroom," she said. "The bathroom," she said, again and again. "The bathroom! The bathroom!" She cheered so blissfully that I thought for a moment she was joking.

According to Octavia's watch, it took us five minutes to hike to the restrooms, which were midway between our cabin and Troop 909's. Inside, the mirrors above the sinks returned only the vaguest of reflections, as though someone had taken a scouring pad to their surfaces to obscure the shine. Pine needles, leaves, and dirty flattened wads of chewing gum covered the floor like a mosaic. Webs of hair matted the drain in the middle of the floor. Above the sinks and below the mirrors, stacks of folded white paper towels lay on a long metal counter. Shaggy white balls of paper towels sat on the sink tops in a line like corsages on display. A thread of floss snaked from a wad of tissues dotted with the faint red-pink of blood. One of those white girls, I thought, had just lost a tooth.

The restroom looked almost the same as it had the night before, but it somehow seemed stranger now. We had never noticed the wooden rafters before, coming together in great V's. We were, it seemed, inside a whale, viewing the ribs of the roof of its mouth.

"Wow. It's a mess," Elise said.

"You can say that again."

Arnetta leaned against the doorjamb of a restroom stall. "This is where they'll be again," she said. Just seeing the place, just having a plan, seemed to satisfy her. "We'll go in and talk to them. You know, 'How you doing? How long will you be here?' that sort of thing. Then Octavia and I are gonna tell them what happens when they call any one of us a nigger."

"I'm going to say something, too," Janice said.

Arnetta considered this. "Sure," she said. "Of course. Whatever you want."

Janice pointed her finger like a gun at Octavia and rehearsed the line she'd thought up, "'We're gonna teach you a *lesson*.' That's what I'm going to say." She narrowed her eyes like a TV mobster. "'We're gonna teach you little girls a lesson!'"

With the back of her hand, Octavia brushed Janice's finger away. "You couldn't teach me to shit in a toilet."

"But," I said, "what if they say, 'We didn't say that. We didn't call anyone a N-I-G-G-E-R'?"

"Snot," Arnetta sighed. "Don't think. Just fight. If you even know how."

Everyone laughed while Daphne stood there. Arnetta gently laid her hand on Daphne's shoulder. "Daphne. You don't have to fight. We're doing this for you."

Daphne walked to the counter, took a clean paper towel, and carefully unfolded it like a map. With this, she began to pick up the trash all around. Everyone watched.

"C'mon," Arnetta said to everyone. "Let's beat it." We all ambled toward the restroom doorway, where the sunshine made one large white rectangle of light. We were immediately blinded and shielded our eyes with our hands, our forearms.

"Daphne?" Arnetta asked. "Are you coming?"

We all looked back at the girl, who was bending, the thin of her back hunched like a maid caught in stage limelight. Stray strands of her hair were lit nearly transparent, thin fiber-optic threads. She did not nod yes to the question, nor did she shake her head no. She abided, bent. Then she began again, picking up leaves, wads of paper, the cotton fluff innards from a torn stuffed toy. She did it so methodically, so exquisitely, so humbly, she must have been trained. I thought of those dresses she wore, faded and old, yet so pressed and clean; I then saw the poverty in them, I then could imagine her mother, cleaning the houses of others, returning home, weary.

"I guess she's not coming."

We left her, heading back to our cabin, over pine needles and leaves, taking the path full of shade.

"What about our secret meeting?" Elise asked.

Arnetta enunciated in a way that defied contradiction: "We just had it."

Just as we caught sight of our cabin, Arnetta violently swerved away from Octavia. "You farted," she said.

Octavia began to sashay, as if on a catwalk, then proclaimed, in a Hollywood-starlet voice, "My farts smell like perfume."

It was nearing our bedtime, but in the lengthening days of spring, the sun had not yet set.

"Hey, your mama's coming," Arnetta said to Octavia when she saw Mrs. Hedy walk toward the cabin, sniffling. When Octavia's mother wasn't giving bored, parochial orders, she sniffled continuously, mourning an imminent divorce from her husband. She might begin a sentence, "I don't know what Robert will do when Octavia and I are gone. Who'll buy him cigarettes?" and Octavia would hotly whisper *"Mama"* in a way that meant: Please don't talk about our problems in front of everyone. Please shut up.

But when Mrs. Hedy began talking about her husband, thinking about her husband, seeing clouds shaped like the head of her husband, she couldn't be quiet, and no one could ever dislodge her from the comfort of her own woe. Only one thing could perk her up — Brownie songs. If the rest of the girls were quiet, and Mrs. Hedy was in her dopey sorrowful mood, she would say, "Y'all know I like those songs, girls. Why don't you sing one?" Everyone would groan except me and Daphne. I, for one, liked some of the songs.

"C'mon, everybody," Octavia said drearily. "She likes 'The Brownie Song' best."

We sang, loud enough to reach Mrs. Hedy:

> I've something in my pocket;
> It belongs across my face.
> And I keep it very close at hand in a most convenient place.
> I'm sure you couldn't guess it
> If you guessed a long, long while.
> So I'll take it out and put it on —
> It's a great big Brownie Smile!

"The Brownie Song" was supposed to be sung as though we were elves in a workshop, singing as we merrily cobbled shoes, but everyone except me hated the song and sang it like a maudlin record, played at the most sluggish of rpms.

"That was good," Mrs. Hedy said, closing the cabin door behind her. "Wasn't that nice, Linda?"

"Praise God," Mrs. Margolin answered without raising her head from the chore of counting out Popsicle sticks for the next day's session of crafts.

"Sing another one," Mrs. Hedy said, with a sort of joyful aggression, like a drunk I'd once seen who'd refused to leave a Korean grocery.

"God, Mama, get over it," Octavia whispered in a voice meant only for Arnetta, but Mrs. Hedy heard it and started to leave the cabin.

"Don't go," Arnetta said. She ran after Mrs. Hedy and held her by the arm. "We haven't finished singing." She nudged us with a single look. "Let's sing 'The Friends Song.' For Mrs. Hedy."

Although I liked some of the songs, I hated this one:

> Make new friends
> But keep the o-old,
> One is silver
> And the other gold.

If most of the girls in my troop could be any type of metal, they'd be bunched-up wads of tinfoil maybe, or rusty iron nails you had to get tetanus shots for.

"No, no, no," Mrs. Margolin said before anyone could start in on "The Friends Song." "An uplifting song. Something to lift her up and take her mind off all these earthly burdens."

Arnetta and Octavia rolled their eyes. Everyone knew what song Mrs. Margolin was talking about, and no one, no one, wanted to sing it.

"Please, no," a voice called out. "Not 'The Doughnut Song.'"

"Please not 'The Doughnut Song,'" Octavia pleaded.

"I'll brush my teeth twice if I don't have to sing 'The Dough-nut —'"

"Sing!" Mrs. Margolin demanded.

We sang:

> Life without Jesus is like a do-ough-nut!
> Like a do-ooough-nut!
> Like a do-ooough-nut!
> Life without Jesus is like a do-ough-nut!
> There's a hole in the middle of my soul!

There were other verses, involving other pastries, but we stopped after the first one and cast glances toward Mrs. Margolin to see if we could gain a reprieve. Mrs. Margolin's eyes fluttered blissfully, half-asleep.

"Awww," Mrs. Hedy said, as though giant Mrs. Margolin were a cute baby. "Mrs. Margolin's had a long day."

"Yes indeed," Mrs. Margolin answered. "If you don't mind, I might just go to the lodge where the beds are. I haven't been the same since the operation."

I had not heard of this operation, or when it had occurred, since Mrs. Margolin had never missed the once-a-week Brownie meetings, but I could see from Daphne's face that she was concerned, and I could see that the other girls had decided that Mrs. Margolin's operation must have happened long ago in some remote time unconnected to our own. Nevertheless, they put on sad faces. We had all been taught that adulthood was full of sorrow and pain, taxes and bills, dreaded work and dealings with whites, sickness, and death.

"Go right ahead, Linda," Mrs. Hedy said. "I'll watch the girls." Mrs. Hedy seemed to forget about divorce for a moment; she looked at us with dewy eyes, as if we were mysterious, furry creatures. Meanwhile, Mrs. Margolin walked through the maze of sleeping bags until she found her own. She gathered a neat stack of clothes and pajamas slowly, as though doing so were almost painful. She took her toothbrush, her toothpaste, her pillow. "All right!" Mrs. Margolin said, addressing us all from the threshold of the cabin. "Be in bed by nine." She said it with a twinkle in her voice, as though she were letting us know she was allowing us to be naughty and stay up till nine-fifteen.

"C'mon, everybody," Arnetta said after Mrs. Margolin left. "Time for us to wash up."

Everyone watched Mrs. Hedy closely, wondering whether she would insist on coming with us since it was night, making a fight with Troop 909 nearly impossible. Troop 909 would soon be in the bathroom, washing their faces, brushing their teeth — completely unsuspecting of our ambush.

"We won't be long," Arnetta said. "We're old enough to go to the restroom by ourselves."

Mrs. Hedy pursed her lips at this dilemma. "Well, I guess you Brownies are almost Girl Scouts, right?"

"Right!"

"Just one more badge," Drema said.

"And about," Octavia droned, "a million more cookies to sell." Octavia looked at all of us. *Now's our chance,* her face seemed to say, but our chance to do *what* I didn't exactly know.

Finally, Mrs. Hedy walked to the doorway where Octavia stood, dutifully waiting to say good-bye and looking bored doing it. Mrs. Hedy held Octavia's chin. "You'll be good?"

"Yes, Mama."

"And remember to pray for me and your father? If I'm asleep when you get back?"

"Yes, Mama."

When the other girls had finished getting their toothbrushes and washcloths and flashlights for the group restroom trip, I was drawing pictures of tiny birds with too many feathers. Daphne was sitting on her sleeping bag, reading.

"You're not going to come?" Octavia asked.

Daphne shook her head.

"I'm also gonna stay, too," I said. "I'll go to the restroom when Daphne and Mrs. Hedy go."

Arnetta leaned down toward me and whispered so that Mrs. Hedy, who had taken over Mrs. Margolin's task of counting Popsicle sticks, couldn't hear. "No, Snot. If we get in trouble, you're going to get in trouble with the rest of us."

We made our way through the darkness by flashlight. The tree branches that had shaded us just hours earlier, along the same path, now looked like arms sprouting menacing hands. The stars sprinkled the sky like spilled salt. They seemed fastened to the darkness, high up and holy, their places fixed and definite as we stirred beneath them.

Some, like me, were quiet because we were afraid of the dark; others were talking like crazy for the same reason.

"Wow," Drema said, looking up. "Why are all the stars out here? I never see stars back on Oneida Street."

"It's a camping trip, that's why," Octavia said. "You're supposed to see stars on camping trips."

Janice said, "This place smells like the air freshener my mother uses."

"These woods are *pine*," Elise said. "Your mother probably uses pine air freshener."

Janice mouthed an exaggerated "Oh," nodding her head as though she just then understood one of the world's great secrets.

No one talked about fighting. Everyone was afraid enough just walking through the infinite deep of the woods. Even without seeing anyone's face, I could tell this wasn't about Daphne being called a nigger. The word that had started it all seemed melted now into some deeper, unnameable feeling. Even though I didn't want to fight, was afraid of fighting, I felt as though I were part of the rest of the troop, as though I were defending something. We trudged against the slight incline of the path, Arnetta leading the way. I wondered, looking at her back, what she could be thinking.

"You know," I said, "their leader will be there. Or they won't even be there. It's dark already. Last night the sun was still in the sky. I'm sure they're already finished."

"Whose flashlight is this?" Arnetta said, shaking the weakening beam of the light she was holding. "It's out of batteries."

Octavia handed Arnetta her flashlight. And that's when I saw it. The bathroom was just ahead.

But the girls were there. We could hear them before we could see them.

"Octavia and I will go in first so they'll think there's just two of us. Then wait till I say, 'We're gonna teach you a lesson,'" Arnetta said. "Then bust in. That'll surprise them."

"That's what I was supposed to say," Janice said.

Arnetta went inside, Octavia next to her. Janice followed, and the rest of us waited outside.

They were in there for what seemed like whole minutes, but something was wrong. Arnetta hadn't given the signal yet. I was with the girls outside when I heard one of the Troop 909 girls say, "NO. That did NOT happen!"

That was to be expected, that they'd deny the whole thing. What I hadn't expected was *the voice* in which the denial was said. The girl sounded as though her tongue were caught in her mouth. "That's a BAD word!" the girl continued. "We don't say BAD words!"

"Let's go in," Elise said.

"No," Drema said. "I don't want to. What if we get beat up?"

"Snot?" Elise turned to me, her flashlight blinding. It was the first time anyone had asked my opinion, though I knew they were just asking because they were afraid.

"I say we go inside, just to see what's going on."

"But Arnetta didn't give us the signal," Drema said. "She's supposed to say, 'We're going to teach you a lesson,' and I didn't hear her say it."

"C'mon," I said. "Let's just go in."

We went inside. There we found the white girls, but about five girls were huddled up next to one big girl. I instantly knew she was the owner of the voice we'd heard. Arnetta and Octavia inched toward us as soon as we entered.

"Where's Janice?" Elise asked, then we heard a flush. "Oh."

"I think," Octavia said, whispering to Elise, "they're retarded."

"We ARE NOT retarded!" the big girl said, though it was obvious that she was. That they all were. The girls around her began to whimper.

"They're just pretending," Arnetta said, trying to convince herself. "I know they are."

Octavia turned to Arnetta. "Arnetta. Let's just leave."

Janice came out of a stall, happy and relieved, then she suddenly remembered her line, pointed to the big girl, and said, "We're gonna teach you a lesson."

"Shut up, Janice," Octavia said, but her heart was not in it. Arnetta's face was set in a lost, deep scowl. Octavia turned to the big girl, and said loudly, slowly, as if they were all deaf, "We're going to leave. It was nice meeting you, okay? You don't have to tell anyone that we were here. Okay?"

"Why not?" said the big girl, like a taunt. When she spoke, her lips did not meet, her mouth did not close. Her tongue grazed the roof of her mouth, like a little pink fish. "You'll get in trouble. I know. I know."

Arnetta got back her old cunning. "If you said anything, then you'd be a tattletale."

The girl looked sad for a moment, then perked up quickly. A flash of genius crossed her face: "I *like* tattletale."

"It's all right, girls. It's gonna be all right!" the 909 troop leader said. It was as though someone had instructed all of Troop 909 to cry at once. The troop leader had girls under her arm, and all the rest of the girls crowded about her. It reminded me of a hog I'd seen on a field trip, where all the little hogs would gather about the mother at feeding time, latching on to her teats. The 909 troop leader had come into the bathroom shortly after the big girl threatened to tell. Then the ranger came, then, once the ranger had radioed the station, Mrs. Margolin arrived with Daphne in tow.

The ranger had left the restroom area, but everyone else was huddled just outside, swatting mosquitoes.

"Oh. They *will* apologize," Mrs. Margolin said to the 909 troop leader, but Mrs. Margolin said this so angrily, I knew she was speaking more to us than to the other troop leader. "When their parents find out, every one a them will be on punishment."

"It's all right. It's all right," the 909 troop leader reassured Mrs. Margolin. Her voice lilted in the same way it had when addressing the girls. She smiled the whole time she talked. She was like one of those TV cooking show women who talk and dice onions and smile all at the same time.

"See. It could have happened. I'm not calling your girls fibbers or anything." She shook her head ferociously from side to side, her Egyptian-style pageboy flapping against her cheeks like heavy drapes. "It *could* have happened, see. Our girls are *not* retarded. They are *delayed* learners." She said this in a syrupy instructional voice, as though our troop might be delayed learners as well. "We're from the Decatur Children's Academy. Many of them just have special needs."

"Now we won't be able to walk to the bathroom by ourselves!" the big girl said.

"Yes you will," the troop leader said, "but maybe we'll wait till we get back to Decatur —"

"I don't want to wait!" the girl said. "I want my Independence patch!"

The girls in my troop were entirely speechless. Arnetta looked as though she were soon to be tortured but was determined not to appear weak. Mrs. Margolin pursed her lips solemnly and said, "Bless them, Lord. Bless them."

In contrast, the Troop 909 leader was full of words and energy. "Some of our girls are echolalic —" She smiled and happily presented one of the girls hanging on to her, but the girl widened her eyes in horror and violently withdrew herself from the center of attention, as though she sensed she were being sacrificed for the village sins. "Echolalic," the troop leader continued. "That means they will say whatever they hear, like an echo — that's where the word comes from. It comes from 'echo.'" She ducked her head apologetically. "I mean, not all of them have the most *progressive* of parents, so if they heard a bad word they might have repeated it. But I guarantee it would not have been *intentional*."

Arnetta spoke. "I saw her say the word. I heard her." She pointed to a small girl, smaller than any of us, wearing an oversized T-shirt that read: EAT BERTHA'S MUSSELS.

The troop leader shook her head and smiled. "That's impossible. She doesn't speak. She can, but she doesn't."

Arnetta furrowed her brow. "No. It wasn't her. That's right. It was *her*."

The girl Arnetta pointed to grinned as though she'd been paid a compliment. She was the only one from either troop actually wearing a full uniform: the mocha-colored A-line shift, the orange ascot, the sash covered with patches, though all the same one — the Try-It patch. She took a few steps toward Arnetta and made a grand sweeping gesture toward the sash. "See," she said, full of self-importance, "I'm a Brownie." I had a hard time imagining this girl calling anyone a "nigger"; the girl looked perpetually delighted, as though she would have cuddled up with a grizzly if someone had let her.

On the fourth morning, we boarded the bus to go home.

The previous day had been spent building miniature churches from Popsicle sticks. We hardly left the cabin. Mrs. Margolin and Mrs. Hedy guarded us so closely, almost no one talked for the entire day.

Even on the day of departure from Camp Crescendo, all was serious and silent. The bus ride began quietly enough. Arnetta had to sit beside Mrs. Margolin, Octavia had to sit beside her mother. I sat beside Daphne, who gave me her prize journal without a word of explanation.

"You don't want it?"

She shook her head no. It was empty.

Then Mrs. Hedy began to weep. "Octavia," Mrs. Hedy said to her daughter without looking at her, "I'm going to sit with Mrs. Margolin. All right?"

Arnetta exchanged seats with Mrs. Hedy. With the two women up front, Elise felt it safe to speak. "Hey," she said, then she set her face into a placid vacant stare, trying to imitate that of a Troop 909 girl. Emboldened, Arnetta made a gesture of mock pride toward an imaginary sash, the way the girl in full uniform had done. Then they all made a game of it, trying to do the most exaggerated imitations of the Troop 909 girls, all without speaking, all without laughing loud enough to catch the women's attention.

Daphne looked at her shoes, white with sneaker polish. I opened the journal she'd given me. I looked out the window, trying to decide what to write, searching for lines, but nothing could compare with the lines Daphne had written, *"My father, the veteran,"* my favorite line of all time. The line replayed itself in my head, and I gave up trying to write.

By then, it seemed as though the rest of the troop had given up making fun of the 909 girls. They were now quietly gossiping about who had passed notes to whom in school. For a moment the gossiping fell off, and all I heard was the hum of the bus as we sped down the road and the muffled sounds of Mrs. Hedy and Mrs. Margolin talking about serious things.

"You know," Octavia whispered, "why did *we* have to be stuck at a camp with retarded girls? You know?"

"*You* know why," Arnetta answered. She narrowed her eyes like a cat. "My mama and I were in the mall in Buckhead, and this white lady just kept looking at us. I mean, like we were foreign or something. Like we were from China."

"What did the woman say?" Elise asked.

"Nothing," Arnetta said. "She didn't say nothing."

A few girls quietly nodded their heads.

"There was this time," I said, "when my father and I were in the mall and —"

"Oh, shut up, Snot," Octavia said.

I stared at Octavia, then rolled my eyes from her to the window. As I watched the trees blur, I wanted nothing more than to be through with it all: the bus ride, the troop, school — all of it. But we were going home. I'd see the same girls in school the next day. We were on a bus, and there was nowhere else to go.

"Go on, Laurel," Daphne said to me. It was the first time she'd spoken the whole trip, and she'd said my name. I turned to her and smiled weakly so as not to cry, hoping she'd remember when I'd tried to be her friend, thinking maybe that her gift of the journal was an invitation of friendship. But she didn't smile back. All she said was, "What happened?"

I studied the girls, waiting for Octavia to tell me to "shut up" again before I even had a chance to utter another word, but everyone was amazed that Daphne had spoken. I gathered my voice. "Well," I said. "My father and I were in this mall, but *I* was the one doing the staring." I stopped and glanced from face to face. I continued. "There were these white people dressed like Puritans or something, but they weren't Puritans. They were Mennonites. They're these people who, if you ask them to do a favor, like paint your porch or something, they have to do it. It's in their rules."

"That sucks," someone said.

"C'mon," Arnetta said. "You're lying."

"I am not."

"How do you know that's not just some story someone made up?" Elise asked, her head cocked, full of daring. "I mean, who's gonna do whatever you ask?"

"It's not made up. I know because when I was looking at them, my father said, 'See those people. If you ask them to do something, they'll do it. Anything you want.'"

No one would call anyone's father a liar. Then they'd have to fight the person, but Drema parsed her words carefully. "How does your *father* know that's not just some story? Huh?"

"Because," I said, "he went up to the man and asked him would he paint our porch, and the man said, 'Yes.' It's their religion."

"Man, I'm glad I'm a Baptist," Elise said, shaking her head in sympathy for the Mennonites.

"So did the guy do it?" Drema asked, scooting closer to hear if the story got juicy.

"Yeah," I said. "His whole family was with him. My dad drove them to our house. They all painted our porch. The woman and girl were in bonnets and long, long skirts with buttons up to their necks. The guy wore this weird hat and these huge suspenders."

"Why," Arnetta asked archly, as though she didn't believe a word, "would someone pick a *porch*? If they'll do anything, why not make them paint the whole *house*? Why not ask for a hundred bucks?"

I thought about it, and I remembered the words my father had said about them painting our porch, though I had never seemed to think about his words after he'd said them.

"He said," I began, only then understanding the words as they uncoiled from my mouth, "it was the only time he'd have a white man on his knees doing something for a black man for free."

I remembered the Mennonites bending like Daphne had bent, cleaning the restroom. I remembered the dark blue of their bonnets, the black of their shoes. They painted the porch as though scrubbing a floor. I was already trembling before Daphne asked quietly, "Did he thank them?"

I looked out the window. I could not tell which were the thoughts and which were the trees. "No," I said, and suddenly knew there was something mean in the world that I could not stop.

Arnetta laughed. "If I asked them to take off their long skirts and bonnets and put on some jeans, they would do it?"

And Daphne's voice — quiet, steady: "Maybe they would. Just to be nice."

EDITH PEARLMAN

Allog

FROM ASCENT

THERE WERE FIVE APARTMENTS in the house on Deronda Street. There were five mailboxes in the vestibule: little wooden doors in embarrassing proximity, like privies.

Nobody liked to be seen there — not the middle-aged widower, not the Moroccan family, not the three old ladies.

The widower got too few letters.

The Moroccans got too many, all bills.

The soprano got some, enough, too much, too little; what did quantity matter. Every concert series in Jerusalem had her name on its list. Do-good societies would not leave her in peace. But the one letter she craved rarely appeared, and when it did come it was only a thin blue square, as if it had been first ironed and then frozen. She extended her palm, the missive floating on it. Decades ago she had indicated with the same gracious gesture, after sufficient applause, that her accompanist might now take a bow. The letter weighed less than a peseta; inside would be perhaps four uninformative sentences in a jumble of Polish and Spanish. She might as well burn it unopened. Chin high, eyes dry, she climbed the stairs.

Tamar, who lived with her grandmother across the hall from the soprano, picked up their mail on her way home from school. Unlike the others, she didn't care who saw her correspondence. She was seventeen. Her parents, in the United States on an extended sabbatical, wrote once a week. A great number of elderly Viennese who had fetched up on other shores wrote to her grandmother. But her grandmother didn't like to go to the mailboxes, or anywhere else for that matter. When Tamar's grandmother did go out — to exhibits, to lectures, to the market — she did so because as a woman of cultivation she was obliged to transcend her dislike of society, though not to conceal it.

Mrs. Goldfanger, on the ground floor, loved society. But she crept from her apartment to the mailboxes like a thief. She wanted to be alone when puzzling out the Hebrew on the envelopes, making sure that everything in her box was truly addressed to Mr. Goldfanger or Mrs. Goldfanger or Mr. and Mrs. Goldfanger or the Goldfanger family; and not to the Gilboas, who ten years ago had sold their apartment to the Goldfangers, newly arrived from Capetown. The Gilboas still received advertisements from tanning salons, which Mrs. Goldfanger felt justified in throwing away. But some morning a legacy might await them in the Goldfanger box. Such things had been known to happen. And then what? She would have to run after the mailman, hoping that he was still crisscrossing Deronda Street like the laces on a corset. If he had completed his route she would have to go to the post office with the misdirected letter, and join the line that backed all the way to the delicatessen; and she would have to explain in her untrustworthy Hebrew that Gilboa, who had just received this letter from a bank in Paris, was away, gone, exiled, and had left no forwarding address.

So Mrs. Goldfanger's relationship with her mailbox, as with many things, was an anxious one. How strange it was, then, that one August morning, having deciphered the first envelope and also its return address, she gathered up all the others without looking at them — let the Gilboas wait another day for their emeralds. She flew up the stairs, a smile on her pretty face.

Mrs. Goldfanger was eighty-five. Her doctor said she had the heart of a woman of thirty; and though she did not believe this outrageous compliment, it strengthened her physical courage, already considerable. She was not afraid of the labor of tending her husband — she could lift him from bed to wheelchair, from wheelchair to bed; she could help him walk when he wanted to. But her sadness was deepening. To diaper him seemed the height of impropriety, and listening to his unintelligible gabbles was some day going to break her thirty-year-old heart. The assistants she hired were often indifferent; if they were kindly they soon got better jobs.

But now . . . she knocked at the door above her own. Tamar's grandmother opened it, dressed as usual in slacks and a blouse. No one had ever seen her in a bathrobe.

Mrs. Goldfanger leaped into the apartment like an antelope. "It's come!"

Tamar's grandmother examined the official envelope and then handed it to Tamar, who had wandered in from the balcony where she was breakfasting in her skimpy nightgown.

Tamar too examined the envelope. "The hepatoscopist has landed," she said.

A year earlier the state of Israel had entered into a treaty with an impoverished Southeast Asian nation. Under the treaty Israeli citizens could purchase the assistance of Southeast Asians for the at-home management of the elderly. The foreigners were not to be hired as nannies, housecleaners, or day care workers — able-bodied Israeli citizens were available for that work, not that they relished it. The Asians' task was to care for sages who had outlived their sagacity.

The employers undertook the expense of airfare — round-trip airfare: workers were not supposed to hang about when their charges died. Citizenship was not part of the deal. Weren't these people already citizens someplace else? The Law of Return did not apply to Catholics, which most of them nominally were, nor to hepatoscopists, which some of them were said to be.

As soon as a bureau was established, Mrs. Goldfanger applied for an Asian.

"What's a hepatoscopist?" she asked Tamar's grandmother.

Tamar's grandmother said: "Hepatoscopy is the prediction of the future by an examination of the entrails, specifically the liver, of a mammal. Properly a sheep, more practically a rodent."

"Oh."

"All those stray cats," murmured Tamar. "Useful at last."

Tamar's grandmother, her lips tight, accompanied Mrs. Goldfanger to a series of office visits. The younger old woman helped the older old woman fill out the required forms. Every time a packet of papers arrived in the mail, Mrs. Goldfanger brought them up to Tamar's grandmother. She settled herself at the table in the dining room. Sunlight slanting through the blind made her rusty hair rustier — more unnatural, Tamar mentioned later. "Henna is a natural substance," her grandmother reminded her.

And now the Asian was here. Or would be here in three weeks time. Mrs. Goldfanger was to go to the bureau at ten o'clock on a morning in September to be introduced to the newcomer and to sign the necessary final papers.

"Shall I come with you?" sighed Tamar's grandmother.

"Oh, not this time." Mrs. Goldfanger paused. "That there should be no confusion," she confusedly explained. "But thank you very much, for everything. I just wanted you to know."

So it was alone, three weeks later, that Mrs. Goldfanger journeyed to the dingy office that she now knew so well. Her hand alone shook the hand of the serious man. Her voice alone welcomed him, in English. *His* English had a lilt, like the waves that lapped his island country. Mrs. Goldfanger, unassisted, told the bureau official that she understood the necessity for employer and employee to visit the office once every four months (later she wondered briefly whether the visits were to occur four times every one month). Her smile beckoned the man to follow.

His satchel was so small. He wore tan pants and a woven shirt and another shirt, plaid, as a jacket. She hoped that cabs would be numerous at the nearby taxi stand; she wanted him to see immediately that the country was bountiful. Providence smiled on the wish: three cabbies were waiting, and the first promptly started his engine. But before the pair could get into the vehicle a schnorrer approached. Mrs. Goldfanger gave him a coin. Joe felt in his own pocket. Oh dear. "I've paid for us both," she told him.

During Joe's first afternoon at the Goldfangers' he spent several hours on the balcony fixing the wheelchair. Because he was on hands and knees he could not be seen above the iron railing, wound about with ivy; but on the glass table lay, in plain view, an open toolbox and an amputated wheel. Coming home from school, Tamar paused under the eucalyptus, squinted through the ivy with a practiced eye, and saw the wheelchair lying on its side, the kneeling figure operating on it. Whatever he was doing was precise, or at least small; it required no noticeable movement on his part. He maintained his respectful position for many minutes. Tamar, under the tree, maintained her erect one. Finally his bare arm reached upward — blindly it seemed, but in fact purposefully

— and the hand without wandering grasped a screwdriver. The girl went into the building.

In the succeeding days there were signs of further industry at the Goldfangers' apartment. The rap of hammering mixed with the mortar fire of drilling. The soprano noticed the new servant standing in front of the Goldfangers' fuse box in the shared hall, his fingers curling around his chin. Soon the stereo equipment rose from its grave; remastered swing orchestras that Mrs. Goldfanger had not been able to listen to for months issued from the open doors of the balcony into the autumn warmth.

"Joe is a wonder," said Mrs. Goldfanger to Tamar and her grandmother. "He's descended from the angels."

Tamar's grandmother narrowed her eyes. The indentured were often industrious. A good disposition was natural to people born in the temperate zone. Sympathy flourished in mild climates; it withered in torrid ones; and in *this* country, amid five million wound-up souls, it was as rare as a lotus. People here had mislaid civility a century ago.

Mrs. Goldfanger gushed on about Joe; Tamar's grandmother kept her knowledge of human nature to herself. "My husband is lucky," Mrs. Goldfanger said.

Mr. Goldfanger's decline had been gradual, though Tamar and her grandmother remembered that he had moved in already trembling. The children in the ground-floor apartment opposite the Goldfangers' had never known him as other than a speechless gremlin, those funny pointed ears, hair sprouted right out of them, and he always looked as if he were going to speak, but he never did, not one word. They had been warned not to mock him.

This family, referred to as Moroccan by everybody in the building, had all been born in Israel — father, mother, three children. The epithet derived from the previous generation and would no doubt abide for several hundred years. The Moroccan mother got vigorously tarted up for the holidays and for nights out, but at other times she hung around in an unclean satin robe. She had apricot hair and freckles and a mischievous smile. Her children were always underfoot — under her feet, under everybody else's. Her husband ran a successful tile business; some of the most praised kitchens in Rehavia owed their gloss to him.

He was artistic — or at least he had an artistic eye — but he was not handy. The entire family, in fact, was all thumbs. All ears and all eyes too; they couldn't help be aware of the cleverness of the Goldfangers' new aide. Such fingers! And so, every ten days or so, when one of their appliances would break down: "Joe! Joe!" they'd call. "That damned toaster!" And Joe, leaving the Goldfangers' door open in case his patient needed him, walked across the hall and diagnosed and maybe repaired the thing, and softly returned.

"We must be careful not to take advantage of Joe," said the mother one morning. The father eyed her with pleasure. Her comments tickled him, as did her languid behavior, so different from the vigor of the women who bought his tiles. She was indolent and forgetful, but she didn't crave much; she'd been wearing that red schmatte since their honeymoon. She loved the children in an offhand way — sometimes she called the older boy by the name of the younger, sometimes the daughter by the name of her own sister. "Take advantage of Joe?" he said. "What do you mean?"

But as usual she couldn't or wouldn't say what she meant, just sat smiling at him across the disarray of their dining table. So he got up, kissed her good-bye, and left the apartment. Across the hall he could hear Joe's calm voice. What do we need with these people? he wondered in a brief spasm of irritation. Didn't the country have enough trouble? Next time he'd take the toaster to the Bulgarian fixer. Then the mood passed, and he thought maybe Joe could use that flecked jacket he hadn't worn for years; a bit too vivid for his own complexion; perfect for a yellow man.

The soprano had friends and acquaintances in the Spanish-speaking community and in the musical one, and she went to a lot of recitals. However, she spent most of her time writing and revising letters to the home she'd left.

> Besides you, Cara, *[she wrote]* I miss most the peasants. Do you remember how they used to welcome me whenever I went on tour? — crowding around the train, strewing my path with flowers? I miss their flat brown eyes.

In fact her tours had been flops. In Latin America, trains to the provinces were just strings of dusty cars. Their windows were either stuck open or stuck closed. The soprano traveled with her accompanist — a plain young woman glowering behind spectacles — and the pair were untroubled by admiration or even recognition. But the singer had imagined throngs of fans so often that the vision

in her mind's eye had the clarity of remembrance. She saw a donkey draped with garlands. Her hand was kissed by the oily mayor of
a town whose cinema doubled as a concert hall. The mayor's wife
was home preparing a banquet. Many people came to the concert
and still more to the banquet, and the floor of the mayor's rickety
mansion rocked with stomping and the room rocked with cheers.

> In this ambitious country there is no peasant, no one to love the earth.
> The collectives pay mercenaries to farm; the countryside is a fiefdom
> now. The giants of the desert are gone. I am quoting my neighbor across
> the hall, a woman of strong opinions.

The soprano scratched her letters by hand, sitting on her balcony.
She spent a week composing each one. For whose sake were those
literary efforts? Tamar's grandmother inquired. Ah, to entertain
her best friend back home, said the soprano, adjusting a soft shawl.
She owned its replica in several shades — the gray of dawn, the violet of dusk, the lavender of a bruise.

> Nobody cares for singing. We have become a country of string players,
> all Russian, all geniuses. Then there's the fellow with a fiddle and a cup
> who stands outside a big department store. He makes a living, too.

"Of course I no longer perform," she'd told Joe.
"Your speaking voice is music," he said, or something like that.

> Joe grew up in a village by a river. The houses were on stilts. He trained
> as a pharmacist.

She imagined him mixing powders crushed from roots. He told
her that in some of the villages of his country the pharmacist had
to behave as a doctor. "Aided by American Police Corps," he'd said.
"Peace Corps, surely."
On the afternoons that she dropped in at the Goldfangers',
she and Joe exchanged tales about high-minded Americans. Then,
when she indicated by a tiny droop that the visit was over, he escorted her upstairs to her door.

> Come to me, Carissima. Bring your damned parrot. Come.

The widower occupied the whole of the top floor. He was sad
but alert. Not for him to be left out when other people were getting
favors.

"There isn't a cabdriver in the whole damned city I can trust," he confided to Joe as they climbed the stairs with the widower's groceries. "The Arabs? Don't make me laugh. The Russians are all crooks. That stuff's not too heavy for you, is it? Some muscles! Still, you could leave one bag on the landing and then go back for it. And I'll take the cabbage," and he grabbed a pale head from the top of one bag, as well as the brochure that had constituted his mail of the day.

The widower was currently a vegetarian. Vegetables are lighter than chickens. Joe usually carried the weekly purchases in one trip, a sack in each arm, like twins. He managed the new television too.

"I don't suppose you play chess," said the widower one day.

"I play chess."

Soon they were playing two or three evenings a week. If Mrs. Goldfanger was staying home they played after Joe had put Mr. Goldfanger to bed. The widower's apartment was a hodgepodge of office furniture and supplies for his stationery store, which was also a mess. The two men settled themselves on straight-backed chairs at one corner of a metal table stacked with cartons.

If Mrs. Goldfanger was going to a concert or a bridge game they played at the Goldfangers'. The widower brought down his board and his chessmen and a bottle of wine and a vegetable pie. Joe provided oranges and tea. The widower set up the game on the living room coffee table. After pie and wine, the widower dragged a hassock to the table. He spent the evening on the hassock, hunched over the set. Joe sat on the flowered couch. Mr. Goldfanger, sitting wordlessly beside Joe, often fell asleep with his head on his caretaker's shoulder. At those times Joe, reluctant to shift his body, asked the widower to move the chessmen for him.

On Saturday mornings, while Mrs. Goldfanger was attending services and Tamar's grandmother was reading German philosophy and the soprano was swimming in the Dead Sea with other émigrés and the widower was playing with his grandchildren at his daughter's house and the Moroccan family, in its best clothes, had pranced off to some celebration, the youngest on Rollerblades — on Saturday mornings, Tamar knocked on Joe's door.

"Shall we take a walk?"

In response Joe posed the question to Mr. Goldfanger.

Mr. Goldfanger looked warmly at Joe.

"Tov," said Joe. His Hebrew was already better than Mrs. Gold-fanger's, but he was too shy to use it with anyone in the building except the Moroccan children. He spoke English with the adults.

Joe pushed the empty wheelchair out of the apartment and out of the building. He parked it under the eucalyptus. He locked its wheel. Then he went back inside. Then he reemerged, walking backward, his hands extended with their palms up. Little Mr. Goldfanger tottered forward, his palms resting on Joe's. Mr. Goldfanger's gaze at first did not stray from his own sneakers, but he gradually lifted his eyes until they met Joe's. The two proceeded to the waiting chair. They executed a quarter turn, and Joe nodded and Mr. Goldfanger sat down and Joe settled him and then resettled him and took his own position behind the chair and unlocked the wheel.

"Here I come," called Tamar from her balcony. She had run upstairs to get a sweater, she said; to grab a book, she said; really to watch the *pas de deux* from above, like a princess in her box.

Sometimes they walked to the Botanical Gardens, sometimes to Liberty Bell Park, and most often to the Promenade, where they gazed across the forested valley at the walls of the Old City.

In English laced with Hebrew they talked about Tamar's future in television newscasting or video production.

"Of course I will live in Tel Aviv."

"I have heard of Tel Aviv. The action is there."

They talked about Joe's past — his island country.

"Little bits of islands, really. In the shape of the new moon."

"Connected?" she wondered.

"There are bridges. Sometimes you need a boat."

"So much water. You must find us dry."

"Well . . . I have heard of the Galilee," he said respectfully.

"Do you have reptiles?"

"Oh, many lizards."

"And jungles?"

"And jungles."

"I've never seen a jungle."

"Before coming here I'd never seen a desert."

If Mr. Goldfanger were asleep in his chair, they might talk about him. In Joe's opinion Mr. Goldfanger, despite or because of his inarticulateness, knew more than most people. "The secrets of plants. The location of water underground."

"Some ministry would pay for that information."

"He is like one of our allogs, grown too old for council duty, but still to be revered."

"Allog?"

Joe thought for a while. "It means a kind of chieftain."

"Allog, all'gim," said Tamar, Hebraicizing it. Then she turned it into verbs, passive and active and reflexive. Joe listened patiently.

"The elderly allog, the wise one, is consulted on great questions," he said.

"Allog emeritus," said Tamar.

Joe was silent again. Then: "I think perhaps you are very clever," he said.

Tamar gave an ashamed whinny. "And the young allog — the one who is still in charge?"

"He makes decisions for the group. Also he acts as troubleshooter. And a sort of confessor, since the churches are not very helpful anymore."

"Is it true that you examine entrails?" she asked quickly.

"That practice died out when the missionaries came."

"When was that?"

"In the sixteenth century."

"Joe was educated by the Jesuits," said the soprano to Tamar's grandmother. "Another glass of wine?"

Tamar's grandmother nodded. "Then he was trained as a paramedic."

"Pharmacist," said the soprano.

A barbed silence followed, gradually softening into a companionable one. There were few jobs for either paramedics or pharmacists on Joe's little island, the two women agreed when dialogue resumed. Joe's wife, a teacher, also could not find employment at home. She worked as a housekeeper in Toronto. Each hoped to be able to send for the other, and for the eight-year-old daughter who had been left in the care of her grandparents and was so unhappy with the arrangement that she refused to go to school. "She is on strike," Joe had said.

"The classroom," Tamar's grandmother observed, "is the crucible of reactionaries."

If Tamar ever went on strike her grandmother would enthusiastically undertake to educate her at home, emphasizing eighteenth-century German philosophy. This prospect kept Tamar in school, most of the time.

But some of the time she was repelled by even the thought of her classmates, greedy and self-absorbed . . . One such day she knocked at the Goldfangers' door.

"Surprise!"

"No school today?" Joe said calmly.

"No school," she lied. "Shall we take a walk?"

Mr. Goldfanger was agreeable. They set out. Tamar suggested that, since it was a weekday and everything was open, they visit one of the downtown cafés where you can browse the Net. Joe said that Mr. Goldfanger would not enjoy that activity. Tamar wondered if he had ever been exposed to it. They were walking while they argued. In the end they just pushed the chair along the busy streets.

They stopped in a dry courtyard to eat the lunch Joe had prepared. A fix-it shop and a dusty grocery opened onto the yard, and a place that sold ironware.

"Delicious orange," said Tamar. "When they did practice hepatoscopy — what did they discover about the future?"

Joe unwrapped a sandwich and handed her half of it. "The discoveries were about the past — about transformations that had occurred. Just one bite, dear man."

"Transformations? What kind?"

"People into fish. Trees into warriors." Men into nursemaids? She waited; but he didn't say that. Caretakers into guardians, then.

"Girls into scholars," Joe said with a smile. "What a fat book."

That fat book was *The Ambassadors*. She was trying to improve her English reading skills. The first paragraph was as long as the entire Tanach.

Mr. Goldfanger was beginning to smell. Tamar picked up the debris from lunch and walked with it to a Dumpster in one corner of the courtyard. Her approach flushed a few scrawny cats.

She turned from the Dumpster and saw, across the yard, that two men had been joined by a third. The third was a beggar, the kind with a story. She didn't need to be within range to hear the familiar patter. Wife recently dead. Children motherless and shoeless and without textbooks; was the foreign gentleman aware that children who couldn't afford textbooks had been known to commit suicide? She drew nearer until she could hear the shpiel directly. How impossible it is to find work in this country that gives all its resources to Ethiopians who are no more Jews than you are, sir. Sir!

Joe was standing now, one hand resting on Mr. Goldfanger's head. With his own head slightly inclined he listened to the beggar. The fellow wore a junk-pile fedora over his skullcap. He held out his hand in the classic gesture.

Joe dug into his own pocket for shekels. The beggar put them deep into his long coat. Then he extended his palm toward Mr. Goldfanger. Mr. Goldfanger laid his fingers trustingly on the hand of this new partner.

"That will be that," said Joe to the beggar, his Hebrew not at all shy.

"Sir," bowed the beggar, and stepped lightly away.

They walked home in sweet silence. On the corner of Deronda Street they ran into the Moroccan woman, and a few buildings later the widower caught up with them. In the vestibule they collected the mail. Joe got a letter from his daughter.

Winter came, and with it the rains. Joe fitted an umbrella to Mr. Goldfanger's wheelchair. That served for misty or even drizzly days, but when it poured they had to stay inside. They listened to music while Joe cleaned and darned. The soprano loaned them her own two recordings of arias — LPs, not remastered.

Joe patched a leak for the widower. He fixed a newel post. He accepted a spare key to the apartment across the hall and put it into his sewing box. One or another Moroccan child, forgetting his own key, knocked on the door at least once a week. Joe baked cookies while Mr. Goldfanger napped. The kids forgot their keys more often.

One afternoon the soprano stopped in at the Goldfangers' after attending a string trio recital. Mrs. Goldfanger was playing solitaire and Mr. Goldfanger was watching her. The soprano sipped a brandy and talked for a while with Mrs. Goldfanger, their voices tin-

kling like glass droplets. Joe, coming in with a plate of cookies, remarked that the visitor looked pale. The summer will correct that,
she told him. She refused his customary offer to escort her upstairs.

At her own door, about to insert the key, the soprano was seized.
She slumped forward; then, with an effortful spasm, she pushed
her hands against the door so that she fell sideways and lay aslant,
her bent knees touching each other. Her upper body rested on the
stairs leading to the top floor. Her head was in majestic profile.

Tamar saw the legs when she herself drifted upward on her way
home from play rehearsal. She didn't scream. She turned and
ran down to Joe's. She beat on the door. Joe opened it. After a
glance at her open mouth and pointing finger, he bounded up the
stairs, removing his jacket as he ran. Mrs. Goldfanger, needlessly
telling Mr. Goldfanger not to move, followed Joe. Tamar followed
Mrs. Goldfanger. The Moroccan woman heard the footfalls of this
small army and opened her door and started up the stairs, her children surrounding her. Tamar's grandmother, whose head cold had
kept her in bed all day, opened her door. She was wearing an ancient bathrobe with a belt. The widower descended from his flat.

The Moroccan husband, coming home from work, pushed
through the vestibule. He saw at first two open apartment doors,
his own and the Goldfangers'. Mr. Goldfanger sat on the flowered
couch, finishing off a snifter of brandy, though spilling most of it.
The Moroccan saw his wife, halfway up the stairs, rising from a nest
of their children. He then saw Tamar with her arm around Mrs.
Goldfanger. He brushed past them all. Tamar's grandmother stood
in her doorway, costumed as a Hassid. Now he saw his old flecked
jacket in a heap on the floor; now he saw the soprano, flat on the
landing where Joe had hauled her. The soprano's skirt was hiked
up and one shoe had come off. A siren wailed.

They were none of them unused to death. The children had lost
a beloved older cousin in a recent skirmish. Television kept them
familiar with highway carnage. The Moroccan father had fought in
one war, and the widower in several, and Tamar's parents had also
served. During her stint in the army the Moroccan mother had
been elevated to assistant intelligence officer, a job she executed
skillfully while seeming to laze about. Tamar would be inducted after high school, unless she joined her parents in the States as they

urged her to do. Three years ago her most envied friend had been blown up in a coffee shop. The two old ladies had sat at many deathbeds.

Joe kneeled over the corpse, attempting mouth-to-mouth resuscitation. Then he said she was gone, and cried.

Joe and his family changed nothing in the soprano's apartment. They even kept the shawls. Their little girl used them to cover her dolls. She went to the local school. She looked like a daughter of privilege in the plaid skirts of the nuns' academy she had refused to attend. She played with the Moroccan daughter. She was picking up Hebrew quickly.

The widower continued his chess matches with Joe. When Joe was working — *he* continued his attentive care of Mr. Goldfanger — they played as before in the Goldfangers' apartment. When Joe was at home they played there. Mrs. Joe cooked a spicy stew. After a while the widower inquired as to the ingredients — meat, it turned out, and sweet potatoes, and nuts. After a further while the widower asked for the recipe. His own cuisine took a promising turn.

They played at a low teak table, elaborately carved. Like the rest of the furniture, it had originated in Latin America and had accompanied the soprano into exile. The walls were still decorated with photographs of the deceased at various stages in her career. The child sat on the floor next to the table like a third player, following the moves.

Mrs. Goldfanger worried that the change in Joe's fortune would alter their relationship. Of course she was happy for him, though she did think . . . she did think . . . well, couldn't the apartment have been left to a family member?

"There was no family," said Tamar's grandmother.

"And she was of sound mind, I suppose," sighed Mrs. Goldfanger.

"Thoroughly."

In fact very little in the building changed. Though Joe lived in the apartment that had been bequeathed to his wife, he was always available for night duty. Sometimes he made dinner on those evenings, more often his wife cooked; and the Moroccan children dropped in, and the widower, and sometimes Tamar, and sometimes even Tamar's grandmother; and when Mrs. Goldfanger came home it was as if a little party were being conducted on her premises. Mr. Goldfanger had always liked a crowd. He became restless only on the brief occasions when Joe left the room; as soon as Joe returned, and their eyes met, he settled into his usual calm vacancy.

As the treaty was renewed and expanded and a citizenship clause inserted, more of Joe's countrymen arrived, to take a wider variety of jobs. One, it is said, became a skilled schnorrer. The noun "allog" entered the accommodating vocabulary. The word became disconnected from the idea of chieftain; but it gained the connotation, at least in Jerusalem, of "resident indispensable." In heedless Tel Aviv it sometimes refers to the janitor.

ANNIE PROULX

People in Hell Just Want a Drink of Water

FROM GQ

YOU STAND THERE, braced. Cloud shadows race over the buff rock stacks as a projected film, casting a queasy, mottled ground rash. The air hisses, and it is no local breeze but the great harsh sweep of wind from the turning of the earth. The wild country — indigo jags of mountain, grassy plain everlasting, tumbled stones like fallen cities, the flaring roll of sky — provokes a spiritual shudder. It is like a deep note that cannot be heard but is felt; it is like a claw in the gut.

Dangerous and indifferent ground: against its fixed mass the tragedies of people count for nothing, although the signs of misadventure are everywhere. No past slaughter or cruelty, no accident or murder that occurs on the little ranches or at the isolate crossroads with their bare populations of three or seventeen or in the reckless trailer courts of mining towns, delays the flood of morning light. Fences, cattle, roads, refineries, mines, gravel pits, traffic lights, graffiti'd celebration of athletic victory on bridge overpass, crust of blood on the Wal-Mart loading dock, the sunfaded wreaths of plastic flowers marking death on the highway, are ephemeral. Other cultures have camped here awhile and disappeared. Only earth and sky matter. Only the endlessly repeated flood of morning light. You begin to see that God does not owe us much beyond that.

In 1908, on the run from Texas drought and dusters, Isaac "Ice" Dunmire arrived in Laramie, Wyoming, at three-thirty in the dark

February morning. It was thirty-four degrees below zero, the wind shrieking along the tracks.

"It sure can't get more worse than this," he said. He didn't know anything about it.

Although he had a wife, Naomi, and five sons back in Burnet County, for the sake of a job punching cows he swore to the manager of the Six Pigpen Ranch that he was single. The big spread was owned by two Scots brothers who had never seen the Six and never wished to, any more than the owner of a slave ship wanted to look over the cargo.

At the end of a year, because he never went into town, saved his $40-a-month wages and was an indefatigable killer of bounty wolves, because he won at Red Dog more often than he lost, Ice Dunmire had $400 in blue tin box painted with the image of a pigtailed sailor cutting a curl of tobacco from a golden plug. It wasn't enough. The second spring in the country he quit the Six and went into the Tetons to kill wapiti elk for their big canine teeth, bought for big money by members of the BPOE, who dangled the ivory from their watch chains.

Now he staked a homestead claim on the Laramie plain south of the Big Hollow, a long, wind-gouged depression below the Snowy Range of the Medicine Bows, put up a sod shanty, registered the Rocking Box brand. The boundary didn't signify — what he saw was the beautiful, deep land, and he saw it his, aimed to get as much of it as he could. He bought and stole half a hundred cows, and with pride in this three-up outfit, declared himself a rancher. He sent for the wife and kids, filed on an adjoining quarter section in Naomi's name. His sudden passage from bachelor to family man with five little hen-wranglers, from broke cowpuncher to property-owning rancher, earned him the nickname of "Tricker," which some uneasily misheard as "Trigger."

What the wife thought when she saw the sod hut, ten by fourteen, roofed with planks and more dirt thrown on top, one window and a warped door, can be guessed at but not known. There were two pole beds with belly-wool mattresses. The five boys slept in one, and in the other Ice quickly begot on Naomi another and another kid as fast as the woman could stand to make them. Jaxon's most vivid memory of her was watching her pour boiling water on the rattlesnakes he and his brothers caught with loops of barbwire, smiling to see them writhe. By 1913, ridden hard and put away dirty, looking for relief, she went off with a cook-pan tinker and left Ice the nine boys — Jaxon, the twins Ideal and Pet, Kemmy, Marion, Byron, Varn, Ritter and Bliss. They all lived except Byron, who was bitten by a mosquito and died of encephalitis. Boys were money in the bank in that country, and Ice brought them up to fill his labor needs. They got ropes for Christmas, a handshake each birthday and damn a cake.

What they learned was livestock and ranchwork. When they were still young buttons, they could sleep out alone on the plain, knees raftered up in the rain, tarp drawn over their heads, listening to the water trickle past their ears. In the autumn, after fall roundup, they went up on Jelm Mountain and hunted, not for sport but for meat. They grew into bone-seasoned, tireless workers accustomed to discomfort, took their pleasure in drink, cigarettes, getting work done. They were brass-nutted boys, sinewy and tall, nothing they liked better than to kick the frost out of a horse in early morning.

"Sink them shittin spurs into his lungs, boy!" screamed Ice at a kid on a snorty bronc. "Be a man."

Their endurance of pain was legendary. When a section of narrow mountain trail broke away under Marion's horse, the horse falling with him onto rocks below, the animal's back broken and Marion's left leg, he shot the horse, splinted his own leg with some yucca stalks and his wild rag, whittled a crutch from the limb he shot off a scrub cedar and in three days hopped twenty miles to the Shivers place, asked for a drink of water, swallowed it, pivoted on the cedar crutch and began to hop toward the home ranch, another seven miles east, before George Shivers cajoled him into a wagon. Shivers saw then what he missed before — Marion had carried his heavy stock saddle the distance.

Jaxon, the oldest, was a top bronc buster but torn up so badly inside by the age of twenty-eight his underwear were often stained with blood; he had to switch to easy horses broke by other men. After a loose-end time he took over the daily operations of the Rocking Box and kept the books, stud records, but in summers turned all that back to his father while he ran as a salesman for Morning Glory windmills, bumping over the country in a Ford truck to ranches, fairs, and rodeos. There was a hard need for cash. The Rocking Box had a hard need for cash. The jolting was enough that he said he might as well be riding broncs. He bought himself a plaid suit, then a roadster, hitched a rubber-tired trailer to the rear bumper. In the trailer bed he bolted a sample-size Morning Glory windmill supplied by the company. The blades turned showily as he drove. He carried sidelines of pump-rod springs, regulators, and an assortment of Cowboy's Pal Deluxe Calendars, which featured campfires and saccharine verses or candy-tinted girlies kneeling on Indian blankets. The Morning Glory was a steel-tower, back-geared pumping mill. The blades were painted bright blue, and a scallop-tailed vane sheet carried the message NEVER SORRY — MORNING GLORY.

"I got a advantage over those bums got nothin but the pictures and the catalogues. I show em the real thing — that main shaft goin through the roller bearins to the double-pinion gear. You can't show that in a picture, how them teeth mesh in with the big crank gears. The roller bearins are what makes it bite the biscuit. Then some old guy don't want a windmill, he'll sure want a couple calendars. Small, but it adds up."

He kept his say in ranch affairs — he'd earned the right.

Pet and Kemmy married and set up off the Rocking Box, but the others stayed at home and single, finding ceaseless work and an occasional group visit to a Laramie whorehouse enough. Jaxon did not go on these excursions, claiming he found plenty of what he needed on his travels to remote ranches.

"Some a them women can't hardly wait until I get out a the truck," he said. "They'll put their hand right on you soon's you open the door. Like our Ma, I guess," he sneered.

By the droughty depression of the 1930s the Dunmires were in everything that happened, their opinions based on deep experience. They had seen it all: prairie fire, flood, blizzard, dust storm, injury, sliding beef prices, grasshopper and Mormon cricket plagues, rustlers, scours, bad horses. They ran off hobos and gypsies, and if Jaxon whistled "Shuffle Off to Buffalo," in a month everybody was whistling that tune. The country, its horses and cattle, suited them, and if they loved anything that was it, and they ran that country because there were eight of them and Ice and they were of one mind. But there builds up in men who work livestock in big territory a kind of contempt for those who do not. The Dunmires measured beauty and religion by what they rode through every day, and this encouraged their disdain for art and in-

tellect. There was a somber arrogance about them, a rigidity of attitude that said theirs was the only way.

The Tinsleys were a different kind. Horm Tinsley had come up
from St. Louis with the expectation of quick success. He often said
that anything could happen, but the truth of that was bitter. He
was lanky and inattentive, early on bitten by a rattlesnake while
setting fence posts, and two months later bitten again at the same
chore. On the rich Laramie plain he ended up with a patch of
poor land just east of the rain, a dry and sandy range with sparse
grass, and he could not seem to get ahead, trying horses, cattle,
sheep, in succession. Every change of season took him by surprise. Although he could tell snow from sunshine, he wasn't
much at reading weather. He took an interest in his spread, but
it was skewed to a taste for a noble rock or other trifling scenic
vantage.

His failure as a stockman was recognized, yet he was tolerated
and even liked for his kindly manner and skill playing the banjo
and the fiddle, though most regarded him with contemptuous pity
for his loose control of home affairs and his coddling of a crazy wife
after her impetuous crime.

Mrs. Tinsley, intensely modest, sensitive and abhorring marital
nakedness, suffered from nerves; she was distracted and fretted by
shrill sounds, as the screech of a chair leg scraping the floor or the
pulling of a nail. As a girl in Missouri she had written a poem that
began with the line "Our life is a beautiful Fairy Land." Now she
was mother to three. When the youngest girl, Mabel, was a few
months old they made a journey into Laramie, the infant howling
intolerably, the wagon bungling along, stones sliding beneath the
wheels. As they crossed the Little Laramie, Mrs. Tinsley stood up
and hurled the crying infant into the water. The child's white dress
filled with air, and it floated a few yards in the swift current, then
disappeared beneath a bower of willows at the bend. The woman
shrieked and made to leap after the child, but Horm Tinsley held
her back. They galloped across the bridge and to the river's edge
below the bend. Gone and gone.

As if to make up for her fit of destruction, Mrs. Tinsley developed an intense anxiety for the safety of the surviving children, tying them to chairs in the kitchen lest they wander outside and

come to harm, sending them to bed while the sun was still high, for twilight was a dangerous time, warning them away from haystacks threaded with vipers, from trampling horses and biting dogs, the yellow wyandottes who pecked, from the sound of thunder and the sight of lightning. In the night she came to their beds many times to learn if they had smothered.

By the time he was twelve, the boy, Rasmussen, potato-nosed, with coarse brown hair and yellow eyes, displayed a kind of awkward zaniness. He was smart with numbers, read books. He asked complicated questions no one could answer — the distance to the sun, why did humans not have snouts, could a traveler reach China by setting out in any direction and holding steady to it? Trains were his particular interest, and he knew about rail connections from study of the timetables, pestered travelers at the station to hear something of distant cities. He was indifferent to stock except for his flea-bitten gray, Bucky, and he threw the weight of his mind in random directions as if the practical problems of life were not to be resolved but teased as a kitten is by a broom straw.

When he was fifteen his interest turned to the distant sea, and he yearned for books about ships, books with pictures, and there were none. On paper he invented boats like inverted roofs, imagined the ocean a constant smooth and glassy medium until Mrs. Hepple of Laramie spoke at an evening about her trip abroad, describing the voyage as a purgatory of monstrous waves and terrible winds. Another time a man worked for them five or six months. He had been in San Francisco and told about lively streets, Chinese tong wars, sailors and woodsmen blowing their wages in a single puking night. He described Chicago, a smoking mass shrugging out of the plains, fouling the air a hundred miles east. He said Lake Superior licked the wild shore of Canada.

There was no holding Ras. At sixteen this rank gangler left home, headed for San Francisco, Seattle, Toronto, Boston, Cincinnati. What his expectations and experiences were no one knew. He neither returned nor wrote.

The daughter, neglected as daughters are, married a cowboy with bad habits and moved with him to Baggs. Horm Tinsley gave up on sheep and started a truck garden and honey operation, specializing in canner tomatoes, in Moon and Stars watermelons. After a year or so he sold Ras's horse to the Klickas on the neighboring ranch.

In 1933 the son had been gone more than five years and not a word.

The mother begged of the curtains, "Why don't he write?" and saw again the infant in the water, silent, the swollen dress buoying it around the dark bend — who would write to such a mother? — and she was up in the night and to the kitchen to scrub the ceiling, the table legs, the soles of her husband's boots, rubbing the old meat grinder with a banana skin to bring up the silvery bloom. A murderer she might be, but no one could say her house wasn't clean.

Jaxon Dunmire was ready to get back on the road with his Morning Glory pitch and bluster. They'd finished building a new round corral, branding was over, what there was to brand, forget haying — in the scorched fields the hay hadn't made. What in another place might have been a froth of white flowers here was alkali dust blooming in the wind, and a dark horizon not rain but another choking storm of dust or rising cloud of grasshoppers. Ice said he could feel there was worse to come. To save the ranchers the government was buying up cattle for nickels and dimes.

Jaxon lounged against a stall watching shaggy-headed Bliss, who bent over a brood mare's hoof, examining a sand crack.

"Last year down by Lingle I seen Mormon crickets eat a live prairie dog," Jaxon said. "In about ten minutes."

"God," said Bliss, who had not tasted candy until he was fourteen and then spat it out, saying, too much taste. He enjoyed Jaxon's stories, thought he might like to be a windmill man himself sometime, or at least travel around a few weeks with Jaxon. "Got a little crack startin here."

"Catch it now, save the horse. We still got half a jar a that hoof dressin. Yeah, see and hear a lot a strange things. Clayt Blay told me that around twenty years ago he run into these two fellers in Laramie. They told him they found a diamond mine up in the Sierra Madres, and then, says Clayt, both a them come down with the whoopin pox and died. Found their bodies in the fall, rotted into the cabin floor. But a course they'd told Clayt where their dig was before they croaked."

"You didn't fall for it." Bliss began to cut a pattern into the hoof above the crack to contain it.

"Naw, not likely anything Clayt Blay says would cause me to fire up." He rolled a cigarette but did not light it.

Bliss shot a glance into the yard. "What the hell is that stuff on your skunk wagon?"

"Aw, somebody's threwn flour or plaster on it in Rock Springs. Bastards. Ever time I go into Rock Springs they do me some mess. People's in a bad mood — and nobody got money for a goddamn windmill. You ought a see the homemade rigs they're bangin together. This one guy builds somethin from part of a old pump, balin wire, a corn sheller, and some tie-rods. Cost him two dollars. And the son of a bitch worked great. How can I make it against that?"

"Oh, lord," said Bliss, finishing with the mare. "I'm done here. I'll warsh that stuff off a your rig."

As he straightened up, Jaxon tossed him the sack of tobacco. "There you go, brother boy. And I find the good shears I'll cut your lousy hair. Then I got a go."

A letter came to the Tinsleys from Schenectady, New York.

The man who wrote it, a Methodist minister, said that a young man severely injured a year earlier in an auto wreck, mute and damaged since that time, had somewhat regained the power of communication and identified himself as their son, Rasmussen Tinsley.

No one expected him to live, wrote the minister, *and it is a testament to God's goodness that he has survived. I am assured that the conductor will help him make the train change in Chicago. His fare has been paid by a church collection. He will arrive in Laramie on the afternoon train March 17.*

The afternoon light was the sour color of lemon juice. Mrs. Tinsley, her head a wonderful frozen confection of curls, stood on the platform watching the passengers get down. The father wore a clean, starched shirt. Their son emerged, leaning on a cane. The conductor handed down a valise. They knew it was Ras, but how could they know him? He was a monster. The left side of his face and head had been damaged and torn, had healed in a mass of crimson scars. There was a whistling hole in his throat and a

scarred left eye socket. His jaw was deformed. Multiple breaks of
one leg had healed badly, and he lurched and dragged. Both hands
seemed maimed, frozen joints and lopped fingers. He could not
speak beyond a raw choke only the devil could understand.

Mrs. Tinsley looked away. Her fault through the osmosis of guilt.

The father stepped forward tentatively. The injured man lowered his head. Mrs. Tinsley was already climbing back into the
Ford. She opened and closed the door twice, catching sudden sunlight. Half a mile away on a stony slope, small rain had fallen and
the wet boulders glinted like tin pie pans.

"Ras." The father put out his hand and touched the thin arm of
his son. Ras pulled back.

"Come on, Ras. We'll take you home and build you up. Mother's
made fried chicken." But he looked at the warped mouth, sunken
from lost teeth, and wondered if Ras could chew anything.

He could. He ate constantly, the teeth on the good side of his
mouth gnashing through meats and relishes and cakes. In cooking,
Mrs. Tinsley found some relief. Ras no longer tried to say anything
after the failure at the train station but sometimes wrote a badly
spelled note and handed it to his father.

I NED GIT OTE A WILE

And Horm would take him for a short ride in the truck. The tires
weren't good. He never went far. Horm talked steadily during the
drives, grasshoppers glancing off the windshield. Ras was silent.
There was no way to tell how much he understood. There had been
damage, that was clear enough. But when the father signaled for
the turn that would take them back home, Ras pulled at his sleeve,
made a guttural negative. He was getting his strength back. His
shoulders were heavier. And he could lift with the crooked arms.
But what did he think now of distant cities and ships at sea, he
bound to the kitchen and the porch?

He couldn't keep dropping everything to take Ras for a ride. Every day now the boy was writing the same message: I NED GIT OTE
A WILE. It was spring, hot, tangled with bobolink and meadowlark
song. Ras was not yet twenty-five.

"Well, son, I need a get some work done today. I got plants a set
out. Weedin. Can't go truckin around." He wondered if Ras was
strong enough to ride. He thought of old Bucky, fourteen years old
now but still in good shape. He had seen him in Klicka's pasture

the month gone. He thought the boy could ride. It would do him good to ride the plain. It would do them all good.

Late in the morning he stopped at Klicka's place.

"You know Ras come back in pretty bad shape in March. He's gainin but he needs to get out some and I can't be takin him twice a day. Wonder if you'd give some thought to sellin old Bucky back to me again. At least the boy could get out on his own. It's a horse I'd trust him with."

He tied the horse to the bumper and led it home. Ras was on the porch bench drinking cloudy water. He stood up when he saw the horse.

"Ucka," he said forcefully.

"That's right. It's Bucky. Good old Bucky." He talked to Ras as though he was a young child. Who could tell how much he understood? When he sat silent and unmoving, was he thinking of the dark breath under the trees or the car bucking off the road, metal screaming and the world tipped over? Or was there only a grainy field of dim images? "Think you can ride him?"

He could manage. It was a godsend. Horm had to saddle the horse for him, but Ras was up and out after breakfast, rode for hours. They could see him on the prairie against the sharp green, a distant sullen cloud dispensing lean bolts. But dread swelled in Mrs. Tinsley, the fear that she must now see a riderless horse, saddled, reins slack.

The second week after the horse's return, Ras was out the entire day, came in dirty and exhausted.

"Where did you go, son?" asked Horm, but Ras gobbled potato and shot sly glances at them from the good eye.

So Horm knew he had been up to something.

Within a month Ras was out all day and all night, then away for two or three days, God knows where, elusive, slipping behind rocks, galloping long miles on the dry, dusty grass, sleeping in willows and nests of weeds, a half-wild man with no talk and who knew what thoughts.

The Tinsleys began to hear a few things. Ras had appeared on the Hanson place. Hanson's girls were out hanging clothes and suddenly Ras was there on the gray horse, his hat pulled low, saying garbled things, and then as quickly gone.

The party line rang four short times, their ring, and when Mrs. Tinsley answered, a man's voice said, keep that goddamn idiot to home. But Ras was gone six days, and before he returned the sheriff came by in a new black Chevrolet with a star painted white on the side and said Ras had showed himself to a rancher's wife way the hell down in Tie Siding, forty miles away.

"He didn't have nothin she hadn't see before, but she didn't preciate the show and neither did her old man. Unless you want your boy locked up or hurt you better get him hobbled. He's got a awful face on him, ain't it?"

When Ras came home the next noon, gaunt and starving, Horm took the saddle and put it up in the parents' bedroom.

"I'm sorry, Ras, but you can't go around like you're doin. No more."

The next morning the horse was gone and so was Ras.

"He's rid him bareback." There was no keeping him at home. His circle was smaller but he was on the rove again.

In the Dunmires' noon kitchen, a greasy leather sofa, worn as an old saddle, stood against the wall, and on it lay Ice Dunmire, white hair ruffed, his mouth open in sleep. The plank table, twelve feet long and flanked by pants-polished benches, held a dough tray filled with forks and spoons. The iron sink tilted, a mildew smell rose from the wooden counter. The dish cupboard stood with the doors off, shelves stacked with heavy rim-nicked plates. The beehive radio on a wall shelf was never silent, bulging with static and wailing voices. A crank telephone hung beside the door. In a sideboard stood a forest of private bottles marked with initials and names.

Varn was at the oven bending for biscuits, dark and bandy-legged, Marion scraping milk gravy around and around the pan and jabbing a boil of halved potatoes. The coffeepot chucked its brown fountain into the glass dome of the lid.

"Dinner!" Varn shouted, dumping the biscuits into a bowl and taking a quick swallow from his little whiskey glass. "Dinner! Dinner! Dinner! Dinner! Eat it or go hungry."

Ice stretched and got up, went to the door, coughed and spat.

They ate without talk, champing meat. There were no salads or vegetables beyond potatoes or sometimes cabbage.

Ice drank his coffee from the saucer as he always had. "Hear there was some excitement down Tie Sidin."

"Didn't take you long to hear it. Goddamn Tinsley kid that come back rode into Shawver's yard and jacked off in front a the girl. Matter a time until he discovers it's more fun a put it up the old snatch."

"Do somethin about that. Give me the relish," said Jaxon. "Sounds like nutty Mrs. T drownded the wrong kid." He swirled a piece of meat in the relish. "Goddamn, Varn, I am sure goin a miss this relish out on the road."

"Nothin a do with me. Buy yourself a jar — Billy Gill's Piccalilli. Get it at the store."

Around noon one day in the wide, burnt summer that stank of grasshoppers, Mrs. Tinsley heard the measured beating of a truck motor in the yard. She looked out. A roadster with a miniature windmill mounted in the trailer behind it stood outside, the exhaust from the tailpipe raising a little dust. There was a mash of hoppers in the tire treads, scores more in various stages of existence clogging the radiator grille.

"The windmill man is out there," she said. Horm turned around slowly. He was just getting over a cold and had a headache from the dust.

Outside Jaxon Dunmire in his brown plaid suit came at him with a smile. His dust still floated over the road. A grasshopper leaped from his leg.

"Mr. Tinsley? Howdy. Jax Dunmire. Meaning a come out here for two years and persuade you about the Mornin Glory windmill. Probably the best equipment on the market and the mill that's saving the rancher's bacon these damn dust-bowl days. Yeah, I been meanin a get out here, but I been so damn busy at the ranch and then runnin up and down the state summers sellin these good mills, I don't get around the home territory much." The smile lay over his face as if it had been screwed on. "My dad and my brothers and me, we got five a these Mornin Glories on the Rockin Box. Water the stock all over; they don't lose weight walkin for a drink."

"I don't do no ranchin. Pretty well out a the sheep business; never did run cattle much. I just do some truck gardenin, bees.

Plan a get a pair a blue foxes next year, raise them, maybe. We got the well. We got the crick close. So I guess I don't need a windmill."

"Cricks and wells been known a run dry. This damn everlastin drought it's a sure thing. More uses to a mill than waterin stock. Run you some electricity. Put in a resevoy tank. That's awful nice to have, fire protection, fish a little. You and the missis take a swim. But fire protection's the main thing. You can't tell when your house is goin a catch fire. Why I seen it so dry the wind rubbin the grass blades together can start a prairie fire."

"I don't know. I doubt I could stand the expense. Windmills are awful expensive for somebody in my position. Hell, I can't even afford new tires. And those I need. Expensive."

"Well, sure enough, that's true. Some things are real expensive. Agree with you on that. But the Mornin Glory ain't." Jaxon Dunmire rolled a cigarette, offered it to Horm.

"I never did smoke them coffin nails." There was a ball of dust at the turnoff a quarter mile away. Windmills, hell, thought Horm. He must have passed the boy on the road.

Dunmire smoked, looked over the yard, nodding his head.

"Yes, a little resevoy would set good here."

Old Bucky rounded the corner, pounded in, lathered and tired and on him Ras, bareback, distorted face and glaring eye, past the windmill truck close enough for dirt to spatter the side.

"Well, what in the world was that?" said Jaxon Dunmire, dropping the wet-ended butt in the dust and working the toe of his boot over it.

"That is Ras; that is my son."

"Packin the mail. Thought it might be that crazy half-wit got the women all terrorized wavin his deedle-dee at them. You hear about that? Who knows when he's goin a get a little girl down and do her harm? There's some around who'd as soon cut him and make sure he don't breed no more half-wits, calm him down some."

"That's your goddamn windmill, ain't it? It's Ras. Tell you, he was in a bad car wreck. There's no harm in him but he was real bad hurt."

"Well, I understand that. Sorry about it. But it seems like there's a part a him that ain't hurt, don't it, he's so eager a show it off."

"Why don't you get your goddamn windmill out a my yard?" said Horm Tinsley. "He was hurt but he's a man like anybody else." Now they had this son of a bitch and his seven brothers on their backs.

"Yeah, I'll get goin. You heard about all I got say. You just remember, I sell windmills but I ain't full a what makes em go."

Out in the corral Ras was swiping at old Bucky with a brush, the horse sucking up water. A firm man would have taken the horse from him. But Horm Tinsley hesitated. The only pleasure the boy had in life was riding out. He would talk to him in a day or so, make him understand. A quick hailstorm damaged some young melons and he was busy culling them for a few days, then the parched tomatoes took everything he had hauling water from the creek, down to a trickle. The well was almost out. The first melons were ready to slip the vine when the coyotes came after the fruit and he had to sleep in the patch. At last the melons — bitter and small — were picked, the tomatoes began to ripen and the need for water slacked. It was late summer, sere, sun-scalded yellow.

Ras sat hunched over in the rocking chair on the porch. For once he was home. The boy looked wretched, hair matted, hands and arms dirty.

"Ras, I need a talk to you. Now you pay attention. You can't go doin like you been doin. You can't show yourself to the girls. I know, Ras, you're a young man and the juice is in you, but you can't do like you been doin. Now don't you give up hope, we might find a girl'd marry you if we was to look. I don't know, we ain't looked. But what you're up to, you're scarin them. And them cowboys, them Dunmires'll hurt you. They got the word out they'll cut you if you don't quit pesterin the girls. You understand what I mean? You understand what I'm sayin to you when I say cut?"

It was disconcerting. Ras shot him a sly look with his good eye and began to laugh, a ghastly croaking Horm had not heard before. He thought it was a laugh but did not catch the cause of it.

He spoke straight to his wife in the dark that night, not sparing her feminine sensibilities.

"I don't know if he got a thing I said. I don't think he did. He laughed his head off. Christ, I wish there was some way a tell what goes on in his mind. Could a been a bug walkin on my shirt got him goin. Poor boy, he's got the masculine urges and can't do nothin about it."

There was a silence, and she whispered, barely audible, "You could take him down a Laramie. At night. Them houses." In the dark her face blazed.

"Why, no," he said, shocked. "I couldn't do no such thing."

The following day it seemed to him Ras might have understood some of it for he did not go out but sat in the kitchen with a plate of bread and jam before him, barely moving. Mrs. Tinsley put her hand gingerly to the hot forehead.

"You've taken a fever," she said, and pointed him up to his bed. He stumbled on the stairs, coughing.

"He's got that summer cold you had," she said to Horm. "I suppose I'll be down with it next."

Ras lay in the bed, Mrs. Tinsley sponging his scarred and awful face, his hands and arms. At the end of two days the fever had not broken. He no longer coughed but groaned.

"If only he could get some relief," said Mrs. Tinsley. "I keep thinkin it might help the fever break if he was to have a sponge bath, then wipe him over with alcohol. Cool him off. This heat, all twisted in them sheets. I just hate a summer cold. I think it would make him feel better. Them dirty clothes he's still got on. He's full a the smell of sickness and he was dirty a start with when he come down with it. He's just burnin up. Won't you get his clothes off and give the boy a sponge bath?" she said with delicacy. "It's best a man does that."

Horm Tinsley nodded. He knew Ras was sick but he did not think a sponge bath was going to make any difference. He understood his wife was saying the boy stank so badly she could no longer bear to come near him. She poured warm water in a basin, gave him the snowy washcloth, the scented soap and the new towel, never used.

He was in the sickroom a long time. When he came out he pitched the basin and the stained towel into the sink, sat at the table, put his head down and began to weep, *hu hu hu.*

"What is it?" she said. "He's worse, that's it. What is it?"

"My God, no wonder he laughed in my face. They already done it. They done it to him and used a dirty knife. He's black with the gangrene. It's all down his groin, his leg's swole to the foot —" He leaned forward, his face inches from hers, glared into her eyes. "You! Why didn't you look him over when you put him to that bed?"

The morning light flooded the rim of the world, poured through the window glass, colored the wall and floor, laid its yellow blanket on the reeking bed, the kitchen table and the cups of cold coffee. There was no cloud in the sky. Grasshoppers hit against the east wall in their black and yellow thousands.

That was all sixty years ago and more. Those hard days are finished. The Dunmires are gone from the country, their big ranch broken in those dry years. The Tinsleys are buried somewhere or other, and cattle range now where the Moon and Stars grew. We are in a new millennium and such desperate things no longer happen.

If you believe that, you'll believe anything.

FRANCES SHERWOOD

Basil the Dog

FROM THE ATLANTIC MONTHLY

IT WAS the 1950s, and in Trinidad, the British West Indies, Winston Rama's mother believed in *soucouyant,* spirits who left their skins and flew about in the night sky clad only in raw pink flesh. She kept a pan of salt under her bed to throw on them if they came to steal her breath away.

Winston's mother had many remedies, many rituals.

If you had an enemy, you put his name on a piece of paper and placed it in your shoe, so that you walked on him all day.

To get children, in addition to prayers to Mary, Saint Elizabeth, Saint Francis, she had done special penance on her knees, and for good measure had her mother, Nenin, prepare rich foods for her to eat — breadfruit and cassava, pepper-pot stew with oxtail, calf's foot, pork, and chicken, all flavored with boiled and sweetened cassava.

To stop having babies, after Margaret and Winston, Mrs. Rama drank a bitter brew concocted by the obeah man, the ancient magic man who lived in the hills.

A piece of bread behind the image of the Sacred Heart above her bed ensured food in the house at all times.

If you dreamed of losing teeth, that was very bad.

Spiders were good. If you fell and cut yourself, you could put a spiderweb over the cut to heal it.

Everything had to be done just so. Monday was washday, and when Winston came home from school, the clothes would be spread on stones in the yard to dry. Tuesday, his mother did her mending and darning, with a solid wooden ball that had been in her family for generations for the toes of the socks, and she made Margaret's dresses, using the treadle Singer sewing machine in the front room, feet plying forward, back, forward, back, her whole body moving with the effort. Wednesday, Mrs. Rama rode the country bus to visit her mother and sisters and their families, bringing them city things — silver-paper pinwheels for the children, big bars of soap for laundry washing, scented talcum powder in tin cans, which sprinkled out from little holes at the top like a metal shower nozzle. And for the men razor blades wrapped in thin paper, orange and white, a tiny picture of two swords crossed, and also Player's cigarettes, already made and lined up in a perfect little box, which later held pins, needles, matches, or ground coriander or ginger. Thursday, Mrs. Rama cleaned the parish church with other women, and Friday was the day the house was done top to bottom, although dust would have sifted up between the floorboards and in through the front door and windows by evening of the very same day.

Breakfast was tea and fried biscuits, sometimes a piece of cheese. Lunch was the same, the biscuits wrapped in brown paper, and Winston had tea sweetened with a drop of canned condensed milk when he came home. At dinner, if he was lucky, his mother prepared pelau — rice and pigeon peas, rice and salt pork, or rice with curried eggplant. At Christmas the treat was dark fruitcake saturated with rum, pastelles wrapped in banana leaf, ginger beer, and roti with curried chicken.

After finishing his homework, Winston would walk up to the Queen's Park Savannah, laze with the other boys under a cannonball tree, and drink coconut water from the coconut truck — the driver took one whack with his machete to crack a coconut open. Little fire stands circling the savannah signaled roasting corn. Margaret, because she was a girl, was not allowed to go out of the house at night, and instead would listen to the BBC on her father's big Telefunken radio if he was not home, snapping it off quickly when she heard his step. She also liked to play tea party with her two dolls, pink rubber babies with eyes that opened and shut and painted-on hair like a brown cap. She was very good in school, and her mother spoke of her going to convent, becoming a nun. At that Margaret would roll her eyes upward, give Winston a conspiratorial look, and silently mouth the word "never."

During soccer season Winston played with a ball he had made of rags wrapped around a stone; in cricket season he used a stick and a can. In kite season he made kites from strips of young bamboo, thin tissue paper begged from the Syrian store owner on the corner, paste of flour and water, and string saved from his mother's packages. He celebrated Carnival with calypso and costume, Christmas with Spanish parang, Boxing Day, the Queen's Birthday.

Of course, every day, until he lost his job, Mr. Rama went to work in the accounting department of Texaco Oil. A Calcutta Indian, descended from grandparents who had come to Trinidad after slavery to work the land, Mr. Rama was the only father on the street who wore a white shirt and a tie. He could add up numbers in his head as fast as Mrs. Rama could say her rosary. And he would give the children a shilling every week for candy, putting his hands behind his back, asking them to guess — which one? When they were little babies, Mrs. Rama told her children, their father would be so eager to see his family that he *ran* the last block home.

Margaret, the more Indian-looking, with her long, straight hair and pale skin, was his favorite. After she died and the rum took him, Mr. Rama, indifferent to what Mabel, next door, could hear, would shout and carry on, calling Winston, his dark son, who had his mother's African features, "old nigger" and "bastard" and other bad names. Winston's mother said it was the drink talking. Yes, Winston, trying hard, knew that bottle had mouth, and he also knew that despite the modest measure of their island life, despite each day's knuckled vigilance, despite the fence his mother put up against dirt and disease, despite humility in the face of fate, empire, and God, there was Basil.

Basil came for every breathing creature, no matter. He could not be outwitted, ignored, or placated. He came in sickness and in health, in age and in youth, in the midst of cheer or sorrow. He came with the cool breeze of late night or on days so hot that even the hummingbird stayed still in the shade. He came with worms that entered your heel and lived in your stomach, eating the food that you swallowed, with mosquitoes whose touch was so light that you did not feel the long needles of their noses injecting their treacherous venom. Basil came when the world held its breath before break of day, and in rolling clouds of thunder. Even his smell was a puzzle. It was the scent of stale sweat and green gangrene, the smell of spent, cold ashes, the smell of overripe pineapple, rancid banana skin, ulcerous pus, rain-rusted tin roof, goat pills, dead cat. Also clean seawater, bicycle spokes, white chicken feathers, pages of *Alice in Wonderland* at the small library on Knox Street, Father McCauley's breath of anise and gin.

Basil dressed like a man, with shirt and pants, but he had the long snout of a dog, yellow eyes as scary as a snake's, tippy-toe goat hooves fitted tightly into human shoes, and jackass ears, which were kept folded under his hat. Basil lingered on corners of city streets, smoking a cigarette, appraising, from under the brim of his hat, the passersby. In the evening he could be found among the slender stalks of green bamboo in the botanical gardens, or perched in the spiky leaves of the prickly palm, or hiding in Old Man Bitter Bush, and in the morning, the day fresh and the streets just filling with bicycles, he could be stumbled over on the savannah, a piece of grass in his mouth, sleeping the way the dead do, his eyes open.

Winston had actually seen Basil three times before Margaret's death.

When he fell through the Grill roof.

When his grandmother, Nenin, died.

Auntie Elizabeth.

Through the Grill Roof

Winston was standing on the roof of the old abandoned Grill, on Abercomby Street, and it was a clear, blue day in December, an in-between time after Christmas and before Carnival. He was ten, at the Tranquility Grammar School, still in short pants. Margaret, who was twelve, was his companion, for she could climb trees, run fast, shoot marbles. They were on that day flying a Chinese kite, *chickichong*, a fighter kite prepared for battle with *zwill* — small pieces of glass — glued to its tail, and paste with ground-up bottle in it on its string, so that when he whipped it across the sky, it could slice the strings of other boys' kites and win.

Winston had made his first communion the year before, and had hoped that his godmother, who had a cookshop in her front room, would give him a bicycle, a Raleigh, but she hadn't. He had hoped that he could save enough from his job at the chemist's on the corner, wrapping packages of medicine in brown paper and string on Saturday mornings, to buy a bicycle, but he had to give his money to his father every week for the house. Winston knew that Mr. Singh, the chemist, would dismiss him shortly anyway. The brown paper was in a long roll, difficult for Winston to rip off, short as he was, with the quick, flipping movement he had been shown, and the string, on a tall cone fixed to a pole, gave him fine, smarting cuts, and then the bandages on his fingers, deducted from his wages, made him even slower and clumsier at his work.

On the Grill roof that day Margaret said not to bother about the job, she was going to be rich when she grew up and would buy him a bicycle first thing. She meant it, cross her heart and hope to die. At that moment, with the wind ballooning out her checkered cotton dress and the strands of her hair playing around her face like the memory of something, she was so beautiful that she scared Winston, and, shuddering, he quickly replied no, *he* was going to be rich and buy *her* a bicycle.

The sky sprouted kites that day, a bunch tailed in brightly colored rag bows from the city streets and another fleet gaily sailed up from the savannah. Some were the colors of flowers. Winston's was plain newspaper, made the night before using thin, pliable strips of young bamboo and flour paste. A kite was nothing compared with a bicycle. If he had a bicycle, he would spend all his time riding around, exploring from morning to night on Saturdays, and on school days he would ride to school, pulling up right in front of his friends.

All of a sudden he felt himself fall. The wind rushed in his ears like the end of the world. He grabbed air, he kicked air. He wanted to scream *help*. His mouth opened.

Hail Mary, Full of Grace.

Thud. He landed on something.

His bowels loosened before the world collapsed.

Seconds, minutes, hours, whole days? A ray of light touched his face. *I am in heaven,* he thought, and a trio, the Trinity — the Father, the Son, and the Holy Ghost — peered down curiously at him. But the Father was none other than his mother, her face drawn together like a rooting rodent, the agouti; and the Son was the Chinese doctor from Frederick Street, Dr. Woo; and the Holy Ghost was his sister, Margaret, crying, "Wake up, Winnie, wake up."

The roof had broken under him, and Winston had fallen through onto dusty cardboard boxes, not the hard floor, not cement. He was alive, and Basil, outside the building, walking up and down, up and down, gnashed his teeth in anger and frustration, let his long, thin tongue out from the cage of his teeth, and hissed, *Zcurses, zcurses, zdrats, zdrats, I am going to eat my zhat.*

Nenin

His grandmother had been with them for a while, sleeping in his mother's room, sharing her bed. Nenin slept curled like a little cat; she was so light that Mr. Rama could easily carry her into the front room and place her in the Morris chair under the wedding photograph hanging by a rope. Nenin loved, longed for, her sip of brandy, measured out by spoon twice a day, morning and night. When Mrs. Rama went to the market or to Mass, Nenin sent Winston and Margaret scurrying all over the house to find the hiding place.

Fee, fi, fo, fum, I smell the blood of an Englishman. Winston would make a big show of his search, looking in the chifforobe, where Nenin kept her teeth, or the kitchen safe, covered by screen to protect from flies. Margaret looked in her father's house shoes, street shoes so old that the leather was as soft as a wool blanket and went slip-slop when he walked about. When Winston found the little bottle of brandy, he would shout out "Eureka."

There it was, behind the statue of the Blessed Virgin or the Sacred Heart above his mother's bed. The Blessed Virgin, in serene blue, her arms outstretched, her eyes cast modestly down, stood on a snake. The Sacred Heart had two little doors. Winston's mother would kiss the image and then close the doors, saying, "Good night, Jesus." In the morning, first thing, she would open the doors, and the heart beaming bright rays looked ready to burst right out of Jesus' body like a red-hot cannonball.

Nenin's brandy, retrieved, administered, replaced, was actually mixed with water, and the last drops were barely flavored, merely tinted. Yet Nenin would smile as if it went straight to her cancer, made it all better. When they could afford it, they took her to the Colonial Hospital for morphine, which the nurse gave her in an injection, followed by a glass of English Beefeater gin. The *Trinidad*

Guardian printed notices all the time asking people to give money for morphine so that cancer patients could be put out of their pain.

Unfortunately, Nenin's pain increased, and she wasn't always able to be taken to the latrine in the yard in time; she dribbled and had to wear a bib, and when she could, she smoked a rough country pipe, stinking up the house so that Mr. Rama said Nenin would have to go. Mrs. Rama arranged for Mabel, next door, to keep Nenin.

"Where are my children?" Nenin would cry. "Where are my lovely ones?" she sang faintly from her pallet on the floor by the window. They could hear her quite clearly from their house, and Margaret, disregarding her father's look, would run outside to the street, calling, "I'm coming just now, Nenin."

Margaret was the one who helped to wash the old woman, stroking her face with clear, cool water from a bowl on the floor and soaping her neck and shoulders with a soft cheesecloth, under her arms with a square torn from one of Mr. Rama's shirts gone to rag. She boiled cornmeal pap with evaporated milk into a thin gruel. When changing her grandmother's gown, Margaret did it quickly and gently, using a sheet to cover her withered parts and the lump in her stomach, which was as big as a soccer ball.

Toward the end Nenin, gazing out at the patch of blue sky from her pallet on the floor, mumbled over and again, "God, I'm ready. God, take me home."

But it was not the rush of golden wings and the angelic host proclaiming that Winston saw hovering in the sky the day Nenin passed. It was Basil, Basil himself, Basil as bird — and not one of the scarlet ibis that clustered in the mangroves of the swamp like little licks of flame, or any kind of nice little bird, but a hard, big bird, a bad bird, a bird of prey with feathers as black as night, as sharp as arrows, crow after carrion, death after life.

Auntie Elizabeth

Winston's favorite aunt came into town from the country to have her baby in the big bedroom where Winston himself had been born. He knew very well where babies came from. He had seen dogs, goats, mount each other, and once, in Woodford Square, two cats. He had heard his father call to his mother at night, "Gouti, I'm lonely — gouti, come to me."

Winston knew what the words of certain calypso songs meant, such as "the big bamboo," and he knew that swizzling on your own in the shower was a sin you had to confess: *Father, I have sinned.* But to do it, finally, man to woman, in the way to make a baby — a child to be baptized, dressed, steadily fed, sent to school, taught his catechism — Winston envisioned as an event full of power and mystery, much like the picture of the train he had seen in the encyclopedia in the library on Knox Street, an engine shooting puffs of steam from either side, entering a dark tunnel ribbed with bands of bone, emerging into an explosion of light, God's light.

Auntie Elizabeth got his mother's bed, the one curtained with mosquito netting, its head and foot bars of metal. Under the bed Winston's mother kept her best things — a toaster from England, in the box it came in; a set of special china plates painted with bright blue windmills, wrapped one by one in white tissue; her wedding dress, wilted and yellowed, bundled into a straw basket; and the Christmas ham, in a string bag covered with brown paper. Margaret cleaned under the bed using a wet cloth tied on a stick. She did the rest of the floor by standing on the cloth in her bare feet and shuffling along, instead of getting on her hands and knees, which was how her mother made Margaret clean when she was watching.

Mrs. Rama spread a rubber sheet on the bed and added a layer of newspapers, and the jalousies were shut tight so that the room was as dark and as cool as the inside of a cave. Their auntie, who had been waiting all the while in the front room in the Morris chair, with a rag dipped in ice water on her forehead, was brought in.

Winston and Margaret, banished from the room, had to go outside and play.

The afternoon was cloudless. The hot sun bore down on the hibiscus bush in the yard with a vengeance. The bush, full of showy red flowers (each corona of petals with a long, tube-like stamen), seemed to be sticking out its many tongues. The air was taut, inscrutable. Winston felt uneasy. The night before, he had dreamt of evil men with knives chasing him, and only at the last was he able to take flight, soar above all harm.

He and Margaret made boats with cork and pins and little triangles of paper snipped from the frail blue airmail envelopes sent by their British pen pals. The boats were set to sail in the drainage stream that ran in the yard along the verandah, between the latrine shared by several neighbors and the front room of their house. After boats they looked at the five stamps in Winston's stamp collection, kept, along with his best marbles and his slingshot, in a cigar box that had on the underside of the lid a picture of an old-fashioned man in a beard. They did times tables as far as they could go, up into the hundreds, all the whole afternoon, trying to ignore the thread of pure glass, the high, eerie wail of Auntie Elizabeth, that cut through whatever their play.

She called for her mother, poor old Nenin gone some one year, and she called on God to help her, save her, spare her. She asked that she could please just die, be buried in town, in Pechier Cemetery, which had a tall iron gate and broken bottles along the top of its wall. She wanted to be forgiven, not forgotten. She wanted to know if anybody had ever loved her, name one. She wanted a glass of cold water, she wanted the priest, she wanted a real doctor for God's sake, she wanted to die, to live, to die.

Winston finally put his hands over his ears. Margaret tried to pull his hands away. They got in a fight. His mother came out of the room, saying, "What are you children doing?" His aunt began to scream again. Winston's mother rushed back into the room. "Hush — hush, hush."

And then the screaming stopped. It stopped. Shortly his mother came out of the room with the baby, wrapped tightly in a blanket like a little package, except its head showed bald. "It's a boy," she said. Now, Winston thought, maybe now they would at least have their evening tea, turn on the radio to the BBC since his father was not home, have a treat of sweet bread spread with tinned New Zealand butter. But Auntie Elizabeth called from the room, "It's not coming out."

His mother said to Margaret, "Get Mabel, next door," and to Winston, "Run, boy, fetch the Syrian down the street to drive your auntie in his car to Colonial Hospital. Run, now."

When he came back, Margaret was holding the baby, and Mabel from next door was holding Auntie Elizabeth's knees open, and Winston wondered if this was like the Black Hole of Calcutta, which he had heard mentioned once, or if it was like the giant ants he had seen in a movie, who swarmed over people, ate them alive — for it was terrible beyond compare. Bloodied newspapers were wadded up on the floor between white enamel bowls of bloody water. The mosquito netting was pulled down and in a dirty pile. The baby was crying. His aunt's skin was going from brown to ash, and her eyelids, fluttering like butterflies, desperately tried to stay open.

"Push, girl, push," his mother instructed.

Winston's own dried placenta, as flat as a pressed flower, as brown as a dead leaf, his mother kept safely wrapped in paper somewhere under her bed. As was the custom, she would give it for safekeeping to his wife when he got married, to be eaten in dire sickness.

"Push, girl, push."

Mr. Vivi arrived. Scooping up Auntie Elizabeth in his big, strong arms, he carried her to the car, gently settling her into the back seat.

"No bother at all," he said.

Not thinking of her agony, Auntie Elizabeth reached out of the car window and put her hand on Winston's cheek.

"You take care of your little cousin, you hear, boy?"

"Right as rain," Mr. Vivi said. "She is going to be right as rain."

Winston wanted to believe in that, in rain, but what he saw was Basil, Basil the Dog, in the back seat, as comfortable as could be, his long tail curled around his neck like a great mapepire snake, and a wicked, wicked smile on his thin, cruel lips.

The baby's father, a cane cutter, arrived the next day and took the baby away, going deep into the bush with his child and getting a new wife the following week, a strong, fat woman with thick flat feet.

The Most Awful

Winston crouched on the tin roof of the house, rocking back on his heels, hearing his mother in her room, humming as if wearing her good funeral clothes were sport. The humming stopped abruptly when she looked up from the window facing the courtyard and caught him.

"Winnie, Winnie, I see you up there. Come down, boy, and dress."

Winston squatted resolutely, wrapping his arms around his knees, holding on for dear life, because he felt that if he did not grip himself hard, he might float up, up, and away, like Superman, or like one of his *chickichong* kites cut loose. His mother came out in the yard.

"Winnie, what do you think your sister will feel if she knows you don't even go to her own funeral, eh?"

To his mother, Margaret was walking up in the clouds, probably looking down and getting heaven ready for the rest of them, much like straightening up the house on Friday. Winston wished his mother were the one who was lying in the coffin on the table with chipped ice packed all around her. Margaret, a honey brown, was now a powdered, painted doll wearing her Sunday dress, which she had always hated for its starched skirt, babyish sash, and guava green color. Two professional mourners, old ladies with no right to long life, were by her coffin, sobbing and moaning as if they were not paid to sit. Moving around the roof, Winston saw through another window his father thrown across his sister's bed, twisted in grief.

The day she died, the nuns from Tranquility had said, "God needed her more than we did."

Winston's father had replied, "God's rump, God's face, God go to hell, you stupid, stupid."

And Winston had wildly agreed with his father. Oh, how he had agreed.

Then Mr. Rama ran through the house beating his head against the walls, knocking things down with one swipe, all the dishes, kicking, swearing, screaming, as if with enough destruction he would be released from grief and Margaret would rise from her bed, saying, "Daddy, stop. You see, I am alive, God is love."

Mr. Rama even spit on the crucifix in the front room and tore down the Sacred Heart above his wife's bed. For naught.

The sickness had started because Winston and Margaret used the drainage ditch as a channel for cork-and-pin boats. The part of the house by Mabel's was sheltered by a large flamboyant tree, and Winston imagined afterward that Basil, already in the vicinity because of Auntie Elizabeth, had spotted Margaret from a limb in the tree, his legs dangling over, julie mango in his hand, sweet juice running from the corners of his mouth. Or perhaps Basil was lingering by the latrine. A wily fellow, like Granddaddy Roach, sitting in the crack, who skittered on the floorboards when lights were out, Basil was everywhere always.

Margaret got a little cough is all. But Dr. Woo came, just to be sure, examined her chest with black rubber tubes dangling from his ears, placing the little metal cup at the end on the smooth skin over her heart, the wings of her lungs, turning his head away as if listening hard to distant music. He told Mrs. Rama that Margaret needed rest, good food, lots of liquids.

Margaret got her mother's bedroom, the bed with the toaster and the wedding dress underneath. They had eaten the ham on Christmas Day, before Margaret got sick, Winston's mother placing the thin slices on the plates with blue windmills, mango relish to the side. For Christmas she had also made sorrel, plantain balls in callaloo soup, souse and cucumber, dark cake soaked in rum. In fact, the night before Christmas even his father had gone to Mass. It had been, all told, except for the death of Auntie Elizabeth, a good year, Mrs. Rama declared at grace, and the year before, except for Nenin's dying, a good year. Looking back, she could find no fault. They had food on the table, clothes on their backs. Margaret in her most hated dress, her braids tied in red ribbons, peeked a look at Winston across the table during this speech, mouthed *hungry*, giggled.

"Mind your manners," Mrs. Rama cautioned. "You want to bring bad luck?"

The day the doctor had to come again, because Margaret's cough would not go away at all, at all, Winston's mother closed the jalousie shutters to keep out the sun and noise, the dirt from the street, just as she had for Auntie Elizabeth. And in the following days Mrs. Rama attended Margaret around the clock, bringing her tall glasses of mauby, chips of ice to suck on from the Syrian's fridge, sea moss to build strength. She made puddings of breadfruit or pumpkin, and rubbed Margaret down with bay rum and Tiger Balm every afternoon. In addition to Margaret's Saint Christopher medal and cross, Mrs. Rama had Margaret wear around her neck a piece of camphor sewn in a little bag on a string for easing the throat, and a little bag of stones to protect the child against the evil eye. At night, when Mr. Rama came home from work, he sat by his daughter's bed, held her hand gently in his, and told her stories about mongoose, tortoise, parrot in the tree.

Winston went to school, of course, but all other times he sat on the floor by his sister's bed and watched. The nuns from Tranquility swept in like birds of ill omen; Father McCauley appeared, pronounced "Be a brave girl"; Mabel from next door said, "Brave my arse, by Carnival you be so well, you be dancing for so, just you wait and see, nuh?" Mr. Singh came with a bottle of tonic from his shop free of charge. The Syrian brought sticks of candy whorled green and apricot. Little girls filed in, Margaret's friends, their eyes wide with curiosity and fear.

At the beginning of her illness Margaret had seemed to know, for she had given Winston her cat's-eye marble, which was worth a good trade of at least five ordinary marbles, and the picture of a champion cricket player she had saved from the *Trinidad Guardian*. She also had a picture of the boxer Joe Louis, the Brown Bomber, who had visited from the States, staying in the Queen's Park Hotel.

When the coughing got worse, Winston's mother summoned the obeah man. He poured rosewater in all the corners of the room, lit incense, chanted spells, and made a mixture of plants gathered near Maracas Beach at three o'clock on a Sunday morning.

"Get that witch doctor out of here," his father had shouted, loud enough that Mabel had to run over and calm things down.

The day Margaret died, rain fell so hard in the afternoon that the drops, like bullets, dented holes in the ground. Then the rain stopped. Then the sun came out, as unrelenting as ever. Then darkness fell, and that was like mercy bestowed on the good, for Winston felt that the cool air was a sign that Margaret would get better. Indeed, her cheeks appeared to gain color that night, and she smiled.

"Look," she said to him when they were alone in the room, "I can still stand." With several attempts, pathetically thin, almost faded to extinction, yet all by herself, she stood on the bed and stretched out her arms. "See?"

But later she got worse, very bad.

Father McCauley was summoned. He gave her the last rites, and with them kneeling around her bed, his mother praying and crying, his father struck down by the unthinkable, and he, Winston, in a fury of grief, there, on the outskirts of their suffering, Basil began his strutting, a little chip-step to a calypso beat.

Oh yes, oh my, time does fly.

The dirty dog thought he was King of Carnival, Emperor of the Caribbean, Ruler of the World, God Himself Supreme.

Oh yes, be my guest, I love you so, don't be slow.

This was before the rum took Winston's father.

This was before — or maybe it was when — Winston knew he had to leave the island, travel over the waters, go to university, learn to do serious battle.

Contributors' Notes

*100 Other Distinguished Stories
of 1999*

*Editorial Addresses of American
and Canadian Magazines*

Contributors' Notes

GEOFFREY BECKER is the author of a novel, *Bluestown* (1996), and a collection of short stories, *Dangerous Men* (1995), which won the Drue Heinz Award and the Great Lakes Colleges Association Prize for best first book of fiction. He is a past winner of the Nelson Algren Award from the *Chicago Tribune,* and has held National Endowment for the Arts and James Michener/Copernicus Society fellowships. He lives in central New York.

▪ I used to play guitar at a ribs place in Atlanta on Saturday evenings. The pay wasn't much — tips and a free meal, to be precise — but I had a great time, made many friends, and brought home a regular supply of ribs (one whole shelf of my refrigerator was devoted to the little white paper cups of dipping sauce they put in the take-out bags). Sometime later, I tried writing "Black Elvis" from the point of view of the guy who hosts the weekly blues jam — I'd run one myself for a few years, so it seemed like an easy narrative position to take — but it didn't go anyplace and I stopped after three pages. I think a year went by before I decided to take another crack at it, this time from the title character's point of view.

For me, the story is partly about having clothes so redolent of barbecue smoke that they almost stand up by themselves, and the silence that comes after an evening of loud live music, like ghosts whispering in your ears.

AMY BLOOM is the author of a novel and two short story collections, the most recent of which, *A Blind Man Can See How Much I Love You,* was published this summer. Her first collection was nominated for a National Book Award, and several of her stories have been selected to appear in *The Best American Short Stories.* She lives in Connecticut.

▪ What began as the story of an unfortunate friendship became crime and punishment in Connecticut, and I was consumed, and horribly taken, by the insightful cruelty and sensible maneuvers of my Iago, my Inspector Petrovich, a bookkeeper and a reasonable woman.

MICHAEL BYERS is the author of *The Coast of Good Intentions,* which was a finalist for the PEN/Hemingway Award and which won the Sue Kaufman Award from the American Academy of Arts and Letters in 1999. The recipient of a Whiting Award, Byers lives in Seattle, where he writes and teaches.

• In a funny way, I often feel unqualified to talk about my own writing, because I so rarely end up with the story I set out to produce. "The Beautiful Days" was supposed to be a brief, uneventful, mild-mannered sort of thing, but as usual the more I tried to make something happen, the more its opposite insisted on occurring. After a while, I stopped fighting the inevitable. My stories as a rule get written in stages, and this one took three to four months to get down. The first ten pages were easier than the last fifteen — I was uncomfortable with Aldo's nasty behavior, I guess, though the logic of the piece obviously suggested it. Where did the story come from? I don't know exactly. I do have fond feelings for the Midwest, for those great trees and big humid summers, and the impulse to write this story arose, in the very earliest stages, out of a nostalgia for that place, and for the strange semimystical feelings it produced in me, years ago.

RON CARLSON is the author of five books of fiction, most recently the story collection *The Hotel Eden.* His novel *The Speed of Light* will be published in 2001. He teaches at Arizona State University.

• I lived in Houston, Texas, when I was a freshman in college, and that year I had a job doing general maintenance at an old motel. Texas was new to me and so was being seventeen, and I found the year lit and exotic in my memory when I came to write about it. My father is a successful engineer, and my mother has always been a poet and what we used to call a "character." She has over the years written on the bottoms of things. The thing I set out to put in the story, that my brother made money that year melting glass bottles, never made the draft.

RAYMOND CARVER was born in Clatskanie, Oregon, in 1938, and he lived in Port Angeles, Washington, until his death on August 2, 1988. His first collection of stories, *Will You Please Be Quiet Please?* (a National Book Award nominee in 1977), was followed by *What We Talk About When We Talk About Love* (1981), *Cathedral* (nominated for the Pulitzer Prize in 1984), and *Where I'm Calling From* (1988). A poet as well as a short story writer, Carver received *Poetry* magazine's Levinson Prize in 1985, and his poems are collected in *All of Us* (1996). In 1988 he was elected to the American

Academy and Institute of Arts and Letters and received an honorary doctor of letters degree from the University of Hartford. His work has been translated into more than twenty languages.

• *From Tess Gallagher:* This story, "Call If You Need Me," was discovered in midsummer of 1999 by William L. Stull and Maureen P. Carroll, husband-and-wife partners in Carver scholarship, when they visited the William Charvat Collection of American Fiction at the Ohio State University Library. There, while examining a box of manuscripts, they found two complete unpublished stories. They phoned me excitedly, on my birthday, with this news. The story was ultimately published in the December *Granta*. These two stories will join three others discovered in March 1999 for publication in a volume entitled *Call If You Need Me*, due out in January 2001.

The story will be of special interest to Carver scholars and readers at large for its relationship to the stories "Chef's House" and "Blackbird Pie," as well as to the poem "Late Night with Fog and Horses." Images and situations overlap and find different vantage points from which to approach what's befallen a couple as they try to repair their marriage by taking time away for themselves in a rented house. The haunting scene of horses coming into the yard at night in fog becomes an emblem of sorrow and tenderness as the couple try to determine whether they will stay together. Carver's signature is the great economy of motion in the story, its poignant details, and how much he is able to suggest of the unspoken and the unspeakable between people who love each other yet, inexplicably, cannot heal what has injured them.

KIANA DAVENPORT is *hapa haole* — half Native Hawaiian, half Anglo-American. She is the author of the novels *Shark Dialogues* (1994) and *Song of the Exile* (2000). Her short stories have been published worldwide and have been included in the O. Henry Awards and the Pushcart Prize anthologies. A 1992–1993 fiction fellow at Harvard-Radcliffe's Bunting Institute, she was also the 1997–1998 visiting writer at Wesleyan University, and has received a fiction grant from the National Endowment for the Arts. She lives in Boston and Hawaii.

• Every family is an automatic piece of fiction. But some stories we don't want to tell. We want to outrun them. With "Bones of the Inner Ear," the past finally came banging on my door at two A.M., demanding to be let in.

This story was harder to write than anything I have ever undertaken. Cutting it down from ninety pages, struggling with it month after month, reinforced my love for writing fiction. We hide behind fiction. We embellish. We vanish. I wrote "Bones of the Inner Ear" hoping no one would believe that it's true.

JUNOT DÍAZ is the author of *Drown* (1996) and was selected by *The New Yorker* as one of the "Best Twenty Writers for the Twenty-first Century." His fiction has appeared in *The New Yorker, African Voices,* and *The Best American Short Stories 1996, 1997,* and *1999.* He is the recipient of a Guggenheim fellowship and the Lila Wallace Reader's Digest Award. He teaches creative writing at Syracuse University, is a member of Dominicans 2000, and is at work on his first novel.

• "Nilda" is about a young woman I knew, back in the day. For a long time I could not deal with my older brother's cancer, either in fiction or in life. This, I guess, is my first attempt.

NATHAN ENGLANDER is the author of the collection *For the Relief of Unbearable Urges* (1999). His stories have appeared in *The Atlantic Monthly, The New Yorker, Story, The Best American Short Stories 1999,* and *The Pushcart Prize XXII.* Born and raised in New York, he has been living in Jerusalem for the past four years.

• My own transformation from religious to secular was slow and studied and utterly unspontaneous. In "The Gilgul of Park Avenue" I wanted to explore the opposite kind of transformation. Not the journey from secular to religious, but the inspired moment, the instantaneous (and purely emotional) understanding that a person is other than what he or she has always known him- or herself to be. I always liked the notion of the gilgul — the Jewish equivalent to reincarnation. I thought this a suitable vehicle for the story, or, more exactly, that the character Charles Luger was the proper vehicle for such a soul.

PERCIVAL EVERETT is author of thirteen books. His most recent novels are *Glyph, Frenzy,* and *Watershed.* He is a professor and the chair of English at the University of Southern California. He lives with his wife on a small farm outside Los Angeles.

• "The Fix" comes from a period during which I experienced a rash of expectations from other people. Friends would call up and ask for advice, assistance. At home, if anything went haywire, I was summoned, to repair bicycle breaks, kill rattlesnakes, and remove slivers from fingers. And so I imagined the character in the story, who, unlike myself, could actually repair everything brought to him. I wondered what terrible things such a talent could offer.

TIM GAUTREAUX is the author of two collections of stories, *Same Place, Same Things* and *Welding with Children,* as well as a novel, *The Next Step in the Dance.* His stories have appeared in *The Atlantic Monthly, Harper's Magazine, GQ, Story, New Stories from the South, The O. Henry Prize Stories,* and *The Best*

American Short Stories. He is writer in residence at Southeastern Louisiana University.

▪ My wife and I were eating supper one night, and over the butter beans and squash I asked her if she could give me a story idea, because I had a little free time coming up. She told me, "Why don't you write one about a priest that has a problem with alcohol. He could get into trouble, maybe get some traffic tickets." It was a great setup. I'm a practicing Catholic, so I knew the details, had been around priests since one dribbled water on my face back in the forties. I had been taught that one mistake led to another, so I imagined a series of escalating misadventures for my brandy-toned prelate. I wrote the first draft and saw that it was about sin and redemption, something I hadn't seen in 150 years. I realized that often forgiveness or redemption comes to priests the same way it comes to everybody who gets it — in an unlikely way, where it's not expected, sort of in the corner of the eye.

ALLAN GURGANUS is the author of the novels *Oldest Living Confederate Widow Tells All* and *Plays Well with Others,* as well as of *White People,* a collection of stories and novellas. His collection of short novels, *The Practical Heart,* is forthcoming. His writing has won the Sue Kaufman Prize from the American Academy of Arts and Letters, the Los Angeles Times Book Prize, the Southern Book Prize, and the American Magazine Prize. *White People* was nominated for a PEN/Faulkner Prize.

Gurganus was recently awarded a certificate of lifetime achievement by Episcopal Caring Response to AIDS. In the last decade, his benefit readings and signings have raised more than $2 million dollars for AIDS research and hospice care. A native of North Carolina, he has taught writing and literature at Duke, Stanford, the Iowa Writers' Workshop, and Sarah Lawrence.

▪ I grew up Calvinist. Such poetry as existed in our Protestant home — cold gleaming hardwood floors — sprang from the joy of jobs perfectly managed. My kid brothers and I rose early on Saturdays, but our father (off to work at six A.M.) had already posted on the fridge today's lists: under each child's name, the inventory "Things to Do by Sundown, if Eating Interests You." I recall nineteen items inscribed there once, in handwriting that resembled briars, barbed wire.

As a grownup, "a working artist," I've tried to redirect this inherited overdirectedness. Like Niagara's energy, there's no stopping it — only channeling, diverting it. So, work is the dynamo combusting the heart of "He's at the Office." The story came to me, like a breech birth, like a pink slip, last line first. The idea enlisted me the moment I entered my own home office. There, I write only fiction; no trivial business letters, no bill-paying busywork, just All Fiction All the Time. That day I decided — even if I were led into this space at age 150, however enfeebled — I could probably pick up exactly where my last fiction had left off, midsentence. "He's at the Office" transferred my own present sunny workspace backward into the pitiless discipline of my father's generation. Hoping to honor those workers who so silently served out their life sentences, I built this little working altar — one the exact green metal of 1940s filing cabinets. The tale is meant both as a praise-song to work (which keeps us all well out of mischief) and as a nod, alas, to all the sexy and enriching mischief that work killed. And why? For a few more hours of time-and-a-half.

ALEKSANDAR HEMON was born in Sarajevo, Bosnia-Herzegovina, where he lived until he ended up in Chicago in 1992. He has been writing short stories in English since 1995. His stories have appeared in *TriQuarterly, Ploughshares, The New Yorker, The Baffler, Granta,* and elsewhere. His story "Islands" was chosen for *The Best American Short Stories 1999,* and his book of stories, *The Question of Bruno,* has recently been published. He still lives in Chicago with his wife, his cat, and an infant laptop.

    ▪ My first job in this country was for a real estate agent who was called Johnny O. I occasionally did some real estate data entry, and since I had no work permit at the time (I can hear the INS agents knocking at my door), I worked for less than the minimum wage. Johnny O. liked me and wanted to know more about "my culture," so he asked me if we had TV and pizza where I had come from. He thought that I was speaking "the king's English," largely because I ended one of my hapless sentences with ". . . and so forth." My employment ceased after I clumsily erased the file that I had been working on for a while.

    Then I worked (legally) as a canvasser for Greenpeace. I canvassed in all of the Chicago suburbs, going through a crash course in the American middle-classness. I talked to people who thought that Yugoslavia (wallowing in blood at the time) was a misspelling of Czechoslovakia. I talked to people who hated foreigners and were not shy to tell me that. I talked once to an ardent Baptist whose daughter was away with some cult (this was at the time of the Waco siege), who kept saying "Amen!" after whatever I said and whose tubercular little dog kept coughing out clots of sludge on my shoes. I talked to some very nice people, but I talked and talked and talked, and there is nothing as depressing as the fall in Schaumburg, Illinois.

    I worked in bookstores, where they were very careful not to give us more than thirty-nine hours a week, lest they have to pay for our benefits. I worked as a bike messenger, huffing and puffing proudly on a Huffy, which I bought in a used equipment store for $80 and which had probably been stolen. I taught ESL in a school whose director told us that he could get an English teacher off the street anytime he wanted, so we shouldn't get cocky. And there were other jobs.

But the worst thing of all was people — and I would often run into them — who thought I was living the American Dream and who expected me to be absolutely exhilarated about being here. This story is for them.

KATHLEEN HILL's novel, *Still Waters in Niger,* was named a Notable Book of 1999 by the *New York Times Book Review.* "The Anointed" was selected for inclusion in *The Pushcart Prize XXV* and one story in a work-in-progress that takes for its subject the critical moment when a book becomes, in Kafka's words, "an axe for the frozen sea within." Other completed pieces in the collection are "Reading with Diana," which recently appeared in *The Yale Review,* and "Avesnes," which appeared in *Michigan Quarterly Review.* Hill lives in New York City and teaches at Sarah Lawrence.

• Not long ago I unearthed from the back shelf of a closet a notebook I had used in my seventh-grade music class. Turning its pages, ink-blotched and written on in large, looping letters, I remembered a teacher, a boy, and the rest of us. The boy has remained for me the figure of childhood sorrow. As such he made his claim, mutely requested a story.

HA JIN has published several books of fiction and poetry. His most recent book is *Waiting,* a novel, which received the 1999 National Book Award for fiction. He teaches at Emory University.

• "The Bridegroom" was willed into existence. By that, I mean I didn't have the story in my mind originally. For several years I was writing a collection of short stories, all set in a city in Manchuria. To make the collection broad in scope, I needed stories of different styles and of different subject matter. Since homosexuality was a relatively rare and challenging topic, I chose to create a story out of the articles and books I could gather about it. The story was very hard to write and probably took me a year to finish.

I wanted a narrator who is compassionate but prejudiced at the same time. To my mind, this might be a good way to make the voice convincing and authentic and to give some depth to the story. I'm glad that "The Bridegroom" is the eponym of my new collection of short fiction, which will be out this fall.

MARILYN KRYSL has published three books of stories and seven books of poetry, and her stories have appeared in *The O. Henry Prize Stories,* a Pushcart Prize volume, *Sudden Fiction,* and other anthologies. She has taught ESL in the People's Republic of China and worked for Peace Brigade International in Sri Lanka and at Mother Teresa's Kalighat Home for the Destitute and Dying in Calcutta. With Naomi Horii she coedits the literary journal *Many Mountains Moving*. Her most recent collection of stories is *How to Accommodate Men*. She lives in Boulder, Colorado.

▪ In Sri Lanka in 1989, six lawyers attempting to bring human rights cases in the courts were murdered. The Sri Lankan Bar Association contacted Peace Brigade International, which offers protective accompaniment upon request, and asked us to open a project in Colombo. During the time I worked there I came to understand some of the ways in which ordinary citizens must attempt to negotiate the civil war between the Liberation Tigers of Tamil Eelam and the Sri Lankan government forces. Many families lose even more members than the family in this story. Rape is rather common in areas where there is fighting, and many young men are "disappeared" by government forces or recruited by the LTTE.

Under these circumstances, it's not surprising that the suicide rate on the island is one of the highest in the world. I was struck by the fact that one of the most commonly used poisons is the seed of the alari, a beautiful flowering vine. The blossom and its poisonous seed: beauty and destruction in one image.

I want to say that from this image the story came into being. But the story also came from a deep longing on my part to honor the suffering of the people I worked with and of others I met and who befriended me, and a longing to come to grips with the complicated ways — sometimes beneficial, sometimes damaging — that Western countries have played a part in that suffering.

Writing the story hinged upon fine-tuning the tone, style, and diction of its first paragraph. I wrote drafts of the paragraph and fiddled with it for weeks, trying to articulate to my satisfaction Vasuki's amorphous sense of history and of the "master countries." Only then could I proceed.

It is a sad irony that one of the Sri Lankans who urged me to write about the civil war, the Tamil lawyer and M. P. Neelan Tiruchalvam, died in a suicide bombing. There has been speculation that he may have been targeted partly because he was a moderate, educated in the "master countries."

JHUMPA LAHIRI is the author of *Interpreter of Maladies*, a collection of short stories. She is the recipient of the Pulitzer Prize, the PEN/Hemingway Award, the Addison M. Metcalf Award from the American Academy of Arts and Letters, and the *New Yorker*'s Book Award for a notable debut in 1999. She lives in New York City.

▪ My father is a reticent man. Throughout my life, however, I have heard him tell one story with distinct dramatic flair: his description of living in Cambridge, Massachusetts, in the summer of 1969, in the home of a woman who was 103 years old. When telling this story, my father always made sure to impersonate the woman, beginning each of her sentences with "Boy," to the point where my family began referring to the woman herself as Boy. In 1997, my father came to visit me at the Fine Arts Work Center in Provincetown and told the Boy story at a small dinner party I had for him. Soon afterward I began to work on a fictional account of what I imagined that period of his life might have been like. In the process I changed several details of the actual events. For example, in 1969, my father had already been married to my mother for three years and had a two-year-old daughter (me); my mother and I were visiting India that summer and joined my father in August. As a result, I had to write myself out of the last scene of the story, for when the landlady declared my mother "a perfect lady," I too was present in the room.

Of course, I had no memory of that visit, or of that time in general. As I wanted the story to be a surprise for my father, I turned to the library instead of to him for my research (my father will appreciate this, being a librarian himself). I am grateful to the Provincetown Library, which obtained, at my request, photocopies of pages from the *Boston Globe* from July 20, 1969, the day of the *Apollo 11* moon landing. For six months I struggled with the story, writing a series of unsuccessful drafts. Then in May 1998 my father went to St. Petersburg, Russia, for five months, to work in a library. While he was away I worried for him, alone in a foreign country after so many years, far from his home and family. At the same time I was thrilled, for it had been a lifelong dream of my father's to visit Russia. It was a combination of those emotions that finally enabled me to tell the story of my father's arrival in America, nearly thirty years before.

WALTER MOSLEY is the best-selling author of many works, including the five critically acclaimed mysteries featuring Easy Rawlins; the blues novel *RL's Dream*, which was a finalist for the NAACP Award in Fiction and winner of the Black Caucus of the American Library Association's Literary Award; the story collection *Always Outnumbered, Always Outgunned,* which received the Anisfield-Wolf Book Award, and its sequel, *Walkin' the Dog;* the science fiction novel *Blue Light,* a national bestseller; and a book of nonfiction published by the Library of Contemporary Thought, *Workin' on the Chain Gang: Shaking Off the Dead Hand of History.* He is also the winner of the TransAfrica International Literary Prize. His books have been translated into twenty-one languages. He lives in New York.

▪ Every now and then a lonely fly from the outside world finds its way into my Greenwich Village apartment. I become aware of the little visitor because of a tiny black flickering in my peripheral vision or maybe a buzzing at the upper edges of a windowpane. Years ago I would spend as much time as it took to corner and destroy this insect invader; I never knew why.

After a while the death toll became inexcusable. After all, I live alone and the apartment is large. Most of the time the fly keeps to itself, and I never leave unwrapped food out. Who would care if this bug and I shared a living space for a few days of its life span?

I began by having simple conversations with my sporadic insect guests. Simple because flies don't seem to have long attention spans. "Hello. How you doin'?" is about all the talk a fly has time for before zipping off to another engagement.

In a way the fly is a perfect guest for a busy writer. A brief hello and then nothing for hours. And then, late at night, when I'm watching television alone in the dark, the resident fly almost always comes to watch with me. He gets right up on the screen, bathing in static electricity, while I recline some feet away.

We both go to sleep at lights out and I'm usually the first one up in the morning.

For some time I wanted to write about this passive relationship, but the story was absent. Then I began thinking about the silly books and movies about Wall Street brokers. These young, beautiful, rich, amoral characters who, it seems, we should all want to emulate.

I worked on Wall Street for years as a computer programmer. I worked with stockbrokers, commodity traders, secretaries, janitors, and mail delivery personnel.

In the movies and books, Wall Street seemed to be made up of WestEuroAmericans with Ivy League credentials. What I remember are Poles, Puerto Ricans, African Americans, Hasidic Jews, and Koreans — to name only a few. We were raw-edged and unsophisticated, worked to the bone and more or less drug-free. There was very little wild sex on boardroom tables and no midweek flights to Monaco.

There was a lot of loneliness on the job and not much emotional support or love. We were working schlubs, even the WestEuroAmericans.

It seemed to me that many of the people I worked with might have had pet flies or button collections. Everybody started the job hoping for a new life, but in the end home was the only refuge.

The story "Pet Fly" wrote itself from that point. I think of it as a real Wall Street exposé addressing the sad (and funny) quirkiness that Hollywood and cutting-edge novels seem to have overlooked.

ZZ PACKER was born in Chicago and raised in Atlanta and Louisville, Kentucky. She attended Yale and received an M.A. from Johns Hopkins and an M.F.A. from the University of Iowa. She is currently a Stegner fellow at Stanford.

- This story was inspired by recollections of growing up in the black suburbs of Atlanta in the eighties. Our parents pumped us with ballet and gymnastics lessons, yet all the models for leotards and tutus were white. Once we were nine or ten years old we began to feel that we were regarded as second-class citizens, no matter what our parents told us. Perhaps as a reaction, most of us developed a wariness toward whites — particularly white girls. In "Brownies," I wanted to capture how such bitterness was inherited and incubated.

I also owe a deep debt to conversations about echolalia with my fellow writer Jake Bohstedt. His work with echolalic children and our discussion of them helped me see my way not only to the end of the story but also to a degree of empathy I hadn't previously felt.

EDITH PEARLMAN's collection of stories, *Vaquita,* won the 1996 Drue Heinz Prize for Literature. "Allog" is her second story to appear in *Best American Short Stories;* "Chance" was selected in 1998.

• While living in Jerusalem I got to know several East Asians who cared for the elderly. I admired their tolerance and tact, qualities sometimes in short supply among Israelis, and I imagined the changes that might occur if these workers had greater standing and wider influence. A year later, back at home, "Allog" began to take shape — but only after the weeks of seemingly aimless wanderings over the typewriter keys that initiate any story.

"Allog"'s characters are composites/inventions/projections, with the exception of the schnorrer: *he* is drawn directly from life.

ANNIE PROULX lives and writes in Wyoming. Her most recent book is *Close Range: Wyoming Stories.*

• "People in Hell Just Want a Drink of Water" was written specifically for *Close Range: Wyoming Stories,* a collection examining the rural character of this sparsely populated western state. I am a collector of regional and local histories, and some years ago read Helena Thomas Rubottom's *Red Walls and Homesteads,* edited by Margaret Brock Hansen and published in 1987, a memoir of Wyoming homesteading days in the early twentieth century. I could not forget a very brief anecdote about a young man apparently castrated by his cowboy neighbors, for those few paragraphs illustrated a stock-raising community's set of mind; the true incident of decades gone became the takeoff point for "People in Hell." In the story two very different Wyoming families confront each other. The boy Ras Tinsley has been hurt in a distant accident and returns home a physical and brain-damaged wreck. His rancher neighbors, the Dunmires, fall into the stockman's knee-jerk response to a crippled or malformed animal — bad genetics. Logically they may know better, but culturally they can have only one response, to remove the bad genes from the herd/community. In the context of that time and place, the Dunmires' response to Ras's sexual exhibitionism is logical and correct.

FRANCES SHERWOOD's fiction was included in the *O. Henry Prize Stories* in 1989 and 1992, and she is a recipient of grants from the National Endowment for the Arts and the state of Indiana. Her books include a collection of short stories, *Everything You've Heard Is True* (1989), and two novels — *Vindication* (1993), exploring the life of the eighteenth-century feminist Mary Wollstonecraft, which was a finalist for the National Book Critics Circle Award, and *Green* (1995), set in California in the 1950s. A professor of English at Indiana University at South Bend, Sherwood is currently finishing a novel about magic.

▪ I was immersed in Trinidadian culture for a good many years. I kept my eyes open and my ears tuned, and for this story I also did a fair amount of research. I have tried to work with the character Winston Rama before, but it never went quite right. Then, I sat down one cold Indiana weekend with my material, and Mrs. Rama led me into the story. Basil, of course, was and is a mystery to me, and that is why I made him so concrete. History is important here as well, because I wanted to show Trinidad before Americanization. The central tragedy, however, is meant to be always and everywhere.

100 Other Distinguished Stories of 1999

SELECTED BY KATRINA KENISON

Editorial Addresses of American and Canadian Magazines Publishing Short Stories

When available, the annual subscription rate and the name of the editor follow the address.

African American Review
Department of English
Indiana State University
Terre Haute, IN 47809
web.indstate.edu/artsci/AAR
$30, Joe Weixlmann

Agni Review
Creative Writing Department
Boston University
236 Bay State Road
Boston, MA 02115
webdelsol.com/AGNI
$18, Askold Melnyczuk

Alabama Literary Review
Troy State University
Smith 253
Troy, AL 36082
$10, Theron E. Montgomery

Alaska Quarterly Review
Department of English
University of Alaska
3211 Providence Drive

Anchorage, AK 99508
$8, Ronald Spatz

Alfred Hitchcock's Mystery Magazine
1540 Broadway
New York, NY 10036
$34.97, Cathleen Jordan

Amelia
329 E Street
Bakersfield, CA 93304
$30, Frederick A. Raborg, Jr.

American Letters and Commentary
850 Park Avenue, Suite 5B
New York, NY 10021
$5, Jeanne Beaumont, Anna Rabinowitz

American Literary Review
University of North Texas
P.O. Box 13615
Denton, TX 76203
$15, Lee Martin

American Voice
332 West Broadway
Louisville, KY 40202

*$15, Sallie Bingham, Frederick
    Smock*

Analog Science Fiction/Science Fact
1540 Broadway
New York, NY 10036
$34.95, Stanley Schmidt

Another Chicago Magazine
Left Field Press
3709 North Kenmore
Chicago, IL 60613
$8, Sharon Solwitz

Antietam Review
41 South Potomac Street
Hagerstown, MD 21740-3764
$5, Suzanne Kass

Antioch Review
P.O. Box 148
Yellow Springs, OH 45387
$35, Robert S. Fogarty

Apalachee Quarterly
P.O. Box 20106
Tallahassee, FL 32316
$15, Barbara Hamby

Appalachian Heritage
Berea College
Berea, KY 40404
$18, James Gage

Arkansas Review
Dept. of English and Philosophy
P.O. Box 1890
Arkansas State University
State University, AR 72467
$20, William Clements

Ascent
English Dept.
901 8th St.
Moorehead, MN 56562
ascent@cord.edu
$12, W. Scott Olsen

Atlantic Monthly
77 N. Washington Street
Boston, MA 02114

www.theatlantic.com
$15.94, C. Michael Curtis

Baffler
P.O. Box 378293
Chicago, IL 60637
$24, Thomas Frank

Baltimore Review
P.O. Box 410
Riderwood, MD 21139
Barbara Westwood Diehl

Bananafish
P.O. Box 381332
Cambridge, MA 02238-1332
Robin Lippincott

Baybury Review
P.O. Box 462
Ephraim, WI 54211
$7.25, Janet St. John

Belletrist Review
P.O. Box 596
Plainville, CT 06062
$14.99, Marc Saegaert

Bellingham Review
MS 9053
Western Washington University
Bellingham, WA 98225
$10, Rosanna Lippi-Green

Bellowing Ark
P.O. Box 55564
Shoreline, WA 98155
$15, Robert R. Ward

Beloit Fiction Journal
Beloit College
P.O. Box 11
Beloit, WI 53511
$14, Clint McCown

Big Sky Journal
P.O. Box 1069
Bozeman, MT 59771-1069
bsj@mcn.net
$22, Allen Jones, Brian Baise

Black Dirt
Midwest Farmer's Market
Elgin Community College
1700 Spartan Drive
Elgin, IL 60123-7193
$10, Rachel Tecza

Black Warrior Review
P.O. Box 862936
Tuscaloosa, AL 35486-0027
www.sa.ua.edu/osm/bwr
$14, Christopher Manlove

Blood & Aphorisms
P.O. Box 702
Toronto, Ontario
M5S ZY4 Canada
www.interlog.com/-fiction
$18, Michelle Alfano,
  Dennis Black

BOMB
New Art Publications
10th floor
594 Broadway
New York, NY 10012
www.bombsite.com
$18, Betsy Sussler

Border Crossings
Y300-393 Portage Avenue
Winnipeg, Manitoba
R3B 3H6 Canada
$23, Meeka Walsh

Boston Book Review
30 Brattle Street, 4th floor
Cambridge, MA 02138
www.BostonBookReview.com
$24, Constantine Theoharis

Boston Review
Building E53
Room 407
Cambridge, MA 02139
bostonreview.mit.edu
$17, editorial board

Bottomfish
DeAnza College

21250 Stevens Creek Blvd.
Cupertino, CA 95014
$5, David Denny

Boulevard
4579 Laclede Avenue #332
St. Louis, MO 63108
$15, Richard Burgin

Briar Cliff Review
3303 Rebecca Street
P.O. Box 2100
Sioux City, IA 51104-2100
$4, Phil Hey

Bridges
P.O. Box 24839
Eugene, OR 97402
$15, Clare Kinberg

The Bridge
14050 Vernon Street
Oak Park, Ml 48237
$8, Jack Zucker

Button
Box 26
Lunenberg, MA 01462
Sally Cragin

Callaloo
Dept. of English
322 Bryan Hall
University of Virginia
Charlottesville, VA 22903
www.press.jhu.edu/journals/cal
$35, Charles H. Rowell

Calyx
P.O. Box B
Corvallis, OR 97339
www.proaxis.com/-calyx
$19.50, Margarita Donnelly

Canadian Fiction
Box 946, Station F
Toronto, Ontario
M4Y 2N9 Canada
$34.24, Geoffrey Hancock
  and Rob Payne

Capilano Review
Capilano College
2055 Purcell Way
North Vancouver,
British Columbia
V7J 3H5 Canada
$25, Ryan Knighton

Carolina Quarterly
Greenlaw Hall 066A
University of North Carolina
Chapel Hill, NC 27514
www.unc.edu/student/orgs/cquarter
$10, rotating

Century
P.O. Box 150510
Brooklyn, NY 11215-0510
www.centurymag.com
$20, Robert K. J. Killheffer

Chariton Review
Division of Language & Literature
Northeast Missouri State University
Kirksville, MO 63501
$9, Jim Barnes

Chattahoochee Review
DeKalb Community College
2101 Womack Road
Dunwoody, GA 30338-4497
$16, Lawrence Hetrick

Chelsea
P.O. Box 773
Cooper Station
New York, NY 10276
$13, Richard Foerster

Chicago Quarterly Review
517 Sherman Avenue
Evanston, IL 60202
*$10, S. Afzal Haider, Jane Lawrence,
    Brian Skinner*

Chicago Review
5801 South Kenwood
University of Chicago
Chicago, IL 60637

humanities.uchicago.edu/review
$18, Andrew Rathman

Cimarron Review
205 Morrill Hall
Oklahoma State University
Stillwater, OK 74078-0135
cimarronreview.okstate.edu
$16, E.P. Walkiewicz

Clackamas Literary Review
196 South Molalla Ave.
Oregon City, OR 97045
www.clakamas.cc.or.us/clr
$10, Jeff Knorr and Tim Schell

Colorado Review
Department of English
Colorado State University
Fort Collins, CO 80523
creview@vines.colostate.edu
$24, David Milofsky

Columbia
415 Dodge
Columbia University
New York, NY 10027
*$15, Ellen Umanksy
    and Neil Azevedo*

Commentary
165 East 56th Street
New York, NY 10022
103115.2375@compuserve.com
$39, Neal Kozodoy

Confrontation
English Department
C. W. Post College of Long Island
    University
Greenvale, NY 11548
mtucker@aol.com
$8, Martin Tucker

Conjunctions
21 East 10th St.
#3E
New York, NY 10003
www.conjunctions.com
$18, Bradford Morrow

Cottonwood
Box J, Kansas Union
University of Kansas
Lawrence, KS 66045
$10, Tom Lorenz

Crab Creek Review
4462 Whitman Ave. N.
Seattle, WA 98103
*$8, Kimberly Allison, Harris Levinson,
    Laura Sinai, Terri Stone*

Crab Orchard Review
Dept. of English
Southern Illinois University at
    Carbondale
Carbondale, IL 62901
www.siu.edu/-orchard
$10, Jon Tribble

Cream City Review
University of Wisconsin, Milwaukee
P.O. Box 413
Milwaukee, WI 53201
www.uwm.edu/Dept/English/ccr/
    tccrhome.htm
$12, rotating

Crescent Review
P.O. Box 15069
Chevy Chase, MD 20825-5069
$21, J. Timothy Holland

Crossconnect
P.O. Box 2317
Philadelphia, PA 19103
xconnect@ccat.sas.upenn.edu
David Deifer

Crucible
Barton College
College Station
Wilson, NC 27893
Terence Grimes

Cut Bank
Department of English
University of Montana
Missoula, MT 59812
$12, Cat Haglund, Pamela Kennedy

Denver Quarterly
University of Denver
Denver, CO 80208
$25, Bin Ramke

Descant
P.O. Box 314, Station P
Toronto, Ontario
M5S 2S8 Canada
$25, Karen Mulhallen

Descant
Department of English
Texas Christian University
Box 32872
Fort Worth, TX 76129
$12, Neal Easterbrook, David Kuhne

Distillery
Division of Liberal Arts
Motlow State Community College
P.O. Box 88100
Tullahoma, TN 37388-8100

DoubleTake
Center for Documentary Studies
55 Davis Square
Somerville, MA 02144
www.doubletakemagazine.org
$32, Robert Coles, R. J. McGill

Elle
1633 Broadway
New York, NY 10019
$24, Patricia Towers

Epoch
251 Goldwin Smith Hall
Cornell University
Ithaca, NY 14853-3201
$11, Michael Koch

Esquire
250 West 55th Street
New York, NY 10019
*$17.94, Rust Hills,
    Adrienne Miller*

Eureka Literary Magazine
Eureka College
P.O. Box 280

Eureka, IL 61530
$10, Loren Logsdon

event
c/o Douglas College
P.O. Box 2503
New Westminster, British Columbia
V3L 5B2 Canada
$15, Calvin Wharton

Fantasy and Science Fiction
P.O. Box 1806
New York, NY 10159-1806
GordonFSF@aol.com
$38.97, Gordon Van Gelder

Fence
14 Fifth Ave., #1A
New York, NY 10011
www.fencemag.com
$14, Rebecca Wolff

Fiction
Fiction, Inc.
Department of English
The City College of New York
New York, NY
www.ccny.cuny.edu/fiction/fiction.htm
$7, Mark Mirsky

Fiddlehead
UNB Box 4400
University of New Brunswick
Fredericton, New Brunswick
E3B 5A3 Canada
$20, Norman Ravvin

Fish Stories Literary Annual
5412 N. Clark, South Suite
Chicago, IL 60640
$10.95, Amy G. Davis

Five Points
Department of English
Georgia State University
University Plaza
Atlanta, GA 30303-3083
$15, Pam Durban

Florida Review
Department of English

University of Central Florida
P.O. Box 25000
Orlando, FL 32816
$10, Russell Kesler

Flyway
206 Ross Hall
Dept. of English
Iowa State University
Ames, IA 50011
$24, Debra Marquart

Folio
Department of Literature
The American University
Washington, D.C. 20016
$10, Carolyn Parkhurst

Forty-nine Words
School of Visual Arts
209 East 23rd St.
New York, NY 10010-3994
www.schoolofvisualarts.edu

Fourteen Hills
Department of Creative Writing
San Francisco State University
1600 Holloway Avenue
San Francisco, CA 94132
www.sfsu.edu/-cwriting/14hills.html
$12, rotating

Gargoyle
Paycock Press
c/o Atticus Books and Music
1508 U Street, NW
Washington, DC 20009
www.atticusbooks.com/gargoyle.html
$20, Richard Peabody and Lucinda
   Ebersole

Geist
1062 Homer Street #100
Vancouver, Canada
V6B 2W9
geist@geist.com
$20, Stephen Osborne

Georgia Review
University of Georgia

Athens, GA 30602
www.uga.edu/garev
$18, Stephen Corey

Gettysburg Review
Gettysburg College
Gettysburg, PA 17325
$24, Peter Stitt

Glimmer Train Stories
812 SW Washington Street
Suite 1205
Portland, OR 97205
www.glimmertrain.com
$29, Susan Burmeister, Linda Davies

Good Housekeeping
959 Eighth Avenue
New York, NY 10019
$17.97, Arleen L. Quarfoot

GQ
350 Madison Avenue
New York, NY 10017
www.swoon.com
$19.97, James Truman

Grain
Box 1154
Regina, Saskatchewan
S4P 3B4 Canada
www.sasknet.com/corporate/skywriter
$26.95, Diane Warren

Grand Street
131 Varick Street
New York, NY 10013
www.voyagerco.com/gs
$40, Jean Stein

Granta
1755 Broadway, 5th floor
New York, NY
10019-3780
$32, Ian Jack

Great River Review
211 West 7th Street
Winona, MN 55987
$12, Pamela Davies

Green Hills Literary Lantern
North Central Missouri College
Box 375
Trenton, MO 64683
$5.95, Jack Smith

Green Mountains Review
Box A 58
Johnson State College
Johnson, VT 05656
$12, Tony Whedon

Greensboro Review
Department of English
University of North Carolina
Greensboro, NC 27412
www.uncg.edu/mfa/grhmpg.htm
$8, Jim Clark

Gulf Coast
Department of English
University of Houston
4800 Calhoun Road
Houston, TX 77204-3012
$22, Marsha Recknagel, Merrill Greene

Gulf Stream
English Department
Florida International University
North Miami Campus
North Miami, FL 33181
$9, Lynne Barrett

G.W. Review
Box 20B, The Marvin Center
800 21st Street
Washington, DC 20052
$9, Greg Lautier

Habersham Review
Piedmont College
Demorest, GA 30535-0010
$12, Frank Gannon

Harper's Magazine
666 Broadway
New York, NY 10012
$16, Lewis H. Lapham

Harvard Review
Poetry Room

Harvard College Library
Cambridge, MA 02138
haviaris@fas.harvard.edu
$16, Stratis Haviaris

Hawaii Pacific Review
1060 Bishop Street
Honolulu, HI 96813
hpreview@hpu.edu
Catherine Sustana

Hawaii Review
University of Hawaii
Department of English
1733 Donagho Road
Honolulu, HI 96822
$20, Jason Minani

Hayden's Ferry Review
Box 871502
Arizona State University
Tempe, AZ 85287-1502
www.statepress.com/hfr
$10, Michael Guerra, Richard Yanez

High Plains Literary Review
180 Adams Street, Suite 250
Denver, CO 80206
$20, Robert O. Greer, Jr.

Hudson Review
684 Park Avenue
New York, NY 10021
$24, Paula Deitz, Frederick Morgan

Idaho Review
Boise State University
Dept. of English
1910 University Dr.
Boise, ID 83725
$8.95, Mitch Weiland

Image
323 S. Broad Street
P.O. Box 674
Kendall Square, PA 19348
www.imagejournal.org
$30, Gregory Wolfe

India Currents
P.O. Box 21285

San Jose, CA 95151
info@indicur.com
$19.95, Arviund Kumar

Indiana Review
Ballantine Hall 465
Bloomington, IN 47405
$12, Laura McCoid

Ink
P.O. Box 52558
St. George Postal Outlet
264 Bloor Street
Toronto, Ontario
M5S 1Vo Canada
$8, John Degan

Inkwell
Manhattanville College
2900 Purchase Street
Purchase, NY 10577
$14, Karen Sirabian

Iowa Review
Department of English
University of Iowa
308 EPB
Iowa City, IA 52242
www.uiowa.edu/~iareview
$18, David Hamilton, Mary Hussmann

Iris
Box 323 HSC
University of Virginia
Charlottesville, VA 22908
$9, Eileen Boris

Italian Americana
University of Rhode Island
College of Continuing Education
199 Promenade Street
Providence, RI 02908
$20, Carol Bonomo Albright

Jewish Currents
22 East 17th Street, Suite 601
New York, NY 10003-3272
$20, editorial board

Joe
1271 Avenue of the Americas

New York, NY 10020
Scott Mowbray

Journal
Department of English
Ohio State University
164 West 17th Avenue
Columbus, OH 43210
$8, Kathy Fagan, Michelle Herman

Journal of African Travel Writing
P.O. Box 346
Chapel Hill, NC 27514
$10, Amber Vogel

Kairos
Dundurn P.O. Box 33553
Hamilton, Ontario
L8P 4X4
Canada
$12.95, R.W. Megens

Kalliope
Florida Community College
3939 Roosevelt Blvd.
Jacksonville, FL 32205
$12.50, Mary Sue Koeppel

Kenyon Review
Kenyon College
Gambier, OH 43022
www.kenyonreview.org
$25, David H. Lynn

Kiosk
English Department
306 Clemens Hall
SUNY at Buffalo
Buffalo, NY 14260
eng-kiosk@acsu.buffalo.edu
$6, Kevin Grauke

Laurel Review
Department of English
Northwest Missouri State University
Maryville, MO 64468
*$8, Craig Goad, David Slater,
    William Trowbridge*

Lilith
250 West 57th Street

New York, NY 10107
$16, Susan Weidman Schneider

Literal Latté
Suite 240
61 East 8th Street
New York, NY 10003
www.literal-latte.com
$25, Jenine Gordon

Literary Review
Fairleigh Dickinson University
285 Madison Avenue
Madison, NJ 07940
www.webdelsol.com/tlr
$18, Walter Cummins

Louisiana Literature
Box 792
Southeastern Louisiana University
Hammond, LA 70402
$12, Jack Bedell

Lynx Eye
1880 Hill Drive
Los Angeles, CA 90041
$20, Pam McCully, Kathryn Morrison

Madison Review
University of Wisconsin
Department of English
H. C. White Hall
600 North Park Street
Madison, WI 53706
$15, rotating

Malahat Review
University of Victoria
P.O. Box 1700
Victoria, British Columbia
V8W 2Y2 Canada
malahat@uvic.ca
$15, Marlene Cookshaw

Manoa
English Department
University of Hawaii
Honolulu, HI 96822
wwwz.hawaii.edu/mjournal
$22, Frank Stewart

Many Mountains Moving
2525 Arapahoe Road
Suite E4-309
Boulder, CO 80302
$18, Naomi Horii, Marilyn Krysl

Massachusetts Review
South College, Box 37140
University of Massachusetts
Amherst, MA 01003-7140
$22, Jules Chametsky, Mary Heath, Paul Jenkins

Matrix
1455 de Maisonneuve Blvd. West
Suite LB-514-8
Montreal, Quebec
H3G IM8 Canada
matrix@alcor.concordia.ca
$18, R.E.N. Allen

McSweeney's
394A Ninth Street
Brooklyn, NY 11215
submissions@mcsweeneys.net
$36, Dave Eggers

Meridian
Dept. of English
University of Virginia
Charlottesville, VA 22903
$10, Ted Genoways

Michigan Quarterly Review
3032 Rackham Building
University of Michigan
Ann Arbor, MI 48109
$18, Laurence Goldstein

Mid-American Review
Department of English
Bowling Green State University
Bowling Green, OH 43403
www.bgsu.edu/midamericanreview
$12, Michael Czyzniejewski

Minnesota Review
Department of English
State University of New York

Stony Brook, NY 11794-5350
$20, Jeffrey Williams

Mississippi Review
University of Southern Mississippi
Southern Station, P.O. Box 5144
Hattiesburg, MS 39406-5144
sushi.st.usm.edu/mrw/index.html
$15, Frederick Barthelme

Missouri Review
1507 Hillcrest Hall
University of Missouri
Columbia, MO 65211
www.missourireview.org
$19, Speer Morgan

Ms.
230 Park Avenue
New York, NY 10169
ms@echonyc.com
$45, Marcia Ann Gillespie

Nassau Review
English Department
Nassau Community College
One Education Drive
Garden City, NY 11530-6793
 Paul A. Doyle

Natural Bridge
Department of English
University of Missouri — St. Louis
8001 Natural Bridge Road
St. Louis, MO 63121-4499
www.umsl.edu/~natural/index.htm
$15, Steven Schreiner

Nebraska Review
Writer's Workshop, ASH 212
University of Nebraska
Omaha, NE 68182-0324
unomaha.edu/-jreed
$11, James Reed

New Delta Review
Creative Writing Program
English Department
Louisiana State University

Baton Rouge, LA 70803
$10, Andrew Spear

New England Review
Middlebury College
Middlebury, VT 05753
www.middlebury.edu/nerview
$23, Stephen Donadio

New Letters
University of Missouri
4216 Rockhill Road
Kansas City, MO 64110
$17, James McKinley

New Orleans Review
P.O. Box 195
Loyola University
New Orleans, LA 70118
$18, Ralph Adamo

New Orphic Review
1095 Victoria Drive
Vancouver, BC
Canada V5L 4G3
$25, Ernest Hekkanen

New Renaissance
26 Heath Road #11
Arlington, MA 02174
wmichaud@gwi.net
$11.50, Louise T. Reynolds

New Yorker
4 Times Square
New York, NY 10036
www.enews.com/magazines/
  new_yorker
$32, Bill Buford

New York Stories
English Dept.
La Guardia Community College
31-10 Thomson Ave.
Long Island City, NY 11101
$15, Daniel Lynch

Nimrod
Arts and Humanities Council
  of Tulsa
600 S. College Avenue

Tulsa, OK 74104
www.utulsa.edu/Nimrod
$15, Francine Ringold

North American Review
University of Northern Iowa
1222 West 27th Street
Cedar Falls, IA 50614
webdelsol.com/NorthAmReview/NAR
$22, Robley Wilson, Jr.

North Dakota Quarterly
University of North Dakota
P.O. Box 8237
Grand Forks, ND 58202
ndq@sage.und.nodak.edu
$25, Robert Lewis

Northeast Corridor
English Department
Beaver College
450 S. Easton Road
Glenside, PA 19038-3295
$10, Susan Balee

Northwest Review
369 PLC
University of Oregon
Eugene, OR 97403
$20, John Witte

Notre Dame Review
Department of English
University of Notre Dame
Notre Dame, IN 46556
$15, Valerie Sayers

Oasis
P.O. Box 626
Largo, FL 34649-0626
oasislit@aol.com
$22, Neal Storrs

Ohio Review
Ellis Hall
Ohio University
344 Scott Quad
Athens, OH 45701-2979
www.ohiou.edu/TheOhioReview
$16, Wayne Dodd

Oklahoma Today
15 N. Robinson, Suite 100
P.O. Box 53384
Oklahoma City, OK 73102
$16.95, Louisa McCune

Ontario Review
9 Honey Brook Drive
Princeton, NJ 08540
www.ontarioreviewpress.com
$14, Raymond J. Smith

Open City
38 White Street
New York, NY 10013
$24, Thomas Beller, Daniel Pinchbeck

Other Voices
University of Illinois at Chicago
Department of English
(M/C 162) 601 South Morgan Street
Chicago, IL 60680
$20, Lois Hauselman

Oxford American
115½ South Lamar
Oxford, MS 38655
www.oxfordamericanmag.com
$16, Marc Smirnoff

Oxford Magazine
Bachelor Hall
Oxford, OH 45056
OxMag@geocities.com
$8, David Mitchell Goldberg

Oxygen
535 Geary Street
San Fransisco, CA 94102
$14, Richard Hack

Oyster Boy Review
103B Hanna Street
Carrboro, NC 27510
$12, Chad Driscoll,
    Damon Suave

Paris Review
541 East 72nd Street
New York, NY 10021

www.voyagerco.com/PR
$34, George Plimpton

Parting Gifts
3413 Wilshire Dr.
Greensboro, NC 27408-2923
Robert Bixby

Partisan Review
236 Bay State Road
Boston, MA 02215
partisan@bu.edu
$22, William Phillips

Pearl
3030 E. Second St.
Long Beach, CA 90803
Joan Jobe Smith, Marilyn Johnson,
    Barbara Hauk

Playboy
Playboy Building
919 North Michigan Avenue
Chicago, IL 60611
www.playboy.com
$29.97, Alice K. Turner

Pleiades
Department of English
Central Missouri State University
P.O. Box 800
Warrensburg, MO 64093
$12, R. M. Kinder, Kevin Prufer

Ploughshares
Emerson College
100 Beacon Street
Boston, MA 02116
www.emerson.edu/ploughshares
$21, Don Lee

Porcupine
P.O. Box 259
Cedarburg, WI 53012
$15.95, group editorship

Potpourri
P.O. Box 8278
Prairie Village, KS 66208
Potporpub@aol.com
$15, Polly W. Swafford

Pottersfield Portfolio
P.O. Box 40, Station A
Sydney, Nova Scotia
Canada B1P 6G9
www.pportfolio.com
$17, Douglas Arthur Brown

Prairie Fire
423-100 Arthur Street
Winnipeg, Manitoba
R3B 1H3 Canada
pfire@escape.ca
$25, Andris Taskans

Prairie Schooner
201 Andrews Hall
University of Nebraska
Lincoln, NE 68588-0334
$22, Hilda Raz

Prairie Star
P.O. Box 923
Fort Collins, CO 80522-0923
$10, Mark Gluckstern

Press
125 West 72nd Street
Suite 3-M
New York, NY 10023
www.paradasia.com/press
$24, Daniel Roberts

Prism International
Department of Creative Writing
University of British Columbia
Vancouver, British Columbia
V6T 1W5 Canada
www.arts.ubc.ca/prism
$18, rotating

Provincetown Arts
650 Commercial Street
Provincetown, MA 02657
$10, Ivy Meeropol

Puerto del Sol
P.O. Box 3E
Department of English
New Mexico State University

Las Cruces, NM 88003
$10, Kevin McIlvoy

Quarry Magazine
P.O. Box 1061
Kingston, Ontario
K7L 4Y5 Canada
$22, Mary Cameron

Quarterly West
312 Olpin Union
University of Utah
Salt Lake City, UT 84112
$12, Margot Schilpp

Queen Street Quarterly
Box 311 Station P
704 Spadina Ave.
Toronto, Canada
M5S 2S8
theqsq@hotmail.com
$25, Suzanne Zelaso

RE:AL
School of Liberal Arts
Stephen F. Austin State University
P.O. Box 13007
SFA Station
Nacogdoches, TX 75962
$15, Dale Hearell

Red Rock Review
English Dept. J2A
Community College of Southern
    Nevada
3200 East Cheyenne Ave
North Las Vegas, NV 89030
$9.50, Richard Logsdon

Redbook
959 Eighth Avenue
New York, NY 10017
$11.97, Peggy Northrop

Riversedge
Department of English
University of Texas,
    Pan-American
1201 West University Drive, CAS 266

Edinburg, TX 78539-2999
$12, Dorey Schmidt

River Styx
Big River Association
14 South Euclid
St. Louis, MO 63108
$20, Richard Newman

Room of One's Own
P.O. Box 46160
Station D
Vancouver, British Columbia
V6J 5G5 Canada
$22, collective

Salamander
48 Ackers Avenue
Brookline, MA 02146
$12, Jennifer Barber

Salmagundi
Skidmore College
Saratoga Springs, NY 12866
$18, Robert Boyers

Salt Hill
Syracuse University
English Department
Syracuse, NY 13244
$7, Caryb Koplik

Santa Monica Review
Center for the Humanities
Santa Monica College
1900 Pico Boulevard
Santa Monica, CA 90405
$12, Andrew Tonkovich

Seattle Review
Padelford Hall, GN-30
University of Washington
Seattle, WA 98195
$9, Colleen McElroy

Seventeen
850 Third Avenue
New York, NY 10022
$14.95, Patrice G. Adcroft

Sewanee Review
University of the South

Sewanee, TN 37375-4009
www.sewanee.edu/sreview/home.html
$18, George Core

Shenandoah
Washington and Lee University
P.O. Box 722
Lexington, VA 24450
www.wlu.edu/-shenando
$15, R. T. Smith

Sonora Review
Department of English
University of Arizona
Tucson, AZ 85721
sonora@u.arizona.edu
$12, Hannah Haas

So to Speak
4400 University Drive
George Mason University
Fairfax, VA 22030-444
$10, Katherine Perry

South Carolina Review
Department of English
Clemson University
Clemson, SC 29634-1503
$10, Wayne Chapman, Donna Hasty Winchell

Southern Exposure
P.O. Box 531
Durham, NC 27702
southern_exposure@14south.org
$24, Jordan Green

Southern Humanities Review
9088 Haley Center
Auburn University
Auburn, AL 36849
$15, Dan R. Latimer, Virginia M. Kouidis

Southern Review
43 Allen Hall
Louisiana State University
Baton Rouge, LA 70803
$25, James Olney, Dave Smith

Southwest Review
Southern Methodist University

P.O. Box 4374
Dallas, TX 75275
$24, Willard Spiegelman

Spindrift
1507 East 53rd St. #649
Chicago, IL 60615
$10, Mark Anderson-Wilk, Sarah Anderson-Wilk, Amy Jorean

Story
1507 Dana Avenue
Cincinnati, OH 45207
$22, Lois Rosenthal (ceased publication)

Story Quarterly
P.O. Box 1416
Northbrook, IL 60065
$12, Anne Brashler, M.M. Hayes

Sun
107 North Roberson Street
Chapel Hill, NC 27516
$34, Sy Safransky

Sun Dog
The Southeast Review
406 Williams Building
Florida State University
Tallahassee, FL 32306-1036
$8, Russ Franklin

Sycamore Review
Department of English
Heavilon Hall
Purdue University
West Lafayette, IN 47907
www.sla.purdue.edu/academic/engl/
    sycamore
$12, rotating

Talking River Review
Division of Literature
Lewis-Clark State College
500 8th Avenue
Lewiston, ID 83501
$12, group editorship

Tampa Review
University of Tampa
401 Kennedy Blvd.

Tampa, FL 33606-1490
$10, Richard Matthews

Tea Cup
P.O. Box 8665
Hellgate Station
Missoula, MT 59807
$9, group

Thema
Box 74109
Metairie, LA 70053-4109
$16, Virginia Howard

Thin Air
P.O. Box 23549
Flagstaff, AZ 86002
jdh4@dana.ucc.nau
$9, Jeff Huebner, Rob Morrill

Third Coast
Department of English
Western Michigan University
Kalamazoo, MI 49008-5092
www.wmich.edu/thirdcoast
$11, Heidi Bell, Kellie Wells

13th Moon
Department of English
SUNY at Albany
Albany, NY 12222
$18, Judith Emlyn Johnson

32 Pages
Rain Crow Publishing
101-308 Andrew Place
West Lafayette, IN 47906-3932
$10, Michael S. Manley

Threepenny Review
P.O. Box 9131
Berkeley, CA 94709
$16, Wendy Lesser

Timber Creek Review
3283 UNCG Station
Greensboro, NC 27413
timber_creek_review@hoopsmail.com
$15, John Freiemuth

TriQuarterly
2020 Ridge Avenue
Northwestern University
Evanston, IL 60208
$24, Susan Firestone Hahn

University of Windsor Review
Department of English
University of Windsor
Windsor, Ontario
N9B 3P4 Canada
$19.95, Alistair MacLeod

Virginia Quarterly Review
One West Range
Charlottesville, VA 22903
$18, Staige D. Blackford

Wascana Review
English Department
University of Regina
Regina, Saskatchewan
S4S 0A2 Canada
$10, Jeanne Shami

Weber Studies
Weber State College
Ogden, UT 84408
$20, Sherwin Howard

Wellspring
770 Tonkawa Road
Long Lake, MN 55356
$8, Meg Miller

West Branch
Department of English
Bucknell University
Lewisburg, PA 17837
*$7, Robert Love Taylor,
    Karl Patten*

Western Humanities Review
University of Utah
Salt Lake City, UT 84112
$20, Barry Weller

Whetstone
Barrington Area Arts Council
P.O. Box 1266
Barrington, IL 60011

*$8.50, Sandra Berris, Marsha Portnoy,
    Jean Tolle*

Willow Springs
Eastern Washington University
705 West 1st Ave
Spokane, WA 99201
$10.50, Christopher Howell

Wind
RFD Route 1
P.O. Box 809K
Pikeville, KY 41501
lit-arts.com/wind/magazine.htm
$10, Charlie Hughes, Leatha Kendrick

Witness
Oakland Community College
Orchard Ridge Campus
27055 Orchard Lake Road
Farmington Hills, MI 48334
$12, Peter Stine

Worcester Review
6 Chatham Street
Worcester, MA 01690
$10, Rodger Martin

WordVirtual.com
1119 North & South Rd.
St. Louis, MO 63103
Brian Cochran

Xavier Review
Xavier University
Box 110C
New Orleans, LA 70125
$10, Thomas Bonner, Jr.

Yale Review
1902A Yale Station
New Haven, CT 06520
$28, J. D. McClatchy

Yalobusha Review
P.O. Box 186
University, MS 38677-0186
$6, rotating

Yankee
Yankee Publishing, Inc.

Dublin, NH 03444
$22, Judson D. Hale, Sr.

Zoetrope; All-Story
AZX Publications
126 Fifth Avenue, Suite 300
New York, NY 10011

www.zoetrope-stories.com
$20, Adrienne Brodeur

ZYZZYVA
41 Sutter Street, Suite 1400
San Francisco, CA 94104
www.webdelsol.com/ZYZZYVA
$28, Howard Junker